The Plain of the Dogs

A. W. Terry

The Plane of the Dogs is a work of fiction.
Names, characters, locations, and incidents either are the
product of the author's imagination or are used fictionally.
Any resemblance to actual persons, living or dead,
events, or locales is entirely coincidental.

Village Books Publishing
Bellingham, Washington

ISBN 979-8-9928198-0-9

Library of Congress Control Number 2025904372

Printed in the United States of America

Book and Cover Design by Jill Flores

To Margot, for her eternal encouragement, support, and patience.
And Fr. Joe for his critical storyline suggestions and
technical advice on the push to the finish.

Slainte!

Chapter 1

ТHE MIDSUMMER DARKNESS of the Arizona high desert was slow in coming, particularly with this miserably hot July night. When darkness there finally did settle in, the half-moon and almost radiant Milky Way still provided enough light to read by. It certainly was not black enough to satisfy the men parked alongside the high chain link and barbwire-topped security fence surrounding the military facility. The fence separated the street from a dozen or so rows of camouflage-painted military vehicles belonging to the Arizona Army National Guard. The moonlight and visibility were still coming from each star of the many millions crowding the velvety sky that seemed to seek them out, bathing them in a soft but revealing light.

The truck in which they nervously sat, a rusting six-wheeled, 2 ½ ton Ford with no working air conditioner, was steamy hot and rank with the sweating men's odor. Fitted with an unmarked aluminum box and a two month out-of-date New Mexico plate, the truck idled just behind a dark green Cadillac sedan parked tight along the edge of the dry and weed-filled drainage ditch that scarred the earth between the street and fence surrounding the Army National Guard post. Another darkened and idling Cadillac was parked in the shadows a block back to east of the truck. Three men were in the truck cab and five more in the green Cadillac. They all wore dark colored coveralls and were gloved. Black ski masks lay across their laps. The men worked hard at being quiet and casually non-descript, failing that with the nervous and incessant checking and rechecking of the assortment of shotguns and short barreled automatic weapons spread through their lot and made more obvious by the fact that the fact that there were even there at all. It all would have betrayed them immediately but for the nearby population's penchant for avidly minding their own business and staying safely behind closed doors after dusk. The man behind the wheel of the Cadillac at the head of the small convoy nervously squinted at his wristwatch again and cursed softly under his breath. He shrugged to shift his soggy clothes and find any kind of comfort.

Each of the men stared intently at a low and flat-roofed red-brick building some two hundred yards on up the street toward the west. The fence they sat alongside ran straight up the high side of the drainage ditch and was joined to the flat-roofed building near where its front wall met the enclosed motor pool. Surrounding the wire enclosure, strong security lights high on metal poles glared and illuminated an expansive asphalt paved motor pool compound, filled with the various trucks, M113 personnel carriers, self propelled artillery pieces, and a dozen camouflage painted M60 tanks that were normally consistent with an under-equipped Army National Guard mechanized unit. The men hardly noticed the array of equipment the wire and light protected though.

Their interest was focused on the street side of the low brick building boasting *Arizona Army National Guard* in raised and painted lettering on a long and weathered wooden sign affixed above its front door.

A single yellowish light glowed dully through a window at the near corner of the building as it had ever since the sun had dipped below the southwestern horizon. One lone vehicle remained in the parking lot that faced and ran the length of the building's street side, a faded red Ford pickup truck, atop tall off-road tires and sporting spots of primer covered repairs. The last of the other full-time National Guard employees had pulled out of the isolated parking lot well over an hour previously. The light still glowed.

One of the men in the Cadillac, smelling of tequila, onion, and gross uncleanliness, seemed to be unable to remain still for even a moment, slumped against the passenger side door and complained incessantly. Finally, he laid the machine pistol back on his lap and almost too low to hear growled, "You think that old geezer will ever quit?"

The driver checked his wristwatch again and returned, "You don't have to whisper. Just watch the light. When it goes out, he'll be heading for the front door within the minute." For the fourth time since they'd parked there alongside the compound, he repeated, "Be careful when we get in there. I want to get in and out as quickly as possible. Remember, the boss says we do it without hurting anyone. For me…and don't you ever forget this…it means your sorry ass is more expendable than the man inside is." Then, after a moment's thought he leaned forward and looked directly into the man's face, "And, listen to me, asshole, you ever try to come on a job smelling like booze again and you'll hurt a long time. I'll see to it. Hear me?" He leaned back into the seat shaking his head in disgust and began staring at the distant light again.

The person using that light, if the man at the wheel of the Cadillac had his information correct, was CW4 Hollis Vander Pool, a crusty and nearing the end of his career Guardsman and the Assistant S4 (supply officer) of the mechanized infantry battalion the armory housed. Vander Pool was also, according to the drunk to whom they'd fed drink after drink, a tough old lifer and one of five full-timers working at the armory. He was a perfectionist and everything had a place for him and that is where it was or someone paid the consequences, almost regardless of their rank, his source said. Everything also had a number, which was the only way Vander Pool ever referred to it. If you didn't speak numbers you, private or colonel, were shit-out-of-luck with Chief Vander Pool. He belonged to the strata in the military hierarchy—warrant officers—that were almost immune to the normal rules of decorum and discipline. Decorum be damned, they were competent and didn't need your approval.

The old Chief Warrant was, again according to the drunk, no fool and tough. Always working late—he had no wife for whom he had to hurry home—Vander Pool packed a Smith & Wesson .357 on a belt rig high on his right hip. The revolver was about the only thing non-regulation about him. The Mexican border was less than half a mile away and only an idiot wandered around after dark that close to the often-breached line of wire and imagination stretched across the sand without something more potent than good intentions. And, as the drunk was fond of saying, the crusty old soldier was anything but a fool. He had said that as if he both admired and feared the old soldier.

The man behind the wheel of the Cadillac shifted in his seat again and held his wristwatch up to the dim street-side glow of the fence's security lighting. Even he was beginning to show frayed nerves. He was just about to spew a few more curses again when he saw the light in the corner office blink off. Thirty-seconds later, the building's foyer light came on and the front door pushed outward. The man had already pulled the Cadillac into drive and was quietly rolling forward, at a low idle, with no lights showing.

CW4 Vander Pool sat in his truck for a few moments, tuning the radio from his morning commute news station to his evening drive-home country music station. He ignored the buckle-up warning light and started to back out of his distinctly marked and reserved slot. He was startled to see the outline of a large sedan close up behind him in the light thrown by his backups. He froze a mere moment, then grabbed for the .357 at his hip. The sound of a shotgun slide racking almost in his ear stopped him mid-movement. As the drunk said, he was no fool.

Vander Pool slowly turned his head to his right and looked down the barrel of a sawn off 12-gauge pump shotgun pointed straight at his face. The size and nearness of the shotgun's open maw caused him to forget looking on past the weapon's muzzle to the man standing behind it. His attention had been bought for the moment and he didn't see or even sense another man move back to the street and switch his flashlight off and on three times or notice the bobtail six-wheeler begin the move toward the lot.

He also didn't see the second Cadillac sedan that followed the truck in until it was stopped in the slot next to him. Two darkly clothed men got out of the back doors of the sedan and the one nearest the truck reached back in and none-too-gently pulled a frightened and spectacled young man in handcuffs out.

"Why, Cap'n Morrissey…" was all Vander Pool managed to say. He could see the disheveled young man was frightened and that he smelled of booze and urine. The front of his clothes were soiled. They were hurriedly ushered back to the door of the armory and, with the barrel of the 12 gauge at his ear, Vander Pool opened the door and quickly shut off the alarm. There was no argument. They were hustled down the hall to a large and heavy gray metal door with two dials on its face. The door opened into a 20x30 foot room-sized walk-in vault and took up a large chunk of the brick building's guts. The silent men who followed them had a large collection of tools and a portable torch just in case the good Chief Vander Pool proved intractable.

There was no argument at the door. One of the men, eyes black as obsidian, stared out of a balaclava with unspoken threat and explained that he knew each one of them had the combination to one of the dials. They were bluntly told to open the door to the arms vault or die for their refusal. They chose to open the door—and quickly. A decision to do otherwise would have been immediately fatal. Vander Pool then opened the locks at each end of a long series of arms racks bolted to the reinforced concrete floor and slid the bar out of the way. Some of the still silent men began hauling the rifles out the front door and into the back of the truck.

Vander Pool managed to put over a small lie, claiming that he did not have a key to the wire cage and tall safe containing the M16 bolts, magazines, and row upon row of .45 autos, but it barely slowed things down. Unperturbed, one of the men merely snapped on the acetylene torch and burned through the locks in two minutes flat. The rifle bolts, handguns and boxes of magazines for both rifles and pistols were quickly loaded into the truck.

The last thing the men did was order Vander Pool to open a locked and barred door at one end of the arms vault. Sitting in the middle of this next room were three heavy wheeled carts, each stacked waist-high with just–arrived metal cases of ammunition, all originally destined for the coming weekend's firing exercise. The carts were hurriedly pushed out the storage space, down the hall, and to the back of the truck, where their burdens were loaded and stowed out of sight in just over 15 minutes. In all, the men had been inside the armory for less than 30 minutes and everything had gone well for them. They were pleased.

The men had intended to just handcuff the two guardsmen to one of the rifle racks and walk out, leaving them to be found and embarrassed by the coming morning's first arrivals. They had almost forgotten what the drunken young captain had said about Vander Pool. He was a tough old man and he had watched as the shotgun wielder grew less cautious—almost careless…almost stupid.

The man with the shotgun shifted the Mossberg to his left hand, barrel up, and twisted sideways to pull handcuffs from his belt. The butt of Vander Pool's .357 was right there in front of him, sticking out of the man's belt and so temptingly close. For a big man, an old and tired man, he struck like a snake. The heel of Vander Pool's left hand smashed hard into the man's face as his right jerked the .357 from his belt. The man bounced off the wall, an astonished and wide-eyed look on his face as Vander Pool jerked the trigger, the muzzle flash so close the man's shirt began to smolder. The roar of the .357, bottled up in the hallway, was deafening. The immediate reaction was startled and confused pandemonium. The old Warrant Officer simply pivoted left and pulled the trigger again, slamming a second man against an empty gun rack and onto the floor, a widening dark stain spreading across his chest.

That's as far as it got. The man managing this raid had a large-framed automatic up quickly and out at arm's length. He dropped into a crouch and fired twice, all within mini-seconds. Pieces of CW4 Hollis Vander Pool's face came off in a bloody spray that splattered across the frightened stare of the now almost sober Captain Morrisey. The shooter stood there a bit, as the men still standing tried to get their bearings and hearing back and nervously glanced jerkily about. Finally, and almost casually, he looked into the blank eyes of the shaking young Captain Morrissey, "You are one unlucky son of a bitch," was all he said as he shook his head. There was no change in his expression as he raised the pistol and shot the young man twice in the middle of his chest.

Holstering the pistol, he turned to the others and, as if it happened every day, ordered their dead associates left where they lay and hurriedly rushed the startled survivors out of the building. They drove off without apparent haste toward the freeway that wound up toward Tucson and, eventually, Phoenix. His only concern was that the dirt on the license plate obscured it enough so that no state trooper would notice that it was expired and enter into the mix.

He commented to his still-shaken cohorts that, "…if I had three men like that old warrant officer, I wouldn't need you." They just sat silently and stared into the darkness.

Chapter 2

THE RAIDING OF ONE NATIONAL GUARD armory and the slaughter that went with it was bad enough that it drew federal agencies like a visit from a sitting president. Unfortunately, the Nogales raid was only part of it. That same night and almost at the same time, a similar raid had taken an El Paso Army National Guard site by complete surprise and an even larger haul of military weaponry had disappeared into the night. This time, a few fully automatic pieces were also taken. And, as the papers and TV also trumpeted the next day, a small armory on the outskirts of Phoenix had also been raided. It felt like a small invasion.

By 9 o'clock in the morning, the politicians were already howling for blood and they didn't even know the half of it, not that they ever did. The media hadn't mentioned the previous day's attack on two large firearms and munitions wholesale facilities in North Carolina and Georgia, it wasn't political enough. At least, the swarms of newly arrived federal agents reminded themselves, there had been no shootings during the other armed attacks. On the other hand, they had thus far not even been able to make an identification of the dead stickup men left alongside Vander Pool and Morrissey on the bloody floor of the Nogales armory.

....

THE FIRST TRUCK PULLED INTO THE FENCED YARD behind the west-end Tucson JDS Enterprises building at a little after three in the morning. Two men awaited them. One, obviously in charge, was a well-dressed and dark man in his early thirties; the other was a big man, well-muscled and over 6'3". Neither of the waiting men looked happy. The big man did not have to; he held their lives in the palm of his hand.

The driver of the dark green Cadillac that followed the truck into the facility got out and hesitantly walked toward the two men. The conversation was short.

"Things went bad in Nogales and …"

The dark man cut him off. "I've heard. How bad?"

"We lost two—they lost two, Mr. Cooper," the nervous Mexican replied.

Cooper shook his head, anger clearly visible, "Alright. Get this stuff consolidated when the other trucks get here. Hide it at the county warehouse. And hear me," he finished, "get rid of those bit players you hired—permanently."

"Permanently?" the man asked with raised eyebrows and a questioning look.

"Before dawn. You know they can't all keep their mouths shut— we can't afford them."

The dark man only shook his head in what passed for momentary disbelief, then turned and walked away, his bodyguard in tow.

. . . .

IT HAS BEEN SAID BY THE MORE OBSERVING and eloquent few recording the history of man's endeavors that there is something of the child in all aviators. Happiness is hard to find but those who take to the sky seem to find that illusive virtue more frequently. It would seem that truly growing up goes against the life-long aviator's grain. At that moment, the phenomenon both helped and hindered a weary and sweating Wes Bailey as he vainly sought a moment's rest in the desert's grimy heat. His mind, trying to push physical discomfort aside, played with and hid among the shadows and shapes there before him in the isolation of the Sonoran Desert. He was in the right place for mind games, for Arizona's desert at summer's dusk is a combination of dusty smells, slowly fading heat, vaguely soft impressions and blurred images that can fill the mind and loosen the imagination. The distant buttes might become darkened, parapet surrounded castles and giant cactus loomed as aged and hapless Quixote-like warriors frozen in timeless and uneven ranks. The rustle of breezes in the cholla and patter of small desert animals scurrying across shifting dunes merged and, in the mind's eye, he could even imagine the ghosts of his yesterdays darkly skulking through the dunes, scab-rock gullies and outcroppings. Despite the pain in his gut, it all brought a slow smile to what otherwise had been Bailey's dour and grim-set face. His imagination was on a tear again; the pills making it difficult to suppress its wanderings. But, he thought, he might as well let it run for the moment. Baley breathed a deep sigh and looked back out into the coming darkness.

The land sloped unevenly downward from where Bailey stood, the desert foothills convulsing in a jumble of rocks, brush, sand, and gullies that meandered off toward the southwest. His tired and slightly bent frame almost totally blended with nearby boulders and the scrub brush surrounding the dark shape of an old twin-engine aircraft. It was still July hot and a powdery and purplish haze hung above the desert floor between the edge of the small airstrip and the hills far to the south. The ever-present armies of saguaro cactus, poking their spiny frames up through the haze, were silhouetted against the sky in the last of the shrinking contrast between sky and earth. Farther out, even they surrendered and were swallowed up in the coming darkness. To the northwest, where the valley widened, a thin shower could just be seen moving down from the hills to the flat, thirsty desert's floor. A heavy quiet began to softly blanket this bit of earth—if only for the moment.

A few lights winked on, scattered splashes across the valley floor, each marking a lonely enclave of humanity sequestered in the anonymous poverty of the dry and gritty solitude offered by the high desert. Far across the flats, the lights of a company town, in the distant past optimistically and colorfully misnamed Silverbell, spread from the skyline down into the deepening and indistinct gloom.

The quietness continued drifting in as a slowly rising tide and the little movement the slight breeze had stirred ceased with the transition from day to deepening and darkly soft dusk. Then the night noises began, first as almost a murmur, made by the few evening birds and, as if on cue, a few skittering ground animals hurrying for safe niches and burrows. As the sun's last rays dropped below the westerly mountain range, even that became lost in the distraction of the click and pop of the aircraft's cooling metal surfaces. There was a distinct smell of oil and solvents, dust, stale tobacco and insecticides that did not fit with the surroundings. But the night breezes soon began, cooler and more comforting, and he welcomed it.

Bailey stood very quietly, not moving at all for a few long and tired minutes. He took an even longer time moving his attention from the quiet desert darkness before him, as if by not doing so he could remain fixed there, lost in the peace of the moment, the jumbled canyons of his memory and, occasionally, his tired imagination.

Finally, he breathed a deep, tired sigh and turned away from his quiet isolation at the slope's edge, taking a last look at the thunderheads to the southwest. It was, after all, still monsoon season and he didn't need to contend with the heavy torrents a storm might bring. Then he trudged back toward the aircraft, carefully moving into the even darker shadows beneath its slouching frame. There was more to do than he could ever accomplish before the dawn came again. His travels through yesterday's haunting memories and quiet agonies would have to wait for a better time or at least be pushed to the back of his mind for the moment.

Bailey knew that he only had a scant few hours left on his promise to put the DC-3 into the air and a few meager hours more to head it south and away from this gritty piece of desert. He fought to stay focused on the tasks before him and found that effort more and more difficult. Farther out in the growing darkness, under a dim and yellowish light, he could see the shapes of two men moving about and hear the sounds of metal on metal, along with occasional soft curses as they labored over the aircraft.

Bailey stopped in the moon-cast shadow of the DC-3's port wing and stared up at the old aircraft's battered and weathered hulk with a care and concern born of ingrained survival instincts and a level of long-held reverence that, in this place and time, drifted toward awe. His perceptions were gathered through the dim light of a slowly dying battle lantern and shaped by memories that fell from over four decades of life in the sky. He tried, and failed again, to remember how many hours he had aloft in craft just like the one before him. It didn't matter. They would be at home with one another—for the time that either had left.

He had to admit to some involuntary amazement that the anachronism before him could still raise its wings to the sky. *Hell*, he thought almost aloud, he knew all the theories of flight and still wondered why things like this old Douglas flew. He wondered about himself too. That he was still here, after almost a lifetime of battered years, to shepherd this corroding old pelican to a morrow's fate was almost a miracle … or perhaps a just another nightmare in the making.

He, like the aircraft, was no youngster and he knew it all too well. He was, well, fiftyish, *if you were kind* and caught him on a more scrubbed and sharply attired day. If you were not inclined to that level of kindness and could be brutally honest, he would be in his 71st year in less than a month and looked, no, felt every day of it and then some. He was tired, so completely bone-weary tired that each step had become a struggle. There had been too many hours squinting through darkened windscreens at obscure landing fields, stale meals in long-forgotten backcountry nowheres, hundreds of long, tedious, sometimes hazard-filled hours airborne to places of which few people had ever heard or cared to hear. Too many sadnesses creased his brow and one bottle too many—a hundred-hundred bottles too many—wearied his mind, weakened his body, and drew deepening lines in his face.

Bailey, Wesley David Bailey, looked and, and at that moment, certainly felt the part he appeared: a graying, creaking old man, growing thick of body, out of place in a world slowly, but surely, passing him by, bitter and, now, terribly short of life's time. Still, contradictions were there for the truly astute, for he had always possessed a certain class and hardness that could be all too easily overlooked by the casual observer. Even he allowed that sorry first-impression to cloak his mind, far too often believing the negative to be true. The growing pain in his belly made most introspection moot and a waste of time; and he could ill-afford to waste the time.

The visual image he presented bothered Bailey very little however. Even in his more youthful days, wearing the tailored and dapper uniforms of half a dozen air carriers he had served, he happily managed to appear as just another anonymous pilot tucked away on the flight deck. He knew that and carried it comfortably, enjoying being simply a face among faces. His fascination was with the skies and the craft in which he plied them. The rest didn't matter. It was the thrill, yet peace, of flight that mattered to him.

Just a half an inch over six feet tall, he remembered always being conscious of an annoyingly persistent roll around his belt line. The crow's feet that tugged at the corners of his eyes didn't add character to a face now beginning to grow puffy with drink, they were just wrinkles on a face growing old. His coarse and graying crown of shaggy hair was beginning to thin and was nearly always unkempt. He smoked too much, ate too many of the wrong things and, by almost anyone's standards, drank too much. He could not have been outwardly more superficial, wasted, perhaps *beige* was a better descriptor, had that been the design of his gods—not that he had actively courted any, at least not these past few decades. Things were different now. He would readily accept help from God—any man's God. And he wondered, day-by-day, hour-by-hour, if it was already too late.

Only a pale and leathery line of a scar that ran from high on his right cheekbone downward across a face that was showing the veins and lines of too much whiskey made you notice Bailey in a crowd. And even that depended on the crowd being a very small and very bored one. He sought obscurity with skill, persistence, and success. The scar might catch your eye though and could not help but make you wonder what misfortune had indelibly drawn it there. But it was a relic of a long past misadventure that he never talked about. Occasionally, while staring into yesterday's space, he would run a slow finger down the scar. He thought about it but, for the most part, that was as far as it went. Its origin was his alone to remember. He knew no one could be more than temporarily interested in one of his ancient failings. That he had *almost* pulled an overloaded B-24 off of a too-short and muddy Malayan airstrip was fit only for barroom tale telling or some footnote to a history dedicated to no one in particular. Remembering that he was more than three fingers into a bottle at the time would only sadden him, particularly when he thought of the ones who died in the shattered and flaming wreckage he had strewn across the swamp beyond the runway.

So, he left that memory alone as much as he could and just let its shame, grief, and imbedded terror crouch there in the darkest recesses of his mind. It didn't matter any more, even to him, that the crash had come after days-on-end without rest and that the booze had only served to make the pain of a cracked vertebra even marginally bearable. It certainly didn't matter to the board of review officers that hung him out to dry after he limped out of the hospital and into their sanctimonious custody, comments, and charges … and predetermined decisions. It only mattered that he'd flown his crew into the trees and most of them into nameless, moldering, graves. They, these old and beloved companions, never left him though—never. Their ageless faces stared into his eyes from clouded dreams and their losses always weighed heavily on his soul's shoulders and continually chipped away at his spirit. It would ever be so, but the time left to withstand the pain was short, perhaps too short.

You might notice the scar though. If so, you would have to see his eyes. They were a surprise and hard to ignore and didn't seem to belong in the remainder of the man's jumbled composition. Once looked fully into, they could never be forgotten.

The man's eyes wrote books, books without words—yet full, from cover to cover. Wes Bailey's eyes were a light and almost translucent layering of blue-gray. They could be, at one moment, the watery and empty eyes of the wasted human refuse he almost always appeared to be—then, at the flip of some invisible switch, become cold, hard, and filled with ice and hazard. They could touch you with warmth and a heart beat later stare through you as if you didn't exist and lock onto some place and time long ago etched in his mind. But you instantly knew they missed nothing; seeing, analyzing, and recording everything. Those pale blue-gray eyes mocked and measured you; taking all of you in and knowing your worth in bare moments—and letting you know it without remorse or hesitation. The eyes may have been just about the only indication there was really something more than what you first glimpsed imprisoned inside the body and mind of what seemed a tired, long past salvage, old man.

Bailey's one consistently salable skill, given his state of moral and physical decay, was an ability to fly almost anything with wings and a propeller. There were over 17,000 hours of pilot in command time to prove that. As long as he was flying it was almost all that counted. He was ever aware of that and kept those skill honed to perfection. The ingredient that sold that skill these years past, considering his interminable affair with the bottle, was the ethic and hopelessly reliable mindset that allowed him to fly *anywhere* for *anyone*. His employers knew he could erase the whole episode from his mind and lips as if it had never happened. Some of his cargoes considered, that silence was a very good trait. It had brought his license to fly and live to the verge of revocation on more than one occasion and jail, or a client's bullet, seemed an almost unavoidable fate. Death had breathed down his neck during, and because of, more than one flight and its cargo. No matter what, his almost monastic trait of silence had certainly kept him alive in a business where life was of little worth and secrecy was far more important than anything, often breath itself.

Now, far too late, he was beginning to choke on that ethic. The time had come, though unplanned and certainly without welcome, to be able to look back on a life with which a man could find some tiny element of honor. He certainly, perhaps cynically, saw nothing resembling that; there was only emptiness and waste. Those thoughts turned around and around in the back of his mind and he found it interfering with his ability to prepare the aircraft to take to the sky again. It was difficult to even think beyond the moment. He squeezed his eyes tightly shut and shook his head, forcing himself to focus on the mental list of tasks he'd pulled from the many the aircraft required and that he had selected as his own to bear or eliminate. He leaned back against an oil drum and wearily stared up at the emerging blanket of bright, twinkling stars, trying hard to regain his focus. He closed his eyes again for a moment and he could hear her voice and vaguely see her outline against the darkness of his memory. Then she was gone. The jumble of thoughts seemed to waver and then sway back into a rationally straight line. He sighed and pushed himself on with the slow examination of the aircraft.

The aircraft he warily circled had been part of the draw for this job though. There was, of late, a conscious and almost desperate search for *what once was* in his life and this old Douglas filled large gaps in that quest and it gave him one last chance to leave something good and useable behind. Despite himself, and deep in his soul, he was beginning to feel a bond developing between the ancient aircraft and himself. He felt once again a small but better part of everything he'd ever been when he wandered down the length of her fuselage, touched the control pedestal, gripped and moved the yoke, breathed in the smells he believed only the old Douglas could possess.

She had a soul. He knew it. That soul had a voice that spoke to him and it spoke to him in a language only he could hear and understand.

To be sure, he was remembering his life as it had been three decades past, but it was better than the *now* he struggled within. His interaction, and it was without doubt an *interaction*, with the aircraft felt good and brought a sharp and instant flush of life to his mind and body. The increasing pain in his gut was ever-so-slightly pushed away from the center of his mind and he would struggle through, no matter what came. He needed to end his time with one lasting and final taste of personal honor. It even pushed the need for booze aside and dampened the fatigue still slowing his mind and body.

The plane's personality was there too and, now that it was necessary, warmed and lent excitement his weary mind. She was without doubt worn, patched, aged, and flown to the wall. Yet, somehow, there was a stately, almost eager set to her frame. But, beyond all that, there was a curious, almost human melancholy, as if the old aircraft regretted all her past sad cargoes and felt embarrassment at the decayed state that now defined her. They, the worn DC-3 and Bailey, fit together as surely as if expressly made for one another.

The look and feel of the old aircraft told Bailey this flight might well be her last. The pain he carried with him was also explicit in that it wouldn't make any difference—to Bailey at least. He pushed his hand into the front of his dirty coveralls and ran his fingers over the warm surface of his Saint Michael, worn nearly smooth by time and touch and carried for over forty years. For a moment, it brought a tiny bit of comfort and hope back to life.

....

T
HE VAGUE SHAPE AND THREATENING PRESENCE of the small and dark Mexican watchdog with the machine pistol, shadowy and indistinct against the night sky, troubled Bailey's thoughts. They somehow grew into a significantly oppressive part of the atmosphere at the dirty little airstrip. The man's aura was both irritating and, somehow, part theater. Sooner, more probable than later, the dance

between them would stop and it would not be pleasant. Bailey had already begun the mental process of finding reasons to hate the little man that he had never met before that evening's yesterday. It would make the coming and unavoidable confrontation easier. It also helped to know that the man underestimated him—a foolish thing for a man to do that played with guns and power.

The confrontation-to-come created little fear for Bailey. He knew his biggest problem lay with keeping Stoudamyre from starting the dance sooner than absolutely necessary. The little Mexican was a problem, just not much of one. It was obvious he, totally soaked in bravado and arrogance, knew little about his charges. When the time came, he would be swatted just like another fly. A picture fuzzily moved across Bailey's mind: a pressed and shiny little militia captain, waving his pistol about and shouting orders as he unloaded paramilitaries on a potholed little airstrip midst the Bolivian mountains. He remembered how the little captain finally focused on him, the only Anglo present, and began pointing the pistol in a more threatening and aggressive flurry of words. Then there was the shocked look on his face and the widening of his eyes as he looked down at the two almost symmetrical red splotches on the front of his so correctly pressed shirt and then back up to the old 1911 in Bailey's hand. Nothing else came; Bailey could remember none of the man's falling or the total silence that followed in the ranks surrounding him. The man's image simply disappeared into the shadows of his mind. And Bailey wished that was all he needed to hide.

He forced his attention back to the aircraft one more time and began to slowly examine it more closely. It seemed to just slouch there, faded and gray, patched and battered, on bald and age-checkered tires. The thought ran through Bailey's mind that he and the old aircraft deserved each other. Descriptions of their physical condition could be made in the same terms and be correct, except that the old Douglas had once been something to be admired. He doubted with the sincerity and certainty of a cynic that he personally had ever been of much actual worth.

Bailey reached up and brushed some of the newly collected dust from an aileron and noticed that after only a short time on the ground the aircraft was already covered with a coating of fine and gritty desert powder. He ran the battle lanterns ever-weakening beam along the fuselage and stopped at the barely visible hand lettering beneath the pilot's side wing window. The words *Shawnee Rose* were faded but visible and he wondered what pretend aerial cowboy had named her that and when, even where. Shaking his head and with a dry smile, he went on with what could best be described as an autopsy.

He had flown scores of aircraft just like *The Rose*. These once proud aircraft, ravaged by years and neglect, had become time-weary and unpredictable. They could be death traps for those who casually flew them. New, this relic had been no different from those in which he had hauled mail in and out of Syracuse, Cleveland, and Tulsa; moved tense and frightened paratroopers cross-channel in '44, sweating and dying legionnaires out of Algeria and the Congo—even Dien Bien Phu. They still flew, even though they both had degenerated to their current sorry state of decay. The budding new drug cartels' outback strips in Colombia and Bolivia provided his home-away-from-home now and, at the same time, kept him in his element. But, they both had to deal with the inevitable; they were worn out. Neither could last much longer. Still, he chose, for the moment, to ignore that, concentrating instead on the fact that he was still flying well past his time.

This particular evening, only the time and location had changed. He was on a narrow little Arizona airstrip, trying to make believe the sad pile of junk before him could become airborne again and serve his employer's purpose. To bend things more to the ludicrous, he loved every second of it. On the debit side of the ledger, he didn't yet know what the cargo was or where it would go. The truth was, he didn't care—and that was all that made it bearable.

Faces, still young, stared out of the darkness, crowding in on his mind, and he could remember them as if it were only moments before that he'd heard their voices. He wondered what his ghosts thought of him now. Noticing that others were within earshot, he chose not to talk to his ghosts this night. His smile was gone. The pain was back.

Bailey rubbed a hand that smelled of gas, dirt and oil, across his face and wished for a drink, a real drink. But there was no alcohol at the strip. His new employers had learned enough of his reputation to see to that. He settled for a cigarette with the rationalization that booze might make him miss a defect that could later on kill him. Considering the sorry condition of the Douglas brought a stark reminder that would be easy enough as it was.

That thought process failed though. He still wanted a drink and the prospect of being dead didn't seem to hold much terror at the moment. Perhaps death would actually be a welcome visitor at some point very soon. At least the pain would be gone. He had just over half of the prescription left of the pain medication the Veterans Administration doctor had provided and that helped for the moment. He wouldn't even have that but for the understanding young physician who'd delivered the bad news. He thought about that for a few seconds and could see the government-green examining room in its dismal entirety again. He could hear, off in an echoing distance, the young man telling him, in polite, caring, and quiet tones, that what caused him pain was inoperable. They could check him in and keep him comfortable; the young man guaranteed that. Instead, Bailey dressed and just walked out. The pills had later and surprisingly arrived by cab at his worn single-wide trailer, along with a note from the young physician that wished him well and offered a telephone number if he needed further help.

He was startled out of his black thoughts by the sound of approaching footsteps. "Hey! … Man!" the shadow with the machine pistol bitched, "You think you oughta be smokin' 'round all this gas and shit?"

It was not really an inquiry, the tone wasn't even very questioning. Bailey's safety was not the issue either. The man's continual nagging was little more than an effort to show who held all the power and that he too was bored. The slim and filthy Mexican seemed to feel his control could be exercised and evidenced only with a constant stream of meaningless jabbering and incessant toying with the machine pistol he cradled across brown and tattooed arms. Bailey couldn't even remember his name. The effort to remember a dead man's name wasn't worth the effort.

When Bailey offered no answer, the man raised his voice a little higher and pushed, "Hey … man … you hear me?"

Bailey's voice was low and flat, its weariness almost liquid, "Yeah. I hear you. Why don't you go somewhere else and … play with yourself … OK? I don't think your owner would like it if he thought for even a second you were getting in my way."

There was a forced and shrill cackle of shallow laughter, then, "Careful how you talk to me old man … careful!"

The little man did disappear from the skyline though. Bailey could hear the crunch of sand on tarmac as he trudged away from the airplane and disappeared into the darkness.

Bailey breathed a sigh of relief; at least he would be left alone for a while. The darkness would fold around him and there would be time to wander through memories while sleepwalking through a perfunctory inspection of the aircraft. *The Rose* had already begun to take on a character and personality of her own. He liked that. *The Rose* and he would be close friends. She had the look and feel of others he'd known and he could remember, almost see and feel, their passage through the skies of all his adult years, though darkly and far away.

Chapter 3

WHEN BAILEY HAD FIRST SEEN *THE ROSE* from a distance, its mottled gray silhouette had almost blended into the surrounding landscape. It seemed a tired old wreck that little could help and certainly not fit for any kind of long and severe trial his tomorrows would certainly bring.

The logbooks told him the plane's airframe had withstood enough flying time to have accumulated over sixty-five thousand hours of flight time and that it had been almost fifteen hundred hours since the overhaul of its newest power plant. It was stretched thin—very thin. He doubted those entries though and just about anything else recorded in the logbooks available in the weathered old derelict. He very seriously questioned where his employers had acquired the craft.

Still, there was a comfortable level of stateliness about the best of Douglas's creations. That characteristic seeped through, even in its current and obvious state of decay. Bailey's fondness for *The Rose* grew steadily as each new bit of her character and personality surfaced.

Both of the R-1830 Pratt and Whitney engines were filthy from oil leaks and caked in dust and grime. At first walk-around, there had been bits of fading green leaves attached to a slim piece of branch wedged into the space between the aileron and the wing on the starboard side and fresh scrapes in the metal nearby. A takeoff or landing that had almost failed seemed the most likely explanation. Bailey shook his head and wondered about the rest of the aircraft and who had flown it last and, more to the point, for what reason.

The time since engine overhauls made for a great deal of nervous uncertainty. Even considering the little that he knew of the destination, he was aware there would be a long over-flight of mountain wilderness and jungle terrain, and that test of *The Rose's* capabilities would be followed by a jump of part of the Caribbean. That would be asking for trouble with the condition that the engines were in—as if there weren't enough problems already.

He reminded himself aloud that he should have gone over to jets—*way back when.* But, God, how he hated them and, at this point in time, it was far too late to worry about that. Now was now and he was too damned old to even consider the 727s or DC-8s that had passed him by. There was only crumbling, old and dissolute, 392 Delta … *Shawnee Rose* to someone a long time ago.

He chuckled at how the name looked out of place now. But it seemed only yesterday that he'd seen strips all over both theatres of the war alive with aircraft just like this one. It only *seemed* yesterday though and even now the memories had a faded and distant look to them. Somehow, someway, after the pain that crowded his body begun to fade with the pills and his *here-and-now* senses were dulled, it all came back, in dirty brown and gray images. The edges of his mind began to fill with the voices and movement of young men in the midst of the confusion and din of war and there was a crushing roar of a thousand engines in a dozen skies. The present seemed to slip away, if only for a little while.

Aircraft—generally those of *The Rose's* ilk—and bouncing from pillar to post like some rootless gypsy, had been too much of Bailey's life. It had shown him most of the civilized—and not so civilized— world. It had also cost him a wife and the regret tied to that had grown to a morose depression that deepened with drink and always lay just below a calm, almost expressionless, veneer. The daughter that left with his wife made the anguish just below that calmness almost unbearable. This trip was for them—*all he had to give.*

Bailey's bare and hurried examination of the panel had turned up a variety of instruments and electronics. Some of the newer pieces were at least twenty years old, the remainder in between ancient and just old. A small smile touched his face momentarily when his mind passed back over what little he knew of his piece of the whole scheme that he was now involved with and how this run-down pile of junk only added to the insanity of it. But, when he sat there on the flight deck's left seat, *The Rose* seemed to fold quietly in around him, as if offering comfort to a friend.

Insanity might well be a good description for it, but he was broke—dead broke—and there had been no other real job prospects when this gamble came up. Since his walk-away from the Veterans Hospital, he had been desperate for work—any work. He had so little time left that, as he often thought aloud, "Any plane, any place, and any time." There had to be one payoff—all in cash. He would not need it where he was bound and it would be his last contribution to the welfare of all that would be left of him. He wished—every moment—that he could be there in person to give them what little he would have left from this flight. He dreamed of seeing them *just one more time.*

....

THE WELL-DRESSED BLACK MAN quietly listened as the man across the table assured him, again, that the aircraft and its load would be ready in less than three days. Everything, he purred, was going well. He had an excellent crew and a full load of the *product* requested. He slid a single key across the table and the black man quickly palmed it out of sight.

"So, check this *sample* out. Number of the locker is on the key. Bus station is two blocks down the street west. I wouldn't leave it there long."

They stared at each other for a few moments, then the black man nodded at him and handed him a folded newspaper that concealed an envelope containing $20,000 in cash.

"Thank you, Mister Cooper. Here is a sample of my wares. I'll see you at the strip day after tomorrow."

The man stood, shrugged his suit jacket straight and said, "Enjoy your drink." He turned and walked off through the tables filled with after-work drinkers and skirt chasers toward the door, his bodyguard falling in behind him.

"Thank you, I will," the black man said to no one, as he reached for the double Irish, neat, and settled back into the chair. He would check the *sample* later.

....

THE MEN WHO HAD OFFERED THIS FLIGHT had known who they were looking for though and Bailey would be the last to ask who had sent them his way. He did briefly wonder how they had gotten to him and he was glad they didn't know quite as much about him as they thought they did.

They—the secretive thugs he'd since come to despise—had found him sitting at a small table near the back of an almost vacant and musty smelling bar that hunkered down sadly among one of city's most bleak, hovel thatched sides of town. He frequented it often. It was about all he had left—except for the memories. It continued to feed his weakness for booze and his solitude was rarely invaded there. The bar's owner, himself a one-time crop duster, considered him a fellow aviator and allowed Bailey to run a lengthy tab. He seemed to feel a certain kinship with Bailey, one aviator to another, with both men long past their prime, usually awash with booze, and struggling with a world ignoring their existence. Bailey always paid up—sooner or later—and that kept the sour mash readily available.

Conveniently, the stale smelling little saloon was just around the corner from the trailer park where Bailey rented a single-wide box of aluminum, plastic and cockroaches that a noisy twenty-four-hour-a-day swamp cooler made almost bearable. There were not many places lower for him to hide his soul and await the end.

He remembered looking up from the last of an imitation of Jack Daniel's when the unwelcome glare of the door opening invaded his morose memories and self-pity. At first, he'd only idly watched the three men file in, looking around as if the smell of the place offended them. God knows, it should have. One of them leaned across the bar and motioned for the frizzy blond building drinks and pulling beers. She absentmindedly polished the counter top between them and wiped her hair back with the hand not occupied with the bar towel while listening to the man. She was little more than a dark shape against the dingy yellow painted window in the saloon's front but it was easy for Bailey to remember, with a grimace, just how homely the woman really was. Then she leaned toward the man and stretched to see beyond the fat trucker sitting there, both elbows on the bar and a beer parked just below his chin. It was apparent she was looking for someone and he had started to wonder who, when she gave a nod of recognition and pointed the hand holding the bar towel directly at him.

Bailey felt his senses involuntarily cringe and the thought that the men might be cops flared for a moment. But all he had unaccounted for were a couple of low-end and overdue movers. No police department worth its salt sent three men out to collect for something that chippy. That thought turned the knot in his gut to ice.

The three men spread through the few tables to almost block Bailey's way out of the bar and then moved slowly toward him. Anxiety overtook the booze and he began to think of his last employers and their illicit cargoes. Two of the men approaching him were obviously hard men and the third was a well dressed, though too warmly so, black. When they were close enough for him to see them clearly, it became obvious they could not be cops. There was no polyester.

One of the heavies, the physically less imposing of the two, stepped closer to the table and momentarily stared through the smoke, his eyes almost comically hooded and drawn to exaggerated slits. He very quietly said, "We need to talk to you—outside—not here." He twanged of somewhere low rent, maybe Chicago, Bailey thought.

The man didn't even ask who he was. That frightened him more than the idea they might be cops. It was suddenly serious and Bailey had no place to run. And running was something he was good at—he'd run from life and all its implications for the better part of his seventy-plus years.

The voiceless half of the white duo merely stood there and looked the bar over, his eyes never still. His whole image was something copied from Hollywood's version of a mobster. He kept his arms folded across his chest, his right hand never straying too far from a bulge the heat and a shoulder holster made prominent under his left armpit. It was the only flaw in his warm, but otherwise correct, blue and gray pinstripe suit.

Bailey vaguely remembered that he gave them a somewhat slurred, four-whiskey, "Wha'for?" and that the man's expression had only hardened. The voiceless one crowded a little closer to the table, while the well-dressed and out-of-place black continued mopping a sweating brow with a large and wilted white kerchief. The talker very quietly continued, "Someone told me you got lots of time in big and old prop jobs. I need someone like that. Real soon." He straightened to his full height and disdainfully added, "And sober."

Bailey's attention had been bought for the moment and he raised an eyebrow and listened more closely, even through the fog the booze had raised and thickened. But the man said nothing else. He just looked at Bailey a hard moment, then turned and walked to the door, pushed it open and stood to one side of the blaze of light stabbing into the dark coolness of the saloon. Letting his two companions exit, he turned and looked back to where Bailey still sat behind his empty glass. The man's stare was a statement that made not following a less than sensible option.

Bailey shrugged, careful to maintain an exaggerated nonchalant appearance and ignored the rising tightness in his chest. He lurched to his feet and, in that same calm, pulled a handful of stale popcorn from the wicker basket on the table, and followed the trio out into the painful brilliance of a July afternoon in Arizona's high desert.

It all began there.

Chapter 4

The Nogales National Guard armory was crowded with white-coated technicians, federal cops of every description, and an overabundance of uniformed Army officers. Little knots of quietly talking investigators and officers surrounded a large square of mess hall tables filling the center part of the drill floor.

Near the entrance, a shirt-sleeved and dark complexioned man listened quietly and intently, a telephone pressed to one ear, the other covered by a hand to dampen the noise. When he hung up, he looked around the room and, spotting who he wanted, caught his attention, and motioned him over. They talked a moment and then walked to the edge of the table. The man reached out and picked up an ashtray and tapped it on the table, then raised his voice above those already talking.

"Gentlemen—gentlemen, could I have your attention?" When the noise of voices ceased, he went on. "I'm Special Agent Obregon." He very carefully didn't say Special Agent of what. "This is Special Agent Bill Simpson, FBI. We've been assigned primary on this." He noticed the other faces around the room showed relief and that they thought themselves lucky. Big cases can make you or break you and this one had all the earmarks of someone's transfer to Butte, Montana … for life.

Obregon went on, "I'll need anything and everything you've got forwarded to Bill's office. I'm from out of town so you can reach me there for the time being."

Simpson stood quietly for a moment, then turned toward two nearby darkly-suited men, "Charley, could you and your partner work with those Army CID guys over there and interview the armory's personnel? I don't expect much, but I do need what you can get on the two victims."

Obregon nodded and said, "Thanks guys, let's get at it." He turned to Simpson and continued more quietly, "Let's get the hell out of here. You probably have more questions than I have answers for already."

....

Looking up at where a navigation light should have been and noting that its glass cover had been sheared off, Bailey thought back on the strange and stilted conversation in the saloon's parking lot. It had been a short but uncomfortable verbal sparring match that had eventually led to the dusty little airstrip out in the middle of nowhere.

First, there had been the almost unbearable heat. Bailey still laughed at the local's, "*Well, it's dry heat,*" routine. 105 degrees was 105 degrees to him; hot was hot, miserable was miserable. There had also been the great effort the two whites put into acting out mobster roles. To be sure, they *were* mobsters, and he thought them barely above the street-level and bottom-feeder sort. Their overly practiced swagger had only bent the meeting toward the ridiculous. Last in the parade of dark humor, a marked County Sheriff's prowler had cruised through the parking lot, the deputy glaring at them from his air-conditioned bubble as though they were already guilty of something and, if not, had something contagious. The deputy quickly moved on to other boredoms though, little about them to hold his attention, but he had inadvertently almost broken up the meeting.

Bailey had done a lot of things you didn't just up and run to the cops about. There had been more than one load of marijuana, a hashish wheel or two along the way and cocaine was the new entry to the world of dreams and uselessness to mankind. That didn't even consider the illegal immigrants and fugitives he'd ferried across half a dozen borders. Some of the flights had been not so lucky as others. One had ended scattered across a rough New Mexico foothills strip and another mired in a soggy Georgia swamp. And there were others that brought the same level of pain—and remorse.

He thought back on those flights for a long and almost mournful moment. The prop-bender in New Mexico had hardly held any terrors. The gear simply wouldn't come down. The hydraulics had leaked so badly that you could smell the fluid throughout the plane so he wasn't surprised when the gear didn't respond to his efforts; neither did the flaps. But a DC-4 is strong and he had brought it in on a long, slow and shallow glide path, holding her nose up and the speed down as much as he could until the belly began scraping the gravel and sod. The old DC-4 had surprised him and tracked almost straight down the worn stretch of grassland strip until it just shuddered, pivoted a half turn to the left, and abruptly stopped.

There'd been no fire and no injuries. The dopers, a couple of them high on their own trash, had moved their haul out in a few short hours, and then torched the old bird. Bailey hated that, aircraft held life to him, but he simply walked away with no more than a sour taste in his mouth and a few glances over his shoulder, warily looking for Border Patrolmen and county cops or, worse, dopers with a change of heart about leaving a witness behind. He'd heard later that the dopers managed to get picked up by the cops before they'd even reached Albuquerque. He was glad that he'd just taken a bus to El Paso and hunkered down in a motel with a couple of fifths of Jack Daniels for company and solace.

The other was a nightmare; a belly-landing in the Georgia swamps just south of Waycross held far more painful memories. He didn't like thinking about it, but found to forget it was impossible. He remembered it with brilliant and painful clarity.

Bailey could still see and feel that flight in its entirety. He had pushed in late and low, ferrying a Beech Kingair across the gulf at wave top level and on up into the southeast's swamplands. The weather had been bad enough to suit his purposes but the human cargo, three Guatemalans—all former military police colonels running for their lives—were airsick and scared. When he'd crossed the coast, they were riding the left front quadrant of a tropical storm that just missed a random name that went with hurricanes. The storm had begun its predictable turn back northeast and was dumping rain from ceilings that never quite reached four hundred feet and pushed hard at him with a quartering tail wind that drove his airspeed indicator into insane and erratic behavior. He knew very well they'd not escaped the radar of all those who looked for his kind, they were just too smart to come out after him in that night's weather.

The original destination had been a small strip on a farm near Valdosta but, when he buzzed by at one hundred feet, he saw that the field and the surging brown river next to it had merged into one dirty and swirling mass. He'd hurriedly circled twice, looking for and not finding anyone on the ground, and then moved on to the northeast, three hundred feet showing, near empty tanks, and a starboard engine beginning to run rough. It only lasted another seven minutes.

He hadn't been high enough to pick up a good signal from Waycross's Omni and know precisely where he was, but the rain had shown a bit lighter and brighter brand of gray sky off to his right. He started to pull the nose of the Beech that direction and had just begun a gentle bank to the right when both engines simply quit. Bailey had the air speed to stay in the shallow bank toward the brightness for a few seconds and then began trying to set up for a bad ending to it all there in the middle of Georgia's swamps. He remembered that the three big-shot colonels in the back had started almost child-like wails and that he could hear one retching. It was only a few moments before the Beech was banging and slashing through the swamp grass, putrid water, mud, and brush.

He remembered that something hard had smacked into his head and that things dimmed for a while, but that he still tried, stupidly and futilely, to keep the Beech's nose pointed down the open trough between the trees. It was a waste of effort; the plane went where the mud and the force of its landing led it. Though seemingly forever, in mere seconds he and two of the Guatemalans were out and slogging through the swamp, desperately seeking high ground.

One of the colonels stayed with the plane. The fat one, with the dumb looking Hitler-like mustache, was left dead. The torn sheet metal near his seat and his face blended together as a single, bloodied and tangled mass but he was still moaning and trying to push himself erect. Bailey had considered the few options left to him and pulled out the same old 1911 he now carried and leaned back toward the surely dying man and shot him, right between the torn metal and the man's right eye. His misery was over; Bailey's just continuing in what had become a familiar pattern.

The two of them that did manage to crawl out of the torn and broken Beech began a search for high ground, but it went downhill from there. Bailey and the sad-faced little colonel from Cuidad Vieja managed to stumble out onto a muddy county road just as dawn broke dimly through the clouds. The other colonel, and he gratefully couldn't remember his name, was somewhere back in the swamp's mud, high water, snakes and 'gators. They didn't even know when they'd lost him; just that one minute he was there and, when they looked again, he was gone. He often wondered if the man had ever been found. Lately, their lost souls had become bitter fodder for his more frequent nightmares … and futile prayers.

Bailey had been paid well and up-front for that trip. The three colonels, running from a change-in-government firing squad, had forged papers and signed the Kingair over to him and given him a briefcase filled with $75,000 in used U.S. twenties and fifties. He'd come away with just over $7,000 in fifties he had, for some reason, stuffed into his flight jacket pockets. The rest was in the swamp with the dead colonel and what was left of the Kingair. Even then, he figured he had still come out ahead. He was alive. The $7,000, well, that was an extra.

A week after they hitched a ride into Waycross with an old black farmer and his pickup truck, Bailey had read that the remaining

Guatemalan hanged himself in an INS holding cell in Miami. Bailey was already laying low in Augusta and doing some ferry work for a local fixed base operator out of his past. It was only by chance that he caught the small article about the Guatemalan. INS was on the verge of shipping the man home and he'd simply pre-empted a firing squad. Bailey, still anonymous, wasn't even on their radar. The tone and color of his life had not improved much since then, just the locations and the paymasters."

....

HIS MIND DRIFTED BACK to the then and there and he recalled that, until this day, at least all his previous customers had been up front about their cargoes. The potential meal tickets bankrolling this venture had only looked him up and down and asked questions about his flying experience. Bailey hoped it wasn't another load of grass. He didn't like hauling grass. Some of it stank to high heaven and often crawled with every bug known to the outback. The crawling things would remind him of the swamp and the dead colonels and he hated it. Worse, the people who sold it and paid for the transport, were the most unpredictable and treacherous lots he'd known. That was to be expected with amateurs, he thought, and *these guys smack of amateur*. Only the guys with big money haul coke or smack. He tried to stay away from them too. A man dumb enough to have a memory is too expendable with the big-time haulers to suit Bailey.

The mobsters' questions were clumsy and completely annoying. Bailey's answers, true or not, seemed to mean little to either of them. The content of the questions had shown they knew little, if anything, about flying. It was evident he'd either been pointed out to them as a pilot to do their kind of work or, perhaps, that they had no one else to whom they could turn. Now they were playing a game designed to establish *position*. Bailey didn't mind a lot if keeping the upper hand did something for them. He was accustomed to being on the low end of things. The equation was simple. They had the money and he didn't. He let them ramble on, really listening only occasionally, and, even with effort, those brief interludes were hampered by the booze.

Finally, after a spate of prodding from Bailey, his questioner had said, "Pretend you're back in Air America, asshole. What's inside the frickin' airplane is secret." He had dropped that as if playing a long held and cherished ace. It did set all of Bailey's alarms ringing, but all he could do was wonder how they had learned of that ill-remembered part of his life and flying time. Very few people possessed that information. After a dragging bit of silence, the man finished with, "Oh, screw it … you'll know if and when the time comes—provided you're in. Besides, if you're not and know more …." He let his voice trail off and, offering a poor, one-sided and humorless smirk, pointed a finger at Bailey and let his thumb fall like the hammer on a pistol. He had made his point and there was no doubt that he meant it.

There was another strained period of silence, while the heat pressed in even more. He didn't like where the conversation was going and was about to give them the best *piss-off* that the booze and heat would allow and just walk away—despite the obvious physical hazards that course of action might hold. It was grass. It had to be grass and he didn't want to haul any more of it. More to the point, there wasn't enough money in hauling grass to meet his very last needs. That came first. At that moment, he'd haul firewood for the devil's fires for the right price.

It was then that the first words finally came from the black. The voice was flat and emotionless, yet deep, and sounded as if had been nurtured in educated soil. There was no immediately recognizable regional identity to it and the tones didn't match the look that combined anger and solemnity on the man's face. There was something about the man that invited—no, commanded— confidence and that he be heard.

"Mister Bailey—Wes, if I may—these men have sold me *something*. At least they say that is so." His eyes flicked toward the two mobsters and offered, with a harsh and stony darkness, an edged message not to interfere. "I know your fear. Narcotics. Yes?" He let the words hang there for a time before going on. "Well, you may rest assured our cargo does not contain any form of narcotics … unless you consider the politics of power narcotic. I personally detest even the most minimal use of drugs and, remember, one transports narcotics into America—not out. Am I correct?" There was a short silence, then, "But I must get my … ah … *purchase* … home. These bloodsuckers will not get their money until I'm safely out of the country." He paused again and looked at Bailey with an almost expressionless face, cleared his throat and said, "… and I do need to get out of the country—right now! It is more imperative that you can ever guess."

The black man paused for another moment, then turned to face the now fidgety mobsters and continued in a more quietly controlled, yet almost forced and mockingly subservient drawl, "So, y'all see, *sir*, we both desire your services; don't we … gentlemen?"

The two white men's anger now began to bubble up, accelerating their case of nerves and they became obviously more uncomfortable. But they did not say a word. It was plain they did not enjoy being pushed from their top-of-the-totem roles, but worked at keeping up a relaxed façade, with appropriately ominous glares at both Bailey and the black man. While the threatening looks were not lost on Bailey, the black man seemed totally unimpressed. It was becoming apparent that *he* might be the one to fear.

Bailey turned his stare to the black man, summoned up a small reserve of bravado, and asked, "Just who the hell are you?"

The black just stared back for a while, seeming to probe beyond the veneer of alcohol and bluster. Finally, he quietly responded, "My name is Guthrie Mubutu … you may call me Guthrie or Mr. Mobutu. My last name might sound odd, coming from your tongue, so, if that troubles you, call me Colonel. I would appreciate it if you did not do so around others who are people not a part of our little … ah, clique … though."

Bailey's mind instantly filled with memories of his swamp-bound Guatemalans and his stomach recoiled, bile and fear-ridden. He almost said aloud, "Not again," but stifled it, though visibly paling. The change in Bailey's expression was not lost on Mobutu and though it puzzled him, he only filed it away for a later time and use. He stroked the ridge of his nose with a forefinger and looked directly into Bailey's eyes for what seemed half a minute, before continuing, "At any rate, while I shall not directly pay you, there will be no pay without me. I suggest we can use each other … for the time being at least."

The voice had begun to sound something vaguely like what Bailey remembered as created in Sandhurst. He remembered a Brit he'd flown with who had gone there. While that was long before Bailey's fall from grace, the sound had stuck there in the back of his mind. His thoughts slipped away to the man for a moment and he wondered where the fates had taken him since the Congo. The black's voice continued and brought him back to the moment. It was obvious he was showing more poise, as if he knew he was winning a little.

"Wes, I must return to a point on the African Continent—Liberia to be exact. But that need not concern you. You are not going that far. I mean no threat, please don't think that. It is just that you will have enough worries getting us across the very roughest miles that Mexico and Central America have to offer. If—and I say, *if*—you make that, and we have all of the Sierra Madres to cope with, probably the Air Defense Forces of Mexico and certainly enough trigger happy people in the Guatemala, Honduras, Belize, Nicaragua corridor to go around, your job will be over. Remember, we cannot prearrange happy welcomes in all these spots for ourselves. In fact, I hope not to stop at all." After a short pause he continued, "I have something to take with me … undiscovered, so to speak."

He leaned back against the fender of the dark Ford sedan and, with some sarcasm, went on, "I've seen our *transportation*. You have your work cut out for you. Considering the aircraft's decrepit state, it will be a long, slow and undoubtedly hazardous journey." At the mention of *transportation*, he had leveled a glare at his two associates that caused an immediate and visible flinching. Yes, *he* would be the one to fear.

"Well, *Guthrie*, just where the hell are *we* going?"

"Mister Bailey … Wes, if I may, I will tell you this much. We are headed for an old military airstrip on the Gulf of Venezuela. It is just on the Venezuelan side of their border with Colombia … near a small place called Cojua. Whatever that quaint name means, the local people call it *The Plain of the Dogs*. God knows why. It is a good thirty kilometers outside the Maraciabo control zone, so local authorities shouldn't present an immediate problem—*if* we get in and out in a hurry. You know those little piss-ant countries are always fighting, so anything could happen. Just know there will be to be motorized barges ready and a freighter nearby to take care of our load. We will, hopefully, meet another aircraft there with additional cargo. Given the strip's proximity to the border, it is restricted airspace. Therefore, it is low, slow … and it is careful. Understand?

"You sound like a man who can fly one of these things yourself. Why do you need me?" Bailey's heart was in his throat. He knew the strip only too well. The old airstrip had long been a departure point for narco-smugglers and the people scattered across the small plats hewn from the jungle had been under the thumb of the smugglers' small and brutal armies for years. They were treated like dogs and remembered as dogs. Their little part of the coastal flats was, and had been for years, called *The Plain of the Dogs*.

Over the last half-dozen years, both Columbia and Venezuela had periodically rained on the smuggler's parade, principally to draw more and better bribes. As a result of the conflict, several of the local villages had managed to arm themselves from battlefield debris and become very aggressive. The Plain of the Dogs had become an extremely dangerous and deadly place to be. The locals were friendly to no one and subservient only to the better armed.

Mobutu grimaced and shook his head slowly, "Alas, Wes, I am a person with many hours in rotary craft—but, I'm sorry to say, not one whit of time in any fixed wing aircraft larger than a Cessna 172, … ever. But, know that you will be paid well, very well. I understand that might be to your style and ethic?"

Bailey only stared back, saying nothing, distaste strong on his face, understanding Mobutu did mean to insult and that he had suceeded. He tried hard to respond with something sharp and biting, but the booze and the fact that what the man said was true silenced him. Mobutu did not yet sound totally confident, but it was obvious that he considered Bailey as someone less than honorable. More, it was apparent he knew that it was only a matter of time and proper incentive until he had his way. They stood and stared at each other for what seemed minutes though was probably only a few seconds. Bailey was caving in, even though he had not said a word.

The black man chuckled without any real humor showing and said, "The airstrip is no Heathrow, but certainly no worse than that from which you'll leave here in Arizona. While the Venezuelan military no longer uses the facility, they once flew patrol bombers out of it—your American Liberators I think—and they took far more runway than you'll require."

Bailey nodded and said quietly, "I know the place very well … been there several times. … wish I'd never heard of it."

Mobutu stared at him and nodded then, after a moment, went on, "Only a few local, shall we say, *farmers* use the strip now and, I hear, some of the villagers are dangerous. I'll no longer be concerned with you once the aircraft is on the ground there. Our friends here have told me that you can keep the aircraft—as long as it never comes back into the U.S. That does sound acceptable, doesn't it?"

Mobutu stared at Bailey a few seconds longer, a smile still playing at the edges of his mouth, before continuing, "I'm sure you've guessed that if the authorities catch you it will surely mean jail—and jail down there will be anything but enjoyable. You should also be aware that if you betray me, these men—or I—will just as surely kill you." The comment came as casually as if he were discussing the weather. Bailey did not doubt for a second that he meant it.

When that had the desired effect, he finished with, "There is even more than a remote possibility the reception at journey's end will be less than amicable. But, you have to get us there first." The last phrase came softly but with the return of the same baleful glare at his companions.

Bailey stood quietly for a moment the said, "You're sure as hell cheerful," then more quietly, "and not much an advertisement for your ... uhh ... *company*."

Ignoring the comment, the black went on, "Mister Bailey, I assume this man has your telephone number. He'll call you in the morning to see if you are at all interested. If you are, there will be much more to tell you then. If you are not interested, I'd suggest you be far away by dawn, perhaps visit Canada—and, Mr. Bailey, don't call the police. I've already told you far too much." It was obvious he already knew Bailey was irrevocably tied to them.

Then the smaller of the two white thugs spoke in a quiet monotone. "Bailey, we do need to know if you're in or not. Tell you what—It will be me that calls in the morning. You be there. You decide not to go, like the man says, make yourself scarce. Understand?"

Bailey didn't respond immediately and the man leaned a little closer and even more quietly asked again, "OK?" Bailey responded with a bare but affirmative nod.

The man straightened and a small smile that didn't quite reach his eyes flickered across his face. He reached into a pocket and pulled a thick fold of bills out and counted off a few. He methodically refolded them while staring into Bailey's eyes. As he reached across and pushed them into Bailey's shirt pocket he half-smiled again and said, "That's better ... *asshole* ... that's better. Now, who you gonna get to ride shotgun with you?"

"I don't know yet. I'll think on it—if I decide to go.

"Oh, you'll go. We can play this silly game out here in the sun all you want. It's the booze talking now, but you'll go. Be ready tomorrow when I call—and have a copilot, you flaming drunk. And I don't want to even catch another whisper of booze 'til this is over—you hear?"

Bailey stepped back as the three men got into the dark Ford and wheeled out of the parking lot. When they'd gone out of sight toward the noise of the freeway, he reached woodenly for the fold of bills in his pocket. There were eight hundreds and four fifties. He refolded them and shoved the bills into a pants pocket and walked back to the door of the saloon. He paused there a moment then turned away and strode the few hundred feet to his drab trailer home.

His mind began to weave its way through the flights of his yesterdays. A copilot. There could be only one—only one.

Chapter 5

Two days—two days and not a whisper of any information on the stolen weaponry. Both Obregon and Simpson were wearied by lack of sleep and futile effort, not to mention a constant hammering from the bureaucrats back east. Their field crews were no better off. They'd gone over available forensics and all the interviews dozens of times Very few hard facts had surfaced, but they'd gathered a lot of frustration, all stacked into dead ends. The two dead men from the robbery were finally identified though, both illegals from Mexico and wanted across the line in Sonora. Nothing more.

"Bill, who we got in the Mob hereabouts? Got a laundry list of who's who?"

Simpson studied his new partner for a bit, "That's something I can handle. It's what I usually work. The local family is run by old man Colisimo, been here for years. He keeps a pretty low profile, even with all the heat that's coming down around his ears lately. Come on up to the Ops room. I'll show you a family tree."

Ten minutes later they were in an inside room on the fifth floor, staring at a white board of names, organizational lines and linked relationships.

"We are pretty sure the names are real; at least they are the ones they've used for the last few years."

He watched Obregon walk slowly along, staring at the hand-written names. "Anybody you particularly looking for? We've been turning up the heat on Colisimo lately. I know most of the players associated with him of any importance by name and sight I guess."

"No, just looking and hoping."

Simpson thought a moment before he said, "You guys don't work the mob, do you?"

"Well, no, not exactly," then he stopped at a name and seemed to stare through it for several long seconds. He poked his finger at the name, "This Cooper, he really an Italian? Oh, early to mid-thirties, slick looking, has a big dumb shit named … damn … oh, yeah, … Jess … follows him around and covers his back?

"Umm … yeah. That's him. Down from Chicago a while back … two or three years. Fairly long rap sheet. How do you know him?"

"Not important right now. I suppose you guys have phone numbers or places they might be found?"

Simpson shrugged and walked over to a file cabinet and leafed through the folders for a while. "Here, he's got an apartment and a couple of phone numbers. We had pen registers on both of them early in the year … nothing came of it." He asked again, "You know this guy?"

"Yes. I need to talk to him. We go back a ways." He saw that Simpson was staring hard at him, and thought a moment before saying, "You don't need or want to know that right now. It's not important anyway. Give me a bit to think on it."

....

BAILEY PULLED A FLASHLIGHT from a slash pocket in the leg of his coveralls, set the almost dead battle lantern aside with a curse, and began to thumb through the DC-3's log books before doing the last of the walk-around that would really determine the aircraft's condition. The plane's history was not unlike his own, checkered at its very best, less than reputable on more than a few occasions and simply missing in others. It, like Bailey, was drifting toward the end of the line.

God! His gut hurt and the sourness crowding the back of his mouth was almost unbearable.

Forcing his attention back to the logbook, he found that the old Douglas had started life carrying passengers for Eastern and then went into uniform as a lease to the Army Air Force in late 1942. He stopped for a moment, remembering his time with Army Air with great fondness. The little postcard-pretty English villages and their friendly people always made for warm memories. He remembered how he was one of the few that had not longed to trade his Douglas for a Thunderbolt or Mustang, knowing that he was where he belonged. He'd flown all over that theatre, from England to Egypt and Russia to the Azores.

Toward the end of the war, he ferried a reassigned general and his staff to the Far East and through, he guessed, necessity, had been ordered to stay. They'd used him as a jack-of-all-trades, ferrying supplies, troops, casualties, and aircraft from one sweating and miserable shithole to another. The sick feeling of watching the tree line rush toward the nose of an overloaded B-24 he'd been returning from repair to service always came back though. It never left. Tears filled his eyes, his gut roiled, and he could hear his heart in his ears, each and every time—without fail.

He pulled his attention back to the logbooks and saw that the '3 had even returned to Eastern after the Military for a time. Within months they sold her again, this time to a leasing company. She'd had her passenger seats ripped out again and had been sent off to South African Airways to haul freight. 392 Delta even made it back to a subsidiary of Eastern again, but only for a short six months in '49. He was, if his memory held true, working on the West Coast then, a young pilot pushed back to the right seat after the war. After that, 392 Delta had served a stint with Fawcett down in Peru, then more freight hauling for Hapag-Lloyd. Most of it was non-descript ash and trash hauling—from one nowhere to another nowhere.

The writing then began to fall into garbled and careless gibberish; some apparently smudged with moisture and fit only for slow daylight exploration. A few entries farther on, he found the names of a few South American companies he recognized and even a U.S. oil exploration company. Most of it had begun to look like careless chicken scratchings and he snapped the log closed with a said-aloud hope that "the damn thing better not be stolen." But, when he thought about it, he laughed and remembered the people who had hired him caused a good deal more worry than the possibility that the plane was on a hot sheet somewhere.

Standing under the chin of the craft's scarred shape and staring up at the antennas sticking down just ahead of the pitot tubes, he thought about the night he had spent trying to talk himself out of going. He had hidden it all under the delusional guise of *weighing the options*. Even then, he's spent more time wondering who would go with him than whether he would go or not. His real thoughts were more on how to get his windfall from this flight to *her*. He wrote and re-wrote the note to go with the money—and still did not have one that satisfied him when he when he laid the pen aside.

....

Bailey remembered that he had been out of bed for almost three hours when 9 AM rolled around. He had lain there and stared at the dimly visible calendar pinned to the wall near the foot of his bed until he couldn't stand it any longer. Then he had showered, gone through almost a full pot of coffee and even considered opening a fresh bottle for a drink. The ringing of the phone silenced that thought and he settled for another cup of coffee.

He had let it ring at least a half-dozen times when it began its nerve-grating barrage promptly at nine. Not wanting to appear anything close to anxious, he had slowly paced the half-dozen steps from the coffee pot on the kitchen counter to the telephone nestled on a dust covered end table in what passed for the trailer's living room. Even with all the contrived nonchalance he could muster, the voice on the other end of the line showed absolutely no surprise when he simply said, "Yeah … I'll go."

There was hardly a space between his words and the man's question that followed, "Who's going with you, flyboy?"

Bailey's, "I have a man. I'll have to get in touch with him first though," was obviously not enough as the man rasped back, "Who? … don't jerk me around … who? I've no time for this crap."

The man's tone in mind, Bailey gave Bill Stoudamyre's name and added where he thought, well, knew, they could usually find him. There was a short silence, then the man said, "OK. He'll do. You take care of convincing him and get'cher stuff together. Have him ready yesterday. OK?" Bailey wondered if the man actually knew who Stoudamyre was, or was just running his power trip on a little more.

The conversation ended with the voice's promise to pick him up at eight the next morning … and for him to be ready and, above all, sober. His newfound employers knew him better than he'd thought. He was angered by his own pliability and, worse, his transparency. But, he had a day to be ready. He doubted he would ever come back.

Bailey thought back on that now as he let his eyes wander along the leading edge of the port wing. *Poor Stoudamyre*, but there had never been anyone else he could have chosen. Bailey's bottle habit had alienated just about everyone but Stoudamyre who, for some reason, continued to keep up his end of a bond of trust the two shared. Stoudamyre was also the only one, save the doctor at Tucson's V.A. Hospital, who knew the growing pain in his gut would one day, probably not too far away, kill him. There was, of course, the chance an aircraft, or the booze, or their new employers, or some other fate, would get the job done first and with less pain. And, he had to remember that Stoudamyre could do almost anything with a DC3, even better than he could himself.

So, Bailey had chosen him over the few remaining names in a thin and worn address book. And why not? Perhaps the Air Force considered him crazy, but Stoudamyre could *fly*, he was loyal to a fault, and there had to be more to his dream than sheparding half-wits with butterflies in their stomachs around the pattern in clunky little Cessnas. Stoudamyre had often told him there were times when he felt that if he had to smile at one more missed approach, flinch through one more sloppy, wallowing turn, unclench one more set of white knuckles from the yoke after a frightening departure stall, he would go crazy—*really crazy*. Though not nearly so ancient he, like Bailey, appeared to have few things to sell other than his flying skills.

Not that Stoudamyre was all that young though. He had managed to reach forty. That was in spite of all the bets by a lot of people who had helped pin the *crazy* label on him.

They, always the great *they*, had always admitted he could fly. He could stand Puff on one wing and chop up Charlie's jungle floor better than anyone they could remember. He could keep the old bird in such a steep and jaw-tightening turn that the mini-guns had time to turn a small patch of the jungle below into a metallic desert, devoid of any and all human life. And there were also a lot of Grunts who owned their lives to him for that flying ability. But he always seemed to haul more people into those far-away cesspools than he ever hauled out. Those times and trials still haunted his sleep and crowded the bottom of his drink—and there was always that.

In places where flyers of that era gathered for a drink or three and lied through hazy and exaggerated memories of those days past, Stoudamyre had become something of a folk hero. Each time the tales were told the lives saved became more numerous, the turns got tighter, the loads heavier, the body count higher, the airstrips shorter, clouds thicker … and Stoudamyre's flying better. But without a war, Stoudamyre's skills had simply no longer been needed—and he always wondered if they were all that real in the first place.

Stoudamyre was prone to long spells of depression even in the best of times. When he was *down*, he was dangerous and he drank just enough to cloud his judgment and make it worse. During those times, the pitiful person he could be, in all its sad color, seeped through the smiling veneer he cultivated.

When Vietnam began winding down, the lack of need for his skills became even more painfully obvious to his handlers. There was no way the Gods the Air Force worshiped had room for him in their upper echelons. So, the folks upstairs made sure that Captain William J. Stoudamyre was thrice passed over for promotion, given an out-the-door and almost retroactive Silver Star, along with severance pay consistent with his rank and service, and then unceremoniously separated from the active Air Force. He became a lonesome man in a lonesome place—and it grew worse, day-by-day.

It was just as well he left though, for there was really no place for him in the peacetime Air Force. The magician with an aircraft became the Bill Stoudamyre without a home and attachments and in search of his own tomorrow. But, first, he just needed a simple job—and that wasn't all that easy. The market was full of experienced pilots—supposedly *sane* experienced pilots.

Work ... herding aircraft ... was where he and Bailey had met however. Stoudamyre had been part of a pick-up crew Bailey had pulled together to ferry supplies to surrounded CIA-led shooters in Cambodia's highlands. It had been Stoudamyre's introduction to four-engine time. Neither of them could fix on the reason, but their acquaintance had progressed to a friendship that had lasted this past decade. That friendship may have been partially based in their mutual predilections to great drunken sprees and seasoned with an all-consuming love of flying—maybe. If so, that is where the similarities ended.

Physically, Stoudamyre was tall and tended toward long bunches of stringy, hard muscles. He loved the role of the underdog and would fight, against idiotic odds, at the drop of an imaginary hat. His prowling of just about any woman's bedroom that would lie down for him had, on more than one occasion, brought his sorry soul as close to death as had any of the Viet Cong's efforts. But, he survived and, somehow, he was never alone—almost never. When he was, you could be sure a deepening fit of alcohol-tinged depression would soon cripple what was left of his soul.

There was a certain taste in those he kept around to ease his perpetual loneliness. They may have not been particularly bright, but they were always had the looks to make up for it. He even married one of his bedmates now and then, though none of them stayed around very long. Their departures only added to his pocket deficit and little alteration of his basic personality was ever accomplished. He, like Bailey, could be a lonely, closing in on bitter, and sad excuse for a man, or so it seemed to the casual observer. They just handled their sicknesses in different ways—except for the booze and airplanes.

It was strange that not a scratch showed on Stoudamyre's tanned and handsome face in witness to his many brawls and binges. Whatever scars he wore were carried inside, out of sight, but far more painful and damaging. None of this seemed to fit an honor graduate of Baylor University once destined for the pulpit. War does change people, even if they don't recognize it themselves.

Bailey, on the other hand, seemed to always be alone; alone with what ever stirred the memories around in his mind. Stoudamyre was one of the few who knew there had been *someone* once. He knew that it had not been one of the great tragedies you make sad poetry of, just that Bailey had never been able to shake her from his mind and her loss may have been the final straw, pushing him over the edge and into his complete fall from grace. It just hadn't worked out for one reason or another and remained a cancer in his composition that grew in direct proportion to his other tribulations and surfaced, for all to see, with an increase in his ability to afford sour mash. The lady, whoever she was, still sat perched on the shoulder of his mind and soul, fondly, perhaps illogically, remembered but never touched, rarely even approached.

Bailey did call her now and then. Once when Stoudamyre had walked in on one of their calls, he'd seen one of the few real smiles ever borne by his quiet friend. But any reference to her brought a muddled reply and a silence so deep and long he would be sorry the subject ever came up.

....

THE PHONE JANGLED FOR SEVERAL UNANSWERED rings and Bailey was just about to hang up when Stoudamyre decided to get out of bed, away from his latest diversion, and answer its noisy interruptus. Within thirty seconds, the pouting little carhop was totally forgotten, despite her best efforts and shiny nakedness.

Bailey had little to tell him about the job offering, but it wasn't a little Cessna and it wasn't beating around the pattern with boring and inept pilots-to-be.

The last little bit of their conversation had given Stoudamyre something to chew on though.

"Bill … uhh … you gotta gun?"

"What kind? Why?"

The *why* was ignored, but Bailey answered, "… a pistol of some kind might work best … need to keep it hidden … and stick a few extra rounds in your pocket."

"Sure, I got a little two-incher I took off of a drunk wetback a while back" He almost giggled, "He tried to … caught me with … that OK?"

"Yeah, I guess. I think you ought to throw it in your gear—and keep it to yourself. We don't need any more problems than the job already has … right now."

Stoudamyre simply said, "Sure" and laughed about getting back to bed with his little friend to await the morrow. As a last thought, he'd told Bailey about a Belgian machine pistol, dismantled and hidden in the back of his closet. The gun had been dumped in the weeds along side of a small strip in southwestern Texas by some dopers. Stoudamyre had found it after the DEA agents had hauled them off and he'd never even thought of turning it in, figuring there might be a *someday* when it would be needed. It was agreed this might be that someday and it would fit somewhere in the baggage.

Bailey had some strong misgivings about the job he had decided to undertake. The people surrounding it had given a new and raw edge to his nerves and he saw no grounds for any form of trust. He didn't know when, or if, that would ever come.

Once he had made up his mind to hire on, he had rummaged through a bureau drawer and fished out another relic that seemed to fit him. The worn government model .45 was lying in his lap when he called Stoudamyre. Bailey sat by the telephone a long while after the call, silent and staring into the dank dimness of his bedroom. He switched on the bedside lamp and took a small framed photograph from the nightstand. He stared at the youngish-looking woman's image, his eyes almost caressing her and the small and smiling girl-child she cradled in her arms. After a few minutes, he sat the photograph back onto the dusty nightstand, stood and reached into the open bureau drawer. He pulled out an ancient silver and onyx rosary, felt its comfort as the links began to slide through his fingers, and slowly began to shake his head from side to side. At last, tears in his eyes, he sat back down and flipped off the light. Then he swung his feet onto the bed and lay back, letting the darkness of the shuttered room crowd in to barely mask the tenseness of anticipation.

....

THE RIDE TO THE DUSTY EAST-WEST STRIP had not shed much additional light on their job. The black was not there for the ride, just the two baby mobsters, still trying so hard to loom larger than life. They had offered few words, only that there would be two days, three at the most to check the plane out before the cargo arrived.

The first real shock came when they turned off the county road, skirted some dunes, and pulled up beside the aircraft they were to fly. Bailey's first thought was that it didn't look airworthy now—*how the hell had it gotten there?*

Bailey watched Stoudamyre become more excited than he could remember and pile out of the car while the dust of their arrival still rolled over them. He did a hurried half walk-around and then pushed the taller of the two mobsters aside and crawled into the open side hatch of the DC-3. He re-appeared in what seemed like seconds, still excited but yelling about the smell and the heat.

"What have you been hauling in this piece of shit? It stinks like a newly dumped outhouse! Man, you must have been haulin' really rotten grass in this crate."

He paused for what seemed to be a breath gathering, then, "Damn, it is crawlin' with bugs. I just saw a scorpion big enough to need shootin'. You need to spray this bucket … and … hey! Wes … you oughta see the crap they got in the panel …. It's even older than you. Crawl on up and take a look. You need to get up here and see what the little old lady from Pasadena used to haul pot in after church on Sunday."

With that, he jumped down and hurried out under one of the big Pratt and Whitneys and stared up at its oil soaked undersides as if seeing some great marvel for the very first time.

Save for the DC-3 and its guard, the airstrip had been empty when they'd arrived. There were no tools and no gas. Worse, the plane cast almost the only shade and there was very little of that.

They had done little with the old craft that first day, except to look at it. There were a few snide remarks about its parentage, but mostly it was just a time to consider, in this case, their folly. It was too late to even think about turning back. The point of no return had been reached and they were not even in the air. Bailey was satisfied though. He was in his element.

Chapter 6

The hectic and hurried four hours spent in the scorching heat at the gritty little airstrip had given them an overall idea of what would be needed to even begin work on the aircraft. A sheaf of scribbled notes, that included everything from engine oil to socket sets and insecticide, was prepared for their handlers as they moved through an initial examination of the old Douglas.

The two over-dressed and sweating mobsters had said very little during the flyers' cursory examination of the aircraft. They just aimlessly and grumpily wandered around and made themselves more miserable in the desert heat. Cooper finally found a tiny wisp of shade about fifty yards down and across the runway and stood there quietly, trying to shrink into its bare comfort. It didn't help much. He watched the two flyers wander around the old aircraft, poking and prodding, taking notes, and laughing as if the whole thing were a joke.

His bodyguard, Jess, noticed his focus on the two men and turned to watch them himself for a few minutes before quietly offering, "Roy, you ought to pay attention to that old man. He can make or break this whole thing. What do you know about him? There's something about him … I just can't put my finger on it."

"Hmm, whadda you mean?" Cooper grumped. "He just looks like an old has-been with too many miles on him to me. I'd worry about the tall dude." He lapsed back into silence and Jess, nodding, followed suit.

Their self-imposed silence still cloaked them as they all stepped back into the car for the drive back into Tucson. Each man seemed lost in thought with no desire to be disturbed. The lulling sound of tire on pavement added to the distance each retreated within himself. Stoudamyre even drifted off into what passed for a light sleep. Whether the sleep was real or not was another matter.

A few generalities had been discovered relative to their employers during the trip though. Bailey and Stoudamyre had learned who their employers were, at least who they claimed they were. The one with the voice called himself *Roy Cooper*. He didn't look like a *Roy Cooper* though. He had the dark look of someone christened Salvatore or Angelo and who probably carried some other names found on any number of police blotters. He also sounded life-long Chicago. That's it, Chicago, Bailey had finally placed the accent. But, it didn't matter. As long as he paid the bills, he could be *Roy Cooper*, Tinker Belle, or any other name he pulled out of the hat.

The very large and muscled half of the duo was simply referred to as *Jess*. He didn't seem very bright and probably wasn't. It was also probable that he wasn't nearly as tough as he'd have the world around him believe, but there was little need to argue over the degree of bruises he could inflict. He must, Bailey thought, have a personality, but it was well hidden. Jess was pleasant to the both of them and seemed particularly respectful to Bailey. That puzzled him. He could feel that the man's eyes followed every move he made.

He watched his employers closely and still, even though he didn't want to admit it, wondered who they *really* were. They were a strange pair, working so hard at appearing relaxed, nonchalant and in charge; all the while creating just the opposite impression. Bailey had watched the two's nervousness build throughout the day and thought aloud to Stoudamyre that they had enough problems without their employer's nerves stirring up more. Bailey decided to simply keep his mouth shut and listen, watching everyone and everything. He had to keep Stoudamyre calm though. His volatile temper could turn the whole operation into something wild and beyond his control.

It was hard not to wonder if the two were in over their heads in whatever this venture was really all about. Cooper had as much as said so once, but he stopped short and retreated back into silence. Finally, just before the ride back into the city ended, he brought it out into the open. It was the first anyone had spoken since leaving the little desert airstrip.

He reached across the seat and touched Bailey on the arm, drawing his attention, "Flyboy, I got a lot riding on this. Understand? *The Man* won't like it if we step on our dicks."

"*The Man?*"

Cooper glared at Bailey for a moment, and then turned to stare out into the desert, an exasperated expression on his face. After a bit, he turned back to Bailey and said in a low and terse tone, "Look, fella, you're not stupid. You know damn well we work for a man a hell of a lot farther up the food chain than you usually see in this desert shithole. Well, that man can buy and sell truckloads of people like Jess and me—more of your kind. Those he can't buy, he buries. You do understand—don't you?"

Bailey nodded slightly and Cooper continued, "I just wanted you to know. You can't afford to screw me around. I can't afford it either—you won't like the outcome, I can assure you."

When Bailey only stared back at him, Cooper finished with, "It's damn well too late for either of us to back out now—even if I do wish we could."

Bailey simply shrugged and replied simply, "OK ..."

The silence broken, Cooper seemed unable not to go on, "Well, *The Man* isn't too happy about us dealing with this jungle refugee, no matter what title he wears. That man is scary—and I do mean *scary*. He's not like the ones running around here with a nose full of coke and three overdue Caddie payments. You can control them. Him? *That* is a different story. I've never seen anyone like him."

Bailey finally responded, "Look, I'm sure you've got your problems. Let's keep them yours. You hired me to fly—and that's all I intend to do. I don't want to know too much about your business problems. It doesn't seem very healthy."

They looked at each other for a moment, then Cooper shook his head and offered a humorless smile before turning to stare back out into the desert that stretched to the horizon and beyond.

Bailey tried very hard to think of nothing—absolutely nothing at all. It almost worked.

When they entered the dirty jumble that was the city"s outskirts, Cooper broke the last of the silence. He sounded very weary and his tough veneer was slipping away ever so slightly. "There'll be a self-contained motor home or camper set up at the strip by tonight. You stay there until the plane goes. We got'cha a creep who says he can help you fix whatever's wrong with the plane … *maybe* … and he can be a half-assed part of the flight crew if you need him. He's … borrowed … a tool van and arranged for avgas. OK?"

Bailey only nodded and Cooper continued, "We're working on an emergency fuel stop down south—a place called *Aqua Blanca*—you know, just in case. It's a little dinky spot on the earth's ass-end just northwest of Vera Cruz. Look it up on your charts. I'd like to not stop there unless absolutely necessary. The cost could get high—get my meaning? I'll let you know if anything changes on that later. You *shouldn't* need it, but you never know. I've also paid some closet cokehead at the Flight Service Station to ignore us when we jump the border, but we gotta be ready and out of here by nightfall three days from now, without fail."

The thought swam through Bailey's mind that a person with money could buy a piece of just about anything and anyone nowadays. He'd certainly been easy enough to buy himself. The thought also followed that paying someone at the local Flight Service Station did not buy much along *this* border. The FSS was probably the least of many federal big brothers that watched this imaginary line in the dirt between brown poverty and white affluence.

"There is one thing more: I've added some security at the strip. That little prick you saw earlier. He'll keep curious fools off of the strip.

You saw him. He doesn't look it, but he's dangerous, so be careful. Oh, and he's got a radiotelephone to call me with whatever you need. There isn't a land line within ten miles." He turned to look back as they passed the little saloon near the trailer Bailey called home and nodded back at it. "Stay out of there—hear me? I don't need any more problems. Get your ass out there and get the plane ready to go. We don't have a lot of time."

Cooper dropped them in front of Bailey's dingy and faded little trailer with, "Don't forget, nightfall—third day." He handed Bailey a business card and ended his one-way diatribe with, "Have me called if you need anything. Just get the damn thing flying … OK?" There was no sound of a sincere request in his voice.

The darkly tinted window slid up and Cooper just stared back through the glass at them for a moment. Then he turned and motioned for Jess to drive on. The dark Ford whispered quietly down the street to the next intersection, turned right and disappeared behind a row of other shabby singlewides hunkered there in the heat.

Bailey and Stoudamyre stood on the sweltering green painted concrete in front of the trailer and avoided looking at each other for a while. Stoudamyre slowly shook his head in wonder, while looking down at a small pebble he slowly moved around with the toe of his boot. After a bit, he looked up and very quietly asked, "What the hell have you gotten us into Pop … huh?"

A few seconds passed before Bailey slowly looked up and replied, "I dunno—I really don't, Bill. It has more than a bad smell though … wouldn't you say?" But there was a grin on his face. The DC3 had bought his attention, almost as much as the cash.

Bailey looked back at the off-white matte business card Cooper had given him and saw that it didn't help much either. Block letters spelled out *J.D.S. Enterprises* and a 682 prefixed telephone number and that was all. Aside from knowing the telephone number wasn't in the city proper, he knew no more than before.

Bailey stared down the road toward where the Ford had disappeared a few moments before and, tapping the card against the thumbnail of his left hand, pushed the thoughts through his mind at an ever-increasing rate. But no solid answers were there and he had to squeeze his mind shut. When the thoughts had finally fled, there were only the suffocating facts known: he didn't like his employers and he would probably like the job even less—whatever it was.

Bailey sighed, a feeling of hopeless resignation flowing through his mind as he turned to go into the trailer. He felt Stoudamyre's hand on his arm and turned back to look into a face split by a crooked and half-hearted smile.

"Wes, I don't like them either, but it's a little flamin' late now, don't you think?"

Bailey gripped his friend's hand against his arm in reassurance before replying, "Yeah … suppose so. Let's get packed—we need to be out there as soon as we can. There is a bundle to do. Oh, stick that pistol in your belt. Won't do you much good in your kit."

Stoudamyre only laughed and shook his head, then pulled his shirt up. The little revolver was there in his belt. "Way ahead of you Pop … way ahead of you."

Three hours later, they were pulling out of the parking lot behind Stoudamyre's apartment complex, their traveling gear stuffed into worn flight bags. The keys to both men's places had been left with Stoudamyre's pouting little carhop, along with the instructions to not forget to check the mail, not to wreck the car—and not to get laid more than twice a day. She only gave them a pouting look of dismissal and slammed the door behind them, sloshing a large glass of red wine as she did.

Bailey still had a smile on his face as he edged the car up to the curb line, "Bill, that little chippy ever get out of bed?"

Stoudamyre looked up the boulevard to their right, murmured, "You're clear," then, "Sure, you suspicious old fart, now and then. One does what one does best, my man … what one does best."

Then the conversation quickly shifted to the business at hand. The ride back to the narrow little airstrip was filled with almost enthusiastic talk about the aircraft. They had both begun to call her

The Rose. Anything about what they might be hauling, or where exactly they were going, remained carefully hidden behind a mass of busy-talk and a mental step back in time.

Bailey, usually very quiet, was unusually talkative as he remembered aloud the first multi-engine aircraft he'd ever flown and how the then almost new DC-3 had been a great, exhilarating, experience, even though it was like flying a barn door during takeoffs. Stoudamyre began to feel more pieces of his friend's life fall into place and the puzzle that defined his fall from grace grew as each part was pulled from his memory and polished with words.

And he hung on every one of those words, as if he were a child, hearing of his father's youth for the very first time. His being had been formed, his skills honed, his dreams painted across a soul's canvas, in a time when men and history leapt to the air in the first, perhaps the last, of the best. There had been more DC-3 time, graduating to the new 4's and, in between, another winter driving DC-3's and a long-past-its-prime Curtis C-46 between Pittsburgh and Atlanta for some always-broke mail contractor. All seemed edging toward the scrap heap, but they handled the freight and mail tucked in their bellies reasonably well.

He had been so very young then and remembered that, long before the polished transports, he'd spent hour upon hour cleaning up after trainers held together with spit and bailing wire just to get time in the air. It had all led to the right seat of some feeder lines, most long since defunct and, later, the left seat and a high number on the seniority list of a couple of carriers propped up now by government bail-outs. Then, still looking fuzzy-cheeked and too young for the role, he'd taken time out to pin on captain's bars and haul gas for Patton's Third Army and to ferry bombers to England and Russia … and drums of gas to the Twelfth Air Force in China … and how it was too soon over for him, despite the carnage and missing friends. There was no mention of Malaya and a B24, none at all.

Bailey came by his love of flying naturally he almost thought aloud. He'd never known his father. Hack Bailey, that image seen only in a photograph, had flown his Boeing P26 Peashooter into the path of his wingman during some bad-weather outside of Olathe, Kansas. Both died in some wheat farmer's frozen stubble field and, worse, were not even found for two days. His Grandfather Chase had taken over the task of raising Wesley Bailey and gladly, at that. He'd never really thought much of his daughter's choice in husbands, Air Corps major or not. The loss broke his mother and she never got over it. But Matthew Chase was up to the task and dove in with a fervor.

Matt Chase was no stranger to flying himself. He'd flown since late in The Great War and that skill never failed him. He captained Clippers for Juan Trippe and Pan American for a time and had only been retired a couple of years when he began to verbally feed Bailey's teenaged mental wanderlust. Hours of sitting on the edge of their porch in Roanoke, hearing of the near and far places Grandfather Chase had been, whetted his desire for the leap to the sky.

Matt Chase had died in '42, but Bailey's thoughts of him were always warm. The man had made him what he once was—not what he felt he was in his present state of decay. It was one of the things that made him hope, on occasion, that there was no afterlife. He would not want Matthew Chase to see him as he had become and have to turn explanations into excuses.

He was in the middle of a verbal memory of the weather over the Himalayas when they reached the turnoff to the airstrip and he stopped mid-sentence, folding his memories away for another time. He suddenly felt very old again and he could feel his gut aching.

They were at once aware that the people who'd hired them were serious, very serious. A pickup truck fell in behind them and followed them all the way in on the narrow dirt track through the sand, cactus, and scrub brush. When the cloud of dust they'd raised moved on by them, a smallish, khaki-clad man slowly dismounted through the driver's door of the truck and approached. There were large patches of sweat showing though his clothing that had picked up a coating of dust little different in color than the original khaki. His face was grim set and pocked from a condition that still showed rough and ugly on his neck. The remainder of his face was mostly hidden behind very dark aviator style glasses and a large oily looking mustache right out of a Spaghetti Western. The most prominent thing about him was an Israeli machine pistol that swung from a strap over his right shoulder. Bailey immediately noticed that the barrel never wavered from a point somewhere in the middle of his chest.

The dark little man, cocky to the point of arrogance, looked directly at Bailey and took over.

"You're Bailey … right?"

With Bailey's affirmative nod, he continued, "… thought so. Seen your picture." Then he added, with a tone of a man disappointed, "You don't look like much."

He nodded toward a square and short-bodied Winnebago camper and, after spitting a stream of tobacco juice at the sand, informed them, "You sleep there for the next night or so. You might get smelly, but nobody goes back into town—for any reason. Anything we need gets delivered."

Bailey looked out of the corner of his eyes toward Stoudamyre and noticed the reddening of quick anger already creeping into his face. The little man talking was the type who could bring out the fight in Stoudamyre and, unfortunately, he was already doing just that. A tight knot grew in Bailey's gut and stayed there.

"We got food enough … and that van over there has tools in it. They tell me that prick is a mechanic," pointing off toward a slight and dirty man trudging toward them. "Looks like another friggin' drunk to me. Oh, and there'll be avgas in by dark, day after tomorrow. I s'pose you gotta enough in the tanks for a short test hop … but I dunno."

He just stood there for a while, as if he was trying to think of what else he had to say and confirmed it with, "Almost forgot … they sprayed all the little crawlies in the plane earlier, just like you said. You might want to open the hatch and stay out of it a while. Safer. Any of them little beasties that ain't dead oughta to be real pissed off about now."

There was a pause while the man pushed the bill of his cap up with the thumb of his left hand, then, "Any questions?" There was swagger and arrogance written all over him. "Oh, we'll get your car back to town, tell me where you want it left and leave the keys in it. Get to it in a day or so."

Without waiting for a response, the little man turned his back and walked away, leaving them standing there in the afternoon's dust and heat. About ten yards away, he stopped and turned back to them. When he was sure he had their attention, he added in a practiced and theatrical afterthought manner, "Friends, don't screw with me around here … even a little bit. I bite." With that last bit of bravado, he ambled off toward the sparse shade of the brush along the edge of the strip.

Stoudamyre muttered, "Ahh, shit …" through clenched teeth and rolled his eyes toward the sky, then turned back to the car to begin unloading their gear. He didn't seem impressed by all the little man's show. Worse, he looked angry. He was dangerous when his temper was arroused and Bailey wondered how the day would end—and if he would be there to see it.

The little man with the Uzi could be a problem—no, he *was* a problem. Either one of the only two possible ends to this relationship would be painful. The question was: painful to whom?

Bailey turned toward Stoudamyre and quietly said, "Leave it alone. The little greaser isn't worth the hassle. Cooper says he is dangerous. Besides, he is our communications for parts and whatever else we may need. Let's get to work on this … this … hunk of scrap metal." Stoudamyre nodded, muttered something under his breath, and strode off toward *The Rose*.

He watched Stoudamyre stalk off through the dust and shifted his focus to the little Mexican who was by then seated on the tailgate of a pickup truck and leaning on a water cooler. Bailey mused aloud, to no one in particular, "We need this; we really need this. Damn."

Their first real walk-around of the Douglas was not a happy trip. Nostalgia gone, the reality of the craft's poor condition sank in and built a drowning silence, while piling the doubt on brick by brick. Three days did not seem nearly enough time to get her really airworthy.

The underside of each engine nacelle was covered in black, oily grime, frosted in gray dust, making them wonder how many oil leaks were masked by the filth. Scores of nicks and dings in the belly and props told of numerous backcountry short and rough landings. Whoever had flown *The Rose* was lucky this was an aircraft tough enough to handle that abuse. But, she was old and everything has a limit. How hard it would be to once again raise her wings to the sky was the question—a big question. Bailey had no doubts whatsoever. Win or lose, he was flying *The Rose* out of there.

It seemed everything needed at least some work or just plain replaced. There was a leak in the brake line to the right main gear and the tires were as bald as the proverbial baby's butt. There were patches in the sheet metal here and there that only added to the gray, oxidized and sad image there before them. They were beginning to be overrun by doubts and the often repeated comment, "Well, they flew it in … didn't they?" didn't even draw a smile or a hopeful thought from either of them.

An hour of tinkering around the outside surfaces later, assuming the fumigation had worked its chore, they stepped up the short ladder and entered the dark and sweltering interior of the DC-3. The stench of chemicals, previous cargoes, and just the aging and moldering of the aircraft, was almost overpowering. Everywhere on the deck lay dead insects and the filth of yesterday's passengers.

Their mood sank even lower as they went over the flight deck. The instrumentation was everything they had feared it would be in both age and mixture, even though it generally seemed intact and covered a good part of their immediate needs. Someone had actually cut a slot for an old and outdated weather radar in one of the panel's blank spots. Most of the remaining panel was very old, but the aircraft bone yards near Tucson and the companies that fed off of them would offer replacements for missing and malfunctioning instruments. That much as least was fortunate.

Bailey's mind drifted off to those aircraft bone yards and stuck there for a while. The pills were making it difficult to stay focused. The bone yards … bureaucratic morticians there would have aircraft lined up for sale or demolition in far better condition than this one, wrapped in shrinkwrap plastic and awaiting a buyer or the torch. He had always considered the bone yards sad and dreary places. There were row upon row of aging aircraft, awaiting the torch, and taking to wing only in the memories of old and gray men. Their only respite, both the old aircraft and old men, came in the occasional and temporary rebirth national emergency afforded.

That sad and shaky assurance aside, there were remarkably few indications of serious malfunctions seen and those they did find would be simple replacement exercises. There had been no run-up as yet to check engines and vacuum driven instruments however. Doubts were in abundance … a thousand doubts.

By early evening, Bailey and Stoudamyre had examined all they effectively could without a power run-up. They had poked and pried, checked and re-checked, and laundry-listed replacement parts and end items, then finally crawled down with a list of things for the mechanic to do or help them do. Surprisingly, particularly to Bailey, none of the repairs remaining to be completed would keep the plane from flying. At that moment, even with all of her shortcomings, 392 Delta could, or *should*, fly right then. *How far* was a far different issue. The plane had been flown into the short strip only a few days before. That considered, there would even be enough battery power to turn the engines over— at least, they hoped so, for there was no auxiliary power unit available and getting one—under any circumstance—would only draw more unwanted attention to themselves and their enterprise.

They both stepped away from the slouching shape that was 392 Delta and regrouped at the tailgate of the guard's pickup truck. There was a water cooler there and even water would taste good right then.

Stoudamyre broke the silence, "Think she'll fly?"

"Probably … sure, but I'd prefer not to try it now. We're short on runway, hot as it is."

"Well, then how 'bout a little taxi test? We can wind her up, run down the strip a ways … check what we've not got around to yet. OK?"

"A little anxious are you?"

" … s'pose so …"

A few more minutes of trying to find some form of relief from the heat and, finally admitting that there was none, Bailey set the cooler's tin cup down and said, "What the hell, why not? At least we'll know— one way or the other."

Bailey climbed back into the oven-like aircraft's belly, squeezed onto the flight deck, and settled down in the left seat. Sweat ran down his face and soaked his clothing as he began sorting through battered, plastic covered checklists. He pulled out three that were in Spanish and stuffed them back into the holder riveted to the sheet metal by his left knee as he shook his head in wonder. He glanced out over the leading edge of the wing root between fuselage and engine nacelle and saw Stoudamyre in an animated and angry conversation with the dark little gunman and the mechanic. Finally, the mechanic nodded and returned to position himself at the port engine, a fire bottle on a wheeled dolly beside him.

Stoudamyre was just squeezing into the right seat as the mechanic looked up under a hand used to shade his eyes and gave a thumbs-up *ready* signal.

"What's the matter down there?"

"Aww … nothing. It's just like talking to someone belonging in an institution, that's all."

Bailey was not sure he wanted to know the real problem, but he gave an almost noncommittal, "Oh?"

"Sorry-assed little wetback didn't want us even starting her until Cooper is here. Must think we're gonna steal this piece of crap. Y'know, I will end up sticking that Jewish popgun up his butt if he doesn't quit waving it under my nose."

"Well, do we run her up or not?"

"Yeah … but, look; Shorty is over there on the mobile phone now. Looks like he's about to wet himself."

The dark little man did look agitated, talking into the handset in an excited manner and pointing toward the aircraft with the hand holding the Uzi as if the person on the other end of the connection could actually see him. Then he shrugged and his shoulders sagged a bit as he pulled the handset away from his face and looked at it as if it had suddenly died.

Bailey looked away from the man who was, by then, leaning into the truck to replace the handset into its cradle. It was obvious he was not a problem for the time being. Bailey looked down at the first line on the check list, handed it to Stoudamyre to complete, who immediately began a long and familiar litany:

"Hydraulic pump selector …" he fidgeted with a switch and said, "Left … check."

Stoudamyre started on down the list, using a forefinger as a marker, "Gear latch."

"Down."

"Flap handle …"

The check list procedure droned on through cowl flaps, deicer boots, flight controls, tabs and props, until Stoudamyre, with a wrinkled-brow look of apprehension, said, "Battery switch on."

Bailey returned, "On" and Stoudamyre hesitated, then read "Booster pumps," while really wondering why he'd allowed the butterflies in his stomach to build to such a level.

They looked at each other a moment, then Bailey turned his attention out the open wing window at the mechanic with the fire bottle and, without the usual clearing command, told his copilot, "Master and ignition," switching to the position marked "*on.*" The sight of the propeller beginning to turn seemed almost a surprise, and yet he had expected it.

Several seconds of grinding, a false start later, and a cloud of gray, oily, smoke erupted into a crashing roar as the engine caught and ran. With a half-hearted smile of relief, Bailey began to work the remaining engine to life and to check the instruments dependent upon power and vacuum.

The instrumentation was such a hodgepodge of junk that it would have been amusing at any other time, but not with the entire interior of Mexico to cross. Bailey cursed to himself as his eyes wandered across the panel. There was an altimeter by some unknown government contractor, an old coffee grinder King Radio and Omni stacked on top of another just like it, a crudely retrofitted DME (distance measuring equipment) by Narco that had the glass facing badly cracked and would be difficult to read. Some Collins equipment, and more contract items on across the panel rounded out the instrumentation. There were not that many instruments to start with, DC-3s had a short panel in their original iteration and this was definitely a pretty basic craft. None of the instruments were original equipment, certainly not the old weather radar. But, then you wouldn't expect an aircraft over four decades old to sport much original equipment. Bailey, in some forty years of flying, had yet to see such a collection of mismatches and potential headaches. Thinking of the aircraft as a whole, he could—in his mind's eye—see a past where it limped across some banana republic's sky, full of bandits-cum-soldiers, beer, pot and, probably, the family goat.

Surprisingly, most of the instruments actually worked—at least they appeared to. How accurately they worked remained to be seen and some pieces, such as the omni, could not be tested on the ground this far from a transmission facility. Stoudamyre continued a repair-or-replace list as Bailey cranked the cowl flaps wide open for cooling and pointed to each working or malfunctioning item in turn, yelling to be heard above the engine noise. They would need headsets when *The Rose* actually flew with the next morning's coolness—without them the noise would be intolerable.

Leaning across the yoke and feeling the throb of the tired Pratt and Whitney's brought a strange sensation to both men's minds. They were surrounded by a bit of history and they felt like youngsters about to step back in time and tide. Reality returned quickly. This was no heroic venture. Judging from the cut of their employers, what lay ahead was definitely on the dark side of the ledger. But, for Bailey, this was life—however temporary.

Stoudamyre pulled himself up out of the seat, slapped Bailey on the shoulder as he lurched off of the flight deck and down toward the open side hatch. Exiting into the dust, he did a quick walk-around to check for leaks they might have missed earlier. Finding none of immediate criticality, he hurried back to avoid the engines overheating before they could run a taxi test.

He plopped into the right seat and nodded to Bailey who, in turn, gave the mechanic a thumbs-up and began easing the throttle forward while reducing the pressure on the brakes. The creaking and vibrating old bird waddled forward and was slowly S-turned out onto the east end of the cracked and pot-holed asphalt strip that was the single runway. After a few kicks on the brakes to line 392 Delta up with the center of the strip, a last check of control surfaces and a short run-up, Bailey nodded to his companion and they began to roll.

The noise was deafening, reminding them again about the need for headsets. The vibration brought immediate thoughts of the aircraft's years of metal fatiguing service. Almost halfway down the strip, the controls grew light and the noise eased some, but there was no indication she was ready to fly. The heat had pushed the density altitude so high that she would fly only with difficulty. There was only the easing of the pressure required to operate the control surfaces. At mid-point, Bailey chopped the power and began to brake to a stop. In the heat, the stop from barely sixty knots didn't take long.

They pivoted on *The Rose*'s bald tires and slowly rolled back up the runway, off to the left and onto the same flat working space on which the craft had originally sat. They grinned at each other as they went through shutdown procedures and as the props slowed and ticked to a stop. Bailey was the last to exit the hatch and make the short jump to the sand. They stood for a while and wondered how well she would fly the next day, for there was no doubt in their minds now that *fly* she would.

....

Mobutu waited a half hour, then strolled past the bus station twice, noticed that there were three busses newly arrived in their slots and that a fairly large crowd of people wandered through and about the large and high-ceilinged building. He waited a few more minutes until there were several people at the lockers, either putting bags in or taking them out, and slowly walked to the locker matching the number was on the key in his pocket. As nonchalantly as possible, he opened the locker, left the key in the lock and pulled the valise out. He turned and walked through the front door as if it were something he did every day.

An hour later he pulled to the side of a gravel road he found near the edge of town and opened the valise. Cooper had been right. It was only a sample. The case held several boxes of obviously military ammunition, a couple of semi-automatic handguns, one, a Colt .45, and the other, a Browning 9mm, along with a M16 broken down into barrel, stock, and receiver groups to fit into the leather case. There were also a couple of magazines for the rifle. They were satisfactory— if units totaled the number Cooper promised. If they didn't, Cooper would be very unhappy with the result of his deceit.

Pushing everything back into the valise, he pulled the car into gear and drove back toward the city center. He simply cruised around for a while, awaiting the fall of darkness. As the sun's last light began to fade, he walked back into the bus station and placed the valise back into a locker, pushed some coins in and locked it. Putting the key into his pocket, he walked back out into the night. He needed some camouflage for the remainder of his stay he thought and drove off toward where he remembered seeing several prostitutes plying their street trade.

. . . .

BAILEY AND STOUDAMYRE SLEPT LITTLE that night, compiling lists of necessities for Cooper and fighting the heat until well after midnight. Still, they were only too glad to see the light of a dawning sky begin to ease in across the ragged hills to the east. The lists had been radio-phoned to the number Cooper had left with them and they ambled back to preflight the craft and get airborne for a test flight while the cool air lasted.

Everything went as the preflight of the day before, only more quickly given their excitement. There were still those things that needed repair, but none that precluded a short flight test. Twenty minutes later, they sat at the same end of the runway and nodded the same nod. It was *time*.

The controls became lighter a bit sooner in the early morning air, making the rudder surfaces effective and the aircraft easier to handle. About two-thirds of the way down the bumpy runway, well past the point of no return, forty inches of manifold pressure showed on each engine and the needle flickered past eighty on the ASI. Bailey lifted *The Rose*, shaking and rattling, but not so reluctantly, into the morning sky.

Looking out across the nose, Bailey could see mile after mile of rough country, gullies, and cactus—no place to land; safety was behind them. He kept the throttles forward, but was looking for a way to slow the climb and ease them back. Trimming for climb, Bailey turned to smile across at Stoudamyre, but never quite made it. There was the whack of something breaking and a vibration that could be felt all the way up through the yoke to his hands. The ear-piercing whine of an engine winding too tight filled the flight deck and grew louder with each second.

"Son-of-a-bitch! We gotta a runaway prop ... governors gone ... starboard! Feather it now!" Bailey yelled over the din.

The engine was vibrating at an ever-increasing rate. It seemed that any second it would pull from its mountings and separate from the wing. The whine of its increasing revolutions was deafening. "Goddamn it! Feather the thing!"

Stoudamyre didn't answer. He was pounding on the feathering button, holding the safety cover up with the other hand and ignoring the beads of sweat beginning to run down his face and into his eyes. Nothing was happening. Both men's eyes went from the instrument panel to the stricken engine and back again as if on swivels. The old aircraft felt as if it was about to die in their hands.

"Hit it again! Damn—she's about to shed a prop … hit it!"

Bailey had lowered the nose of the aircraft instinctively when the prop went wild. He had kept the port engine's throttle as far forward as he safely could and jerked the starboard back. The instinct was to shove the throttle of the operating engine all the way to the stops but that would, in this old craft, quickly tear it to pieces. He fought that instinct and rapidly began trimming for single engine flight, all the while standing on the rudder to counteract the yaw. Just hanging onto the bare eight hundred feet of airspace they had above the rocks and gullies, he was slowly pulling the aircraft around in a smooth, ever-so-shallow turn to try and bring the runway back within reach. He knew that at any other time and place that would be wrong. With a thin few hundred feet of altitude in the high desert air, he would have preferred to have kept it pointed dead ahead and try to build some more maneuvering speed and altitude—a bit more safety cushion. The gullies and buttes that cut across his path made that a poor option and he elected to chance a stall and let a little altitude slip away and try to get the aircraft's nose headed back toward the flat piece of sand and rock the runway ran through.

There was a change in the sound coming from the stricken engine and Bailey winced at the thought of the prop blades separating from the stricken engine hub and flailing their way through the thin metal surrounding the flight deck. He noticed Stoudamyre had pulled his hands back toward the yoke and was no longer pounding on the feathering control. He was swearing, almost in a chant, and making no sense whatsoever.

The runway could just be seen to the left and over the nose of the struggling craft. Noise from the runaway propeller had lowered in intensity and he could see from the corner of his eye that it was slowing to a stop. Bailey reached for the gear handle and began setting up for a short final and downwind landing. There was no time for a pattern. He also noticed that he was soaked with sweat.

A DC-3 will fly a long way on one engine and it is not even too difficult to land one in that condition—given adequate airspeed. But *any* malfunction during a takeoff is an extreme hazard. That departure stalls kill more pilots than any other maneuver was heavy in Bailey's mind just then. They were lucky the aircraft had been empty. Had it not been so, it is probable they would have ended up scattered across some of the terrain off the end of the runway. The sour taste in Bailey's mouth told him it had been close.

The problems of less than a minute before began to shrink. The immediate threat was gone. *Time* became the enemy. Less than thirty-six hours lay between then and the time Cooper had designated as departure time—*that* was the problem. It would be difficult under the best of conditions. Now, with a new obstacle, it seemed to crawl toward the impossible.

The end of the runway flicked past and Bailey let *The Rose* touch down and begin the roll down the rough asphalt, shutting down systems as she went. Finally, when he'd braked to a stop after trundling her back into the work area, Bailey released the yoke and signaled for Stoudamyre to finish running down the checklist. He let his head fall forward and cradled it in his hands for a few moments. After a few empty and black thoughts, he pulled himself up and hunched down through the belly of the craft to the side hatch. He wanted his feet on the ground—even this ground.

Chapter 7

BAILEY WALKED AWAY FROM THE AIRCRAFT with thoughts of the near disaster tumbling him into an instant and almost paralyzing depression. And there was fear. He never expected fear. He concealed his shaking hands by pushing them deep into the pockets of his coveralls. Making things physically worse, the medication he'd taken less than an hour before the flight was not even touching the pain setting his gut into a burning turmoil and the flood of adrenalin had kicked it into high gear. He found it hard to concentrate on just being alive, let alone the aircraft's many flaws.

New, the DC-3 was a strong and reliable aircraft, but age and wear had made it brittle and any problems could not help but be cumulative, even contagious, and certainly deadly. The runaway prop might be only the beginning. Had the engine shed its prop at just the right moment, it could have of chopped its way right into the flight deck with him or start the loss of a wing. As much affection as he felt for *The Rose*, there was a certain wariness and mistrust that began to build and blacken the edges of his thoughts.

He stood stock-still and warily stared at *The Rose* for a long while. She seemed to stare back at him over her nose and he heard himself say aloud, "You don't want to do this, do you?" He almost expected an aloud reply. In his mind, there was one.

Stoudamyre looked at him questioningly, shifted his gaze to the aircraft and then back to Bailey, "… You talking to her now?" Bailey just stood there and didn't answer, he wasn't sure he could at that moment.

Stoudamyre paused beside him and stared up at the aircraft. "She really doesn't, you know … want to fly for those creeps, I mean." He stood there silently for a thoughtful few seconds, before saying, "Is it too late to pull out? There's just something here that feels really bad."

At last, Bailey rubbed his sweating palms along the legs of his coveralls and his thoughts focused on how the incident had filled him with the metallic and acidic taste of fear. He'd thought the recent months spent fighting and becoming accustomed to the finality of the illness growing in his belly would have suppressed any fear he might have of death. It was so certain and so near … but he was wrong. Death was still the black and ugly void even the almost blind faith of his Catholic ancestors had been unable to erase. And yet, there was a hopeful feeling and need of life and he quietly began rejoicing in that.

He very slowly turned to stare into Stoudamyre's eyes, "Yes, it is too late. It will take some real luck to get out of this hole right now. And I need some cash to …" and stopped, refocusing on that around him and seeing the mechanic approaching, a look of question on his face. He spoke in quiet and firm tones, his voice flat and edged, "You stay the hell away from that little wetback. I know you want to walk on him, but don't do it right now. It'll come soon enough"

The mechanic looked from one to the other before asking, "What happened?"

"I don't think she likes me anymore. We'll have to treat her with a tad more of tenderness." Bailey drolly offered, as calmly as his racing pulse allowed, "We … damn thing had a prop run away. I was beginning to think it might visit me, right up there on the old bird's beak for a minute."

The mechanic pursed his lips and quickly glanced up at the aircraft and back again, "Well, that I can handle—if you got feathered quick enough."

"Had problems with that too. Bill almost pounded the fucking switch through the sheet iron before it worked. Check it out … we can get another at some shop up around Litchfield. Someone will have to run up there tomorrow anyway."

"Yeah … sure. I gotta list going." He paused, looked around furtively, before almost whispering, "Uhh, Wes, I need to talk to you and Bill first chance we get … away from the little shit with the gun. Soon as you can, OK?"

The man looked worried, very worried, and Bailey stared at him a long time before he asked. "You … the prick who gave these … *pleasant people* … my name?"

"Porteros. My name is Porteros—but most folks just call me Mack." He looked around again before going on, "Yeah, I am. They came and asked for someone—thought it kinda had your name all over it and, anyhow, the guy they asked for first was sitting in jail up in Flagstaff. They said there were some big bucks in it if I could find someone. I knew you were out of work and had the time and tickets they were lookin' for—so, shit, man … I didn't mean for it to turn out like this."

He seemed to be almost pleading and Bailey found he was too drained of all physical energy to be angry with the man. "I wondered how they got wind of me. Where do I know you from? You look kind of familiar."

"You don't exactly … actually … I worked at Borderair when you did … back before it went broke and sold out. I was fresh outa the Air Force. You probably never even saw me though." He dropped his gaze and stared at the ground for a few seconds before going on, "Folks never have. Anyways, I know some of the things old man Simmons had you do, fixed the airplanes up after you came back. Figured these guys couldn't be no worse than that." He forced a short laugh, then said, "Screwed that one up, huh?"

Bailey watched the man fidget for a moment before letting him off the hook and asking, "What do you mean?" His voice was flat and still held little hint of forgiveness.

The man's eyes turned toward the little Mexican with the gun approaching and ended the conversation with, "Later, later," then more loudly, "OK, I'll get right on it. We'll probably have to order up a replacement governor for the prop. Might even need a new prop with gearing."

Bailey nodded affirmatively and watched Porteros walk off toward the aircraft, his attention riveted on the old Douglas, the presence of the puzzled looking Mexican carefully and obviously ignored. "What now," Bailey thought aloud, "What else can go wrong?"

The little Mexican hitter stopped in front of them, looking from one to the other for a moment, then asked, "What happened? Whadda we gotta do now?"

Still expressionless, Bailey turned to the man, bile rising in his throat, "You sure use *we* a lot for some asshole that just sits around on his butt and gathers dust."

The little man ignored the insult and continued, "Can you fix her? I mean, soon? She's pretty rundown …" His voice trailed off and he wore a heavy look of worry that seemed out of place on him.

"I can't—*he* can," as he nodded toward Porteros. "At least I think he can. Just leave him alone and quit waving that shooter under his nose and we'll find out soon enough."

He felt a wave of nausea sweep over him and he sat down very slowly on an overturned oil drum, wiping his face on the back of a dirty sleeve. He could sense the desert around him begin to tilt crazily and spin off slowly as he struggled to maintain his balance. After a queasy moment, the bit of earth he occupied slowed its spin and stopped, his vision clearing and the faintness disappearing.

The worry on the Mexican's face deepened and, after a moment, he said, "Sure, man, sure. I don't get paid no quicker'n you." Then, in what could have passed for real concern, "You OK fella? Shit, you look … bad."

Bailey, staring at the sand between his boots, quietly replied, "Yeah, just let me alone for a minute. It's just hot, that's all."

The Mexican stood for a moment, just staring down at Bailey and considering his dismissal, then draped the Uzi's web strap over his shoulder and walked away toward the truck. Bailey noticed him using the mobile telephone a bit later, but was soon too occupied with controlling the returning nausea and pain raging in his stomach to care. After a few weary minutes, he rose shakily and moved to the water cooler, poured a small cup of the tepid liquid and downed two more of the painkillers. One pill at a time would no longer dull the pain. He'd have to chance the loss in physical agility and quickness of straight-line thinking.

He would also have to face running out of pills. But at that moment it didn't matter anymore. Within ten minutes, he was back at the aircraft, the long list of deficiencies crowding everything else out of in his mind.

The work on the aircraft went on for two more hot and sweaty hours before Porteros and Bailey had a chance for a brief bit of unobserved conversation. By the time they had finished talking there was even more reason to regret having accepted their current employment circumstances.

Bailey could see that their little watchdog had headed for some of the sparse shade that existed here and there along the edge of the strip. He nodded toward the man's disappearing shape and asked, "OK, what's on your mind, Mack?"

Porteros swiveled around, looking for the small Mexican and asked, "Where's he at?"

"Don't sweat it … he's over there … by the cholla. Now, let's hear it."

"So's you're not operating blind, y'know—you ought to know this whole job has gotten more fouled up than you can even imagine. These two small-time creeps paying the bills are only part of it."

Bailey noticed the man's voice quavered a bit as he sped toward the end of his urgent ramblings and his words took on a slight, almost buried, Spanish accent to the words. He listened, but was anything other than sure he would trust the man.

The man went on, "They work for some big-time mob boss that's supposed to have had the run of the valley for years. They claim the man has been on top of the pile for maybe twenty years, even more. That has to be Colisimo, can't be no one else. He's all over the papers these days and every hack on the evening news has him just a step or two ahead of the Feds. He's a man who can't afford any more problems right now. These fools have screwed around and got themselves crossways with him."

He paused for a bit and ran a hand through dark and tousled hair, then continued, "Word's out—and I don't know how they can keep from knowing themselves. They are dead meat and just ain't had enough sense to fall down and let someone toss dirt in their faces."

"Sounds like we may be unemployed pretty soon then—that right?"

"Unemployed? Hell, you can't be that damn dumb. More likely, we're gonna be dead if we don't find a way to get the hell out of here—and stay a long time gone." He looked around for the little gunman again then nervously back to Bailey.

Bailey waited until he knew he had the man's attention before asking, "You know what you're talking about?" He motioned for Stoudamyre to join them, holding out a hand to stop the man's flood of words until he arrived.

"Look, I heard the big mean dude talkin' to the wetback with the machine gun. They're gonna ice us if anything at all goes wrong. Even if it don't, I'm almost sure I heard him say to whack us at the other end—*no matter what.*"

Bailey's eyes were expressionless, his voice low, "You're sure?"

"Damn straight. Well, at least as sure as I can be. When you're as puckered as I am right now you listen hard. This has gotten way out of hand. They've sold that African a bill of goods. He thinks this is just the first load of a whole series. Well, that just ain't so. What will be showing up here is all they got and I hear they maybe had to knock off a couple of National Guard armories to dig up what they've got as it is."

"Armories? Hell, no one has done that since Dillinger."

The look on the man's face was of absolute fright. "These pricks got more heat floatin' around this pile of cactus than you can shake a stick at. Feds are everywhere. From what I can make out, it ain't just the FBI. I mean, there're some of those heavy hitters from other sneaky-Pete outfits with three letter names diggin' around too. I hear old man Colisimo is fit to be tied. He ain't a guy to piss off and don't like things to be complicated at all. He's been the big shot around here a long time and he did it by keeping things running smooth and quiet. Money talks and he's got it. Now even the other families are on his ass. It sounds like some of these Feds don't play by the rules he's used to either and that's got the old man on the run. That, all by itself, just cooked the creeps that hired us. That's the only good news in all of it, but it won't help us much."

He paused to catch his breath, then rushed on, "You ain't had a chance to watch that black guy bankrolling this mess, have you?" He looked hard at Bailey and then finished with, "The story is, he is one dangerous son-of-a-bitch. I only seen him twice and he walks like he sure as hell owns the earth he stands on. Scary—real scary. I watch Jess even walk a long way around him."

Both Bailey and Stoudamyre were staring hard at the man whose fear was obviously roaring out of control as his tale tumbled out in jerky sentences. There were a few moments of heavy silence and the man's fear began to spread across his eyes and garble his speech.

He went on, sensing their disbelief, "Guys, I know what I'm talking about. I've been around these lice since I was a kid."

Stoudamyre replied first, "Armories? We're hauling guns?" He made the word *guns* slide out as if there was no way he could believe it and almost began a laugh.

"Yes, guns … you stupid shits! What did you think?"

"Hell, dope I could figure, people on the run maybe, but … guns? You can't haul enough guns on this crate to make a damn bit of difference in anything worth talking about. Who're they kidding?"

"I already told you, the black guy thinks this is just load number one. I heard him talking to Cooper about another load being gathered up somewhere down in South America. That plane is supposed to meet us wherever we're goin'. Our guy some kinda big shot in … Nigeria … Liberia … one of them, I think. Smells like upper crust army and talks like some kind of bigshot…"

"How do you know all this stuff, Mack? If it's all true, you're either one of them or a Fed's dream come true—maybe both?"

Portero's eyes were black and glazed pools of fear and he looked around in little and jerky movements for the little Mexican with the gun again before going on, "Yeah. You're right. Both. I been fixin' these crates dopers move stuff in for so long they all forget and run their mouths around me. Besides, my brother was in pretty tight with them. 'Cept he used what he hauled and got hisself crossways with a state trooper up near Phoenix—got two bullets in the face for his trouble and probably earned them. These guys just think I'm just part of the frickin' scenery now. I hear a lot of things 'cause of that."

"Been snitchin' for the Feds, huh?"

"Uh, well … oh, hell, what's the difference? We're so close to buyin' it that it don't make no difference now. So, yeah, I been talkin' to the Feds. They caught me big-time wrong. Didn't have much choice. Anyway, a few days back, this DEA guy I know brought a new guy to see me … some spook who said he knew Cooper from … somewhere … way back. I sorta put what he dropped with what I already heard on the street and that makes what I been tellin' you make add up. We are in bad trouble, man … bad trouble."

Bailey started to tell the man he was right when the movement of the little Mexican approaching caught his eye. He nodded toward the man and murmured, "Quick, get on with it …"

"I heard most of what I know before I got out here. I tried to take a quiet run, but too late. Like I said, we're in trouble."

"OK, let's get back at it, for now."

Stopping beside the ladder leaned against the wing's root, the Mexican shifted the Uzi's strap to his right shoulder and yelled up at them, "Hey! What you guys doing … just sittin' there? This piece of crap ready to fly?"

Bailey looked down at the man, the pills dulling his ability to even pretend fearing him, "Back off. We're just figuring out how to fix something."

The man turned and wandered off toward the pickup truck and the water, seeming to be satisfied with their answer.

They glanced at one another but no one spoke and they just turned back to the engine with tools in hand. Bailey murmured as Porteros left hearing distance, "Bill, where did you hide your shooters?"

Stoudamyre's eyebrows arched and he whispered back, "Come to that, huh? Shit. I guess this is gonna get interesting. Well, I still have the peashooter in my belt. The other is in my B4—easy enough to get at I suppose."

Bailey whipped his face with a dirty sleeve and breathed, "Later … later, but keep it close." He dropped back into the sand, brushed his hands free of grit and walked off toward the tool van. The worn old .45 in his belt, hidden by the coveralls, took on new meaning and began to have a certain comforting feeling. He dug to the bottom of his tool bag and fished out another loaded magazine and tucked it in a side pocket of his coveralls.

....

Roy Cooper paused briefly looked each way along the street then, hesitated only a few more seconds before pushing through the front door of the musty smelling little café. The aging and tacky greasy spoon and black coffee boon to the antacid business had never been much good but now, only a few months away from the wrecker's ball, it had become even worse. The building housing the cafe and a row of other small shops just squatted there midst the dust and filth though only a block from the Civic Center's chic new construction.

Cooper could see the graying, mustachioed man seated in the very back booth and that he didn't even acknowledge his presence. He wore silvered aviator style sunglasses that kept Cooper, or anyone else, from knowing if he had even been noticed.

Cooper turned back to the street and stared out a moment, looked around again and hurriedly moved down the gritty floor between the two rows of dingy '60s avocado-green Formica-topped booths. He stopped at the edge of the worn and gouged tabletop and looked down at the man, who casually took off the silvered-sunglasses and nodded Cooper into the stained vinyl bench opposite him.

Cooper hadn't stayed at the front door long enough. Just as he seated himself, the man he had long thought his closest, perhaps only, friend pulled to the far curb in the driver's seat of a new and shiny metallic-gray Lincoln Town Car. His passenger, a slim and dark man, burned even darker by the sun, peered into the filthy little café through small binoculars and swore.

Carlo Malette laid the binoculars back on the seat between them and stared a long, quiet moment at Jess before asking, "You're sure that's a Fed he's talking to?"

"Well, Mister Malette, uhh, yeah, I am. He was one of the guys that used to hire us when we were back in Chicago. You know, when the big guy had us do jobs for the spooks. I … I'm sure he was the one we got Hank T. and Carly Jankowitz to do the job for … well, on that little island big wig."

Malette waved Jess quiet and said, "I don't want to hear about that shit. Ancient history. Outa my league anyway and we stay outa that kind of crap anymore. But, that's him, you're sure?"

"Yeah, I'm sure. Him and Roy always kind of hit it off. But, just the other day we were talking about the old days and Roy told me it'd been a year or so since he'd talked to the guy. You know that Roy's been getting' in bad with IRS and he might be doing some trading. But … dammit … he says he's not seen the guy since Chicago."

Malette ran fingertips along the edge of his lower lip for a moment, winced and said, "Well, Jess, the dumb shit lied."

"What are you going to do?"

There was another silence before a slow, knowing grin spread over the man's face. "Jess, I think you've been working with a dead man. All that's left to arrange are the details." He leaned back into the plush leather upholstery of the Lincoln and stared hard at the face of his wristwatch for a long moment, then shook his head in mock-sadness and turned to Jess with, "Mr. C. will have him put down—he'll have to. This must be the reason for all the Feds running around here now. Jesus … the old man is fit to be tied. I sure as hell wish I was somewhere else right now!"

Malette turned to the Jess and nodded and he dropped the Lincoln into drive and pulled out into the thin traffic without another glance at the Café's glass front. Malette drew his face into a thoughtful scowl, then glanced at Jess and said, "Keep your mouth shut about this. I'll talk to the boss soon as I drop you off and see for sure what he wants done. Above all, don't even think of letting Cooper know we talked or he'll run. Why don't you just get lost for now … stay away from him for a few days. Check in with me now and then though."

Almost an afterthought, Malette asked, "Where did he get this *Roy Cooper* business? The little wop forgot how to spell his name?"

" … and Jess …"

"You done good. Your ass is safe. The old man will know you're loyal now for sure. There's always something in it for the few loyal people. You should know that," he lied with a perfectly straight face.

As Jess wheeled Malette's Lincoln up the freeway ramp outbound from the city, the Malette deftly peeled through a large sheaf of hundred dollar bills from his inside coat pocket. At $2,500 he quit and dumped them in the driver's lap, then laughed at the muscle man's tight-jawed stare straight down the road.

"Hey … come on Jess … don't sweat it. You do something, you get something. The asshole has got to be sellin' us out. You want him singing to the Feds 'bout you sometime? He might leave your balls hanging out there in the breeze at any old time. I'd be willing to bet you're right and he's trying to get up from under his IRS load … probably wants to run. Besides, I think you ought to know, the boss was already considering laying out a hit on the both of you for bringing all the heat down around us with those armory jobs. You just did yourself a big favor coming to me like this … am I right?"

"Yeah, Mister Malette, you're right. I just …" and he stopped mid-sentence and was quiet as they rolled on out the freeway.

At the next exit, the pale green Ford that had been following them dropped off to the right, took a frontage road and was replaced by a jet-black Firebird and, a little farther back, a slightly rusted, tan Chevrolet pickup truck. The unknowing leader of the entourage sped on, out into the high Sonora.

....

Cooper had an uncomfortable tightness in his throat that forced his voice up a bit higher than usual and he could feel the other man's awareness of it … see it in his cold stare. Obregon just didn't up and call without a reason and he was afraid the reason centered on the small desert airstrip he'd just left. He was right on both counts.

Obregon pushed and plied with questions, looking for little truths and half-truths that would help put together the whole. Then it struck Cooper: Obregon knew there were guns moving, but had no idea *he* was personally involved. Cooper felt himself relax a little and lies to each question came easier. He could even smile a bit.

Mike Obregon had been staring hard at Cooper, trying to pick out the reasons for the man's nervousness. But, then it was suddenly gone. The man was dirty—he was *always* dirty—but why had he been wrapped so tight and why had it suddenly disappeared? There had only been a little more anxiety the day he'd watched police bust him for a Chicago shooting. No, he was in the middle of something now, big or small, and didn't want it queered. He wondered, only briefly, if Cooper was the one behind the gun thefts.

The mental dance went on for almost half an hour with Obregon making no real gains. He was ready to call it quits by the time their cups of rancid coffee had been sipped at and pushed aside. Cooper had feigned ignorance to almost all of his questions. The pale green Ford had already returned to its original position at the curb, just three slots back of Cooper's parked car. By the time he was able to move out into the strung out traffic, his host of a minute before had moved to the curb's edge. He followed Cooper with his eyes and when the car had passed to his right, gave a barely perceptible nod to the two men in the Ford. They pulled into traffic four cars behind Cooper and disappeared from sight with traffic and distance.

"You were watched."

Obregon ran a hand through his graying hair and turned toward his cover for the meeting, a tall, rangy, deeply tanned man in faded jeans and a casual shirt over his belt. He winced and returned an almost unenthusiastic, "Oh?"

Obregon fished a cigarette from a jacket pocket and began to hunt for a match. When the man in jeans, David Simpson, snapped a lighter in front of Obregon' s cigarette, he continued, "Thought you quit. Yeah, you were, Cooper's partner and old Carlo M. You know about him. They had binocs on you. Couldn't warn you. Saw it too late. If I had a guess, I'd say they think Cooper is ratting them off. Griff and that local dude are on them now—looks like they are headed out toward Colisimo's ... probably drop Jess off somewhere on the way."

"Shit!" was the best Obregon could muster up.

"What the hell is going on, anyhow?"

Obregon thought a moment, then replied, "Not sure—but it looks like I might have messed Cooper up—and the rumor has it that he is already in deep trouble. Jesus ... we're watching them, they're watching us—we're following them ... what a circle jerk."

"Yeah, well ... anyway, he have anything to say?"

"Not exactly a fount of information. He says he's heard *nada* ... it is more what he *didn't* say. He never could lie worth a damn. More to the point, if that many guns are moving, he'd know. I am beginning to wonder if he is in or close to the operation himself."

When Simpson just stared back and didn't answer, Obregon continued, "Cooper was into illegal gun sales back in his early days with the Chicago bunch. Not big, y'know, small lots, a dozen pistols here, a crate full there; but he knows where to start—and he is in big money trouble right now, more with IRS."

Simpson pushed a grunt out that passed for a laugh and said, "You mean your sorry-assed stoolie may be the guy we're after? Now, ain't that the shits."

After a bit, Obregon shook his head and answered, "I don't know. Wouldn't be the first time. We better keep a tail on both him and the folks that are following him around. It might turn up something." Then, for the third time of the day, "Do you always have to sound like a damn spade? Detroit really rubbed off on you."

Simpson shrugged and, again, ignored the complaint, then began wondering where the people would come from to mount an around-the-clock surveillance of this size.

Obregon thought back on how he'd never liked these stateside operations. He didn't belong here. He'd been out-of-country so much of the time that English was almost a second language. The Company's mandate forbade operations inside the U.S., not that it didn't happen, and as long and as well as he knew the man he was working with, he really didn't trust *anyone* from the Bureau all that much. He also knew the feeling was mutual. They were in competition for the same government dollars, much of the same information and, as much as the Agency said otherwise, the same publicity. The dearth of information passed on to him, working with people often found as adversaries, the darkness of it all … wasn't good. He stood silently for a bit, then flipped the half-spent cigarette toward the gutter.

"Let's go to the barn. We've got some things to think about."

The ride to the Federal Building was quiet as each man tried to piece what he knew into some sort of whole picture. Even when they reached the imposing federal edifice, the silence was still not broken all through the ride up the elevator to Simpson's divisional conference room and until they'd finished a half-hour of note and file review.

Finally, Obregon slapped a leather-bound notebook down on the long, mahogany-topped table and, when Simpson looked up, said, "We have to have all the power players here, particularly our immediate seniors. This is dumb. We're operating blind—and sure as hell out of our league."

"Well, what *do* we know? I mean, what do we know that makes this so special?" Simpson asked.

Obregon toyed with the pen he held for a moment before answering, "It is a feeling as much as anything. Hell, I've never been given so little to work with … and all this hush-hush crap over what seems at first brush to be a couple of armory jobs. How come they didn't tell us about the munitions thefts back east? Are they a part of what we're doing? We had to find out about that on our own—and by accident. It's like they tried to cover that up. Why?"

"So … what's new about being a mushroom in this business?"

"Dammit, look. All we know is *someone* is moving guns … a good-sized pile of them. Not enough to start anything big with, but still a lot of guns. People wanting this much usually just buy them from one of the big arms dealers. There's a bunch of them. Now we have some National Guard armories knocked over, one in Nogales and one up in Phoenix—and don't forget the one in El Paso … and a couple of back-east dealers in light military armament get a dent in their inventory; all something for the locals and the FBI, maybe ATF."

He stared into space for a moment, then went on, "This isn't in my line of work at all. I deal in … well, you know. I'm not even supposed to be here, yet here I am, on the quiet and packing hardware. Man, I can't even remember the last time that happened. All we get is smoke blown up our kilt about the stuff not being headed south to stay. What the hell does that mean? My outfit usually briefs better than this when we hire someone to mow the damn lawn. And … this '*Oh, yeah, boys—there was some automatic stuff stolen back east that could be coming your way* and that came only after they knew we'd found out on our own.' I think we're being had and had good."

"We still don't have much, pard, not much at all—just bits and pieces."

"Cooper nearly went to shit when I talked to him today, never really loosened up until I let him think he was in the clear—which, I might add, he damn near is. I don't have squat on him right now. If you add it all up, we've got some kind of fairly large weapons movement and I don't have a clue about who is doing it or where it's going. We can't do much more unless they tell us what is going on and where their information is coming from."

"Fat chance," but Simpson nodded in agreement and pointed toward the door to the next office with, "You can use the SCAN line in my office."

The calls lasted no longer than three minutes each and they could have been talking to the same person each time. The answers and instructions they received to the calls were almost identical. Both agencies brass had instructed them to cooperate with each other and to maintain surveillance on what seemed half the city's suspected underworld. A team of the taskforce even had the discomforting job of following a couple of City Vice-Narcotics Squad detectives through their nightly rounds. They were also to have a closed conference set up at ten the following morning, with only the SAC, themselves, and their immediate subordinates present. An undetermined number of big wheels from Washington would be in to brief them on what they each called, "A matter that could be embarrassing—if handled indelicately."

As seven in the evening slid around, they locked their stack of scribbled material in a safe behind Simpson's desk, pulled on light jackets to hide their handguns and headed out for a double Wild Turkey—or two.

Chapter 8

Cooper checked the time, mentally noted that it had been an hour since his last try, and dialed Jess's number again. Ten rings and no answer later, he slammed the phone down and began pacing the floor again.

He'd driven by Jess's apartment earlier and found it locked up tight, his car not in its customary slot, and no answer at the door after several minutes of pounding on the door. Jess was gone, just plain fucking gone.

He stopped at the window and stared down at the sparse traffic for a long minute, then focused his attention on the dark blue van parked half a block up the street to the right. It had been there the last time he looked and hadn't moved. He tried to remember if he's seen it in the neighborhood before and drew a blank.

He watched the van for a few more minutes, paranoia building, then closed the blinds and crossed the room to room to a narrow writing desk. Opening a drawer he lifted out several folders and retrieved a stainless Sig 9MM hidden below them and pushed it into his belt. A second magazine for the pistol lay there and, after considering it for a moment, he picked it up and dropped it into his sport coat pocket.

Cooper took the stairs down to the parking garage, slipped out of the building, and walked the three blocks to where he'd parked his car on a side street. He had to find Jess.

….

THE MEETING, LIKE MOST MEETINGS stuffed with desk-bound bureaucrats, got underway half an hour late. By some previous agreement, Pete Hollister, the Bureau's short and pudgy Phoenix SAC, chaired the gathering of glum-looking spooks from the several agencies. He moved the conversation around the table clockwise and asked what each participant had to offer, nodding like some ventriloquist's dummy as each agent talked and ticked off facts and assumptions—more of the latter than was comfortable. A few figments of some very active imaginations and outright lies rounded out the offerings.

Obregon sat directly across the table from Simpson and watched as his partner's expressions too often mirrored how he himself felt about the, as he put it, *circle jerk*. The upper echelon was not listening; it seemed they never did. He could tell they were too busy thinking about they would say when their turn came and, when it did, they could have well been reading from identical scripts. Then he found out why.

The silence at the end of the table-circling show-and-tell had lasted only thirty or forty seconds. The short silence was deafening, but the agents had offered all they had. That was precious little. The Agency's man, Director of Operations Dan "Gunnar" Jorgensen, cleared his throat, received a nod from Hollister, and pushed his tall, bulky, and darkly dressed frame upright.

Staring down at the thumbnail he tapped a cigarette against, he very quietly and in a bourbon baritone, said, "We haven't been all that open with you folks." It had the feel of a staged and insincere confession.

That admission, a self-serving mixture of half-lie and half-truth, still drew a series of quiet murmurs and raised eyebrows from his audience and brought everyone's attention to his end of the room. Looking around the table as he stuck the cigarette in the corner of his mouth and lit up, he raised his voice a few decibels and continued, "There's more to this than you could be readily expected to know. I'm sorry we haven't read you in sooner." He flicked the ashes from his cigarette into the vicinity of the glass ashtray at his right and went on, "But, it's getting out of hand now and we have to lay it all out in the open. Your calls tell us we may be a little behind the power curve … and have, figuratively, screwed ourselves."

Obregon winced at the militarese term *power curve* and wondered if all bureaucrats had their pet jargons they retreated into when they were short on real answers.

Jorgensen paused only briefly, then said, "Let me fill you in … and then we'll see if some new ideas surface."

With that, he moved away from his place and began to walk slowly around the long table and the people seated there, leaving a pall of smoke behind that almost hid the prominent *no smoking* signs hung from each of the four walls.

"You're all aware of Liberia's location on west coast of Africa?" It was meant as a rhetorical question and he continued with only a short pause, "They've had their problems of late, sandwiched in there between Sierra Leone, Guinea, Ivory Coast and the deep blue. There's fighting going on all around them, a lot of it generally in the nature of tribal insurrections that has been liberally doused with Islamic undertones and terrorism. Their government has wavered between going to shit and something even worse. Well, mid-year, this last time around, things seemed to steady up a bit. A large part of the government fell in behind one man, an ex-teacher and a fairly new guy on the political scene named Alex Saint Claude. His man in the *permanent* bureaucracy, if there is anything permanent in Africa except revolution, greed, and poverty, is—or was—a Colonel in the army by the name of Guthrie Mobutu—no relationship to the last Mobutu that made a name for himself in that neck of the woods and became famous through death."

Jorgensen had managed to wander back to his own place at the table, seemingly content with his geo-historic lecture. After a pause for effect, he flipped open a manila folder and tossed several copies of a black and white photograph onto the tabletop. The image was of a serious looking black man in a military uniform of obvious United Kingdom derivation. "This is the good Colonel Mobutu."

"For the physical stuff, he's about 5'11", slim, maybe 170–180 pounds, a little gray … oh, yeah, he'll be fifty-four years old this year. Not much, I know."

"Mobutu got his military upbringing in the service of Her Majesty," he continued, *Her Majesty* spoken with a poorly delivered British accent. "He served everywhere England could find to send troops until, early in the 70s, he just up and went home to his own people."

Going back to his move around the table and beginning a new cigarette, he went on, "He was an SAS Captain, the Limey version of our Special Forces, and it took him a long time to get there. He's been in Malaysia, Palestine, you name it, very experienced and, I might add, *very* good at his trade. Truth is, if he had been white and even a little bit upper crust, he'd have been a Brigadier, still with the Brits and we probably wouldn't be having this little conversation now."

As if that called for a pause for emphasis, he slowly walked back to the head of the table before going on, "When his own government saw what he was all about," motioning to the ceiling with the thumb of the hand holding the cigarette, "straight to the top—or almost to the top. They've got a small army, but there are only two above him. His position is something like, well, the maneuver brigade commander in one of our divisions. He commands all of the combat troops Liberia can field. He is, at least in Liberia, something of a big shot." He paused for another moment, wondering if dredging up his own army background had impressed his audience.

"That's just the so-called exterior. This man is bright and determined. That still doesn't tell you much about him and I know that—a few pictures, a paragraph written for a medal, how tall, how old. Again, gentlemen, I know that's nothing." The intended appearance of humility didn't fit the man at all—nor did it come off that way.

Obregon watched the man struggle to stay in character for his act and could only grit his teeth. He wondered if the men sitting around the table really knew how many of them he would take down with him if he failed.

Jorgensen looked around the table for a moment and almost mumbled, "It is, however, about all I can tell you about the *him* of it." Obregon had the faintest of feelings flicker across his mind that Jorgensen held a great deal more information on the man and just chose to hold it tight to his vest. The niggling discomfort was unsettling. He didn't just distrust the man; more to the point, he despised him.

Jorgensen continued the role of historian in a patronizing tone that indicated he enjoyed the part and that it made him feel somewhere on a higher plane than the group he kept circling and covering in more than one kind of smoke. "But, while Mobutu seems to be doing fine, things are never really smooth in these governments. They rise and fall like the tide. This one just might be on its way out now."

Shaking his head, in mock pity, he lamented, "This regime is less than a year old and there is already a rebel move afoot in the back country and even within part of the army. Mobutu and those loyal to him are up against it, but good. They need a little of everything, no, make that a *lot* of everything."

Obregon shifted uneasily and muttered under his breath, "What in God's name has that got to do with us?"

Jorgensen only stared back at him for a moment and Obregon found himself wishing the words had not come out. The hard-eyed look from Jorgensen was nothing less than a threat.

Jorgensen leaned forward, his weight supported by both forearms on the back of his chair, still looking right at Obregon. "Everybody wants a toehold in Africa these days, something bigger, better, and more profitable than the colonial days, but with a lot less of the responsibilities possession of a colony once held or occupation does now. Industrialized nations are particularly hot to get their hands on the minerals that even the poorest country there seems to have in abundance and can't, for one reason or another, take advantage of in a productive fashion. Y'know, it's pretty tribal, hard to centralize. We had the inside track and blew it. A great number of the people in charge there are descendants of slaves who returned to Africa after our Civil War. They wanted to go back to home and roots but they tried to build a government just like the one they left behind here in the States. We have traditionally gotten along well with them—not now though—something of a standoff exists."

"What do you mean?" Simpson asked, "Who are the players this time?"

"Well, some of the usual," Jorgensen answered, "but not all. Cuba hasn't been involved this time and I don't know why—unless it is their economy, which is really in the toilet. China won't sell them guns and neither did North Korea for some reason. That left us on one side and what's left of the Eastern Bloc on the other ... at least for the time being. The politicos and media don't play it that way, but the Eastern Bloc is beginning to fragment and is not much of a conventional threat there right now, particularly with Russia getting the short end of the stick in Afghanistan. So, what else can I say?"

The short, fat, Bureau man forced a laugh and smirked, "Well, isn't that new? But, what the hell difference would that make now? I mean, all the big-time thinkers say the Warsaw Pact could be headed for an implosion and, if you believe the academics, will not be coming back to life soon if it does crash. And you're right, that little fracas in Afghanistan is not helping them. Anyhow, they've been mostly selling all they can make to the Arabs—for oil and U.S. dollars."

Jorgensen passed his disapproving glance across him for a second before going on, "We've essentially cut a deal with Russia and convinced her remaining allies sometime back that they shouldn't give the rebels—or the current power for that matter—weaponry of any kind. By the same token, they've pretty much done the same to us. It is kind of a good publicity, bad publicity thing. They really don't have the ability to help anyone right now anyhow, not without a lot of cash or some other ready resources up front. At the same time, we have sort of stepped in it—painted ourselves into a corner with our own State Department bullshit rhetoric in that toothless piece of crap we call the U.N. and can't even give the weapons away free."

A thin, mirthless smile creased his face and he concluded, "So, apparently, the principal arms producing nations are either not interested or have their noses out of joint for some reason or another. The Liberians are having a hell of a time scratching up weapons—and I'm not talking about major weapons systems, just rifles and bayonets with which they can fight bows and arrows and a few other assorted popguns." He stopped pacing a bit before going on, "Can you believe these folks don't have a single combat aircraft built in the past twenty years? I'm not even sure those are airworthy—and they are old pieces of shit the Frogs sold them in the first place."

Jorgensen sat down and whispered to Hollister for a moment; he, in turn, leaned over and spoke quietly into the intercom. Within three minutes a youngish secretary appeared with a tall vacuum coffee urn and a tray of cups. She looked the room and its occupants over carefully, as if memorizing the faces, while arranging the coffee service on a wheeled cart and moving it to the edge of the table. Then she quietly disappeared through the door again, without having said a word.

Jorgensen waited until she closed the door, looked around the table, and went on, "Part of the problem is the financial state of the Liberian government. They're hurting … in debt to the outside world for millions and an inflation rate that would knock your eye out. They wouldn't have gotten the loans to begin with if each of the greedy suckers making them didn't have an eye on the minerals there. They're really putting the pressure on them to pay up now, hoping to get an inside deal on the minerals there so they can cart them off to more appreciative owners."

Jorgensen continued what was beginning to sound like a current affairs lecture, "Of course, there are problems with over-flight of unfriendly neighboring governments even if we did want to help them, except from the sea, of course. That also assumes you can find someone interested in, and capable of, coming up with enough of the right kind of weaponry to be of use—and, again, they'd be taking a chance on the Liberian's paying ability."

Jorgensen was filling cups with hot coffee and passing them down the table as he talked, "But now they are getting desperate. The government is about to curl up there in the dust and die. Our sources say Saint Claude trusts few people. Mobutu, for good or bad, is an exception. Saint Claude has laid some squirreled away U.S. bucks on him and sent him shopping on the illegal market. And don't think we're talking about street kid's zip guns. There are half a dozen dealers, here and around the globe, that could outfit small armies at a moment's notice—but for cash only. The two outfits hit in North Carolina fit that category. Pistols or artillery pieces, you name it, they got it. I doubt Mobutu has enough hard cash to interest very many of the sizable dealers though."

Then he put the purpose for the whole dialog on the table, "You won't like this, but we think Mobutu entered the States, via St. Thomas, San Juan, and Miami, two weeks ago. He's *been* using the name of *Joseph Bannock*. The name and history belonged to a guy we think was killed near Monrovia about a year ago in a garden-variety car wreck. Now the cheese gets really binding; we lost track of him about four days ago." He breathed a sigh that sounded almost like pain.

Tapping the table with his lighter as he went for the pack of cigarettes in his pocket again, Jorgensen finished, "That doesn't leave too many places to look when you get down to considering what he is here after." Pointing at Obregon, he said, "We think *your friends* are where he eventually went." Lighting up, he went on, "I know there are lots of other gun dealers out there, but we have sources in most of them and they have pretty much been ruled out. That brings us back to your people. And ... well, we have a snitch there too ... pointing a finger."

He was silent for a long minute, then went on, "We cannot afford—the country cannot afford—for *anyone, anywhere*, to believe, with any hint of certainty, that this agency, or this government, furnished the weapons he does find. We have been selling our souls lately to make things work on that continent and the embarrassment would be a killer. Worse, we gotta a little shit sitting in the oval office now who just doesn't understand *our* world and his main advisors came from the same … leftist kindergarten … where he was potty trained. This could be *bad*."

Jorgensen paused, exhaled a cloud of smoke, and began nervously tapping the arm of his chair with the lighter. Finally, he went on, "Obviously, what is said here will not leave this room—but, I'm telling you now—I don't care who gets burned, I intend to see that … man … out of the country and out of our way. Nobody wants to see Mobutu … well … hurt, but if it becomes necessary …" He left it just hanging there in the air, the implication plain enough.

After a moment, he turned and nodded to the man on his left who, thus far, had not said a word. The man stood up and began, "I'm Steve Bronkowski … from the Agency. Normally, this would belong to one organization or another—never both, certainly not all of us here today. But, we're short on time and don't have enough resources from any one agency here to handle this. None of us can go it alone on this one, maybe not all of us put together." The man had the tone of a know-it-all and, after only a few seconds, it began to grate.

"Until one, or the other, gets the nod from the Hill, and the manpower to handle it, we'll do it this way," and he began to scribble on the whiteboard he'd pulled up on its dolly.

An hour and a half later, when they walked out into a blazing hot day, there was a whole system of cross-agency partnerships and relationships formalized, and a tight plan, at least on paper, of operations under the temporary control of Jorgensen. Resources from the other two main Federal intelligence gathering entities were being called in, along with investigators from the FBI, INS and Customs, and an around the clock surveillance scheme was underway. Everything else was on the back burner … and they all felt like the blind, collectively leading the blind.

. . . .

T HE WOMAN HAD QUIETLY CLOSED THE DOOR to the conference room and walked across the hall to her desk. She punched a button on the phone and held for a few seconds. When the telephone at the other end of the connection was answered, she simply said, "I'm running out to the pharmacy for a minute. Can you catch my calls?" She hung up and picked up her purse and headed down the hall.

Ten minutes later, she entered a phone booth and dialed a number from memory. The man at the other end listened quietly as he looked out across the desert floor far below him. When she'd finished talking, he politely thanked her and hung up.

The young woman left the telephone booth, stood for a moment studying the passing foot traffic and looking at the faces in passing cars. After a few minutes, she crossed the street to a Walgreen's and was back upstairs in the Federal Building within another fifteen minutes. A blue plastic bag with the name of the pharmacy prominently displayed was on her desk. She went to busily shuffling the stack of meaningless papers in her inbox with calm efficiency, disregarding all else around her.

Chapter 9

Colonel Guthrie Mubutu, with growing-stale identification as Joseph Bannock, was less than half a mile from his hunters' table during their long and drawn out session on how he could be run to earth and removed from the equation. He had closeted himself as unobtrusively as time allowed in a motel that was one of many buried in the neon of tourist lodgings along the east-west corridor of Interstate-10.

His time was spent repeatedly and unhappily thumbing through the few typed and marked up flimsies provided by Cooper at the bar that passed for a manifest of the weapons he'd been able to scratch up with the promise of his government's few precious and carefully hoarded U.S. dollars. The list was pitifully short for someone about to fight a war.

Mobutu could only pray this miserly cache of weapons was, as promised, just the first shipment and that his own man, now scouring Paraguay, Bolivia, and Argentina, was having better luck. The mobsters that had prepared the list he studied made numerous references to a *second* shipment, even a *third*, and tried to raise the price at every turn for the most minute of reasons. He was no fool and would believe the additional shipments when and if he saw them. Trusting the mobsters he dealt with was foolhardy and he found doubting, even disliking, them came far easier. His *benefactors* had assured him the weapons were not stolen. He knew that, at least in part, was a lie, not that it would make any difference if law enforcement caught him.

He found his mind shifting again to the man he sent to South America and worrying with the thought that he'd had no communication with him for over two weeks. The anger he carried at the extortionist prices, along with the figurative stench of the underworld shysters who demanded them, overcame his worry over the missed contacts and he went back to reading through the inventory lists again.

The list was disorganized and short. Among the items on the list were a number of almost new M16s, which, he mused, were probably stolen from the armory of some local National Guard organization. The four-hundred plus M16A1s and half a hundred M60 light machineguns at least encouraged him a tiny bit. They would replace the aging and worn Garands and Browning Automatic Rifles carried by one of his battalions. There were also, amongst all the military hardware, over a hundred blued commercial Browning 9 MMs, still in the manufacturer's wrappings, just like the old Hipower he had carried for years and that now lay atop the bedside table. Over two-hundred older Government Model .45 Colt products rounded out the list of handguns, all obviously originally part of some military unit's issue. The remaining few M79s and 81 MM mortars, with only a few rounds of ammunition, were more frustrating than encouraging. Finding more fodder for them would be difficult, though it was at least possible. He was pleased with the amount of ammunition however. Some of it was commercial and he knew the fifty cases of 5.56, sixty-two cases of belted 7.62, along with the miscellaneous grenades and extra magazines, would be sufficient only in the short term. A few repair parts, several additional boxed double cases of .45 and 9MM rounds, and a few other odds and ends, filled out the list.

Down near the bottom of the list was a notation that the M16 bolts were tagged and boxed separately from the rifles. That alone told him the weapons were stolen. He knew American Reserve and National Guard units stored bolts and rifles separately, a practice totally unacceptable—even suicidal—in his little, nearly always unstable, country. It must, he thought, be wonderful to live in a country that could fear its population so little.

It was all small stuff—very small stuff. He'd seen more ammunition than the lists held fired into the air by drunken tribesmen celebrating national holidays, the birth of sons, or the fact that it was … well, Wednesday.

He put the list aside, levered his fit frame up out of the chair, and paced around the room for a few long minutes. Returning to the list, he began going over it again in boredom mixed with anxiety. There was hardly enough armament for a lightly armed infantry battalion— even in his country. There were far too many calibers and not a heavy machinegun in the lot. Worse, repair parts were in terribly short supply, and that was being optimistic.

Mobutu thought back to his service in The Crown's forces and remembered how much better turned out even those traditionally austere combat units were. But, it took very little to alter the course of history in the whole of Africa, even less in small and poor Liberia. A well-armed battalion of infantry, thrown into the battle at the right moment, could well carry the war one way or the other. Looking back at the list, he realized it would have to be done quickly, for there was precious little to do it with—and when that was gone he doubted there would be more. The promises of additional loads of weaponry seemed more mirage than fact. He began to think on how he would make the mobsters trying to fleece him painfully pay for their deceit. That brought a small smile to his face.

He let his eyes and thoughts wander around the drab little motel room again. He felt the walls closing in and wondered how much worse prison would be and he began to pace again. After a few minutes, he stopped at the bottle of Bushmills on the bureau, poured a small drink, neat. He hated ice in a drink. He looked at it thoughtfully, then poured a bit more, smiled, and went back to pacing, winding tighter with each step. He felt very much like a man who had failed, and failed when it could be least afforded, by the president he served, his country, or himself.

Mobutu, with mock amusement, thought how well it all fit together though. He recalled that, throughout history, all his country's wars had been little ones. So, all it took to succeed, or fail, was a ... *little*. He even allowed himself a short daydream about being the man of the hour, bringing that *little bit* needed to bear on issues at the right time and place. But he was a realist, and the daydream quickly fled.

The difficulty he'd had in finding a sponsoring or cooperative government in the Western Bloc had puzzled him at first. He'd thought the United States would have quickly jumped at the idea. After all, more than a few of well-connected officials owed him large and long over-due favors. That did not even consider that Liberia had long been a willing center of indirect U.S. influence on the African Continent.

Liberia had, he reminded himself, received some of its very life's blood from America. Long lineage lines bore names found in any American telephone book. In fact, the Captain he'd sent to South America carried *Davis* as a family name. It was said that Captain Davis was the descendent of slaves once owned by the president of the Confederate States of America. President Saint Claude, with his French surname, seemed almost like an outlander in this sea of Anglo names—Mobutu even more so.

But Mobutu was *Kru*. Neither he, nor any of his direct ancestors, had been unfortunate enough to become slaves—to anyone. He never would. His family had always been there in Liberia's thin-soiled flatlands, scratching out a meager subsistence with a few goats, skinny cows and only a few more rows of maize and millet. That long-held agrarian façade veiled the totally unreconstructed warrior beneath.

Guthrie, named after the hometown of a worn and weary Oklahoma Baptist missionary who had helped a midwife with his birth, had been one of the more lucky Kru youth. Considered bright, very bright in fact, certainly eager and persistent, he'd thrived and gloried in the material usually force-fed his missionary school peers. Among them, Guthrie was always the light they followed. By the time he was in his mid-teens, the schoolmaster recognized extraordinary promise in Guthrie and began searching for a better vehicle to further the young black man's education.

His headmaster by that time, the overly reverent Jacob Watson, had serious visions of Guthrie becoming a homegrown and personally molded disciple to help Christianize a very primitive and dismal corner of God's earth. He saw a monument—not so much to God, but to Jacob Watson. Guthrie would be something he could always point to as evidence of his successful goodness and godliness, not to mention missionary zeal.

Guthrie Mobutu, much to Watson's chagrin, wasn't a *something*. He was a *someone*. And a real, thinking, someone cannot always be depended upon to live as the would-be modelers of their clay would have it. Jacob Watson wept when Guthrie left to join the British Army, then hit the bottle and roundly cursed his departing protégé for having no gods whatsoever.

Guthrie Mobutu then became something more of an oddity—a proud, classically educated, young black man with a warrior's instincts, successfully serving and competing for the few successes available in the Crown's Territorial Army. Before long he found an obscure slot in the regular army. Not that he was readily accepted, he wasn't. The very last of the Mau Mau wars still burned in his more seasoned fellow soldiers memories during his early time in British hobnails. Through that particular time of his life he was, on more than a few occasions, roundly hated—but that hate was always mixed with more than a little fear. Guthrie Mobutu was a combat soldier, a damn good one, and the British Army has always respected good soldiers, whatever their roots.

After a time, he was posted to a regiment that had a long and colorful history and, at the time, damn little else to recommend it. The regiment was made up of a collection of mixed-bloods and hard drinking Irish, in separate companies of course. Most of them were fleeing poverty, hard-to-feed families, or perhaps damp jail cells. He was a sergeant by then and spent long hours in the actual practice of *command*. He had to—his lieutenant was a roaring drunk and forever dropping hints about his IRA past when in his cups. The IRA connection was a lie, but he was always in his cups, so the lie was bigger than the man. Mobutu had no choice but to command or the understaffed mob of misfits would have fallen apart. It was not an easy task, but he gradually grew the unit's capacities. The Irish, so often in their history a target of prejudice, practiced it with fervor themselves.

As poorly hung together as this unit's command structure was, it was sent to Malaya toward the end of the Communist insurrection that weighed so heavily on Parliament's sleep and digestion. Mobutu's lieutenant lasted exactly three days and, in the very first of his in-country bottle binges, stepped into an insurgent's booby trap. He, or rather what was left of him, was scraped into a body bag, along with a significant portion of the radio operator who died with him and shipped back to Ireland. There they could pretend he was a fallen hero and bury him among other pretend heroes.

Guthrie's work had not been without recompense. He then became even more of an oddity—a black lieutenant, a lieutenant of the line at that and, worse, up from the ranks—all in the service of the Crown.

He had found his calling. Before long, it was an honor—albeit a dangerous one—to be sent to that *terrifyin' nigger lieutenant's outfit.* His skills brought him more than a little intra-service acclaim and all that came with it. His unit was recognized as killers—pure and simple. Twelve years, a school tour, and a police action and a half later, he wore Captain's pips, held a slot on a promotion list to Major, and was the operations officer of a unit within SAS.

Then, he left. Mobutu just turned in his papers and left; bowing to no one. He took his discharge papers and a freighter out of Liverpool, needing the rest and relaxation of the voyage, and returned to Monrovia. He took his attitudes, skills and notoriety with him. Liberia proved to be *almost* grateful. The British Army thought him entirely mad. He was, of late, inclined to agree with them.

The motley army he became a part of made him wince in the pain only a self-inflicted wound can bring. But, it did need him. God, how it needed him. He responded in a manner so very typical of him. He threw all he had at making the simple folk populating his new army into what the name implies. He was not unsuccessful and the labor had its benefits. By the time this desperate arms hunt had blundered onto the horizon, Mobutu was a full Colonel, third in command of all the tactical forces Liberia could field and with a considerable level of financial wellbeing. More to the point, he was a *real* Colonel, not like the ex-sergeant who had just been pulled from the throne.

That fool had cloaked himself with the title and office of president and the rank of colonel on the same day he had betrayed the sitting president and slaughtered his way into office. Idi Amin did it, why couldn't he?

Fortunately for all concerned, except the deposed imitation Colonel, Saint Claude now had the man safely locked away in a tiny and filthy cell at a well-guarded post on the outskirts of Monrovia. There he could neither claim rank nor office of any type and had only his delusions to keep him company. He would be lucky to live out the month—and that, unfortunately for him, was of absolutely no concern to anyone outside his squalid, vermin-infested cell.

Mobutu had wisely and carefully developed a host of friends in just the right places on the way up—and, on the other side of the coin, his share of enemies. Saint Claude, the new president, loved him like a brother, actually more like a brother-in law, which he was. Mobutu had met, fallen in love with and married Julianna Saint Claude well before her brother had made his successful grab for the presidential palace. Saint Claude had and kept close connections with the last U.S. president's cabinet even before his assent to office. Together, they saw to it that Mobutu had made several profitable and career enhancing side-trips on his hurried path to Colonel. The short course at the Leavenworth's Command and General Staff College and Fort Rucker's helicopter training were among them. He taught as much as he studied. On both sides of the Atlantic he was considered by all he met and worked with to be a skilled leader of warriors.

The enemies had their slice at him too. The Brigadier he reported to, when he felt like it, had only recently been promoted over him. Necessary *Tribal politics* they called it, with a knowing look and disinterested shrug. It was really more of a pointed warning from those who feared or, more probably, envied him and was intended as not-too-thinly-veiled advice that he should remember his place in the overall scheme of things.

The Brigadier was an obese, over-his-head, semi-literate, pretender. The repulsive and disgusting fool belched at the table, farted in church, drank incessantly and, in the month before his promotion to brigadier, murdered his wife to make way for someone half her age and certainly better looking. Then, after many false tears and days of dramatic and public breast-beating, he executed her witless bodyguards for the crime. But, Mobutu was not without patience, intent, and guile. He would bide his time. The Brigadier would regret everything—everything—even things he was only thinking of doing.

....

Mobutu folded the creased read and re-read stack of paper again and stuffed it back into the soft leather briefcase that lay open on the motel room's single table. He heard it rattle the key to the rental locker at the bus depot and thought of the satchel of *samples* stored there. He looked at his watch, noting that within two hours he had to put more change in the locker's coin lock to avoid some caretaker's finding of the case and bringing another variable into play: the police. Mobutu feared the police that most U.S. cities fielded. They were all armed, generally thought for themselves, and were allowed real curiosity, something never permitted in Liberia. That made them unpredictable and dangerous.

It was imperative that this small cache of weapons he'd bought find its way back to Saint Claude and the army that was about to move on the rebels. In fact, he planned to be there with them. They needed him. Without this *sample* though, there'd be no money for more and he had promised the sellers much more. And that was a lie. The need to succeed welled into an anxiety he'd never before felt. He had to struggle to remain even outwardly calm.

But here he was, in America's southwest, trying to be invisible. Easier said than done. The mixed-blood, Black and Mexican whore on the bed still breathed the slow rhythm of sleep and Mobutu shook his head with a faint smile. Whores, and Irish whiskey, were a fault he had both picked up and almost discarded while in British uniform a long time ago. At least the whores had been discarded; he'd not seen a reason to forgo the appreciation of good Irish. He had no reason to interact with the former.

Now, in this endeavor, he needed to keep a very low profile; to go completely unnoticed. He worked hard at looking like a traveler, become an everyday tourist, and someone of no particular interest to anyone. On his first day in the city, he had circled a run-down neighborhood of a business and entertainment district block twice, then picked up a streetwalker who was dressed less garishly than the others. He paid her to pack some of her other even less flashy clothes and bought three days of her time. Julianna might even understand— *this time.* Of course, he would not be foolish enough to ever bring up the subject. There is expediency and there is stupidity—he did not practice the latter.

Not that he hadn't enjoyed the woman, he had. The white stucco house on the small green and flowered hill in Monrovia, where his Julianna held reign, was a long way from the heat of the American southwest. He was content with remembering that, on a very few occasions, a cold-hearted, but very secret, bit of sex was better than none at all.

This was his second day with her. He knew she would talk with the other prostitutes about the strange trick she had been shacked up with and sooner or later the local police would begin to wonder who and what he was. If nothing else, her pimp would be looking for his walking piece of cash flow. Of course, he was expendable. But, by then he hoped he and his small armament treasure trove would both be out of the country. Since that was less than two days away, he didn't worry as much as he should have.

Thirty-six hours. That's all he needed. Thirty-six hours and he, along with the small arsenal he'd been able to gather, would be gone. The worn-out old DC-3, its shabby, down-at-the-heels, pilots, along with the meager weapons cache he'd bought—would all be gone. It couldn't happen soon enough.

In all his years of service, there'd never been a mission quite like this. And there had been some unusual ones, particularly during his posting to the commando unit. Now he was made to feel more like a criminal than a soldier, certainly not like someone third in command of his country's whole army. He shook his head in tired and sick disgust when he remembered that this time, he, in fact, was a criminal. He rationalized, not very successfully, that it only counted if he were caught. If he were, there would be no medals, no celebrations, no mention in dispatches—just jail, or perhaps a bullet, certainly disgrace. He tried hard not to even entertain the possibility of that eventually.

Mobutu looked back at the woman again and hoped her pimp wasn't looking for her too hard. He didn't need another complication right now, certainly not in the form of some erratic pimp, pushing hard at hanging onto his imagined street image, while trying to bring his day-to-day income back into the stable. It was a well-founded fear, but his thoughts about moving to another motel were just too late.

Downstairs, on the street side of the building, a skinny, thirty-something black man, in almost iridescent green polyester, crawled out of the cool of his equally bright colored Lincoln low-rider's fake leopard skin upholstered interior and strutted into the motel's office. This was only the seventh stop he'd made while looking for his *woman* and the cocaine he'd snorted twenty-minutes or so previously allowed him to feel the beginning twinges of just plain *mean*. His fuzzy mind, only four days out of the county jail on a ninety-day sleepover, saw another pimp on his turf—and that *someone* would pay for his intrusion.

The pimp's description of *Charley*, particularly the white streak in her hair, was good enough to allow the clerk to place the whore Mobutu had checked in with two days previously. It was also enough to make him start worrying about his continued employment and, worse, the cops.

This was a motel full of tourists and travelers, not a slum surrounded cathouse and the twenty-dollar bill the pimp casually flipped over the counter really wouldn't pay for much damage and did very little for the clerk's mood. The motel may have bordered on being a shithole, but he made his living there. He eyed the sawn-off shotgun beneath the counter and wondered if he'd need it. He did finger the phone for a long moment, trying to decide which call he should make first. He settled on his roomers, hoping to move the shooting out of his building to someone else's property, and punched in the numbers. The cops would come next.

Mobutu had just stood and let the robe slip from his shoulders and was stepping toward the shower when the jangle of the phone stopped him. Puzzled, he stared at it through another ring and then started toward it. He was aware the phone had awakened the woman and saw her sleep-touched smile at his nakedness.

Pressing the phone's receiver to his ear, he heard the desk clerk's rapid fire, "Man, there's a 'nuther nigger headed your way," and the room was suddenly filled with the crash of the door flying open as its jamb splintered. The clerk had taken a few thoughts too long to call.

Mobutu appeared unfazed, even calm. His hand lay atop the familiar cool metal of the suppressed Browning 9MM he had concealed beneath a folded and carefully smoothed towel next to the telephone. He already knew, without a doubt, the pimp would soon be dead. But, it was a complication he didn't need and brought the police into play, so he waited.

He turned his head to the noise and stared, with a controlled calmness, at the skinny black hunched there with a little nickel-plated automatic in his hand. The man had the pistol out in front of him and was trying to lean forward on the balls of his feet, crouched over like some television gunfighter. He was too full of cocaine to make his theatrics or his balance work. The green polyester and wide eyes would have been funny at any other time and place.

The cocaine and the exertion of kicking in the door made standing still an impossible task for the spaced-out pimp and small beads of sweat stood out on his forehead. Mobutu calmly turned his attention back to the phone and said quietly, "It's all right. He is a friend." Then he slowly hung up the phone.

He looked back at the pimp in the doorway and, still calm, said, "Come in. Please, close the door."

Mobutu's calmness only served to enrage the black more but, for some reason he didn't even recognize, he pushed the door shut with his heel and stepped on into the room. His voice wound higher and ratcheted tighter, while spittle frothed at one corner of his mouth. He began to stream profanities at the world in general and poked the handgun farther out toward Mobutu, who had not yet turned completely around to face him. The woman was sitting bolt upright, wide-eyed and totally silent.

"You black muther … you got my woman! Turn your sorry ass around and look at me … you … you … dead!" and Mobutu turned to face the pimp at the same time a quiet cough and a metallic clatter was heard.

The pimp's arms jerked back and his eyes and mouth went wide with both pain and fear. The first signs of blood began to show around a small and dark hole just left of the center of his forehead. He could not even struggle with death. His head lolled backward and he seemed to almost collapse in on himself as he fell straight down to the floor. Mobutu turned to the still silent woman and shook his head sadly.

She clutched the sheet up under her chin, trying to hide behind it in sudden, almost ridiculous, modesty and fear. Her eyes were even wider and flitted from his face to the blued automatic in his hand. It was obvious she knew what was next.

The woman pushed one hand out in front of her, palm out, moving it from side to side as part of the plea her lips started to form. Only a strangled, "N … n … no …o" came out, then he raised the Browning and pulled the trigger. She never closed her eyes. She simply flinched and fell forward; her legs doubled under her, and lay still.

Mobutu became aware of the smell of urine mixed with acrid powder smoke. Then, to no one that could hear, he quietly said, "I'm sorry. I really am … but …" and he forced his lips into a straight, tight, line and shook his head slowly.

He stood there for only a moment, staring at the bare back of the dead woman. A flood of complete sadness filled his soul. Then he quickly moved about the room, putting together everything that was his.

Less than five minutes later, he'd thrown his belongings into his luggage, dressed, wiped clean what he could remember having touched and picked up the shell casings. Then he quietly strolled down the back stairs to his rented car and drove out of the parking lot. He could just hear the approaching police sirens in the distance.

. . . .

THE GRUMMAN SMOKED A LONG WAY down the blistering hot runway before lifting into a sky marred by only a few scattered thunderheads crowded down tight against the horizon to the southwest. The pilot pulled the aircraft's nose steeply upward and then banked in a wide, accelerating turn toward the northeast. By the time assigned altitude was reached, the aircraft was at maximum cruise and bound as directly for Dulles International as scheduled traffic and long rows of storms from just east of the Mississippi to Cape Hatteras would allow.

Jorgensen had crowded his bulky frame into a leather recliner anchored behind a smallish "L" shaped wooden desk that was hinged next to an oval window overlooking the starboard wing. He stared out of the dark and cool cabin's interior at some unimportant spot along a line where desert met sky and let his mind withdraw into deep and troubled thought.

He was outwardly quiet but the facts and inferences of the day's meeting whirled endlessly through his thoughts. He was sure that *almost* everyone in attendance at the conference had been convinced he was the same in-control, self-assured, man he always had been and that, as usual, he had all the available and relevant facts. More importantly, they *had* to know his interest was national—not personal. That was important. Then, he again reminded himself that he had convinced *almost* everyone. Neither Obregon nor Simpson had looked pleased or convinced—and, that … asshole … *Obregon*, he was a problem from a long way back. Still, Jorgensen managed to practice the strong, aloof, almost icy, exterior—even now, when there was no one to watch that made any difference.

He could imagine everything unraveling, coming apart in front of those he most wanted to believe him infallible. Twenty five years of struggling up through the murky layers of the intelligence community could all come crashing down around his ears in moments with just one wrong move. He had to think, to neutralize the negative issues crowding in on his personal fiefdom's borders. Turning to someone for help was difficult; he trusted no one. He considered trust in another human a personality disorder and, to him, a defect someone in his business could ill-afford any time and any place.

He played the scenarios and few open options as he saw them. He stacked reputation against reputation, position against position. But, there it was, he had to neutralize both Mobutu and Obregon; they were the only real obstacles he had to overcome. Then he thought a bit closer to home and wondered if Duncan was a part of the mixture. He hadn't even considered him, but he could only move so far and so fast.

The players on the ground there in the desert came back into focus and he thought of Cooper and remembered that he was totally expendable, and deservedly so, just another mobster awaiting a place in the sand. But what about that local man from the Bureau ... Simpson, was it? Suppose Obregon had given him enough information to act on his own? But he had no ... power ... and would have less with Obregon dead. He might be able to bet the odds and decided to consider him too marginal a player to waste energy on at the moment.

No, only Mobutu and Obregon really mattered at the moment. But, if he had to remove them, why not just make a clean sweep? He liked that solution and it didn't even create a bump in his thought process. He knew he had to act—and very soon. He could handle whatever was left over when, and if, he found it necessary.

The Senate would meet in less than ninety days to turn thumbs up, or thumbs down, on everything he'd struggled for these past years. He would be one of the few insiders ever to reach the director's chair and have any hope of holding on to it. His course through this rough sea began to be unequivocally clear. And death paved the way.

Still, Jorgensen's only physical movement was an occasional blink and the pushing of an ice cube through the amber of his drink with an index finger. Appearances were important. A cigarette lay smoldering amidst the ruins of its two predecessors in an ashtray just to his right. It all contributed to the blue-gray pall already surrounding the man. His mind was far away—and on unpleasant things.

The silence had its own heavy impact and made the two young and almost identically dressed aides he'd brought to the southwest with him fidgety and nervous. They had been around the Agency just long enough to know that Jorgensen was a man who made things, exciting and interesting things, happen. They wanted to be there when it did. It would be a both thrilling and career-building place to be. Both actually believed what he'd told them about picking them as aides because of their fine records and potential. Their wagons were irretrievably hitched to his star. They would do anything to please the Director—anything. And, while it didn't cross their buttoned-down minds, just about *anything* might well be asked of them—and soon.

They occasionally glanced at each other in questioning anxiety, constantly flipping through, without really seeing, the several magazines scattered around the cabin. Their Director's disapproving glance had quickly stilled them however, and they were left to sit in a tense and restrained silence. The kraal around their presumed *mentor* was too thorny and high for penetration and they'd not been around long enough to be welcomed inside uninvited.

The two young men were simply *baggage*. They just did not yet understand that. Jorgensen kept them around as loyal gofers, for appearances sake, as trappings of his office—and because they had not been with the Agency long enough to have the slightest chance of belonging to any of the cliques dangerous to him. He also kept them around because they were expendable. They would never become part of the inner circle. He was his own *inner circle*.

Some long and quiet minutes into the flight, near the western edge of the Houston control zone, Jorgensen seemed to blink out of the shadows into which he had withdrawn and pushed his empty glass out at the nearest aide. The young man in the tan tropical suit hastily grabbed for the glass and retreated toward the small bar that was a piece of the bulkhead separating flight deck from cabin. Before the obedient lap-dog had even reached the bar, Jorgensen had another cigarette going and had picked up the secure radiotelephone's handset at his right elbow. When the fresh scotch was returned, he merely motioned it to the tabletop, nodded perfunctory thanks and continued talking into the handset. The young man quickly and subserviently retreated out of earshot.

Jorgensen sat for a while after completing the call, seeming to still be buried in the deep thoughts that had darkened the trip to that point. Then, he brightened for a moment, smiled across his anxious aides' faces and slid his chair into a reclining position. "Wake me when we're fifteen minutes out," was his only comment. He closed his eyes and dropped into a silence that passed for relaxed sleep to his aides. It actually masked frayed nerves, an acid ridden, knotted stomach, and a mind swirling with the doubts that nurtured the beginnings of something alien to Jorgensen: fear.

The tired and bleary-eyed Langley evening desk officer at the other end of the connection had merely taken notes and replied with simple, "Yes sirs" and "No sirs." The conversation, virtually one-way, had lasted only a little over ninety seconds. When it was over the desk officer made three calls.

One was to the swing shift supervisor in Central Files, another to Jorgensen's deputy, reached at a noisy Georgetown party full of Beltway movers and shakers, and the last to the Station Chief in London. None of the calls were long and they were to the point. The desk officer's final action was to notify the standby flight crew and order a helicopter for a pickup at Dulles International.

....

The Grumman's final approach into Dulles was made through a squally and bumpy summer's evening sky that fit well with Jorgensen's foul mood. Ground Control quickly directed them to an isolated pad next to which was parked an idling helicopter. The helicopter pilot waited out a passing rain shower to begin a low and hurried flight to Langley. Even with his roundabout route through the gaps in the squall lines, they were only a few minutes beyond the time he'd scheduled when they touched down on the helipad.

Jorgensen ordered his aides to get some sleep and be in early the next day, then strode down the long and empty hall toward a closed door with a small ribbon of light showing at its base. They were shut out again and the lapdog twins, in their matching tan outfits and matching hopes, stared disappointedly after their master as he stalked off. Then, they too gave in to the night and walked back out into another rain shower.

Jorgensen pushed the door open and entered the space he had called his own for the previous four years. This had been his lair ever since a carefully maneuvered promotion to Director of Operations. The place had been *Gunnarized*, with one wall of books, more for show than anything else, that faced another wall of framed photographs depicting places far and near, forgotten and not forgotten. The room was carefully, but with apparent haphazard logic, strewn with easy chairs, a comfortable and ancient mahogany desk, a small bar, an authentic multi-colored Navajo throw on the floor, and all the other things you would normally expect to see in a man's den or library. But, then, this was Gunnar Jorgensen's *den*. Nowhere was the influence of a woman, any woman, in evidence.

William—Will—Duncan, Jorgensen's deputy, looked over the top of the newspaper he pretended to be reading, eyes full of question and quietly commented, "With the storm, I wasn't sure you'd be in—took me away from one hell of a party. I do have the files you wanted though."

Jorgensen stepped to the desk, pushed the file folders aside, and laid his brief case on its glass top, dropped his jacket across the chair behind it, and turned toward the bar at the far end of the room. He didn't need another drink. His stomach was already sour, but "Drink, Will?" came out easily.

"No ... oh, hell, a beer will do."

Jorgensen opened the small fridge under the bar and fisted two cans of cold domestic label beer out from among the bottled water and assorted mixers. Crossing back to his deputy, he casually remarked, "I really don't like this weak piss much, but they're being struck by the Teamsters and the Local had pickets out the other day. Just couldn't resist buying and flaunting some. But, you know what I think of unions. I didn't jerk you out of a kiss-ass party with those Capitol Hill mutts this time of night to talk about that. Gotta problem."

"Something come up in Denver?" The question did not have the ring of genuine concern and it had long been obvious that there was nothing Will Duncan wanted more than to see the great Gunnar

Jorgensen's balls on the chopping block, figuratively at least. In Duncan's mind, his Director was a crude and dishonorable misfit, ill suited to hold his posting. Duncan was a logical man. Each time he told himself of Jorgensen's shortcomings, he assured himself that no petty jealousy had prompted it. That made it so.

"I wasn't in Denver—the problem is down on the border, near Tucson and Nogales … for the moment." Moving a magazine to make room for the beer, Jorgensen continued, "Here's the fifty-cent tour." He took a short draw on his own beer and, wincing as he did, settled back into the comfort of the old fashioned overstuffed chair. The beer had a nasty taste to it, particularly on top of the scotch, but he wanted Duncan comfortable for what was to come.

"You're aware of the quiet off-the-books operation we've got going on out there—it's moved, for a lot of reasons, on south to Tucson and environs. Well, some things have come up with the potential to embarrass the hell out of us. One of those not-so-long-ago things we pulled off has come back to haunt us. It could really bite us right on the ass, particularly with the appropriations battle going on in the Senate."

Instantly aware of the constant use of the words *we* and *us*, Duncan didn't say anything. He just sat quietly and merely arched his eyebrows, while he continued staring at his one-time underling. He knew it wasn't about appropriations—it could only be about a much-touted nomination and its confirmation hearings.

Jorgensen could read the look and the thought crossed his mind that he trusted Duncan even less at that moment than he did the day he'd taken over the Deputy Director's job and been saddled with him, a left over old-regime plank holder. He knew Duncan had expected the promotion and not getting it had made him an angry, envious and alert enemy. But, circumstances now dictated they work together, even if it was necessary to constantly keep his back to the wall.

"We have a man, Guthrie Mobutu, here to buy the stuff of which you build small armies." Seeing the look of recognition, he nodded and continued, "Yeah, he's the same nigger that fed us all the information on Saint Claude's predecessor … and, yes—he just *might* be the one who handled that U.N. do-gooder. All that slipped by some of our minor front office twits when he came here looking for arms. He had no time to bargain and the next logical step was the illegal market."

He paused for a moment, frowned, and slapped the table with the flat of his hand. His voice was very low and hard. "Look, I don't have any idea whose desk this landed on first—but I want them out of here, maybe driving a bus in South Dakota, perhaps scraping paint in Omaha … wherever. Whoever it is, they are too stupid to be one of my people. But, screw it, that can come later." He finally looked Duncan in the eyes and went on, "Anyhow, he found a dealer –and goddamn quick, you gotta give him that. He cut a deal with one of those Chicago Wops that we used to know. They were sitting out some heat down in Tucson and Phoenix. I hate to admit it, but we've also subbed some … ahh … *business* out to them in the past. We've stepped in a real bucket of shit here."

Duncan interrupted him, "You're telling me we've got people involved on both ends of this?" He wanted to laugh and it showed in his eyes. Jorgensen was in trouble and it was the kind of trouble he doubted anyone would think of blaming on Will Duncan. It didn't have his style or mark on it. He had a chance to stand vindicated and anyone with two brain cells could see that he should have been given the Deputy Director's job in the first place. The problem was, blame or no blame, if Jorgensen went, with the Senate Intelligence committee hot after the Agency's hide, he just might be booted out the door too. No, that was a very likely probability. That South Carolina senator heading the Intelligence Committee already hated his guts. He felt himself begin to cave in and recognized he and Jorgensen might just be cut from the same cloth afterall.

"Shit … that's only part of it. We can only assume they have made their deal and can carry it out. At this point, it is a real mess. The locals are looking at it because it smells like a dope deal—and, you have to admit, it could look that way. As for Cooper, you can find him in the files as *Leonetti* and in another place as Colleto. He's the guy from Chicago. He has traded in guns before—'spect he is just staying true to form. So far, the on-the-ground folks haven't tied him in to the armory heists. They aren't stupid though and he'll soon be on their radar."

He paused a bit before going on, "He's not the real issue though. Number one problem is Mobutu. Number two … we'll get to in a minute. Mobuto is enough of a problem all on his own."

The air in the room was increasingly growing heavy with the electricity of Jorgensen's intensity. "You can see we have to have help from other sources, but we can only have it if they don't understand why they're helping and it would be nice if no one around here knew them."

Jorgensen leaned back into the chair and stared at the wall above Duncan's head. He was quiet, as if he was thinking, but that was strictly for show. He already knew what he was going to do and how he would do it.

He looked back into Duncan's eyes and the thoughts came out as newborn. "Will, you know the new Director over at the Bureau would just love to leave us swinging in the breeze. He's working with us for now, but who knows how long that will last. The real problems can come from having one or the other of those people out there caught and needing to trade on us to get out from under the axe. Both Mobutu *and* Cooper can hurt us … Mobutu the most. There's a strong likelihood it'll turn to real fecal matter, given the poor press of late—and there're too many people who know even a little bit for it not to turn sour sooner or later."

There was a short pause before he went on, "One of our men out there called in Cooper to check out some rumors of an arms deal. He's snitched for our guy before. The agent didn't know the prick was involved until too late."

He paused a moment then went on "Unfortunately, they were seen talking by Colosimo's number one dog robber. I have no doubt they will try to drop a cap on him if they can get to him first. Of course, you know we can't depend on that. They could screw the whole thing up and get everything plastered across the press."

The jargon he'd dropped into irritated even him, but it seemed to fit the uncomfortable situation he found himself in now. His deputy's emotionless stare made him want to squirm even more.

Looking down to the cluttered tabletop, he finished with, "so what we've got is simple: two folks out there who can hurt us, one *real* bad, *if* or when they end up in any place where some reporter, nosy cop, or ambitious politician can talk to them. As far as I can see, it's too complicated not to get fouled up."

"Gunnar, I don't think *we* can afford the heat." The emphasis on *we* was pure sarcasm.

"I am as aware of that as anyone," Jorgensen whispered back. The only assumption available was that his deputy was inwardly gloating over one major fact: both of the *problem children* had been in Jorgensen's stable during his time in the field. He sat for a long and quiet moment then, in a matter-of-fact tone said, "I'm bringing in a *solution*."

Duncan looked across the table at Jorgensen, a puzzled look on his face, and then asked, "Such as?"

"Kirkpatrick—from the London office. I pulled him off of his current assignment and temporarily closed down the operation in Poland. He'll handle a *hard* and *permanent* solution for us. He'll be here early tomorrow for a briefing.

The room was dead quiet for so long both men became uncomfortable. Finally, Jorgensen pointed a thick finger at Duncan and, in a flat voice, said, "You might want to be somewhere else. I don't want you around for this. It is not your kind of game."

Duncan looked shocked and jerkily glanced around the room, as if expecting to find someone listening. He forced a controlled and tight calmness before saying, "I must say, you have brought in the best. If there *is* a *best* in that business I guess it would have to be him. He's a dangerous man, certainly the kind of insurance you hate to use indiscriminately."

He sat quietly for a few seconds and then mused aloud, "How did we ever sink low enough to do business this way? One day, you will hear the roaring crowd out there in the streets … and they will be coming to get us. What's worse, they will be right. Goddamn it, they will be so right."

Jorgensen didn't even look up at him again. He just quietly said, "I thought about it for a long time, believe me. At first, I just wanted to let it ride, let things fall where they may … but, I don't need my nuts fried right now. I … come to think of it … you, can't afford any loose ends like that either. They'll have to go. Everyone … everyone."

"*Everyone*? Wait a minute … you can't be serious. What in God's name are you thinking of?" Duncan let it sink in, ever so painfully, that he had now been dragged in and was a very culpable part of everything that happened from there on out. Worse, he began to dwell on how easily they had started to trade in lives—even the lives of their own.

"Yes—everyone … particularly that fucking Obregon. He's worked on this too long … and he knows far too damn much. You know damn well he'll never play ball with me—too much bad blood … so …" He shrugged and looked away, not wanting to see Duncan's disapproval but feeling it anyway.

He began turning excuses into reasons and said, "Remember, I'm the one who pulled him back from Venezuela. Fouled up his operation … didn't mean to, but it caused two of his friends and sources to end up dead. He'll never let that go and he just couldn't see the new man left in place down there as an ally. All he could see was a bunch of murdered Indians, not commie guerilas … too goddamn idealistic. It is not just a job for him."

Duncan stared at him long and hard, his eyes like to shiny pieces of ice that mirrored only disgust. Then, almost in a whisper, he said, "Damn … we're eating our young now. At this rate, it won't be long before the little scum in the street win—we will self-destruct."

He straightened up and glared across the space and into Jorgensen's face, "Gunnar, know that I do not agree with this—at all. I think you have gone too far this time."

They were both quiet for a moment, then Duncan said, "We've not eliminated one of our own since, well, since that fool was caught selling out our agents to East Germany … back in the '60s–70s … and that order came straight from the Oval Office. I can't believe we're sitting here … in an office of our government … *America's* government … planning one of our own men's death, particularly when he's right and we're wrong—dead wrong." He shook his head slowly side to side and lowered his gaze to the floor, his voice trailing off into a whisper.

He was quiet for bit and, when Duncan looked back up, Jorgensen's face showed almost dead eyes. Before Duncan could say a word, he stopped him with a tight and edged voice, "Ok … just do as you're told, you spineless sack of shit. If I go down the toilet—so will you. I'll see to it. Don't you ever forget that."

Duncan slowly pushed himself to his feet and said, "OK … OK. Is that all?" There was no response and he finished with, "If it is, I think I'll go home and—throw up." When Jorgensen shrugged, he turned and stalked out the door and into the night. Duncan's footsteps were audible long after Jorgensen had ceased to listen.

Jorgensen got to his feet and very slowly, almost aimlessly, wandered around the room, stopping here and there to stare at a photograph or a memento, as if stroking some old memory could pull the smell of success, perhaps a bit of honor, from the depths of despair now surrounding him.

No relief came and long ago thoughts slowly and painfully creased his brow. A thick and suffocating sadness filled his soul and he remembered how his time in this secret world had actually begun with a true desire to serve. He could see a younger version of himself proudly wearing his country's uniform—then saw it dissolve through the years that had changed him into what he had now become. Worse, he could not even describe this end game in any terms other than vile.

….

JORGENSEN LOOKED AS IF HE'D SLEPT when in his clothes when Kirkpatrick was ushered into his office the next morning. In fact, he had. His disheveled look startled even his secretary, and she had seen him in just about any stage of dress and undress possible. She stared at him with an odd mixture of amusement and wonder as she ushered the tall, hard looking man into Jorgensen's office.

Kirkpatrick, however, never exhibited even a glimmer of surprise. He was well acquainted with his host. Over the long years, they had worked together a number of times. He did not like Jorgensen, but that never interfered with work.

He was called under only the most urgent of situations; a situation calling for the very efficient and certain permanent resolutions. That was Kirkpatrick's role in life. He was, very simply, an *executioner*. About that issue he had no illusions. He was good at his job and knew it, even though he and his methods came from what he chose to call the *old school*.

The new breed of final solutions, and Kirkpatrick hated them, used poisons that left evidence of heart attacks, sophisticated substances that masked the truth and drugs of every type and description—and explosives that were wantonly indiscriminate. Kirkpatrick, instead, was a mechanic. A shooter. He usually did his work up close, face-to-face, in the most personal of ways. It was said that he might have even enjoyed his work. Whoever had said it—was right.

Jorgensen led the way back into the interior of his personal cave and offered Kirkpatrick a chair at the edge of the large and ornately carved mahogany desk. He nervously ran a hand through tousled hair and let his eyes dart about the room to see if it was still obvious that he'd spent the night there. It was. First, and foremost, there was the smell. A room that's been slept in has a smell of its own. Then, the couch had not yet completely reshaped to hide the imprint of his body and there was a half-empty glass on the low table in front of the couch … and there were his rumpled clothes. But mostly, there was the smell … a sour, dank, remembrance of someone who needed a shower, shave, and clean clothes.

Kirkpatrick had not yet spoken and Jorgensen moved to seat himself behind the desk. He always wanted the desk as a shield when he was unsure of himself and he was, at that moment, very unsure of just about everything. He thought about how right out of the book that was, then dismissed the amateurish psychology.

He wiped his palm across the stubble on his chin and wondered how to start. Kirkpatrick made that easy by arousing the animosity that always lay just below the surface between the two of them, "Well? I'm sure you didn't roust me all the way back from the comforts of Europe's finer spots just to show me you have sworn off showers and fired your tailor."

Jorgensen started to retaliate, but choked back the words. He needed the man and Kirkpatrick was the best for what he had in mind. All that he could do was tell him that was needed and hope Kirkpatrick wouldn't spend too much time wondering why.

He pulled a deep red colored folder from the center drawer of his desk and opened it, sliding the contents out on to the desk's glass top. The several photos that spilled out were face down. "We have a nasty problem than needs immediate handling. In Arizona."

"Arizona? Why would we have a problem there? The last I heard, we don't do business this side of the pond. I do not like contending with local cops—they get persistent, you know that. What kind of problem can cactus and rattlesnakes be anyway?"

Jorgensen bristled again. There was only one kind of *problem* Kirkpatrick would be called in for and the man knew it. Calming, he continued, "The problem is complicated enough to take a long time explaining and won't make any difference to you anyhow. You only need to know the players—and the people who no longer need to be in the game."

Kirkpatrick was making it impossible for the dance that allowed assignments to be made in euphemisms and stilted non-language. He had to come right out and say what he meant. God, he'd forgotten how much he hated Kirkpatrick, but he managed to stick to business in a way that almost seemed dispassionate and only a matter of official involvement.

He began to flip through the photos, laying them face up on the desk and naming each, briefly detailing his own short-form version of their role in the game being played out in the southwestern desert. He paused at Guthrie Mobutu's photo and laid it aside. "This man is a real professional—no pushover. Whatever you do, don't underestimate him and don't try him face to face. He just might win and we can't afford that. I think he may have killed a local pimp out there for some reason—just as I left yesterday—probably because the man endangered his cover. I don't want the local bulls or our on-site people catching him first; and they are looking and looking hard. He can talk too much to all the wrong people, but, just the same, be damn careful."

He stopped again at Roy Cooper's photograph. "This is little more than a small-time Wop cutthroat. He isn't bad with his tools but he's not in your league. Cooper does know he's on the griddle; so the man's head will be on a swivel … make things a little harder. He uses this guy for muscle," pointing to the photo of Jess, "the guy is just big and stupid. Oh, I forgot, Cooper's real name is Leonetti. You'll find it in the packet. They both know too much. His boss apparently thinks he's a stoolie for us, which he is, so he may get removed for you." He had been careful not to mention his own relationship with either Mobutu or Cooper.

Moving on to the last two face down photographs, he paused a moment before beginning to turning them over. "These two, well, they're the biggest part of our collective problems. I need them done and I don't like it. You'll like it even less. You know one of them I think."

Jorgensen looked across the desk at Kirkpatrick, staring intently at the hard and cold strength that was there and wondering if the man believed a single word of his tale. Kirkpatrick's physical façade was truly impressive for a man into his middle years. He was square at the shoulders, with a thickness to his arms that spoke of strength. His gut was still flat and he was tall, nearly 6'3". The man's face showed only one small scar and that blended with an eyebrow. He had dark, gray flecked, combed straight back, hair, an almost roman nose and close-set, even teeth. His eyes were an uncommon and cold concoction of blue and green—and ice. There was no softness to him anywhere. He was harsh, hard, and direct.

Jorgensen studied the back of the photographs and finally looked at Kirkpatrick and went on, "These men ... these men are *supposed* to be on our side." Then the biggest lie of all, "They've gone over." He flipped the first photograph over and said, "This is Obregon. He's ours and I think you know him ... from Bolivia. He has been dealing with Cooper on the guns." He noticed Kirkpatrick's slight expression of recognition and incredulity when the photo fell face up and knew his own believability was beginning to slide downhill.

Turning over the other photo, he forged ahead with the lie, his voice become slightly stilted and tighter, "This is Simpson. He is a Bureau man. They started out on this together and must have seen a chance to cut a fat hog. They both know enough to burn us and cough up a dozen agents in place. I can only believe they've gone rogue. They have to go. Any kind of trial ... is out of the question."

"I know this little unpleasantness is ... not the norm ... shall we say?" Reaching back into the desk drawer, he pulled out a plain white piece of paper with a single line of type on it. "This is outside of normal budget recording lines, of course. I transferred $250,000 to your account in Zurich ... completely untraceable ... as usual." There'll be another $100,000 when your little housekeeping chore is completed."

He reached into the drawer again and handed Kirkpatrick a thick and unmarked brown envelope. "Here are some operating expenses ... $35,000 ... cash. You need to leave as soon as possible—take a commercial carrier under a different name and ID. Don't let anyone stand in your way."

Kirkpatrick reached out and stacked the photographs, one atop another, slowly and carefully. All the while he stared directly into Jorgensen's eyes. Jorgensen thought any moment now the man would call him what he was—a liar. But he didn't, and when the stare was finally broken, the remainder of the paper was pushed back into the dark red folder and Jorgensen finished with, "All the information we have on them, the what, where—all that bullshit—is in the folder. I won't … don't have to … tell you what to do. The only stickler is *when*. It needs done yesterday."

"Anything else?"

"Well, I can only assume they've got a plane somewhere down there and someone who can fly it. See to them too if need be. You be the judge—God knows you've been paid enough. Report only to me on this—skip Duncan. He hasn't got the balls for this. Here, take this."

He handed Kirkpatrick a second small slip of notepaper with a phone number scribbled across it, "Call me at this number each night—late. I don't care if it wakes me up."

"Jorgensen," Kirkpatrick said as he stood up.

"Yes?"

"Do you know what an asshole you are?" then he turned and without looking back, almost ghosted from the room.

Jorgensen knew then that Kirkpatrick was sure he'd been lying to him. That made him the most dangerous of all and Jorgensen knew that he'd have to silence his hired assassin too, but only when the man had finished his assigned dirty work. Both ends would be difficult—very difficult.

"Will Duncan was right" he thought aloud, "One of these days the roaring crowd will come," and added, "with blood in its eye."

Chapter 10

Cooper's mind had been fully awake for what seemed hours. All his senses whirled with fear and confusion but he still had not even tried to offer much physical movement. Feet crossed at the ankles and hands folded behind his head, he lay staring through the blankness of his bedroom's muted-white ceiling.

After a long time, he finally rallied enough to reach for a cigarette from a pack on the nightstand and glanced at the red numerals on the clock radio beside his bed. He saw that it was 8:17 AM and settled back against the pillow again. His thoughts battered one against another as he struggled to put aside the gnawing uncertainty and numbing fear that almost immobilized him.

The brilliant morning light forced its way through the blinds and drapes telling him it was already growing hot outside. He unconsciously pushed the sheet down his body, leaving the brownness of him exposed from the waist up. The motion roused his companion only a little and she mumbled something unintelligible and then dropped back into the steady, almost purring, sound of sleep. Cooper turned toward her for a while, tried to pull her name from the confusion ruling his mind, gave up, and resumed his troubled and unfocused glare through the ceiling.

Something was wrong—really wrong. What that was evaded him, yet enveloped his every thought. Jess—Jess, his slow-witted and muscle bound right arm was simply missing. He'd suddenly dropped out of sight, at least out of Cooper's sight, and at the worst possible time. The few members of their crowd he'd seen had only offered that Jess was just *around*. Still, there was no answer on the phone and all his pounding on the door went unheeded. His car hadn't been in the driveway all the day before and it seemed he was being avoided as if he carried the kiss of death. And, maybe that was the part that was true.

Why? What the hell was wrong enough wrong to see him isolated like this? He knew old man Colisimo was not particularly happy with the arms venture, but he didn't seem *that* upset when he'd last seen him. Colisimo had simply told him to be careful and that times were getting tough. The sudden appearance in Tucson of Obregon and his questions created some anxiety, but only briefly. Obregon didn't seem to know what was going on and he had only mentioned the guns casually and in passing. None of what he knew added up to the sudden isolation in which he found himself now. Cooper went over and over anything that had happened of late, trying to make sense of the confusion. He was in a business that didn't tolerate mistakes and the thoughts swam through his mind that his fleecing of the Colonel from Liberia was not one of those *mistakes*.

He did know one thing—and struggled to make the thought go away. His goal now had to be to just stay alive. He was far in over his head and there were no friends or back-up resources around to help. He longed for the anonymity of his days in Chicago in a way he never thought possible. But, that too was gone—forever.

Bits of his yesterdays kept popping up in the middle of his thoughts—the old days in Chicago, the days at the bottom of the ladder as a small time enforcer, even earlier days with not two dimes to rub together. Worse was remembered of the long hours he'd spent awaiting the beck and call of the head of the family or one of his lieutenants, fearing the call that could have meant a *hard and lethal contract*. He had always dreaded that and, thankfully, there had only been a few of those calls and less that resulted in fatal blood. The days of open warfare between the lesser families, particularly in Chicago, had almost ended by the time he was put on the payroll. That was good. His severe and very Italian mother's impact on the family's upbringing made the deaths of others bring guilt—and a flood of nightmares. But, he had always toed the mark, shown respect to those who had already made their bones, and been loyal, while he did *exactly* what he was told to do. Now it was like he had been excised, cut out of the whole, marooned in the middle of nowhere—and the fear-tinged questions were: *Why and what the hell can I do about it?*

As much as he needed it, he wasn't even sure he wanted the answer. He dwelt on that too, for in his circle the answer was often fatally final. He could feel his pulse rise with that thought and he hear someone say, "What the hell have I done?" and realized that it was his voice and it was filling a mind beginning to whirl in panic. It jarred him into a total awakening and caused him to chill as if blanketed in a winter's cold, not the desert heat.

Cooper checked the time again and reached for the phone and pushed in the number of another person whose actions were also troubling him. The line buzzed just once at the other end a pleasant female voice came on with, "Malette Imports, may I help you?"

"Yeah, honey, this is Coop. Is Mr. Malette in?"

"I'm sorry, Mr. Cooper, he is in conference right now. Does he have your number?"

"Dammit!" Almost yelling into the phone as his anger flaired, "I've been trying to get through to him since yesterday morning now! Who's he in conference with—the fucking Pope?" He slowed for a second and then finished with. "… and you know damn well he's got my number."

"I'm sorry, sir," the voice becoming harder and more clipped, "He left explicit instructions not to be disturbed." She might as well have said, "… especially by *you.*"

"Yeah, yeah, sorry," and as a wasted afterthought, "Tell him old Coop called, OK?"

He could hear her voice offering something as the phone was angrily slammed back into its cradle. The storm running through his mind now was not really of anger though; it was of fear, a deep, crushing, fear.

Cooper's little friend for the night was sitting up in bed now, watching him with a puzzled expression on her face. She was still fairly attractive in the day's light, so he was sure he'd not downed too much Cognac the night before. Her sandy blonde hair was a bit tousled and her green eyes showed of sleep but were clear. The woman's face was unmarked and young. She brushed a wisp of hair away that had fallen across her eyes and struggled with a cheery, but hoarse, "Good morning …" He smiled in spite of himself and, avoiding a name because he still hadn't remembered it, replied, "Why don'cha jump in the shower before we rustle up some breakfast. I've got some things that need to get done today. I'll have to get rolling. OK?"

She nodded, leaned over and gave his cheek a quick nuzzle, pivoted around and slid out of bed. Watching her disappear into the bathroom, he thought aloud, "Damn, I wonder who she is? Not bad … not bad at all." Then his thoughts were returned to the problems of the day.

He had other things to worry about; someone—something—had placed him on the outside and he didn't know why. Worse, being on the outside with Malette, once you had been on the *inside*, was tantamount to being dead. It was rumored that Malette had a string of old mine shafts out in the desert that served as burial sites for people that had only *irritated* him.

Malette was not someone who inspired immediate fear by his personal presence. He was just another self-centered little thug with other people to do his down and dirty work. The problem was that he did push the buttons for the entire hierarchy and that gave him power—raw, almost unchecked, life and death *power*. Cooper both admired and feared it. He wanted that status for himself one day, but at that very moment it could just as easily stretch him out for the ants. That chilling knowledge didn't help him much, but what was really wrong still eluded him. He would naturally expect trouble if he somehow failed in the weapons sale scam, but that was still on track as far as he knew. There had not been the slightest deviation from the rules in any of his dealing with old man Colisimo, not so much as a single dollar skimmed from the many that flowed through his hands and, God knows, he'd thought about that enough times. That was the trouble with money: a little bit only made you want more—a lot like booze.

There were more Feds in town than he'd seen since his arrival and he wondered if that was part of the problem. Old man Colisimo was in the papers at least twice a week and a couple of his men had received Grand Jury subpoenas. That had to hurt. The armory robberies were ill-timed, to say the least, and the one in Nogales had really gone sour, but the Feds invading the high desert didn't seem to be the kind that would handle that sort of crime. He wasn't even really sure they were there. He may have been jumping at shadows. Jess had said they were there though and in force. But, he thought silently, *what the hell would he know?*

The feeling, all of it bad, was still building and almost crushing his ability to think. His own partner was there, yet *not*. It was obvious he was avoiding Cooper. He'd never expected that from Jess. The man up the chain between himself and Colisimo, Malette, hadn't returned any of his calls. His secretary framed poor excuses, even got snotty, but the return calls never came. Two of Malette's very closest associates had made obvious attempts at avoiding him in a downtown parking garage the night before. It all added up. He was out. *Out* was dead. The sour taste in his mouth was worse than what could have been left from the last night's Cognac—it was *fear*.

Cooper pushed the cloud of anxiety from his mind and began to methodically go over the arms sale he was trying to finish. There were some problems with it, but nothing that a little care and work wouldn't cure. They did have the guns, though he had to laugh when he thought of someone planning a war with no more than the gray and dirty little aircraft could haul. He had really sailed one by the Liberian Colonel with this one. The trip was supposed to be merely a showing of what he could deliver. In reality, there were no more guns. But, just where could the Colonel go to complain? He did wish he hadn't listened to Jess about the robberies though—too much heat.

And that tough old man they killed in Nogales, he hated that. And, there on the ceiling, he could vaguely see his own mother's face and ghostly disapproval. She was sadly shaking her head and her eyes pierced his soul.

The aircraft had been something of a sublet from one of Colisimo's many other organizational fingers. The DC-3 was old but it could stand one more trip, if what the two down-at-the-heels pilots said was true.

Guns were surely no worse than the tons of smoky dreams the old aircraft had hauled in her past. Besides, the plane was hot in half of Central America, known far too well to go back long enough for a load of more marijuana or cocaine.

The trip could not help but be a difficult one though—down across Mexico to Guatemala, Honduras, and Belize, then a long jump over the Gulf to a landfall in Venezuela. The first leg of the trip from the little desert strip to its first stop, if there was one, had to be one of the worst hurdles. They would be low, right on the ground, skipping through mountainous and desolate high country that offered little in real navigational help and would certainly kill you if you made a mistake or went down. He was glad he was not going with them. There was fear that plan might be falling by the wayside too.

The pilot, even with his drinking habit considered, seemed the person who could make it work. The old man seemed to actually relish poking around the old DC-3. Bailey couldn't be too bad at his trade, for he did have the craft in the air on the second day at the strip, even though there had been some engine problems. True, it wasn't *really* ready to go yet, but it was close and getting closer all the time. Still, Bailey bothered him; there was just something about him that nagged at Cooper's thoughts. Jess had even mentioned a concern with the man. He couldn't put his finger on what it was though, just *something*.

He tried hard to look at the pilot as a source of trouble and, after some thought, dismissed him from his mind for that potential. Instead, he found a growing, though close-held, admiration. The man was obviously anything but stupid, though he hardly seemed the type to cause many problems. Bailey was reserved almost to the point of shyness and he seemed to really need this job. There was a yellowish caste to his skin that caused Cooper to wonder about the man's health. But that was none of his business and he let that thought quietly die.

The other pilot though—Stoudamyre—he could be the real sore spot. He had, Cooper thought, a visible level of recklessness in his eyes that would eventually lead to a problem. The man did have a gun. The little Mexican hitter, hired as a guard and watchdog at the airstrip, had said he'd seen one—a small short-barreled revolver of some kind. They had decided to let it slide though; figuring the matter wasn't worth the confrontation just yet. Maybe later it would be, just not now.

The phone's shrill ringing brought Cooper out of the deep world of thought within which he buried himself. The phone was only starting its second ring when he grabbed it up and offered a tentative *hello*, almost as a question.

"Pard? Jess here …"

Cooper was out of the apartment and gone within twenty minutes. He shared the shower with his night's companion and hurried the confused young woman out into the sun ahead of him and left her standing on the curb, covered in his parting flurry of apologies and several hundred dollar bills slapped in her hand for breakfast, transportation and the inconvenience. He still couldn't remember her name.

....

STOUDAMYRE'S CLOTHES AND HANDS WERE STAINED and filthy with oil and grease, all ground together with the ever-present dust and grit. He had spent several hours tightening oil line fittings, torquing down bolts to stem the flow through aged and brittle gaskets and, last, changing the oil in the Pratt and Whitney radials. He was tired and it was more than just hot. Beneath the oil, grease, and dirt, was a sweating, miserable man—a man whose temper grew shorter and more volatile by the minute.

His temperament was not aided in the least by the running monologue from the short and dirty, Uzi wielding, little guard. He was, at that moment, standing just barely in the shade of a wing, eyeing the work going on and pulling on a black and foul smelling cigarillo. He rarely stopped talking and all of it seemed just irritating words designed to fill empty spaces in the air. It was a mistake he was not bright enough to comprehend.

Stoudamyre could feel his temper sliding out into the open and it was too late for him to stop what would happen next. He wasn't even sure he wanted to at the moment. He was within three feet of the little Mexican, just a quick step away. He coiled and started to reach for the man just as a hand was laid roughly on his shoulder. He jerked away and pivoted to whoever was behind him and found he was staring directly into Bailey's face.

"Over here—I need some help." Bailey's face was sternly serious and it was obvious he had seen the fuse set for an explosion. The request for help was merely intervention. Firm intervention.

They walked away from the little Mexican, toward the tool van, with Bailey's grip tight on Stoudamyre's arm. "Bill, I'm telling you, and you damn well listen—stay away from him. I know you can take him out but, so what? What happens then?"

"Damn! I despise that little shit … he just keeps pushing …"

"I know—but, we'll be out of here tomorrow and he isn't going … under any circumstances. I promise you that."

"You're sure? OK—OK. I'll stay cool," and they stopped at the water can, protected by the shade of the tool van and waited while his anger seeped into time and the sand. Bailey popped two more pills and stalled over the two cups of water it took to down them.

….

DEPUTY JILLIAN RYAN STARED OUT into the desert without seeing the barrel cactus, tall saguaro, spiny brush and occasional stunted Palo Verde whip by the window of the patrol car. The air conditioner whined and clattered, working full time just to make the tan Ford's interior was barely tolerable. She could faintly hear her partner's voice droning on about something she had not quite gotten the drift of yet and it probably didn't amount to much anyway. He talked too much and she didn't want to respond, or even hear him for that matter. She really wasn't capable of concentrating well enough to listen intelligently at the moment. Her mind was crowded with other, more immediate, intimate, and painful, things.

At that moment, the jumbled list of problems was topped with how sick she felt. Her stomach was crawling with constant reminders that she was in her second month of pregnancy and her mind was almost drowning in humiliation. Worsening the situation, as of the night before, she was alone.

After an early-evening screaming match, Kip Rawlings had grabbed a few of his things and stormed out. She never even had a chance to tell him she was pregnant. Now she doubted she would have told him anyhow. That factor would have only further knotted their increasingly rocky relationship.

The fight had been over the same thing that started all their other verbal warfare. Kip wanted her off of the Sheriff's Department. He didn't think it was the place for a lawyer's wife, if she was ever to be that. She wanted to remain there and keep her own form of regimented independence. Now she had to be independent, especially with his child growing in her.

Dave Cass finally raised his voice enough to break through the self-imposed barricade she'd built and she turned to look at him. She was at once aware that, even with the air conditioner, she was a hot, sweating, mess. The cotton uniform shirt she wore stuck to both her back and the car's plastic seat covers. The thought that she should buy one of those beaded wooden hot weather inserts for the car seat crossed her mind and was dismissed with the knowledge she would soon be off the road and, more than likely, out of a job. The department didn't take kindly to its few women deputies actually being women. Pregnant and single ones were even less welcomed to the club. This morning she noticed her pregnancy was already beginning to thicken her waist to the point that it made the straps on her newly arrived protective vest uncomfortable. She had left it in her locker at the station.

"What, Dave?" Her eyes still ached from crying and there was a slight and tired blur to her vision. She noticed a scratchy hoarseness to her voice. A night of fitful sleep, crying and staring into the dark, along with the tearful and loud argument, had left her hollow and tired. She could not remember ever feeling so miserable. The voices of her so-called *fellow* officers echoed in her imagination as she envisioned the taunts and *almost-out-of-earshot* comments that would soon fill the substation.

"You sure you feel OK? I mean, you look kinda bad."

"Thanks a lot—I really needed that. It's nothing, really. Nothing. My mind is just somewhere else."

"How's Kip?" Cass ventured, trying to keep the door through her gloomy silence open.

She could feel the tears begin to bunch, then choking them back, very quietly replied, "We—we don't see each other anymore ... and I don't think I'm in the mood to talk about it just now. OK?"

"Jeez, kid, I'm sorry. Didn't know." He let that trail off and focused his attention back on the road. "If I can help, you know, just ask."

Cass, too, was wondering what would happen when the rest of the Department found out his partner was pregnant. He knew she was—he just didn't know how to tell her he knew. Doc Wenderfeldt's nurse, over a hasty *I've-got-a-secret* cup of coffee, had breached that confidence the same day Jill had learned of the misfortune herself. This was a small community. Secrets were hard to keep.

He was more worried what his wife would say. She had never liked him working with a woman—particularly Jill. She might have tolerated a homely one, but, no, not Jill. Cass's wife had become about two axe handles across the behind and anyone that had Jill's looks was more than a threat. But, right then, all he could really think of now was how the *poor broad* was really up against it.

There would be a time, he knew, when the boys in the locker room would rag him about it being *his* kid. That would be all right for a while. He could laugh that off. After all, it wasn't as if he hadn't fantasized enough about bedding her on his own. But, God, she was miserable now. Anyone could see that. And she was his partner … she *was* certainly closer than his jealous, bitching and wide-assed wife.

His attention refocused on work as something caught his eye. Off to the left side of the road he saw a gray metal shape showing above a dune that lay about a quarter of a mile out in the desert. Rolling on down the blacktop, he placed the shape as the rudder of a fairly large aircraft. Cass knew it would be sitting on what was the old and abandoned McMillan Oil Company strip. There had been only an occasional drug runner and the Border Patrol in and out of the strip for years now. Student pilots didn't even bump in and out of there anymore. It didn't feel right to his cop's mind.

He ran several ideas through his mind, wondering why the aircraft would be there and what to do. He let his cynical half win and decided it was probably narcotics … dopers … low-rent thugs and potheads. But, narcotics—any sort of narcotics—was big money along the border and any number of old airstrips saw frequent and illicit use by the drug runners who made more in a day than he could bring in all year, off duty job and all. This corridor, below and up through the Avra Valley, all along the boundary to the National Forest, if cactus could ever be a forest except in a politician's mind and moneybag, was especially bad.

In Cass's mind, there was little else this might be and he wished for a partner who wasn't half sick, beat to hell, and totally pregnant. Dopers rarely went without shotgun riders and he was afraid Jill would be more of hindrance than help. But dopers usually just fought each other and ran at the sight of cops, rarely stopping to fight. He eased off the accelerator and pulled slowly onto the right shoulder. When the tan Ford stopped, he picked up the mike, keyed it, and said, "2 King 5 … we'll be out, suspicious circumstances, at the old McMillan strip—on Dunbar Road, about ten miles southwest of Crissman's store."

The following blurb of static was interpreted as the communication center's acknowledgment. It was, in fact, the last of an overriding radio transmission made by 2 King 2, an adjoining patrol unit. 2 King 2 was twelve miles away and stopping for a mid-afternoon cup of coffee and a cold lunch. No one, save Pima County Deputies Cass and Ryan, know where they were—*almost no one.*

"What's the matter, Dave?"

"There's a plane—I think—back on the old McMillan strip. Let's ease on back and have a look."

"Dopers?"

"Maybe—who knows? They'll have the sun behind them and we can move in close. I'll go over the last bit on foot. Cover me at the radio."

"Dave … how long could it take to get help? I mean, if *we* needed it?"

That should have stopped him, but it didn't. "A while longer than we've got if it gets dicey," then he added with a small smile, "That's why they pay us the big bucks, isn't it? First we gotta see what we have. Then we'll order up the cavalry. OK?"

It was all wrong and she knew it, so did he. But she only nodded as he swung the Ford around in a broad turn and rolled slowly toward the potholed, gravel and dirt track that split from the highway and wandered through the sand and cholla toward the small strip hidden behind the dunes. The little Mexican with the Uzi watched them all the way in.

Cass edged the Ford slowly onto the dirt track and moved ahead just above an idle, trying not to raise a dust cloud. He slowly moved up behind the last small rise before the dune adjoining the strip and stopped. Easing the doors open, they both stepped out onto the sand.

Ryan had the cord to the handset stretched to its fullest and the mike at its end in her left hand. She unsnapped the strap over her revolver, eyed the shotgun in its rack, but dismissed the idea of getting it out.

Dave Cass whispered across the top of the car, "Keep your eyes open, kid." He turned, hunkered down, and padded off toward the dune shielding the airstrip.

Ryan felt terrible and it was hard to keep her mind on what was happening. She found her stare after Cass, as he hurried toward the sandy, brush flecked dune, had become unfocused and her thoughts wandered back to the problems destroying her once comfortable world. She would catch her thoughts drifting off and pull them back again and again only to feel them float away, entangled in the depression she felt at the moment. She could see the back of her partner just going out of sight between the left edge of the dune and occasional Palo Verde. Everything seemed all right. A day's rest, some sleep and she could sort it all out.

Ryan was leaning on her right arm, laid across the top of the open door, and had a foot cocked up on the door ledge, trying to gain some bit of comfort. She still held the mike in her left hand. A gentle breeze coming up from the valley floor gave a bare hint of coolness and she was grateful for it. It was still hard to keep her mind on what was at hand.

There was a scratching sound of something moving through the brush to the right and behind her. Her senses instantly sparked alive and she started to whirl toward the sound. The reflex to draw her weapon had just began to bunch. It was too late. An arm snaked around her neck and a hand smashed across her mouth and nose, stifling any sound and shutting off her air mid-breath. Her head was jerked roughly backward and, at the same time, there was a sharp, burning, and paralyzing pain low on her right side just above her belt.

Ryan knew the pain was from a knife, even though she couldn't see it, and yet there was still life. She tried to push pack into who ever held her, to get space, to move free of the pain, but her legs were collapsing, turning to water—*and the pain*—the pain was almost blinding.

The knife was jerked sharply upward and the flood of new pain surged into grayness—a nauseous grayness—and she retched. It was if she were suspended on the blade and slowly being sliced in two. Suddenly, she felt the blade pull free and heard an almost sucking sound as it cleared flesh and cloth. Then the hand holding it appeared in front of her face and the disembodied arm pressed her back tighter against her assailant. The hand across her mouth and nose released quickly and dropped down the front of her body and grabbed a fistful of shirt. Her lungs still felt empty, yet even with her mouth free, she drew no air, made no sound and things crawled almost to slow motion and became blurred. She was spun around and dropped heavily onto her back into the sand, her head cracking onto the car's door ledge. Even trying, she still made no sound and was unable to breath.

The dark man above her swam in and out of grayness. She could only strain, wide-eyed, to see who had caused so much pain. She was dying—and knew it. There was no longer any fear, just pain. The man loomed closer and pulled the radio's microphone from her hand and she saw him move the knife in and with a quick slicing motion, sever its cord. There was a tug at her waist and the man's hand came away with her service revolver, but he was still out there in the blurred fog of pain. She wanted to move, but couldn't. The face came in again and she could see that he was dark and swarthy in appearance and that he had a one-sided leer.

The man drifting in and out of focus came even closer and she felt him grab a handful of hair and force her head back over the door ledge, toward the floorboard of the car. She could see the stained blade come toward her face and go out of sight below her chin. There was a sharp pain below her left ear and she realized her throat was being cut. Then there was nothing.

The short, dark, man leaned over the deputy's body for a few seconds and saw that the blood only pumped a few times from the gaping red slash across her neck. He still smiled as he reached farther down her body and wiped the blade across her trouser leg. He breathed, "Stupid broad ..." to no one in particular and turned away, still hunched over, and moved back into the brush. The thought of how easy it had been to destroy the deputy widened his smile.

Dave Cass hurried back from his overview of the plodding activities at the small airstrip. It was strange that someone would be doing what appeared to be major maintenance of a DC-3 out here in the desert, but he'd noticed nothing readily identified as illegal. He'd puzzled over it a while then written down the license numbers of the tool van and a pickup truck, then the tail number from the DC-3, and scurried away. He would return to the car, pull out of the area, and run some records checks before calling in more help.

He was sure no one had noticed him and felt they could back out of the narrow dirt track undetected. Glancing toward the car, he was puzzled not to see Jill Ryan where she had been when he'd left. A few seconds later, he noticed the tan of her uniform trousers lying stretched out below the car door and a brief glimpse of her arm in the sand, limp and palm up.

His pulse suddenly raced and he broke into a run toward her side of the car. He did all the wrong things and ignored the brush along the side of the road, grabbed the door's edge, and swung around it to look down on all the horror he could ever imagine. His voice choked in his throat and he felt about to vomit. He just stared at her for a while. Her eyes were still open, but clouded and blank. They looked out of place above the wide and obscene slash across her throat. Then he saw the large patch of blood in the sand near her right side and noticed that her revolver was not in its holster. His eyes teared, but he woodenly reached into the car to pull the mike out.

He still ignored all that surrounded him. Shock seemed to nearly paralyze his thoughts as he stared at the severed end of the mike cord. Then a wild rush of fear grabbed at his chest. He was alone now. Whoever had butchered his partner was still there—somewhere.

He garbled, "Oh, fuck ..." and clawed for his revolver, spinning around to frantically and wide-eyed search the brush for whoever had slashed the life from his partner. There was no anger yet—just fear.

There was a smashing pain in his chest and somewhere, away in the brush, he could hear the staccato hammering of a submachine gun. The force of the bullets tearing the breath from him pushed him back into the side of the patrol car before moving upward above his vest into his neck and face. He slid down the side of the car and across the body of Jill Ryan, and rolled, face down, into the sand.

When he'd settled and became still, the dark little man walked out of the brush and looked down at them. He shook his head and grunted as if it wasn't possible to believe the sight. He straightened, looked around and, as a needless afterthought, pulled the revolver he'd taken from Jill Ryan's belt and shot each of the deputies again. He threw the revolver into the car, turned back toward the airstrip as he glanced over his shoulder for traffic out on the blacktop. He felt tall and strong and powerful and he was still smiling as he plodded through the sand.

Just over the dune, on the wing of the DC-3, Stoudamyre's head snapped up at the sound of the double blasts. The noise from the generator was winding down and it was the first sound he'd really been able to recognize that hadn't come from their work. He looked toward the highway where he'd placed the sound. Reaching over to the aircraft's fuselage, he slapped the side of the cabin where Bailey was laboring over the installation of a reconditioned altimeter head.

Bailey's sweating face appeared at the open window with, "What'cha need?"

"I know I heard some shots … then some more, two, I think. I can see what looks like a cop car … over there," and he pointed off toward the road and a tangle of cactus and dry twisted brush.

"Ahh, come on—why would cops be shooting out there?"

"Hey … here comes that sorry little wetback. He's been over there—and he's still got that goddamn Uzi. That asshole … God knows what he's done. I have to take a look."

Stoudamyre stepped to the trailing edge of the wing and jumped down into the sand below before Bailey could say a word. Brushing his hands against his coverall legs, he kept his eyes riveted on the approaching man with the submachine gun and started walking toward the dune he remembered the car was behind. He was aware the dark little man was swinging the muzzle of the Uzi up toward him and that his slack smile quickly slid into a one-sided smirk.

Bailey watched Stoudamyre for a short moment, knew he and the little gunman would collide, sighed heavily, and hurriedly pulled his way off of the flight deck and down the DC-3's belly to the side hatch. Stopping just at the edge of the light pouring in through the open hatch, he reached inside his coveralls and pulled the .45 automatic from his belt. He looked at it a bare second and jacked a round into the chamber, let the hammer down softly and stuck the automatic back into his belt. This time he didn't zip the coveralls back up. Shaking his head and with a slight groan, aware his stomach was again surging with pain; he stepped into the light and jumped the short distance to the ground.

The little Mexican shifted his gaze to him for a moment and then flicked it back to Stoudamyre, who was almost to where the man had stopped and set himself. The muzzle of the Uzi was raised even more toward the middle of Stoudamyre's chest.

"Where you think you're going flyboy? You need to get your ass back to work." The threat the voice held was real. He must have been convinced his threatening presence and the Uzi would intimidate Stoudamyre. It didn't and it took him a few split seconds to realize that. As Stoudamyre drew abreast of the little man, looking as if he were sweeping on by, he suddenly swung his left arm out stiff, crashing into the man's chest, with all the force of his upper body, momentum, and the twist of his shoulder could muster. The blow sent the filthy little Mexican sprawling backward into the sand and scab rock, the Uzi clattering a few feet farther on, sliding through the sand. The look on the little man's face was pure, breathless, surprise and shock. The wheezing sound his lungs made as they emptied would have been heard yards away. His hand instinctively flew to his chest as if it were on fire. But, it took only scant second for him to recover and the look of surprise was quickly replaced with one of rage. He rolled over to his knees, cursing, lunged for and grabbed the Uzi, taking a few moments to shake the sand from it. He didn't even look up at Bailey, who had hurriedly closed to within fifteen feet of him.

The gunman whirled toward Stoudamyre's back and screamed in an almost falsetto voice, "Stop, you piece a' crap, or I'm gonna blow your goddamn head off!"

Stoudamyre didn't stop and it was already apparent the little man intended to shoot him whether he did or not. He raised the Uzi up to his shoulder, canting his head to look down the sights. Bailey felt the big .45 in his fist and yet couldn't remember drawing it. He knew there was not time enough to make the fifteen feet or so in time to use the gun as a club and he stopped, bringing the automatic up in both hands and stroking the hammer back with the thumb of his left hand. He yelled just once, "Hey … Greaser!"

The man's head jerked up from the sights to look over his shoulder at the sound behind him. He saw Bailey looking across the top of the big automatic straight into his face. The little man wondered if he'd had the weapon all the time and, at the same time marveled at how big the hole in the end of the barrel was. Then he saw the flash and knew for only an instant that he had been worrying about the wrong man all along.

Bailey saw and heard the bullets impact flesh. The first round struck just below the dark little man's right shoulder blade. The man took a half stagger on forward and turned, falling onto his back, his face toward Bailey. The muzzle of the Uzi swung up and the little Mexican tried to center it on Bailey. His mouth was working wordlessly.

Bailey lowered the sights of the .45 to a point just above the man's mid-section and scarcely felt the big automatic's next two jumps. The little Mexican convulsed and was still. Bailey looked down at the man again and felt weak, nausea rising in his throat, but it had nothing to do with the Mexican. There was no emotion for him. He shook his head slowly and again eased the hammer down on a live round and, with hardly a glance back at the dead Mexican, hurried after Stoudamyre.

When Bailey had cleared the edge of the dune, he could see that Stoudamyre had been right. A marked Pima County Sheriff's car sat in the middle of the narrow road leading to the strip. Both doors were ajar. There was silence except for a low mumble he could hear coming from behind the car. When he drew closer to the car, he could tell what he'd heard was Stoudamyre and he was moaning over and over, "Oh, God … Oh God" in a voice that seemed filled with agony.

He rounded the front of the car as Stoudamyre slowly and gently pulled the body of a large uniformed man away from that of a woman deputy and stretched the man on his back in the sand. He looked up at Bailey, his eyes brimming with tears, his voice choking, almost childlike as he whispered, "Look at 'em … look at 'em. The dirty s on of a bitch cut her throat—why'd he do that? The little fuck better be dead!"

Bailey started to reply and got out, "He is …" when the grinding, dust-raising slide to a stop of a car on the dirt track jerked his head up and stopped his response. Before either could really move, Jess was stepping out of the dust cloud … and he had a short-barreled, sawn-off shotgun in his hands.

….

AT AN OLDER MOTEL ON THE EDGE OF THE CITY, half a block off of a boulevard oddly titled *The Miracle Mile*, Guthrie Mobutu was taking his bags out of a newly purchased, three-year-old Dodge sedan that he'd just parked in front of unit number 6. He had bought the car with cash and a forged California driver's license, using a new name: Donald Kemper. He registered under the same name, listing his occupation as a sales representative—from San Diego. The name of Joseph Bannock would no longer serve him well.

Chapter 11

Cooper stepped from the passenger side of the vehicle and made a conscious and very obvious effort to move deliberately, slowly, making sure he retained his balance and eye contact with Bailey. He was in the wrong place to touch off the firefight any erratic move might cause. His every move became fluid, non-threatening; each word smooth and in what he hoped was a calm monotone. He was really anything but calm.

Before stepping away from the car he pulled the metal-rimmed dark glasses from his face and tossed them back onto the front seat, then slowly closed the door. He raised both hands to shoulder height after motioning for Jess to stay where he was. Only then did he turn and slowly walk between the cars to the front of the Sheriff's cruiser, squinting as he faced the sun and clamping his mouth shut against the dust that still hung in the air.

Jess leaned across the top of the car, the sawn-off double-barreled shotgun pointed at Bailey. His eyes were hidden behind dark glasses, but his head swiveled ever so minutely from Bailey to Stoudamyre and back again. There was no doubt that he would use the shotgun.

Cooper was the other extreme. He had moved his hands back down and held his jacket open to show he was unarmed and not an immediate physical threat to anyone. There was obvious fear and nervousness etched on his sweating face, but he kept on moving around the front end of the Sheriff's cruiser.

Neither Bailey nor Stoudamyre moved as he approached. Bailey still had the .45 out, but it was pointed downward toward the ground. He wondered if he could get a shot off before Jess could use the shotgun and if, in the end, it would even matter. Quietly and slowly, he eared the hammer back again and resolved to find out nonetheless. Stoudamyre had his hand inside his flight suit, his fingers wrapped around the grip of the little Smith and Wesson revolver hidden in his belt. There were no doubts in his mind about anything. He had every intention of taking Cooper with him … at the very least.

Cooper very gingerly stepped around the front of the cruiser and looked over the top of the door at the two deputies stretched out in the sand. It seemed to take a second or two for it to soak in and then his hand flew to his mouth and he jerked his head away, his only epithet, "Oh … Jesus …" His face paled and the shock looked real. Bailey, puzzled, thought it a strange reaction for one who had made a living in the Mob and surely must have killed before. He involuntarily murmured, "Well, I'll be damned …" in a low monotone.

Cooper slowly looked back at the bodies again, then eased around the edge of the door and almost gently moved Bailey aside. He stood over the lifeless bodies of the deputies and stared down at them as if he might cause them to disappear with the sheer force of his will. He'd not said anything since his initial exclamation.

He finally broke the silence with an almost strangled, "What—what happened here? Jesus, who did this?"

Stoudamyre started, already on an angry roll, and said, "Your sorry-assed little greaser did this bigshot … that little thug you let run around with the big gun."

"You mean Ramirez?"

"Who gives a damn what his name is—was—you hired the little jerk and he did this!" Stoudamyre's anger mounted as he talked and the rage brought a knife-edge to his voice. His right hand was suddenly no longer inside the flight suit, but pointed at Cooper. The revolver he clutched in a white-knuckled fist was no more than five feet from Cooper's face. The hand that held revolver trembled with the anger of their master and caused Cooper to fear that the intensity of his emotion alone would cause the gun to go off.

Cooper looked away from the gun and saw that Jess was still there with the shotgun. Had he not been between Jess and Stoudamyre, the situation would have already exploded.

"Jess—Jess, get that goddamn wetback here—now! Jesus Christ … we're totally screwed now." Cooper tried to add an in-charge formality to his voice and failed. When he saw Jess hadn't moved, he spat out again, "Now! Jess—move it, Damn it."

The big man behind the car looked at his two adversaries for a few seconds more and then brought the shotgun back off the top of the car and lowered the barrel toward the ground. He shook his head as if he didn't believe his orders and started to walk off toward the aircraft.

Stoudamyre stopped them both with, "Your Goddamn greaser is dead, big shot." He paused a moment before going on, jerkily nodding toward Bailey, "This old man just blew his sorry ass away." Stoudamyre's anger was still hot and growing even more so. Cooper feared that at any second his whole scheme was about to come apart there in the sand.

"You hear me? Your flunky's dead. Now what the hell you gonna do with this mess? That creep of yours just wasted these people for no fucking reason. He just got us all killed."

"Easy, easy," Cooper buttered the words out, "We have to sort this out, take care of the problem …"

"Sort it out …Take care of the problem?" Veins bulged at Stoudamyre's temples and the revolver he pointed at Cooper's face danced almost spastically. "Take care of the problem? Just what the fuck are you gonna do? You gonna bring 'em back to life? You think the cops will quit 'til they got somebody for this? Why should they?" His voice suddenly went low and flat as he said, "I oughta take your spaghetti ass out right now."

Cooper's words and tone had been designed to defuse the situation, more importantly, to gain control again. Neither was happening. It became apparent that mistake had been piled upon mistake now everything had fallen to pieces before it really had a chance to begin. He felt the chill of fear run up and down his spine and a swirling nausea gripped his insides.

And then it became even worse; Bailey now had the .45 up and at arm's length in both hands. It could all be over with the twitch of a nervous finger. Things seemed frozen there for what seemed a long while, though it was only a few seconds. Finally, it was Stoudamyre who both broke the silence and stalemate. He swung the muzzle of the revolver down toward the ground and loosened his grip with the other hand. There was a shrug, then he raised his eyes to Bailey's face and said in a low, barely audible whisper, "Pop, what'er we gonna do? What the fuck are we gonna do?"

Bailey slowly turned his gaze toward Stoudamyre and lowered the .45, easing the hammer down with his left thumb. The flash point had been passed and there had been no explosion.

Jess looked at his partner for a cue and, seeing none, stood for a moment with a look of indecision on his face. Then, he too cashed in, popping the barrels of the shotgun open and tossed it back into the front seat of the car. It was almost totally silent.

Bailey finally very quietly said, "Cooper, I want you to understand something."

Cooper looked up from the bodies, his face showing pale and chalky through the overlying tan. All the bravado of the first day was gone and he quietly said. "Yeah ... sure, what?"

"This is all your doing, every goddam bit of it. First chance we get, we split and then you're on your own. I don't give a damn what happens to you or your load of crap. You can't know what you're doing or this would've never happened. Like Bill told you, you've probably gotten us all killed. Now, keep that ape of yours away from us in the meantime—and know that I will not fry for your mistakes. OK?"

When Cooper didn't immediately reply, Bailey turned to walk away, then thought better of it, faced Cooper again, and went on, "... and don't play any cards that aren't on top of the table. You might win the hand but you'll bleed to death doing it. I don't have a damn thing to lose—you do."

Cooper looked at Bailey without really seeing him. All he could think of was that everything was coming apart, hell, already had come apart. A shaky deal to begin with, old man Colisimo putting a hit out on him, Jess ... Jess maybe working for the other side and, worse, these two deputies dead and to complicate things, was this old man with the ice-cold eyes and big automatic. He wondered what else could and would go wrong—and when.

At least the sorry little Mexican made no difference. He knew just about anyone in his business could buy people like him anywhere. He would never be missed. At worst, he would just be another illegal's bones found in the sand.

He did know he had to strike some kind of deal with these two men and at almost any price, particularly the old man. He was the real rock of the two, booze and all. Bailey had moved, in Cooper's mind, from a worn out old has-been pilot to something much more in the space of bare seconds.

"Bailey—Wes—let's you and me walk and kick rocks for a minute, figure something out, can we?"

"You forgetting someone?" There was edged antagonism in Bailey's voice.

"Yeah, well, you actually ... do the talking for the both of you, don'cha?"

"He wears his own head, Cooper. I'm not his mother."

"Yeah, but ..."

"Go ahead," said Stoudamyre, weariness in his voice as he motioned them away, "I'll stay here a minute ... keep an eye on old big shot's food taster ... go on." He motioned them away and turned his back.

Bailey shrugged, shook his head in resignation and walked off toward the aircraft with Cooper.

....

Mobutu's lack of familiarity with Western systems had begun to take its toll. He quickly recognized the need to change cars and had easily done so within two hours of fleeing the shooting at the motel. It took, however, less than half that time for a city traffic cop to spot the old car where Mobutu had dumped it on a side-street just three blocks from the used car lot where he'd bought the sedan he now drove. The three patrol units assigned to check nearby car lots found where he had purchased the Dodge, with cash, in a bare twenty minutes. It had only been four hours since he had erased the two lives back in the motel room. Now every police unit in the City of Tucson, the County of Pima and, probably the State of Arizona, had Mobutu's description as well as every detail State Motor Vehicles could provide about his new vehicle.

Only patrol unit 2-King-5 had not answered radio's roll call to acknowledge the receipt of the information. The county dispatcher, only mildly concerned, informed the shift commander just like it said to do in the book. Both the shift commander and the dispatcher wrote the lack of contact off to the patrol unit being in an area of poor reception. The county was large and the terrain was rough and difficult, that seemed a logical explanation.

At 4:28 PM, two west end city police officers spotted Mobutu's newly acquired vehicle parked in front of an off-boulevard motel unit. Now the locals' lack of knowledge about Mobutu began to show and work against *them*.

There is always the chance things might have been different if a thorough composite of Mobutu had been released to the local law enforcement agencies involved in the search. But that had not happened. Obregon had cringed inside when he'd given them Mobutu's physical description and deprived them of all else that was known of the man. The local police had no idea the man they searched for had made a decades-long living fighting—and killing—people much more dangerous than they would ever be.

But the Feds flooding the area had been expected to find Mobutu themselves, not counting on the local poor cousins luck and their abilities. It had not worked that way at all.

The black and white unit had drifted on by, circled the block to the right and coasted to a stop just far enough forward of the cement block wall that bordered the motel's driveway to allow the officers to see Mobutu's car. Not being anxious *cowboys*, they quickly called for a sergeant and a backup unit. Two Vice Squad detectives passing nearby also heard the call and responded. It looked like an easy pinch and easy felony pinches draw extra cops just like accidents and fires draw curious crowds.

The Sergeant, knowing only that he was dealing with some black man that had killed a pimp and his product, placed everything there before him in the wrong context. He assumed this was just the surviving half of a street-brother against street-brother shooting. He was sure he had all the firepower he would ever need and then some. There was, after all, only one black man in the motel room, nobody special. He sent one of the vice detectives to the manager's office to determine which room Mobutu was in and began building a hasty and informal plan to dig the man out.

The unit that had located Mobutu was pleased. As first on the scene and the assigned unit, it would be *their* name first on the booking sheet for a felony pinch and it had been a long dry spell. With any luck, their shift commander would spring for a couple of special duty furlough days if the man inside the plain little motel room really was the suspect in the homicide and if they handled it right. After all, this *was* a homicide arrest, its importance be damned. Most of their fellow patrol officers would consider the original shooting a fortuitous act of *population pruning*.

Mobutu felt, rather than saw, the net begin to move in tight around him. He never knew why those feelings came, they just did and those feelings had kept him alive a long time. This time he was removing some clean clothing from the large suitcase that lay open on the bed. An overpowering urge to seek cover, to take flight, all liberally soaked in apprehension, began to grip his insides. There was, most of all, that feeling of dread and the metallic taste of adrenaline. He hated the feeling. Someone usually died.

He laid the shirt he held back on the open maw of the suitcase and walked to one of the windows fronting the room, stopping just beside it and using the cinder block wall as protection. The edge of the fading curtain was slowly pushed aside so that anyone outside would be unlikely to notice the movement and that he was watching. The narrow slit allowed him to see almost all of the parking lot off to his right, including the entrance from the street and perhaps 150 yards of the four-lane, north to south, boulevard that fronted the motel. To his left, the entire parking lot was visible. His senses, developed through long years of close combat, were right. This time being *right* brought a feeling of despair to him. What he assumed were honest, work-a-day policemen stood between him and the completion of his mission and safety.

He watched as a rather shabbily dressed, bearded man walked from the manager's office toward the street. As he moved along the far side of the parking lot, the man kept glancing at what Mobutu felt sure was the room he occupied. The man immediately turned left at the point where the driveway met sidewalk and disappeared, but only for a moment. He stepped back into view within a few seconds, another man with him. He pointed across the driveway and parking lot, hesitated a moment, then both stepped back out of sight. The second man was dressed in the blue-black of a uniformed police officer and a bright flash of sergeant's stripes shone on his sleeve.

Mobutu had started to turn back to the room when the Sergeant popped back into view. Mobutu stopped and, from a grandstand seat, watched the man deploy his troops. At a gesture from the Sergeant, two officers sprinted across the driveway entrance and out of Mobutu's sight. They ran hunkered over, as if that would make them invisible. One had a shotgun, held at port arms; the other held a revolver in his right hand.

They had no sooner left his view than the shabbily dressed man reappeared again, this time in the company of another man. The second man was taller, similarly dressed, and had a scraggily beard. His hair was shoulder length and topped with a floppy brimmed leather hat. His sunglasses were so dark they looked black. He held his right arm stiff to his side and limped stiff-legged and clumsily. Mobutu could catch the sun's glint on the barrel of a long gun he tried to hide tight against his leg on the side of the limp. When they were about 45 degrees to his left, the limping one brought his stiffened arm up with a pump action shotgun in his clinched fist, the limp immediately disappeared, and he jogged the few remaining steps to the cover of a parked car. His partner moved up and crouched behind the hood of the same car. He leaned his elbows on the hood and held a large automatic in his right hand, its barrel resting across the palm of his left hand.

Mobutu turned his attention back to the head of the driveway in time to see the Sergeant motion the remaining two men into position. One went behind a car almost out of his view to the right and the other, also with a shotgun, dropped in behind a pickup truck that had a black rubberized tonneau cover over its box. The truck sat almost immediately behind and some thirty-feet away from where Mobutu had parked the Dodge sedan he had purchased earlier.

He hadn't come to America to kill its policemen, but he had to get away and the cache of small arms had to go with him. Policemen, he sadly thought, had always been expendable. He didn't doubt his own abilities, but to storm out into their ready guns was suicidal. A diversion—he needed a diversion.

Then, without conscious motivation, the will to survive and the instincts honed to razor sharpness over the years exploded into a flurry of activity. He bet everything on his guess of how these men, bent on his capture, would react to the right surprise.

Moving back to the suitcase, he grabbed large handfuls of its contents and tossed them on the bed, uncovering a 9 MM submachine gun that was already assembled except for its barrel and magazine. He quickly twisted the barrel in and shoved a magazine into place. He placed the two remaining magazines securely into his belt. The

Browning was stripped of its suppressor and holstered on his hip. The briefcase, containing numerous bricks of $100 bills meant to buy the arms, was moved to a point beside the door where he could pick it up as he ran out. Then he unlocked the door. Now he was ready. He only then became aware that he was soaked in sweat.

The old feeling was there. He'd felt the same way when entering a firefight in Malaya, Aden, or in his own country's backcountry. The senses were tight and it seemed he could hear things he couldn't, or shouldn't, hear at other times. His taste was more acute and he could *feel* things before he saw them. Surrealistic, yes, surrealistic, that was a good term for it all. He found himself softly cursing under his breath.

This time there was another feeling flooding through his senses though. He felt this fight was wrong. This adversary wasn't *the* enemy but they stood in his way. If he was willing to die for his mission, then they became unfortunate impediments along an already rough and hazardous road. He went back to the window and made a short appraisal of the parking lot area. There were no innocents afoot, no bystanders to become victims.

He turned back to the room and made a last survey. It was a poor place to die; there was no honor to be found. The small motel room had two opaque windows on the side away from the street, one in the bathroom and the other on the back wall alongside the bed. The window in the bath swung outward and was open about six inches for ventilation, allowing Mobutu a partial view of the weed and debris strewn area behind the "L" shaped motel complex. About ten yards to the right of the bathroom window, he could see the legs, waist and right arm of one of the officers. From the muted whispers, he assumed the other officer was somewhere to the left.

Mobutu went back to the suitcase on the bed, pushed all the clothes back into it and moved it to a point near the window on the back wall. He took a deep breath, exhaled slowly to drain the tension, and went back to the bathroom window. The officer was still standing in the same spot.

Sighing deeply again, he drew the Browning, thought about it a moment and then twisted the suppressor back into its threads. He took the car keys from his pocket and placed them between his teeth to have them as easy to get to as possible. Then he laid the barrel across the window jamb and sighted at a point just above the officer's knee. The man would never know how lucky he was this day. He would live.

Mobutu was barely conscious of squeezing the trigger and the recoil of its firing was hardly noticed. The officer screamed in pain, covering what sound the weapon's report made, and twisted to his right, falling out of his view. Mobutu did not wait to see more. He pivoted toward the bed, grabbed the large suitcase and hurled it through the translucent glass of the window on the back wall. He could hear two quick shots and the gibberish of startled yelling in the area behind the motel as he ran for the door, stuffing the Browning into the open-bottomed holster and grabbing the submachine gun, bolt drawn, with his right hand. He threw the door open, scooped up the attaché case, and burst into the bright sunlight, the machine pistol up and ready to fire. The folding stock was clenched between elbow and body to steady it.

He'd been right about the officers and their reaction to surprise. They had thought his break had been out the rear of the building and now he had a slight advantage. One of the officers to his right was just about to go around the edge of the building, intent on helping those in the rear. He was completely out of position and effective handgun range. His partner was standing up with a startled look on his face and his shotgun lying untouched on the pickup truck tonneau cover. One of the plainclothes men had started to run around the parking lot to the building's rear and was caught, flatfooted and awkward, in the open, and not twenty feet from Mobutu's gun. He shifted direction, began to turn back, fell and tried to squeeze into cover next to a car's wheel. The Sergeant had also left his cover and stood in the center of the driveway, some ninety yards away and of absolutely no help to his men. Mobutu thought it strange that he would notice the surprised and foolish looks on their faces and, at the same time, felt regret. These were his type of men—servants to their people, not enemies.

Mobutu swiveled the submachine gun toward the mid-stride plainclothes man, now back on his feet and moving to his right out in the open, and chopped his legs from under him with a short and low burst. The man sprawled sideways against the car to his left, screaming in pain, his handgun skittering under the car as he fell. Mobutu raised the barrel and raked its fire across the hood and windscreen of the car the other plainclothes man crouched behind and heard him yelp in fear and surprise as he dropped behind its cover. Mobutu sprinted for the dodge, turning the gun toward the uniformed office now grabbing for the shotgun he'd laid on the tonneau cover. One round struck the man's shoulder and fragments flayed his face, spinning him away from his cover and toward the ground. A few shots were snapped at the officer near the end of the building and the man lunged for the protection of the building. The sounds of the machine pistol's fire crashed and rattled back and forth between the buildings in a sharp and deafening tirade.

Mobutu threw the attaché and machine pistol through the open window of the car, jerked the door open and leapt in. Time was more than important now; it was everything. The policemen would begin to recover and react at any moment. They were not amateurs. They could and would kill him if given time to recover. He rammed the key in and cranked the starter. It caught on first touch and he squealed the car back out into the lot and headed for the street.

The Sergeant stood in the middle of the driveway, his revolver out and aimed at the oncoming car. Mobutu didn't swerve; there was no time for that. The Sergeant fired one shot that ricocheted off of the chrome trim at the top of the windscreen and a second through the windscreen to Mobutu's right before throwing himself to one side to escape being run down.

Mobutu punched the car across the two northbound lanes of the street, accelerator floored, and bounced over the near curb before clawing through thirty feet of median to the southbound lanes. He sideswiped a small Japanese car, causing it to spin a half turn and broadside a FedEx van, then he crowded the Dodge into a too-narrow space between two southbound trucks with their horns blaring and airbrakes straining. There was another squeal of tires and a pall of smoke as he swerved into the right hand lane, forcing a cab onto the shoulder and into some potted trees fronting a restaurant. He glanced at it momentarily through the rear view mirror as he sped on through thinning traffic to a westbound frontage road. That road linked him with a freeway ramp several blocks on to the west.

No one chased him. He slowed to an inconspicuous speed and headed out into the desert. It was a full two minutes before one of the dazed and shocked officers at the motel interrupted normal radio traffic and began telling the rest of the world of their embarrassing misadventure.

····

"Bailey, you've been around, ... ever see a man that *really* knows what deep shit is?" Cooper asked, without expecting a reply. "Well, you're looking at one right now that does."

Bailey didn't respond and Cooper went on, "You're not much better off, you know ... think about it."

"Tell me—you like to talk." Bailey could only stare at the man, disgust painting a much worse portrait than he actually looked upon. He still toyed with the idea of simply shooting him and driving off to ... nowhere.

Cooper stared back and seemed to understand what Bailey was thinking. After a few moments he went on, "Well, you're out here to haul something you have to know is not straight ... two cops get whacked and you claim our little wetback did it. That's good; we even know it's true. Only thing is—he's *dead*. He can only talk to his maker as he passes by on the way to hell. The cops will want someone they can look in the eyes to pay for this and *you* are as available as I am.

What kind of trouble does that look like?"

"Look, you miserable ass, we're just here to fly your trash. And it looks to me like it's you who has the alligators up around your belly. Anyhow, this isn't getting us anywhere. We can hate each other until hell freezes over—but, some other time. We—you and I—need a way out of this, so we need to think instead of standing around running our mouths."

Bailey's eyes had gone even colder and he stared at Cooper for a long and quiet moment before going on, "I wish I could bring those two cops back, but I can't and a simple walk away went out the door when your little psycho killed them in the first place. Where the hell did you get him anyway?" He really didn't expect an answer.

Cooper looked hard at Bailey with something of surprise on his face, just beginning to really take the measure of the man, then shrugged and lowered his gaze toward the sand, muttering simply, "Yeah … yeah, I know." He turned and walked to the galvanized water cooler on the nearby pickup truck's tailgate and took a long, thoughtful time drawing a cup of water and then downing it. He thought about telling Bailey that he was right, that he was in more trouble than the two flyers, but how dead can you get? If Colisimo did have a contract out on him, Bailey and Stoudamyre would both be just—*gone*. And what were their chances if they tried to go on with the job? God … If what had happened up until then was any example, there would be no winner.

But there were few choices and turning back wasn't one of them. "Bailey, faint heart never filled a flush. We've got to go on. I could tell you our chances were not great—but you already know that. You also seem to know my boss has ordered one done on me. I think I know why now but it doesn't make any difference to you. If we don't make this good, we're all dead … for damn sure. Old man Colisimo doesn't screw around. I go—you go, OK?"

"What's there for us? Bailey asked.

"You're gonna bargain now? Damn. How about, you could live—maybe …"

"I—we—could *live* if Bill and I took that pickup truck over there and split for Mexico too. How about that? You want to try and stop us? You might end up like the wetback and probably should."

"Maybe you'd make it—not likely though," Cooper paused, then decided to gamble on Bailey's keeping it quiet—or, more likely—not being around later to talk about what he would be told.

He stared at him a few seconds before saying, "Let me lay a few things on you. I've only been here, I mean locally … in the Valley, for a few years—three years, come March. I was sent down from Chicago to cool off. I got crossways with some state cops on a tear up there. Old man Colisimo owed the boss a favor or two. But, he really didn't want me 'cause the boss had farmed us out to some Federal spooks a time or two—when the price and place were right."

Pausing a long moment before going on, "He doesn't like Feds— of any stripe. I think he did it to keep some one near and dear to him from getting deported—not sure about that though. That made us a problem in the first place. But he took us both anyhow—Jess and me—and told us about what he owed the boss. He didn't beat around the bush and wanted us to know right off the bat that he didn't owe *us* a damn thing. He made it clear that if we so much as stepped an inch sideways, our next address would be at the bottom of some farmer's well or an old mine shaft. My old boss is dead now. I don't have a clue who made that happen. He got a dozen .22s in his back and face … and Colisimo didn't waste a minute telling us again that he sure as hell doesn't owe us spit!"

"Lord knows, you've got your problems—told you that before. And besides, don't we all have some crap coming down now?" Bailey offered the last bit not really as a question but a statement, and went on. "I need to know what we're hauling—for sure. No guesses, no maybes. Then I need to know who we have to look out for—other than cops—and where, for sure, we are going." Bailey knew the answers to most of those questions but he wanted to hear it from Cooper.

"Is that all?" Cooper asked, sarcasm flaring in his voice, and started to turn away.

"I guess—for now. I hate to admit I don't know enough about what's going on to ask good questions," Bailey replied. "except, who's the black guy that was with you—and what did he mean about having to get something back to Africa? You can talk to me or die right here and now."

This was something new for Cooper. He'd never tried anything on a scale this large before and none of his jobs had been so complicated. None had certainly ever come apart so badly. And these two flyers— he'd never had to deal with people like them before either. He usually hired people who did just what they were told. Neither of these men seemed in the least intimidated and one of them, at least, was dangerous, very dangerous. The Mexican had found that out far too late.

Cooper was desperate now and he was mentally thrashing around for a plan, even a thread of an idea. Most of all, he wanted to live. If there was money that could be made on this venture, life would be so much the better for it, but staying alive came first.

No real and logical plan came, but small bits of a scheme's outline did begin to fall into place. It was rough—and only something to start with—but it just might help find a way out … with a little luck.

This flyer could get them, all of them, to where the black colonel wanted to go. After that, he wouldn't be needed any more. He wouldn't necessarily need Jess either. That would be hard though. He had been an almost constant companion for more than ten years. He, and perhaps Jess, could take the money and split for someplace in Europe, perhaps Paris, or Geneva. Then, well, he'd worry about what happened *then* later. Jess would be a tough issue though. But, they had to get to Venezuela first. Above all, they had to get to, what was it called? Yes, they had to get to the Plain of the Dogs.

Cooper reached into his pocket for another cigarette and turned to walk around the plane. Cupping his hand around the match as he light the cigarette, he kept his silence a few moments longer and ignored the mechanic who was nervously picking through some tools spread across a tarp stretched under the plane's starboard wing. He did mark in his mental notebook that the mechanic needed to join the dead Mexican before they left Arizona.

Exhaling a lung full of smoke, he stopped next to the open side hatch of the plane and turned back to Bailey. "Wes, in about an hour and a half," pausing to glance at his watch, "two bobtails will show up here—packed with guns, all kinds: rifles, pistols, light machineguns, ammunition … parts, a few grenades and grenade launchers. It is mostly military type stuff."

He took another pull on the cigarette and went on, "that black you met is some kind of big-wheel in Liberia's army and he bought the stuff. I sold the junk to him. I got it from, hell—what's the difference where I got it? He pays off when the stuff is out of the country. He thinks this is just load number one. You gotta help keep him thinking that way. There won't be a second load and now I have to get out too … didn't plan on that. We split our take at the other end, that's all."

Bailey closed his eyes and bits and pieces of the crash in the Georgia swamp flooded through his mind. He started to answer, but the noise of a fast moving car jerked their attention to the road. When the car skidded into the dusty road toward the airstrip, both men began running toward the Sheriff's cruiser.

Mobutu saw the Sheriff's cruiser too late, slid sideways to a stop, threw the car into reverse and started to back out of the narrow road toward the highway. Then he saw Bailey and Cooper running toward him, both waving their arms frantically.

He stopped, eyes flitting to both sides of the road. It seemed safe but, the police car? He still had his hand on the machine pistol when Cooper reached the door, gasping for air from the sudden exertion.

"We got trouble, Guthrie—lots of it." The exertion had caused small sweat beads to pop out on his forehead and he mopped at it with his handkerchief before continuing, "We have to get out of here, soon as the sun goes down." He nervously eyed the bullet hole in the windshield but said nothing about it.

"But, the police …?" Mobutu asked, looking at the Sheriff's cruiser, "What happened here?"

"The rotten little wetback guard killed them. Would you believe it? And one of 'em is a woman … for damn sure someone will fry over that. So we have to get out of here … and fast, or it will be us."

Mobutu winced at both the deed and the vulgarity describing it and pushed the car door open. He did not hurry as he walked to the spot where the two officers lay and his expression did not change as he looked down at them. Twenty years of worse had prepared him to show no emotion.

When he raised his head to speak, a dark sadness came to his eyes. "I too have had problems with the police." Then his shoulders seemed to sag a bit and he said, "This is an unhappy day; honor has flown." Then he finished with, "Yes, yes, we must leave as soon as possible.

. . . .

"2-KING-5, 2-KING-5, RADIO TO 2-KING-5. Your location please …" There was only a long silence and the operator shook her head as she looked up to the patrol watch commander's face.

"No luck—we've been trying for almost three hours now."

"Ok—put the word out to anyone who might cross their sector and move, say, five cars over to that side of the county and start looking. They might have run afoul of an armed illegal out there in the weeds. Check their calls for a hint. Get a bird up—and ask for some volunteers to over-fly that area. Oh, phone the Border Patrol; they're all over 2-King-5's sector every day. I'll be down in the Chief's office."

Chapter 12

CARLO MALETTE HAD ENJOYED STANDING at Colisimo's right hand for almost ten years. He had spent that decade always being the one who was called for almost anything. Still, he had not yet earned the right to be a confidant, certainly not to be a friend. He was there because Colisimo needed someone in between himself and the masses, someone to fill the role of a *stalking horse*, someone absolutely expendable.

Carlo had been in that precarious, but profitable, catbird seat ever since Pete Alcala had gone to the walls for tax evasion and trying to bribe a federal district judge. Pete's flashy lifestyle and lapses in paying off the right people at city hall sent him to the Federal Penitentiary on McNeil Island, a rock in the frigid waters of Puget Sound. Pete had a bad temper and an even bigger mouth and, once inside, he'd forgotten that no one there gave a damn who he used to be. He was just another fat little con with a big mouth and dreams of what once was.

One afternoon, he lost an argument with a petty stickup artist from somewhere in the sticks of Idaho. When the guards found, him he was stuffed in behind a boiler in the laundry building. There was a homemade shank broken off in his back. The sharpened piece of plastic had been ground out of a toothbrush and tape wrapped around the blunt end to make a handle. It had done the job as well as Toledo steel—and it was disposable.

Carlo had, by default and necessity, moved up to the big time and inherited Alcala's share of the pie and power. He enjoyed it too, with all the tailored suits, big cars, women, money, and the constant attention of minor vice cops and just as minor wannabe journalists. It all fed an already oversized ego. In fact, and more to the plus side, a couple of the empty headed skirts that had been in Alcala's stable now tended to Carlo's frequent needs. Most of all, he enjoyed the power he exercised—even if it wasn't really his.

Colisimo still made him pucker though and with good reason. A row of perspiration beads showed just above his mustache to emphasize that at the moment. His kept his voice appropriately subservient as he said, "That's about all I know, boss. Jess swears the man with Cooper was a Fed … not the FBI though—one of those no-name spooky guys. He says him and the Fed have known each other for a long time now. It doesn't sound safe. I think you would be right to do something quick. You might even have the hammer dropped on him."

"Do you now, my sweaty little man," it was not a question and Colisimo's eyes were as hard and cold as granite. He waved a hand as a gesture of emphasis, then went on, "Maybe, Carlo, maybe. Our friend in Chicago wouldn't have liked it but, God rest his soul, he is no longer with us." Colisimo crossed himself, then shrugged out of his crisp linen jacket, carefully draped it across the back of a chair, and continued, "My little bird at the Federal Building does say some big guns are in town, the FBI and some of those other three-letter agencies. She says it's confusing and impossible to get really close to … only that they're looking for some guns and an African. Why did you wait two days to tell me? Do you think I read minds?"

He paused a moment, and then went on, "Most of those agencies she says are floating around here now don't usually operate in our part of the world and they sure as hell don't ever talk to the FBI, arrogant bastards that *they* are. Nothing they do is ever this open and they have their own rules—so there must be something big and it has to have big time backing."

He paused again, cocking his head to one side and giving the appearance of a teacher questioning a stammering student, " … and what do we have that's really that big?"

Before Malette could answer, he went on, "The answer, Carlo, is *that* is not the right question." When his underling only stared at him, he said, "The *real* question is, what are we doing that is different and, at the same time, big enough to draw any heat from all from these different agencies."

"Well, sir ..." mopping his forehead with a handkerchief rapidly growing soggy, "Sir, it's ... it's ... "

"Yes, Carlo, Roy Cooper's little gun running deal. He's gotten tied up with the wrong people. That fool was sent to me. I was supposed to keep him on ice and safe for a while. I was told he was a bright boy, maybe just a little too big for his britches. And ... I guess that's more than true."

He stopped and stared into Malette's eyes causing him to shudder and his mouth turn dry, before going on, "There's all the money he'll ever need to be made right here, just sitting on the Mexican brown, coke and weed trails. I don't even mind him running a load of grass on his own now and then. Hell, I would not even be too upset if he did skim a little off the top now and then. I expect that from you mice."

He walked to a sidebar and began pouring a single cup of coffee from a silver service. The move was not lost on Malette. He knew he was being lectured; reminded of his place, disciplined, and the perspiration on his upper lip became more bothersome.

Colisimo returned to his place at the window. He stood there, back to the room, looking out over the desert floor that stretched out below his mountainside retreat. He didn't look back at Malette again, but calmly went on, "No, that bright, enterprising young ... fool ... had to go and sell a piddling load of guns to some African and draw Feds like flies to carrion."

"I suppose he's the one who hit those National Guard armories last week? Stupid—really stupid. I understand he lost a couple of bottom-feeders in that enterprise. Too bad he wasn't one of them."

He paused, then said, "No matter—Carlo, I just can't afford the heat right now. Did you know Cookie caught a Fed going through my garbage last week? *They were actually going through my garbage.*"

He sniffed, wiped delicately at his nose with a white linen handkerchief and spat out in icy and hard tones, "Cooper has been *yours* to worry about. I gave him to you. *You* dropped the ball. Now, *you* take care of the problem—and tell me when it is done. Don't make me talk to you again." He turned back to stare out at the desert and Malette became little more than a piece of furniture.

Malette recognized his dismissal and was glad to be alive for it. He turned and slipped out the door, hurried on through the cool hallways of the house and out the front, a faint but growing nausea crowding his throat. His driver had the car pulled up under the breezeway's shade and was lounging against a fender. The driver bounced away from the car and opened the door for Malette, remarking, "That sure didn't take long." Taking a look at the nervous mobster's pale and sweating face, he added, "Everything OK?"

Malette nodded without replying and stepped into the car's cool interior. He was silent during the ride down the narrow and winding road from the ridge top and through the remainder of the trip to his downtown office. It would have done little good to have told Colisimo he'd only just learned Cooper was probably responsible for the armory heists and worse, that he didn't know where he was at that moment. Those were his personal problems, no one else's. Admitting it would have only made him look stupid. Cooper had been put in his care—and the child had run away from the sitter. He reached into a pocket, retrieved a packet of antacid tablets and popped one into his mouth. He'd been using more of these lately. The thought crossed his mind that perhaps he wasn't cut out for this job after all.

Jess had told him that the plane was supposed to leave sometime after dark this very night. Time was short. Stupidly, he'd let Jess go and now he didn't even know where he was, let alone the aircraft. After his driver had dropped him off in front of the building, Malette took the elevator up to the top floor and entered an office with gilt lettering on the door announcing, "C. Malette, Imports." He nodded at the bored looking receptionist almost without seeing her and went on through the waiting room to his office. Shutting the door, he immediately dialed the number for "J.D.S Enterprises." When the connection was made, he said, "Get Jack for me."

No one asked who he was and, after a short pause, a man came on the other end of the line with a raspy, "What can I do for you Mr. M.?"

"Jack, a couple of things have slipped through the cracks, no … turned to shit. I need to know for sure if Cooper had anything to do with the two armory heists. If he did, who did it for him and where they stashed the stuff. *Right fucking now.*" His voice was low, almost in a whisper, "I've lost track of Jess and he knows, so he'll do if you see him first. I also need to know where he's stashed that damned old DC-3 we loaned him. Got that?"

"Yeah—I'll get right on it."

"And Jack, I need to know right now—this afternoon, hell, yesterday!"

"Uhh, sure. Tough order boss. I'll do my best."

"Given what's going on, I'd suspect Cooper is leaving the country, so when you find where the plane is, have a few dependable guns ready to go. Call me as soon as you know, OK?" Malette cringed at the content of his conversation, his lines had been tapped and he wasn't sure the surveillance still didn't exist was only a pen register. Fear is a strong motivator though and, at the moment, he was as frightened as he'd ever been.

"Got'cha." The line clicked dead and Malette turned to pace back and forth for a time before sitting into the chair at his desk and aimlessly shuffling suddenly meaningless papers from the so-called legitimate side of C. Malette Interprises. It would be dark in a little over four hours. Time was short. He popped another antacid tablet and grimaced as burning acid crowded the back of his throat. He was beginning to understand why Pete Alcala had always been in such a bad mood. But Acala was lucky, he didn't have to fear death anymore.

....

Kirkpatrick watched the two men amble down the Federal Building's front steps and compared their faces to the two black and white photographs in the folder. They were heavily engrossed in animated conversation and seemed oblivious to everything around them. They would be *easy*, he thought, they should be more awake than that. And the cynical edge to his mind told him that now the dogs were turning on each other. In all his years as a *permanent solution* for the Agency's people problems, he'd never had to exercise his skills on one of their own. This situation was not good—but maybe it would be the last for him.

He continued to watch as the men, still talking, got into what was supposed to be an undercover car, parked, for everyone to see, in a *Government Vehicle Only* slot. They quickly eased away from the curb and headed westbound in light traffic. They could wait. Mobutu and the man who now called himself *Cooper* were first on the list.

His mind began to wander a bit and he mused that after this assignment maybe he really would try living in Hong Kong, perhaps Singapore, at least for a while. He was too well known in all the wrong circles to return to the U.K. proper if he opted out—and that included any of his old haunts in Western Europe. That would be even truer if this job drew any real media attention—and it surely would.

He also knew he could never go home again, no matter how much he longed for that. He regretted that every minute of every day. Dublin would be lovely and suit his heart and soul, but he'd probably be dead there within a week. No, he could never go home.

He followed Simpson and Obregon out into the traffic and as far as the second intersection, memorizing every detail about the car and scribbling the license plate number on the back of the folder beside him. Then he turned onto a side street and circled back to the boulevard that fronted the Federal Building. Heading back toward mid-town, he stopped at a bar, parked and entered the dark coolness it offered. He found the dimly lit payphone near the back door and thumbed to a page in a small notebook he fished from an inside coat pocket.

Carlo Malette answered the private telephone on his desk with its second ringing.

....

Mobutu said very little as Stoudamyre, his voice sounding weary and dispirited, described what had happened. He shook his head in sad disbelief when the officers' death was described. When Stoudamyre finished, Mobutu turned to Cooper and, in a flat and terse monotone, said, "You have disappointed me—this is a disaster. I do not brook incompetence happily if at all. Ordinarily I would deal with you right here and now. You deserve it. But, we all have problems at the moment. There are—I hope—alternatives you have thought of?"

"Yeah—uhh—well, nothing with guarantees I'm afraid. We need to get our butts out of here as soon as we can load—soon as it gets dark enough, I mean. That should be around nine, nine-thirty. What did you mean ... *you* had trouble with the cops?"

"Mister Cooper, someone seems to know I am here—probably *why* I am here." He thought for a moment, a puzzled look on his face, and decided to leave out the confrontation with the police at the motel. He also knew the last thing Cooper needed to know about was the killing of the pimp ... and his *property*. He simply finished with, "I had a small encounter with the police—with some difficulty escaping and finding my way back here."

"Anybody hurt?"

Still avoiding describing the firefight, Mobutu replied, "Do I appear hurt?"

Before Cooper could question him further, he asked, "I must assume you plan to come with us, Mr. Cooper? It only seems logical now."

"Nothing is logical any more—but, yes, I do need to get the hell out of here. Sometime yesterday would be just fine."

"Failing that ...?"

Jess had been almost completely silent since the initial confrontation with Bailey and Stoudamyre, yet he was the first to think and talk in methodical and rational terms.

"Roy, we have to get these stiffs out of here—and damn quick. If the trucks show up and see this cop car, they'll just keep on going. You know they will."

Cooper turned his head toward Jess and said only, "Ideas?"

"Well, back when I was looking this place over, I found a side road down past the gully. It runs back up toward that ridge." He said, pointing toward a rust colored ridge some two miles distant. "The road drops down into a swale near the end that I could dump the car in … maybe make it look like the two cops caught an illegal and they knocked each other off somehow. It won't wash if they got any brains and when they really look at it for two minutes, but if they find them before we get out, it might give us some breathing room."

There was no reply from anyone for a moment and then Cooper quietly said, "Let's do it." No one else offered any help as they began loading the deputies and the Mexican into the sheriff's cruiser.

Bailey motioned to Stoudamyre and said, "Come on, let's finish what we started and try to build some sort of flight plan if we can."

"Some flight plan, Wes, we can't even call in and ask about the weather."

....

THE CHIEF CRIMINAL DEPUTY and the Lieutenant commanding Second Watch anxiously hurried back down the hall toward the small room that served as an Emergency Operations Center. The briefing for the Sheriff had been short but as thorough as the little available information allowed. All that was really known was that two deputies, Cass and Ryan, were missing. They had not been heard from for over four hours. Something was wrong but, to that point, no one knew what.

"Are you going to set up a full EOC (*Emergency Operations Center*)?"

"Yeah, if that's OK. I don't like this at all. Those two are as dependable as clockwork, so I want to find them—quick."

OK—go ahead. I'll drop by the desk and have the Sergeant call you in a dozen or so off-duty troops. They'll report to you in the patrol assembly room."

"Fine, sir … I'll keep you posted. Will you be in your office?"

"Yeah—or on my pager. If you need anything, just call." Then he added, "Have you talked to their families? I'd hate to have some fucking reporter call them first."

The Lieutenant started to turn and go into the EOC, but he stopped, seemed in thought for a few seconds, and then said, "No. Not yet. Cass's wife is in Phoenix, according to his Sergeant. Oh, and that lawyer who's Ryan's squeeze was in here a couple of hours ago. He said they'd had a falling out and he needed to talk to her. He was pretty upset, but he doesn't answer his phone right now. He's got one of those goddamn brick cell phones, but he doesn't answer that either. I suppose he'll be back in here in a bit though. Saying the guy was upset is kind of an understatement. Say, what do you know about what went down over on *The Mile*? Is that part of our problem?"

"I don't know. All I heard is that the PD had some black holed up in a motel room. He came out swinging and kicked their ass. They never even got off a good shot and three of their men were wounded … nobody dead though. The guy's supposed to have killed a pimp and some broad over in one of the I-10 motels. He sure doesn't sound like just another street shooter, but you never know"

"Oh? … wonder who he is?"

"Beats me. Sounds like the guy spotted the units setting up on him and decided to shoot his way out—had some kind of submachine gun. Lucky nobody got killed—with all the lead flying around. They claim it was as if he tried not to kill anyone. It seems to have stirred up a whole hornet's nest of Feds though. Walt says they've called in a bunch from other offices, borrowed Border Patrol and Customs plainclothes guys and he says there are some here that the SAC won't even introduce. Strange, I know, but we've got our own worries, so screw them. They never tell us shit, so they are on their own."

The lieutenant looked at the floor for a bit, then said, "No obvious connection to our problem though?"

"Not really. Our two deputies were not answering before this happened."

"OK, well, you never know," and he closed the door to the EOC and beckoned through the large glass window separating the room from the communications center for the Chief Dispatcher to join him.

....

O BREGON SLID INTO THE FRONT SEAT beside Simpson and nodded for him to drive. He reached down and turned the air conditioner up to the last notch and settled back into the seat, folding a piece of scribbled-on paper. When Obregon had pushed the piece of paper into the litterbag that was hanging from a clip on the dashboard, Simpson asked, "What was the call, anything important?"

"I don't know … strange call. A friend of mine, back at Langley, he sounded really nervous. No, a little scared is more like it. He said to watch out, Old Gunnar has sent a *hard hitter* out and to be really careful. That's all he'd say—he even hung up when I started to ask questions. Wonder what's going on?"

"Geez—I dunno. Sounds like a dime novel. You spooks are weird people … know that?"

"Well—whatever. He did say this African we're looking for once did a job for Jorgensen, long time ago. He didn't say what—if he even knew."

Simpson only nodded his head and remained silent for a long while. Then he brought up what was on both their minds, "You know we're going to have to talk to the local bulls sooner or later."

He exaggeratedly cringed at the idea, "That sure as hell isn't gonna be pretty. How are we going go about that?"

"Can't say as I know … they'll be royally pissed when what we left out hits the table. You damn sure can't blame them. Jesus … They could have had someone killed this afternoon—and when they find out we held out on them, it'll get worse."

"Nothing like righteous indignation and a bleeding ego," Simpson added, "You have any friends in the PD?"

"Hell no … I'm not supposed to be here. Remember? And, anyhow, except for a vacation, way back when, this is the first time I've ever been here." Obregon laughed when he said it, but he didn't mean it. In sixteen years with the Agency, he'd never worked more than a few days at a time outside of Latin America.

Simpson chuckled and said, "Well, I've a couple of folks that would talk to us if we really get in a bind. Most don't want too much to do with us after the civil rights investigations we did out here a couple of years ago. We sent almost half of a patrol watch before the Grand Jury—a few guys went to jail for some petty crap. One guy, on the hook for nickel and dime stuff, hung himself. They don't like us very much; guess I can't blame 'em. I suppose we could talk to Matthews over in the Sheriff's Office though. He can probably relay for us or broker a friendlier meeting."

"With what we have to say, it won't remain friendly long."

"Probably not. Here …" he said, motioning toward a corner restaurant whose reader board announced $2.00 Margaritas and refrigerated air, "Let's grab a bite to eat and I can give him a call. We have to make some things happen—in a hurry."

....

STOUDAMYRE COULD SEE THE ALUMINUM BOX of the empty truck just disappearing around the dune as he motioned the second truck back to a point against the open hatch of the aircraft. The work of moving the heavy and roughly crated armament had patches of sweat soaking his clothing and the dust whipped up by their movement had left him gritty and filthy.

He had expected the weapons to arrive in standard and uniformly sized crates but, that had been anything but true. The weaponry had come from National Guard armories and had been in racks when taken. They had simply been picked up or cut free with a bolt cutter and thrown in piles on the floor of a truck. The crates they were now in carried every conceivable label from toys to medical supplies. Only the ammunition and the weapons brought from Cooper's contracted thefts in the east were uniformly crated and weight labeled. With over half the crates showing no weights, the work of a weight and balance scheme for the aircraft became a guess-and-by-God exercise.

Bailey watched the crates being pushed through the hatch and skidded into a tie-down position with some anxiety. He turned toward Stoudamyre and mused out loud, "You know we'll be lucky to get this thing off the ground. Damned if I know where the center of balance is."

Stoudamyre nodded, "I'm not sure I care anymore. Do you realize what we're into now? Man, if we get out, we can't ever come back and, goddamn it, I like it here in the good old U.S of A. Worse than that, if we get caught, we're deader than last year's Potomac promises."

"Face it, friend, we don't have a lot of choices left right now. The folks who hired us are probably not in this for the money anymore either. It's about staying alive and they're running too. Only Mobutu knows where he's going. We're their way out for now, so we have to make the best of it. I don't know about you, but spending the rest of my life in the slammer isn't what I had in mind."

Stoudamyre stared off into the distance a bit, then asked, "You've been around a long time—ever have a deal go this sour before? I mean, that thing with the deputies was … awful. Somebody *ought* to die for that one."

"Somebody did, if you'll remember … but, exactly like this? No—I guess not. I like cops … had an uncle once who was sheriff in a county in Oklahoma's Cookson Hills. Some small-time bootlegger shot him—left him crippled. Always liked him."

He seemed to be deep in thought, his brow wrinkled, eyes focused on some point long ago. After a bit he very quietly said, "Down in Colombia once … some piss-poor and grubby soldiers showed up when we were about to leave with a load of weed and a couple of illegals. They just wanted to squeeze a bit more money out of guy who'd contracted the run. … I'm damned if he didn't just open up and whack 'em right there on the tarmac. Good old America's bad habits are big business down there and they just wanted more of the action."

Bailey looked like he was staring through time and space at the incident, winced and shook his head, "The guy never even broke a sweat. He just had his crew take them somewhere else and dump the lot of them in the bushes. He wanted to use the airport again and they were expendable, the buzzards could have them." He stopped a while, shook his head again as if clearing the thought, and finished, "But—no, nothing like this."

"I feel sick all over—I mean, those poor cops—and that black dude … all he's trying to do is keep his grubby little country alive. And here we are, sitting on this big pile of crap …"

Bailey's voice was firm, though his expression was almost blank as he pulled Stoudamyre around to look him in the face. "Don't dwell on it. Our choices are few and none of them worth a damn right now. If you really want something to think about, think about when the time comes that no one needs us to fly this crate anymore."

Stoudamyre's eyes were sad and he seemed to be searching Bailey's face for some form of comfort or encouragement as he quietly said, "I'm not sure I care about that either—not anymore."

"Well, I do, I've got at least one thing left to do, so let's stick to business. If the gas gets here for the top-off, we'll be out of here in less than two hours. Let's make it less than that if we can. Move your ass. I've got no more babysitting time left in me."

He sounded harsher than he'd wanted to and the effect on Stoudamyre was not lost. The younger man seemed to grow smaller, like a child being scolded. He bit his tucked-in lip and looked at Bailey apprehensively before saying, "OK, OK, Pop, but we have to get away from these assholes as soon as we can."

"Agreed. If you get a chance to do it, put that machine pistol up on the flight deck."

"OK, " Stoudamyre said, as if ending all thought of the matter, "let's get this old sweetheart a last going-over." He stood there looking over 392 Delta's frame once more, before saying, "You ever notice how she seems to sit there and stare down her nose at you? Man, if these things have a soul, we *are* stepping all over it now."

Bailey arched his eyebrows at the question, looked across at the drab shape of the aircraft and replied, "Who knows—who knows, maybe she does. Let's get at it." His thoughts seemed to drift for a moment, floating on painkillers and old memories. Only half aloud, he said, "Yeah, she's got a soul. They all do. This one's just tired."

They walked under the starboard engine nacelle as the mechanic, who still looked almost too frightened to function, stepped down from a ladder positioned against the leading edge of the wing. He had a piece of copper tubing in his left hand, a small adjustable wrench in the other. He was covered in grease, oil, sweat, and dusty grime. The frightened man looked down at the tubing and began talking as if the piece of oil line was the center of the conversation. "This one is cracked … it'd come apart about the time you strained her with the load you got here."

Looking up at the belly of the aircraft, he nodded his head toward it and said, "Hear her pop and crack … groan? She's saying she has had enough. The old bird is almost human. Don't push her too hard—I swear she is looking for a place to die and I don't want to be with her when she finds it."

He glanced back at the tubing he was turning over and over in his hands and moved on to his real concern, "Look, you guys have give me a chance to get out of here. I heard Cooper talking—he's gonna ice me. They can't just let me walk away. I'm screwed."

Bailey looked at the man for a moment before saying, "I

understand your problem buddy. You will go along as my engineer. I saw Cooper eyeing you too. Enough people have already died. We'll find a way to ease you out later. You can find your way home or go wherever you want."

"Thanks fella, thanks."

"Just make sure what you're doing now is done right. That crap they're loading now won't fly all by itself, and it sure as hell won't float—so, pay attention to business."

"Oh, sure—for sure. I know it don't look like it, but this old broad ain't in that bad'da shape—spooky as it is. Don't know that it's meant to do what you want it to or not, but the weed freaks who used it kept the guts up pretty good. Avionics ain't much, but who you gonna talk to down where we're going?"

The man stopped his nervous chatter as Cooper and Jess drove up, returning from disposing of the Sheriff's cruiser and its grisly contents. Bailey turned to look at Mobutu, who was standing near the rear of the unloading truck. He was staring at Bailey with an almost expressionless gaze. When their eyes met, the black man lowered his eyes and shook his head slowly and sadly. Bailey saw that he had a submachine gun slung, barrel down, across his shoulder his forearm resting in the notch between breach and folding stock. He had decided to play the game until the last card.

. . . .

SIMPSON SLIPPED ONTO THE BENCH across the table from Obregon, enjoying the chill feeling of the cool plastic against his back before that too turned to sweat. To Obregon's questioning expression, he offered, "Matthews has a fifteen-minute session with the Sheriff and then he'll be right down.

"Good."

"Says he's got a search going—a couple of deputies missing out in the boonies somewhere."

"Oh? He know why?"

Simpson shrugged and didn't verbally reply, looking up as a tired and frazzled waitress approached. When they'd quickly placed an order for iced tea and a light lunch, the task of organizing their information for the Sheriff's captain began.

"You know, your SAC is really going to be pissed when he finds out we've spilled this to the locals," Obregon murmured, a slight smile on his face, "and it's not like we have so damn much to tell them."

"Well and good, Laddie," Simpson replied, in a mock Irish brogue he was growing more fond of daily, "but that bloody old fart doesn't have to work out here. We don't stand a chance of finding Mobutu without the locals."

"Yeah, well, true, but—what *do* we have to talk about?"

Attention riveted to the notes before them, the two men barely noticed the waitress return with their order.

There was a leak of the arms sale—but from whom? And Mobutu, or was it Joseph Bannock? What *was* the last name he used? The man had strange lack of background—really strange. It was interesting for both to note that the man had once had some kind of a working relationship with Jorgensen ... Jorgensen. He was the center of it all.

Simpson brought that last thought to mind with, "... wonder why Jorgensen didn't mention knowing this African first hand?'

"Dunno. It must seem strange to be sending the bloodhounds after him now. I'd bet it's giving him fits."

Simpson didn't answer for a moment, before marginally changing the direction of their thoughts with, "What about, what's he called ... Gunnar? You have any idea what he is actually like?"

Obregon thought back across what he knew of the man, of the facts and of the rumors that had made the man. "Well, he's a pretty ruthless man from what I know. Been mostly in the covert side of things—ran some pretty hairy gigs in very touchy places."

"He came out of the military. Other than that, there's not much I can say—except, from my time with him, I don't like him much and I guess it's mutual. He got me pulled off of a really important job down south on nothing more than a rumor. Thankfully, we usually work on a compartmentalized basis. A lot like you, if you don't need to know, they don't tell you. But, I've picked up a bunch of rumors, not much else that I can verify. We did work fairly close on a couple of operations a long ways back. He can be an old-school asshole—real nasty tempered."

"*Rumors*—ah, yeah. Well, we all thrive on them."

"Anyway, Matthews will be here in a bit. How much do you want to drop about Cooper. He's your ..." Simpson stopped as he looked up at the strange, open-mouthed expression on Obregon's face. It was as if someone had turned on a light somewhere in the deep recesses of his mind.

"What's wrong—you swallow a fly or something?" Simpson asked with a small chuckle.

Obregon's face seemed to darken, his eyes taking on a worried, yet thoughtful, look. "I ... I think some things are beginning to make sense—that shouldn't, at least I wish they didn't." he said, the words coming out slow and haltingly. "I think we've got some serious problems. That call about the hitter makes some sense now and fits in—and that's the worst of it."

"*Makes sense?* What the hell are you talking about?"

"I'm not sure I can explain—totally—but, here goes. Try this on for size: remember how Jorgensen avoided admitting he knew Mobutu?" Without waiting for a reply, he went on, "Well, you *know* he does—worked some operation with him a long time ago. From what I hear, if the right folks got hold of it, they'd fry his socks. Anyhow, think about this scenario; suppose Mobutu came looking for help, and it got by Jorgensen or gets shortstopped in the front office by some newbie? He's the man to see for that kind of thing. But, what if some low-level flunky turned it down out of hand?"

"So what? Man, there must be a whole herd of Third World folks wanting the stuff new governments are made of and I'd imagine the lot of them are pretty much just camping on the Agency's doorstep."

Simpson shrugged and dumped a spoonful of sugar into the tall iced tea in front of him. "Tell me something new and exciting."

"Wait a minute, I'm not done," Obregon retorted, raising one palm from the table, fingers extended, to quiet his companion. "Jorgensen's operation misses the guy, or is told to miss him or just fucks up, and he hits the illegal market. Now when and if he gets caught, who looks foolish? And even if he doesn't get caught and it makes headlines? *Right* … our big cheese, *Jorgensen.*"

"Looking foolish is nothing new for your friendly local bureaucrat lately, now is it?"

"Maybe not—but it is for Jorgensen—and for all intents and purposes, he is *the* hotshot in the Agency. He runs operations and the big boss is temporary—a fill-in after Moss died. Jorgensen is big stuff. On the Hill twice a week; photo ops with POTUS, he can't afford all the little Mobutus of the world leaving egg on his face. I hear he is even the President's first choice to run the whole shebang permanetly, maybe higher."

Simpson didn't speak and Obregon continued, "Think about this, now that Mobutu is on the illegal market he gets together with our old buddy Cooper and he comes up with some of the goodies."

"Probably in part from the Mesa and Nogales National Guard rip offs—right?"

"Yes—and now the clincher. I first got Cooper as a snitch through Jorgensen. He worked for the mob in Chicago and took a piece of overseas action or two for us … something nasty down in the Caribbean. Looking back, the operations were probably more in Jorgensen's best interests than anyone else's."

Seeing Simpson's look of disbelief, he went on, "I know, I know … we don't do those sorts of things. *But suppose we did.* That means Cooper can talk and so can Mobutu. Worse, what if they both talked? I don't know why it didn't cross my mind until now. Jorgensen can get burned from both sides—and bad."

Simpson rested his chin in a cupped hand, with his elbow on the table and said, "Now that Jorgensen is up in the gray flannel daylight world it would be a pretty problem, wouldn't it? I'm sure our elected princes' dog robbers would cover it up, but Jorgensen would sure as hell be history." He paused a moment and went on, "So you think that's why the hitter is here—to take out Cooper and Mobutu?"

"Has to be—and that's not the only side to it. How many folks do you think know about this? I mean, have enough information to put the pieces together just this far?"

Simpson had a startled, wide-eyed look about him as he replied, "Well, we do, but you don't think ...?"

"That's right, old buddy—*we* do. You might say we're in the big leagues now. I'd say there's a good chance we have as much to worry about as Cooper and Mobutu."

"You can't be ... flippin' ... serious, Christ! Man, you work for the guy. I don't think I believe this." Simpson paused, he was now gripping the edge of the table with both hands, but he continued, "You can't tell me that man is crazy enough to start whacking his own men—and, hell, I'm from the Bureau. Remember? Can you imagine the stink if someone from your agency *even touched* one of the little Irishman's men?"

Obregon only arched an eyebrow and said nothing.

Simpson sputtered on, "God ... that'd even raise the ghost of old J. Edgar. My outfit would never stand still ..." then he stopped when it finally sank in that if Jorgensen were going to have him eliminated, he would not be at all inclined to tell the Bureau of his plans and certainly never admit it later.

Obregon hesitated a moment, then said, "I don't know, maybe the call has me thinking in circles ... getting paranoid. The Agency is not what it used to be—maybe it never was. Strange stories drift around and about our little rat maze."

"You guys look happy—what's going on?" the broad shouldered and thick-bodied uniformed Sheriff's Captain had approached unnoticed and stood at the edge of their table. After a short pause, he slid into the booth beside Simpson so that he could look across the table at Obregon.

"Who's your friend, Dave?"

"Oh, Cap'n Matthews, meet Mike Obregon. We're working together for a while."

The look on the captain's face told them he'd accepted Obregon as a Bureau partner of Simpson's and he ceased to even acknowledge his presence. He turned to Simpson and in a tight voice said, "I'm on a short leash, the officers missing and all, what'cha got?"

....

THE LAST OF THE WEAPONS CRATES and cases of ammunition were being horsed through the yawning hatch into the aircraft's interior. The inside working space was dim and sweltering. The three Mexican swampers were showing the strain of working in the oppressive heat, their faces drawn and tired, their clothing drenched in sweat and crusted with salt and dust.

Mobutu and Stoudamyre busied themselves fastening down the nylon cargo nets that lay across the crates with lines through pad-eyes in the decking. They used rope and flexible cable to tie down crates where no netting existed. Bailey edged past the gritty laborers, excused himself by Mobutu and squeezed into the left seat of the aircraft. He began to examine the handiwork of the mechanic again.

The work appeared to be satisfactory. The man had been chosen because he professed some knowledge of instrument repair in addition to the usually sought mechanical abilities. He probably regretted that now, but he'd plodded along, doing *acceptable* work for a man so thoroughly saturated with fear. Bailey would try to see that the man survived—somehow. He was beginning to think that might be a tough thing to pull off, if it was even possible at.

He slid the side window fully open and, for a moment, watched the two young men with the pump truck topping off the tanks. The noise of the rental truck back against the side hatch being started up diverted his attention for a moment, and then he focused back on the panel. His fingers ran across the instruments and a mental picture was formed of what worked well and what didn't work at all. It was difficult. The pills made the panel swim about in his blurred vision.

His hand explored on across the panel and pedestal, touching a familiar lever, a knob, or a switch, and he could feel the stirrings of life in the old aircraft. The memories were dark, ancient and many, all pushed together into a confused mass. He imagined the pulse he felt was of a worn and melancholy aircraft, regretting its station in a life and slowly withering away. Almost instinctively, his hand moved back to the pedestal's knobs and levers. They had a long-held familiar feel to them and he knew he could reach out and touch them on the blackest of nights. Pitch—left, mixture—right, throttles—center … and, there, the trim wheel … all so familiar, so long a part of his life.

Bailey raised his eyes to the overhead electrical panel and moved his right hand up to touch, with almost a caress, switches for propeller deicer, pitot heat, battery master and a thousand memories. He was at home in this old and decaying aircraft. They felt as one together. *Shawnee Rose* was ready to go—how far she would go was another question. But, then, how far *he* could go was even more of a nagging question. He didn't think there was much time left. He looked back over his shoulder, saw no one watching, and groped in his pocket for the amber plastic pill bottle. He quickly removed the top and stared at its contents. There were not enough pills left for him to have one now. He'd have to stand the pain a little while longer. He recapped the bottle and pushed it back into his pocket.

Mobutu was watching though and his gaze saddened for the moment. There was nothing he could do. The thought crossed his mind that he may have misjudged Bailey, just how much was another question.

Bailey switched battery power on and tuned the top receiver to a frequency that should be Tucson's ATIS channel. The reception was weak and he had to strain to hear the recorded weather. The scratchy voice offered cloud cover, altimeter, wind direction and speed and a warning about moderate turbulence to the south, all preceding the edge of an oncoming tropical storm moving in from the Gulf, trying to wear itself out on the eastern Sonoran desert. Bailey thought about it for a moment and was forced to disregard it. There was no choice; they *had* to go.

He could see Stoudamyre and Cooper on the ground to his left, both engaged in an animated exchange with Cooper. Cooper pointed here and there about the strip. Stoudamyre didn't look happy and the Belgian machine pistol he had kept so well hidden was now cradled under left arm. He completed the flight deck checks and moved back downs the narrow aisle between crates and exited the aircraft to join them.

"Glad you're here … we need to talk about *sanitizing* this place as best we can.," was Cooper's greeting.

"Just how *sanitary* do you mean, Cooper?" Before he could answer, Bailey firmly said, "The mechanic goes with us. Understand? I need him."

Cooper's answer was blunt enough, "Well, I can't leave him here—alive that is." Shrugging, he finished, "You want him, you got him," and walked off toward the small group gathered at the back of the gas truck parked in the narrow road behind two bob-tailed trucks. There was a short and animated conversation, with Cooper pointing out individual tasks before turning to walk back toward the aircraft. The three trucks in the road started up and left almost immediately. The swampers that came in with them hurried about the worksite, policing up tools and other material. Within twenty minutes, they'd thrown a collection of tools into the open hatch of the aircraft, stuffed the rest into the tool van and one of them had left with it.

That left two drivers to move three cars and the camper or burn them. They were one car and the camper away from leaving the airstrip as empty as they'd found it.

"Which ones do we leave, Mr. Cooper?" the smallest of the remaining swampers asked. "When we leave, we don't want to come back."

"I understand. Leave the Dodge and the camper. It's already hot and the camper has a dead battery anyhow. If you don't get to it, we'll torch them before we leave. Drop the other two somewhere downtown and split. Wipe them down good … and … thanks." Cooper slapped the man on the shoulder and pulled out a wad of bills, peeled off several and stuffed them into the man's shirt pocket.

The men were gone in mere minutes, leaving the dust to settle on the narrow track and almost complete silence to cloak the airstrip. Cooper walked back and watched Bailey and Stoudamyre as they studied a stack of Sectional charts. The Phoenix Sectional lay open atop the others. Stoudamyre had a pad of paper on his knee and a pencil he kept pointing at the chart and then scribbling down short notes as Bailey and he talked.

"Well, it's *all* rough south of here, no matter how you slice it—'specially since we need to stay so damn low," Remarked Bailey, "I'd like to have a real altimeter setting before we go. I hate clouds with rocks in them."

"Yeah, ain't no way to stay low through some of it though—and what about the storm coming in off the Gulf?"

Bailey shrugged dismissively and, pointing to a spot on the map, continued, "We can shoot out to the right through here, probably fix a position off of Robles and Basalt, then head down the valley between these two ridges. That puts Keystone on our left at about sixty-eight hundred ASL and this peak also on our left at some seventy-seven hundred plus."

Stoudamyre ran a finger down the route from Tucson to the border and said, "OK, but it gets iffy pretty quick here on the south end toward the border. The floor comes up to meet us and we're in and out of a restricted zone that could get an Air Force fighter up our ass just about any old time."

"That's not the real problem. There's nothing but guesses and luck to navigate on. We'll be too low to fix on Nogales and there's a couple of peaks in there … here," he jabbed a finger at two peaks clearing five thousand feet standing like sentries along their path to Mexico.

"I suspect it'll be too dark to just trust our eyes. Not much of a moon and some overcast … damn!"

Stoudamyre pushed the chart away from him and opened another, titled CH-22, and spread it over the Phoenix chart. "Damn … will you look at this stuff?" Stoudamyre ran his pencil from the point they intended to cross the border south and east across the mountainous center of Mexico's Sierra Madres and shook his head. "We can't handle this low and at night and make any real plans on having a nice breakfast tomorrow. Jesus, old man, just look at these peaks, we're in deep shit."

Cooper had been looking over their shoulders at the charts and wasn't totally sure of the reasons for their concern. A flat, multi-colored chart didn't relay it very well to the unknowing eye. He pushed closer to the chart and pointed at one of the small magenta circles that seemed to pepper the surface of the chart. "It doesn't look all that bad. Didn't you say these are airports?"

Both Bailey and Stoudamyre had a first impulse to simply dismiss the man's question, but remembered that he was going along, sharing the danger, and thought better of it. They looked at each other and, as if on cue, Bailey began, "Yes, and no—these are airports … well, airstrips—of sorts."

"They're not as close together as they seem and not one in twenty is regularly lighted. They're all short and some haven't been repaired or maintained in twenty years. Some date way back to World War II or earlier."

He stopped for a moment, judging Cooper's reaction, then went on, "Most of the rest are private strips for outback ranches or mines and a few belong to some very dangerous people. Most of rest belong to the military—and you know we don't stop there. What's left are just full of run-of-the-mill dopers—you know about them, don't you? Want to land on one, heavy as we are, in the dark? Take our word for it; it is the shits down there and we don't want to even try and stop at one of them."

Cooper started to ask another question, then remembered he hadn't liked the answer to the last one he'd been nervous enough to ask. He decided the fear of not knowing would not be as great as the fear of knowing, nodded at Bailey in acknowledgment and backed away.

Both flyers turned back to the charts and began plotting headings. Stoudamyre even had a smile on his face.

. . . .

KIRKPATRICK PAUSED AT THE DOOR and looked at the gilt lettering before going in. He smiled at the pretentiousness of the seemingly legitimate term *Imports* as he thought of all the poison Malette actually brought in across the border. Of course, his knowing that might help him to persuade Malette to cooperate just then. Persuade was a very broad term in Kirkpatrick's vocabulary however.

It was cool, almost cold, in Malette's office. His face belied that however. Little beads of sweat stood out above his mustache and on his forehead. It was obvious that Kirkpatrick was one of the last men on earth he wanted to see just then.

"It's been a long time, Carlo. Let's see, about four years?"

"Cut the crap—I'm kind of in a bind for time right now. What do you want?" He tried to sound totally calm and in control of himself. He wasn't calm though and he certainly wasn't in control—of anything. Kirkpatrick was the only man in the world he feared more than Colisimo. He tried not to show it, as he worked to slow his heart rate and respiration. He failed. Miserably.

Kirkpatrick could see that and his voice turned immediately to ice and he almost spat out, "OK, Guinea, I'll tell you what I want. I want one of your greasy little jerk-offs ... Cooper, or whatever he calls himself, and I want him right fucking now. If you cough him up, I get to go find someone else I'm looking for and you get to go home tonight. Now, I don't think you'll miss either of the little shits I'm looking for, so don't concern your sweaty little head about it. That quick enough?" He was looking straight into Malette's eyes and it was very plain that not answering would be unacceptable—even painful, probably final.

"Aww, Christ, Man! I'm already wearing the guy around my neck like a Goddamn albatross. The Boss sent me out to find him less than an hour ago. He wants him handled and he wants it done right now too. I don't know where he is or it wouldn't be an issue. Honest. I got folks out looking for him now." He was nervously scratching at his forehead with the fingers of his right hand. Then he said, "OK, you can have him—but I gotta see what happens myself. I'm fried otherwise." He added again, "I gotta see it—you understand that?"

Kirkpatrick almost smirked across the desk at the man's sweaty nervousness and thought how much he looked like a cornered weasel. "You don't suppose your fools will find him anytime soon do you?"

"I expect a call any time now, really—any minute."

"That's good, Guinea, that's good. Suppose we just wait. You don't mind do you?" Kirkpatrick settled back into the softness of the chair and continued a bleak smile at Malette. It was only then that Maletta noticed the polished blue automatic in Kirkpatrick's lap and the chill spread throughout his body.

Chapter 13

Time dragged on slowly for Malette, each minute stretched into ten. He found it impossible to remain calm and sit still behind the expansive mahogany desk that fronted his throne and he traded the chair for pacing up and down the floor. His eyes kept flicking to the telephone, as if willing it to ring. Every few minutes he checked his wristwatch and low expletives came more frequent. Kirkpatrick didn't move—not even an inch.

This time it was 6:35 PM, only three minutes since he had last looked. Sweat soaked the back of his off-white linen suit and had begun to create a darkened mass that ran together with a similar soggy stain edging down from under each arm. He popped the last antacid tablet from a roll he had opened only half an hour before and pulled another packet from a half-empty box in a desk drawer and continued to pace.

Kirkpatrick just ignored him. He seemed so relaxed and oblivious to everything around him. The top of an expensively and ornately lacquered coffee table served as an ottoman for his polished shoes and his head rested back against the soft leather of the high-backed chair. An open copy of the New York Times lay across his lap. It was unread, serving only to cover the silenced 9mm-short Walther automatic lying loosely in his hand. He enjoyed the discomfort that seeped from Malette's pores much more than he could understand.

The telephone shrilly interrupted Malette's nervous glance back at his wristwatch at 6:37 and he knocked over an acrylic piece of non-art from the desk that held pencils, pens, and note pads in his grab for the handset. The contents of the container scattered across the floor between the desk and the chair that Kirkpatrick seemed to lounge so unconcerned upon. From the corner of his eye, he saw Kirkpatrick move the newspaper aside that was covering the automatic.

Malette noticed his own voice seemed at least half and octave higher than usual when he breathlessly croaked into the mouthpiece, "Malette here ..."

"This is Jack. We found him, Mr. M."

"Yeah? Where? It's late—we have to move."

"About an hour out, probably less. There's an old private airstrip—used to be owned by an oil company. We've used it a time or two ourselves. Coop's been using it for a drop—kinda regular lately."

"Which way, Jack? I need—we need—to get out there *now*."

"Remember when we brought that twin Beech and the dirty little bastard the Feds were looking for back from Panama about a year ago? Well, that's the strip."

"How'd you find out?" Malette queried.

"Oh, Jake and I *managed*. We found someone who helped load the damn plane they're using. Pure luck. I had to squeeze him a little—but he got real talkative in a hurry. Seems he's had a heart attack though ..."

"Fine, who cares?" Malette said, "When can you be ready to go with some muscle?"

"We're ready now. How about we meet in the parking lot of that tavern out at Five Corners in twenty, maybe thirty, minutes? That OK?"

Malette turned to Kirkpatrick and, with a nervous smile, said, "See? I told you my guys would find him. You satisfied? Now, I gotta go—my ass is on the line."

Malette turned back to the telephone and began to terminate the conversation with, "I'll see you there quick as I can ..."

The man on the other end of the connection interrupted him. "Mr. M., you're not gonna like this, but that little wetback Coop hired whacked a couple of county cops. This swamper I talked to said things were spooky as hell out there. You know there'll be cops everywhere pretty soon—you can bet on it, so be careful. I checked our … man … downtown and he says they got half the law in the county looking for them. It's gonna get dicey. Someone will get hurt."

Malette dropped the handset back into its cradle and, with an expression showing almost pure panic, said to Kirkpatrick, "Christ … that dumb shit let some cops get killed. There'll be hell to pay. Colisimo will have my …"

Kirkpatrick still seemed relaxed, almost disinterested, and, with a half-smile, said, "Sure, Guinea, sure. Well, *anything* can go wrong just about any time. You should know that by now. It's a rule for our game. Show me on the map where you're talking about," and he spread a Tucson area road map across the top of Malette's desk. He was anything but relaxed. All those years he'd spent in and out of places anyone would peg more dangerous than Arizona … and now things were getting more fouled up … dangerous … much worse than anytime he could remember.

Malette glared at him for a short moment, then spun the map half around, orienting it to be able to recognize its landmarks, and pointed to a spot on the map. "There, right there. You satisfied now?"

"Only if you're sure, Guinea, only if you're sure."

Malette hated the continual needling from the man, but it was not the time to argue the point. More than his pride was at stake. He started to tell Kirkpatrick he had to go again when the man asked, "Who is going to meet you at … where did you say?"

"Shit, man … his name is Jack Bitterman … he does *things* for me. The tavern he's talking about is out where 141, 12 and State 17 cross and the National Forest road heads off into the desert. What the hell do you care?" Malette was growing almost apoplectic in his need to leave and he came around the desk and moved toward the door.

"Thanks, Guinea. I'll give them your regards." Kirkpatrick raised the automatic and pulled the trigger twice, scarcely hearing its asthmatic cough. Stopping only to pick up the ejected shell casings, he turned, and without looking back, hurried off through the door. He was folding the map as he passed the receptionist's desk. He smiled and nodded as he went out the door without saying a word.

Malette hadn't even heard the muffled cough of the suppressed automatic. The shock and searing pain caused him to reel back against the desk and fall to the floor next to the coffee table. A small pool of blood began to form on the carpet beside him as he tried to push himself upright. The pain in his chest was a raging fire and he could scarcely move. He struggled with one of the pencils scattered about the floor and scrawled across a piece of the notepaper just two partial words. Then his body slowly went limp, rolling slightly to his right, and covered the paper. The pain began to move into the distance and the grayness closing in around him slowly became black.

Kirkpatrick had walked on through the outer office without speaking to any of the office personnel he passed on the way. He doubted that most of the office crew even noticed him enough to remember his race. Emerging from the front of the building, he unhurriedly ambled across the almost empty side street to his rented car. He noticed a telephone booth a few steps up the block, checked the time, and decided to make his nightly check-in with Jorgensen. Forty-five seconds later he was talking to the Langley operator. The message catch told him that Jorgensen was not available in his office but was expecting the call and that a relay would be made. Some moments later he was talking to Jorgensen.

"Where are you? The sound isn't too good."

"I'm on my way to Tucson. I need to see for myself how things are going," Jorgensen replied.

"You getting antsy? Don't you think I can handle things?" Kirkpatrick would not waste a chance to rub Jorgensen the wrong way.

"I can be on the ground in a little over two hours. That aside, give me an update on what's going on—and save your bullshit for some other time."

Kirkpatrick quickly thought about what was needed to brief Jorgensen and how long it would take. He gambled that no one had discovered Malette yet but, when they did, there would be cops. He didn't want to be there when they arrived. He started to just hang up, thought better of it, and said, "I assume this line is secure—I mean your end of it?"

"As good as it can get using a relay. Why?"

"Quick and dirty, then I have to get off the line and out of here. So listen, I'll say it just once. It's soured here even more than you thought. Some cops got whacked, some others hurt. My source here just met with a really untimely and unfortunate *accident*. Your friends are about to leave from a little out-in-the-weeds strip near here for parts unknown. I'm headed out there now—that's all I feel like taking the time to talk about now."

"Jesus … that's enough," came from Jorgensen, "can you pull it off?"

"I think so. Probably. How can I get in touch with you, quicker and without going through the desk next time?"

Kirkpatrick scribbled down the radiotelephone number and hung up without acknowledging Jorgensen's message. He sat for a brief moment in the car, looking at the road map, then made a quick U-turn and headed toward the southwest and a state road that cut through the low range of rocky, brush-covered mountains locally dubbed *The Tucsons*.

....

T HE SLOW, PAINSTAKING, AND SO FAR UNREWARDING work within the County's Emergency Operations Center was beginning to take its toll. Darkness was not far away and the missing deputies had still not been located. The patrol shift commander and the communications Sergeant were both coffee-logged, anxious, and weary. They also knew the patrol units were beginning to get frantic, dodging here and there, checking any place that might hide the missing unit and making central coordination increasingly difficult.

Worse, the coming darkness would ground the aircraft and they were the better part of the search resources. At that moment, some were already taking chances they shouldn't. They flitted in and out of canyons filling with shadows to check on a flash of light, an unrecognized patch of color—anything. The feeling grew that when they found the unit, the news would be bad.

The Sergeant checked the time again, looked down a long printout of negative search replies and decided it was time to walk across the street for a sandwich and, he grimaced, more coffee. He leaned over the top of a console and nodded for the Chief Dispatcher's attention, told him of his intentions and left the communications center. The Patrol Watch Commander had preceded him by about thirty minutes.

He was halfway down the hall when one of the secondary operators from the center came running after him yelling at the top of her lungs, "Sarg! Sarg! They think they found them!"

She was still yelling, but he wasn't hearing her anymore. The Sergeant was quickly back down the hall and bursting through the EOC's door with, "Where? Who's got them … they OK?"

"One thing at a time, Sarg, the Chief Dispatcher calmly said as he remained intent on a field unit's transmissions. He reached for the face of the console and flipped a toggle, twisted a knob, and the units voice could be heard. It was scratchy and the noise of an aircraft's engine could be heard in the background."

"… a gully and it's flipped on one side. I see someone … down. No one is moving. I can't get any closer without joining them … sorry."

The Sergeant turned to the out-of-breath little operator who'd chased him down the hall and was now in the EOC beside him. "Get the Shift Commander back down here and page the Sheriff—I *think* he's on the pager anyhow. Try him on the air and call his home too if need be. And, let's see … oh, that'll do for now. No, wait, call the Chief Criminal Deputy, get Captain Matthews, and have a homicide team alerted. Got that?"

She didn't answer him, turned on her heel and hurried to a vacant telephone and computer terminal. The Sergeant turned his attention back to the dispatcher.

"Where?"

"Some twenty plus out on 17. A reserve named Whalen spotted the car. He's by himself in a Cub. The patrol unit is up a gully on a side road … turned over, I think."

"Anything else?"

"Yeah, well … he was going to check it out if he could find a place to land close, but there isn't one. Closest thing is that old strip off to the west. We could get a medevac in there if we have to, but he says there's an old DC-3 and a bunch of people at the strip."

"They *could* be the reason the car's where it is. He think they saw him?"

"Probably. I'd count on it anyway. But, I thought they might be involved somehow so I told him not to overfly them at all anymore. Here, come 'round and look at this." The dispatcher smoothed a heavily marked-up map across the worktable to his right. "I've got a two-man unit in a 4-wheel-drive Bronco, let's see … here," and he pointed to a spot farther out on 17. "They can come in from this side and not be seen by the people at the strip—maybe—and get in there in, say, twenty minutes to half an hour and give us a report. Most everyone else is deployed between here and the strip or on to the south."

"Fine. Good job. OK, let's start pulling them together … just in case there's a connection between those at the strip and what's happened to our unit. Where do you suggest?"

"Well, about five miles shy of the airstrip there is the old Iverson cattle pens. I don't think they are working there this time of year. They've got a good sized asphalt parking lot we can stage on … we used it during the fires last year. It's a good place to set a 'copter down too."

"Yeah, you're right. Get one ready for the air now, so we can get a field commander and some troops out there in a hurry—Sheriff will want to go too. He'll be one pissed-off SOB. Borrow a bird and crew from the National Guard or Border Patrol if need be. Head any unit south and west of the city there. Strip districts if you have to … OK? Oh, and we'll need a scene commander, so make sure you get in contact with Captain Matthews pronto."

"Good as done," the dispatcher replied and turned to the console, the transmitting light went on and he began talking.

The Sergeant turned to another dispatcher who was off-console for the moment and motioned him over, "Bob, grab a pad and pen and meet me at my desk. Oh, we ever get hold of Cass's wife?"

"Still a *no*, boss," the dispatcher said over his shoulder as he headed back for his desk and a pen and paper.

The Sergeant turned the situation over in his mind for the few moments it took the man to return, then said, "I want a secondary log kept of everything that goes on—everything—by time and by incident. Don't lie, but make it sparse though, and that means no editorial comments or leaks to your buddies in the press. We'll need it for briefings and public release. Keep the Chief Dispatcher on duty but get him some backup … and correlate the log with their work. Get a public information geek down here—for the fucking press. Alert University Medical Center's emergency, we might need them. Let's see … suit me up a SWAT team, notify patrol they'll have to extend shifts … use pool cars for oncoming troops. Call the City— ask for any patrol units they can spare … and notify the Border Patrol again. Call the FAA, we might need someone to track an airplane on radar. Got it all?"

The man nodded affirmatively and answered, "Anything else?"

"Oh, there probably will be … but later."

….

Bailey stood near the open hatch, looking up at Stoudamyre and pointing to the last of the tie downs being completed. "Make sure there's a second line over those crates … they're heavy. We need to be moving—fast. You can bet the Cub that circled out by the butte belongs to the law. There's no way he could have missed us."

He had all but completed the pre-flight and began taking the last hurried walk-around of *The Rose*. As he began that last pre-flight walk-around, his mind, almost numbed by the pain medication, began to wander, not so much through space, but time. The cloud of dust each step kicked up reminded him of so long ago and far away. He could hear the noises, engines cranking, men's voices, and almost see dozens of khaki-clad airmen hurrying between rows of aircraft poised for flight. He had to struggle to bring himself back to the then and there.

He wasn't aware of it, but his voice had pulled both Stoudamyre's and Mobutu's attentions to his slow walk around *The Rose*. They watched him momentarily before going back to pushing the aircraft toward ready. The apparent affection he felt for the aged aircraft had become visible enough to be a source of amusement for even Stoudamyre, who probably understood it more than most. Bailey carried on a running monologue directed to the aircraft as he moved from point to point around the pre-flight. There were even remarks about *The Rose* talking back when the surfaces began their evening chorus of creaks and pops.

Within twenty minutes, the last of the interior work had been completed and Stoudamyre stepped down the short ladder and joined Bailey at the makeshift table where he was completing the last of a rudimentary flight plan. Shadows were lengthening and it would soon be dark enough to go.

"How's it look, Wes?"

"It's going to be dark tonight—only a quarter moon and we'll get clouds soon enough that will make it even darker," Bailey replied.

"That's not too big a big of a problem … unless there's something else. Is there?"

"There is, smart ass. I've picked up some more weather and it could get really bad south of here—south and east, anyway. There's what is left of a tropical storm—a damn deep low that just never turned hurricane. It's coming in off of the Gulf. Lots of rain, towering cumulus to God knows where and some pretty nasty wind and turbulence that just might tie a knot in old Rosie's tail." Bailey still stared at the map and tapped the plotter against the table's edge. "I've had to fly in that kind of stuff before … and sometimes it turned out bad."

Stoudamyre craned his neck to see the chart better and, after a moment, said, "Can we get around it at all? Maybe swing a little to the west and come in more to the south?"

"No … the weather's moving west and north enough—almost north-northwest actually—should put the worst of the weather to our left and front as it turns north, then east. Swinging more to the south would put us over the central Sierra Madres—and love this old bird like I do, I still won't trust her that much. Anyone who does is a fool. We can't haul enough gas for everything anyway. I expect the headwinds will hurt our range quite a bit anyway. We'll probably have to make that stop Cooper wanted to avoid."

"Then, it's a *go*." Stoudamyre replied. It was not a question.

"Yes. I'd like to be out of here in less than half an hour."

"Will it be cool enough to for us to get off of this sorry patch of weeds?"

"Maybe … maybe yes, maybe no—and I figure we're right at gross for takeoff at this density altitude. I know damn well we're over 28,000 gross and your guess is as good as mine about the way we did the weight and balance job. We just might be hanging on the ragged edge of a stall for a bit, but we just don't have much of a choice. Trust to luck—whatever *that* is." He did not sound convinced.

"Well, we've a little wind coming up the valley. We can take her down to the other end of the strip, run her up before we kick loose and … push her hard." Stoudamyre had a slight grin tugging at the corners of his mouth and, as he turned to walk back to the aircraft, said, "… bet you five bucks we make it—how 'bout you?"

Bailey just shook his head and then said, "Sucker's bet. Get the rest of the junk on board. Passengers too. We'll know in about twenty minutes, won't we?"

....

THE SHERIFF HAD MANAGED TO BE AIRBORNE and bound for the staging area within a few minutes of his receipt of the dispatcher's call. The description of the scene at the overturned prowler car was devastating. He was in a rage—a helpless, frustrated, and futile rage.

The details of conditions at the wrecked prowler car had left little doubt in the mind of the cagey old career cop that it had been no mutual-loss shootout. They had been left there with that intent, but he was not buying it. That a connection with the airstrip activity existed was not a sure bet either, but he'd pass up nothing at that point.

The plan of attack on the airstrip was simple. Time saw to that. It would be dark within minutes. He had to hit the strip before it was fully dark or risk losing everything. The stream of sheriff's cars left the staging area headed for the airstrip within fifteen minutes of his arrival. The deputies now had the fire of loss burning within them. They needed little encouragement to hurry.

....

KIRKPATRICK SAT BEHIND THE WHEEL of the rental car and silently watched the parade of sheriff's prowlers scream past, all headed toward the airstrip. He'd only been there some ten minutes and had hardly had time to convince Bitterman that Malette had sent him when the first car, emergency lights flashing, whisked by. There was no doubt where the run would eventually end.

Bitterman had brought four men with him, all packed into a van and heavily armed. They had just begun to talk about how to overrun the airstrip when the multitude of sheriff's equipment roaring out the highway changed the options.

When the eighth marked sheriff's car had gone by, Kirkpatrick turned to the man and said, "Looks like we don't go that way today. How's that for an understatement?"

"Yeah, well, I'm not real hot on moving without Mr. M anyway. Where did you say you're from?" Bitterman asked.

"At this point, what difference does it make? Take your folks back to town and lose them before our bad luck here turns into a shroud. I'll amble back on my own."

Bitterman looked at him for a silent moment before saying, "I'll go back 17—you might want to go 141 through Avra Valley or the National Forest. OK?"

"Sure."

Bitterman slid out of the car and took a few hurried steps to the van. They were out of sight in less than two minutes.

Kirkpatrick decided to just wait for a while and see what developed. He was close enough to the airstrip to see a plane if one landed or took off and he knew the harried deputies were not looking for him. He felt relatively safe—for the moment.

....

Stoudamyre pulled the large hatch in 392 Delta's side shut and hurried up the narrow companionway to the flight deck. Both props were turning and vibration and noise filled every nook and cranny. He leaned toward Bailey and yelled, "Let's move her!" before pulling a headset on.

Bailey blasted first one prop, then the other, to move *The Rose* off the hardstand and roll out onto the rough asphalt strip. They trundled, rattling and shaking, toward the far end and a chance to use the little breeze that did find its way up out of the valley floor below. A bit-by-bit preflight check was attempted on the fly as the roll continued.

At the far end, Bailey stood on the left brake and blasted the right engine to turn the aircraft around in a squeaking and waddling turn. As he began the turn, he could see a row of flashing lights on the highway beyond the dunes. By the time *The Rose* was pointed down the center of the narrow runway, he could see that the lights were police cars and that there were many of them. He also saw the first one take the left that would bring them onto the little airstrip. He slapped Stoudamyre's arm, pointed to the lights, and pushed the throttles forward against the stops without a run up and felt the old craft begin a slow acceleration.

The road onto the small strip intersected the tarmac some three hundred feet short of the west end. The old DC-3 had just strained through 40 knots when the first sheriff's car skidded up to the edge of the strip, quickly followed by another, and then many others. Then half of the right side of the narrow ribbon of runway seemed to erupt with flashing lights and cars. Bailey could dimly see uniformed men spreading along the runway beside the cars as he kept the throttles fire-walled and the DC-3 picked up speed slowly, ever so slowly.

The aircraft was sluggish, heavy from the near gross weight load and its poor balance. Bailey struggled to bring the tail up and gain enough speed and lift for a takeoff. Normally coming up by itself, the tail-up position was made difficult by the load and heat. *The Rose* whined, roared, shook and struggled to fly and Bailey sweated and strained with her. Half way down the runway, the tail finally came up and the noise changed pitch. There was the smell of hydraulic fluids and of engines overheating all rolled into one. The vibration became finer and the RPM went into the red, manifold pressure powered through 46 inches and cylinder head temperatures approached the far end of the scale.

The sheriff's cars loomed close, their flashing lights brighter in the gathering gloom as some of them began pulling onto the runway and into his path. Bailey gritted his teeth, unsure the aircraft would clear them and began to slowly pull the yoke back.

He became conscious of Stoudamyre yelling at him, then pointing toward the deputies along the side of the runway. There were flashes of light winking here and there amongst them. Only then did he realize they were shooting at the aircraft, but he still couldn't hear the reports even though he knew the aircraft would be hard to miss. A slapping sound, followed by the whistle of airflow, only served to emphasize that. He could hear Stoudamyre cursing and see his hands clench and unclench, wanting to take the yoke, but not daring.

Bailey had the throttles against the stops and it seemed he was physically trying to lift *The Rose* over the police cruisers trying to block the runway. He heard himself say aloud to Stoudamyre, "I killed my crew last time …" and he wondered why that was there at the front of his mind at that particular moment. And then it seemed that the cars on the runway were passing out of sight beneath the nose of the straining aircraft as he pulled *The Rose*, protesting, into the air. He screamed at Stoudamyre, "Gear up—now!"

The Rose mushed awkwardly upward, nose high and the stall warning blaring, with the noise and vibration growing as they struggled to stay in the air. Bailey pushed the nose down, just short of sliding back into the rocks and brush and kept the throttles hard against the stops and *The Rose* kept flying.

"Milk the flaps up—slow, dammit!"

The Rose was flying. Airspeed was slowly, but continually, creeping upward. Half the valley's width had been crossed before a hundred and twenty knots crept under the needle and Bailey began to ease back on the throttles as the last notch of the flaps clanked home. Still low, he began a gentle turn to the left and flew into the deepening darkness.

….

Kirkpatrick watched the shape of the DC-3 rise above the far horizon and heard the very faint reports of gunfire. He grinned and shook his head in mild surprise and, grudgingly, admiration. The aircraft carried no lights, but he could just make out its turn to the south and down the valley. He walked to the lone telephone booth near the far side of the saloon's parking lot and dialed through to the number Jorgensen had given him.

"They're airborne –don't know how they did it, but they did. Half the sheriff's department got in the way of me doing anything, sounded like a small war. What next, Bigshot?"

"Best I can tell, you're thirty, forty minutes—tops—from the transient terminal at International, *if you step on it*. Be there. There are not a lot of places they can go for what they want. We'll pick them up and follow. I'm in a blue and white Grumman Gulfstream II and have some hired help. So, get moving."

Kirkpatrick looked at the dead telephone for a while, then placed it back on the hook and returned to the car. He sat for a moment and thought about just disappearing on to the west. He had a safety deposit box in San Diego that housed money and several unused passports with clean names. Maybe Hong Kong or Singapore was right for the time.

But he was waiting on Jorgensen when the Grumman whined up to the passenger pad at Tucson's transient gate. They had sucked up fuel and were clear of Tucson airspace in another thirty minutes.

....

Matthews stared intently at Simpson, waiting for an answer and letting impatience show at the edges.

"Captain, we have a mutual problem. You're gonna be pissed— and rightfully so—when you hear what I've got to tell you. I can only hope you won't be too fried to listen and give us a hand. God knows, we need all the help we can get."

Matthews face darkened and he continued a thin-lipped stare at Simpson without saying a word.

"Cap," lapsing into the familiar, "We have what you might call a real ball-breaker of a problem. It got this bad because we withheld information you needed."

Matthews' eyebrows went up a notch and he leaned back into the booth, still silent.

"That black we were looking for—the one the city police found? We should have told you more than we did."

"What do you mean?" The scowl on Matthews' face told that his anger was rising.

Simpson glanced at Obregon, then went on, "He was—is—no part of a simple pimp-on-pimp shootout. It looks more like he had the whore with him purely as cover and it went wrong."

"Huh? What the hell are you talking about?"

"I'd guess the pimp went off half-cocked when his whore didn't check in and found them at the motel. He made the same mistake the city cops did—underestimated Bannock. By the way, his real name is Mobutu, Guthrie Mobutu. He's a Colonel in the Liberian Army."

Simpson felt Obregon's eyes on him and the look said, "Say no more," but he brushed it away with, "Pard, we don't have much choice now—do we?" It was not really a question.

"Cap, this man Mobutu is a real warhorse. He could eat the everyday copper for breakfast, anywhere, anytime. He's soldiered in places we'd never want to go, probably some we've never heard of and he is one tough son-of-a-bitch."

The silence was painful. Then Matthews shifted in his seat and looked directly at Simpson, his voice flat and very low, "You sorry bunch of bastards—you never deal from a straight deck. I don't know why I ever talk to you anyhow. You expect us to do your dirty work, but you can't even bother to be honest with us." The anger began to deepen on the Captain's face and his rising voice was causing the customers to turn and stare. It was obvious the Sheriff's Captain didn't care. "What the fuck do you want us to do now? We ... damn!"

Obregon raised a hand to slow Matthews, and began to talk slowly and quietly, trying to keep the conversation in the booth. "Captain, we need help from both you and someone in the city police department. We thought you might be able to run interference for us with them. I'm beginning to wonder now. You know as well as I do about their attitude toward Feds—any Fed. We need Mobutu badly ... and right fucking now." He was surprised at how calmly that came out.

"Look guys, I'd like to help" the words dried on his lips for lack of reality, then he went on, "… no, that's not true. I'd like to let you assholes stew in your own juices. Love to, in fact, but you know that's not how I work. You do have to understand that I'm in a bind right now."

"I understand you've got a couple of deputies missing—been out of sight for a few hours?" Simpson asked as a rhetorical question, already knowing the answer.

"Yeah, and it's coming on dark. We've extra crews out and some aircraft looking over the desert and the west and south slope of the Tucsons and the ridge across the valley. It doesn't feel good. I wish we had an idea what's going on."

"You don't suppose there's a connection between our man and your deputies do you?" asked Obregon.

"Dammit—I don't know, but, no, not really. The deputies handle a section way out on Highway 17. I suppose anything is possible though." Matthews replied. "What you guys want is hard to sell …" he was interrupted by the beep of his pager and reached down to turn the tone off and pull the device from his belt. He squinted at the digital message across the pager's small LED inset and quickly pulled himself to his feet and hurried back to the pay phones at the rear of the restaurant.

Simpson, and Obregon, when he half-turned in his seat, could see Matthews' face as he spoke into the telephone. They tried to decipher the changing expressions, as Matthews seemed to listen more than he talked. After about forty-five seconds, he hung up the telephone and walked back to the booth. There was a grim and anxious set to his face.

"I gotta go. We spotted the deputies and it doesn't look good. Some things have already been set in motion—and I need to get out there." Almost as an afterthought he added, "You guys are a fucking jinx—but, you can see a Lieutenant by the name of Hanson, *Al Hanson*, over in the PD's patrol. He is one of the night shift commanders. He might talk to you, feds or not—pretty sharp, but he is a straight guy. He will be pissed, God, will he be pissed—so don't run your mouth. Tell him I sent you. Gotta go."

Obregon and Simpson sat very quietly and stared at each other. Obregon almost whispered, "It's getting tight—we'd better get at it."

Simpson flipped a ten-dollar bill on the table and followed Obregon out the door.

Chapter 14

BAILEY BANKED *THE ROSE* SLOWLY AND SMOOTHLY left, the altimeter reading telling him it was a bare five hundred feet to the cactus, gullies and scab rock spread out below. The airspeed indicator finally flickered across 140 knots, creeping slowly upward, as they maintained a straining and gradual climb. He reached across and touched Stoudamyre's arm, drawing his attention, before pulling up an earpiece to his headset. He leaned toward his copilot and yelled above the din, "We've got about ten minutes before both of us have to stay here on deck. I'm going back and check on things while I can. Keep the present heading and ease us up to a grand. I'll be back as soon as possible." He let go of the yolk, pulled his hands back, as he said, "OK, you've got it."

He nodded when he saw that Stoudamyre had the controls, then dropped his hands to the armrests and pushed himself up out of the seat and leaned back and off the flight deck. Entering the cabin, he found Mobutu, to the right, appearing engrossed in releasing his lap belt. Bailey could see Cooper at the far end of the narrow path through the stacks of crates and boxes. He was staring intently at a small splotch of red on the calf of his right leg and dabbing at it with a handkerchief. Porteros was standing in the pathway between Bailey and Cooper, pulling a length of strapping down tighter across a wooden crate, seeming to be unaware of all else around him.

Bailey could just see the top of Jess' head behind a crate marked *Electronic Equipment* in large yellow letters. He turned again to

Mobutu, who stared back at him, a stolid sadness in his eyes, as he nodded toward Jess.

Bailey stepped around the crates to where Jess had strapped himself into a canvas, pull-down seat riveted to the fuselage uprights. He was canted against a crate to his right, chin resting on his chest. There was a trickle of blood running out of the hairline and widening across his cheek, eventually creating a large splotch on the front of his shirt. Both of his eyes were open and seemed to be staring at the aircraft's deck. There was the glaze of death in his eyes.

Bailey knew there was no use, but he leaned toward Jess and gently shook him. There was, as he expected, no response. A faint whistle drew his attention to a small and round hole in the aircraft's skin, directly behind where Jess's head would have rested during takeoff. A one in a hundred shot; a 100% shot for Jess.

He looked back toward Cooper and saw that he'd been watching him as he examined Jess. There was a look of dread and questioning on his face and he was beginning to get to his feet again. Bailey slowly shook his head from side to side and watched Cooper struggle up and limp toward him.

Cooper bent down and pulled Jess' face up, looking into his open, dead, eyes. He went down on one knee, still very gently holding the man's face between both hands. He looked into the man's colorless face for a slow moment, before he muttered something barely audible that the noise of the aircraft covered. After a moment, he ran his hand over the dead man's face, closing his sightless eyes.

When Cooper stood up, there was a flat, almost expressionless set to his face. His eyes were deep pools of lusterless black. "I really liked the guy—even when he tried to sell me out. We're getting off to a crappy start ... what the hell do I tell his folks?"

Bailey didn't say anything, just looked at the man. He shrugged and started to turn away, but Cooper reached out and grabbed his arm and went on, seeming to have a need to keep talking and say something—anything. "We kinda grew up together—east, then, later the south side of Chicago. My old man—his too—was connected. We have to bury him right. I owe him that." Then the expression on his face changed almost immediately, as if it had never happened.

"I hope you're around to do it, but I don't have time for this." Bailey interrupted before he could go on and he turned away to make a circuit of the aircraft, looking for damage. Finally, after finding nothing of any real significance, he shuffled back toward the flight deck. Stoudamyre looked up as Bailey slipped back into his seat and began to buckle his lap belt. "Everything OK?"

"Not exactly. We lost a passenger. Jess is dead."

Stoudamyre looked at him and only a questioning, "Oh?" formed, nothing more.

"*The Rose* has a few holes—just from the cop's popguns. She'll whistle and leak a bit, but fly just fine." He was looking out at the dark mass that was everything from the horizon down. The sky, dimly lit by a quarter moon, was more and more becoming a canopy of blue-black velvet, sprinkled with patches of stars here and there and blackened by thick clouds everywhere else. The darkness from below seemed to reach up and clutch at the aircraft, trying to pull her down and swallow them all. The fates had given them a poor night for low-level flying. All they needed now was bad weather; and it seemed that too was undeniably ahead.

"Ease up another two hundred feet. The valley floor rises here. Damn, it's black out there. I wish we'd been able to get a good altimeter setting before we left—we're just guessing now."

Stoudamyre looked across at him and said, "*Great, just ... fucking ... great.*"

"Bill, come over to 185 degrees. We want to pop over the saddle in the ridge line just here," and he pointed at a spot dimly visible on the chart between two high points in a long and rough ridge of peaks. "These two peaks to our right are both at almost 5,000 feet ASL and the ridge to our left has a first peak at 6,900, where the observatory is, and goes on up to over 7,700 a bit farther on. We should hit the border about five miles east of Horse Peak ... there just west and south of San Miguel. We need to keep low, but remember, even the ground here is over 3,000 feet above sea level—so the clouds might damn well have some rocks in them. See if we're high enough to pick up a bearing off of Tucson or Nogales … anywhere. I've got the ship."

Stoudamyre nodded and replied, "OK, You got it," and raised his hands from the yoke, then turned his attention to the radio stack. He paused in his fiddling with the knobs for a moment, turned on the old and tired weather radar, hoping for more than scatter from a near and rough terrain but not getting it. He went back to the omni and began toying with a signal that faded in and out, causing the needle to swing across a wide sector uncertainly.

After a few minutes, he pointed toward the radio stack and raised his voice enough to be heard, "Wes, I think that's Nogales … at 108.2 … off at about 119 to 122 degrees … maybe. Tucson is over the ridge behind our port wing and I can't raise Robles … might be shut down. There ain't jack shit in front of us. I'll see if anything else pops up, but where do we go if a problem comes up?"

A few moments of silence went by, then Bailey turned to his copilot and, conscious that Mobutu had moved up to stare out the windscreen between them, said, "Look across the bottom of the Phoenix chart. There are six, maybe eight, small private strips within twenty miles. They'll all show restricted, probably real short and no lights. There's one." He was pointing at a spot titled *Rancho Chula Vista*. "We'd never find it in the dark anyway. If we could, the Mexican Army would be on us like stink on …"

Mobutu leaned closer and queried, "Then, you say it's on—or nowhere?"

Bailey only nodded affirmatively.

"You are right, of course," Mobutu continued, "and do you have any suggestions of how to handle our late companion?"

Stoudamyre looked up toward Mobutu, his face set and eyes hard, "Open the hatch and throw the son-of-a-bitch out. No one will miss him."

"No!" Cooper had crowded up behind Mobutu and was staring at Stoudamyre. "We will *not* just throw him out. If we get caught with what's on board this piece of shit, a stiff won't make any difference. I'm gonna bury Jess right. Don't screw with me on that."

Stoudamyre shrugged and murmured, "Do what'cha have to, asshole …" then turned back to the dark that lay ahead.

….

"GRUMMAN 212 ALPHA, we understand you have permission to penetrate Mexican airspace. Your destination?"

The tall, sandy-haired pilot looked toward his copilot and slowly shook his head before answering, "Tucson radio, I'll get back to you on this frequency in … five."

"Roger 212 Alpha. Come up on 126.3 and talk to Mazatlan center."

"Ok, Tucson … in just a couple …"

The pilot shook his head again and said, "You've got it. I'm going back to see what the hell Jorgensen is up to." He popped loose from the seatbelt, pulled his way out of the cramped flight deck, and entered the main cabin of the Grumman. Jorgensen had the handset of one of the several scrambled radiotelephones to his ear and was talking while intermittingly sipping at a drink.

"That would be great, Eduardo … yes. Thanks. No, absolutely not—not on Mexican soil. You know me better than that."

Jorgensen listened for a while, reached for a pen and scribbled on the notepad for a hurried moment, then laid the pen down. He stared at the few lines of scribbled handwriting and nodded, almost in boredom. He leaned forward and said, "Force them down? No-o, no … I'd rather not do that Eduardo … unless we have to, of course. Sure. I understand. I'll call you back in about thirty minutes … and, Ed," lapsing into the familiar, "I really owe you big on this one."

Jorgensen rolled his eyes upward in mock exasperation, and finally motioned for the pilot. He handed the man the slip of paper and said, "Can you read my scratching? Call Mazatlan. We gotta play the game. They'll hand you off to some Mex Air Force dickhead in Hermosillo …so play along. OK?"

"Where *are* we headed, Mr. Jorgensen? Tucson wants to know. Actually, it would nice if I knew … we have to know where to herd this beast"

"Well, you can ignore those useless fucks in Tucson. We're a bit further up the food chain than they are. Just hope the good General keeps a short leash on his fighters. He looked back at his notes and said, "He says our fools crossed the border at a place you'll find on the map just east and north of a place called *Rancho Chula Vista*. Grab your charts. They're low and appear to have turned to a heading of about 120 degrees magnetic now. They can't be doing 180 knots … probably less, loaded like they must be. See if you can intercept … OK?"

The pilot knew dismissal when he heard it and bent back onto the flight deck. As soon as he was seated, a hurried search of the flight bag produced a chart labeled CH-22. After refolding the chart to show the border area from Nogales to the Gulf of California, he began to study the area dotted with a number of small magenta circles containing "Rs" that designated short and restricted private airstrips. "Jorgensen's Mexican friends think the DC-3 crossed here," pointing at the chart, "and are low and slow along a general heading of 120 degrees. Where are we now, Pat?"

"About ten miles south of Nogales … I'm doing a slow 360. Where do you want to go?"

"How fast can a loaded DC-3 go? Shit, I've never even been in one, let alone flown one of the old crates." Without waiting for an answer he went on, "180 knots … maybe 190? … probably less? Head down here toward Magdalena, let's put that fancy new radar to use— try and pick them up." He laid the chart across his knees and began sorting through his flight bag for another one that would adjoin CH 22 on the east.

. . . .

THE LITTLE DESERT AIRSTRIP WAS ALIVE with flashing emergency lights and angry, frustrated, swearing, Sheriff's deputies. The half-hour since the aircraft had managed to escape their fire had scurried by and confusion still reigned. The Sheriff's helicopter sat mid-strip, its blade slowly ticking around. The Sheriff himself stood midst a small knot of his closest aides, hands jammed into his pockets and a dark and angry look chiseled across his features. His eyes followed two deputies slowly going through the Dodge sedan parked near a clump of brush near the strip's north edge. One of the deputies detached himself from the search and was walking slowly toward the Sheriff.

"Yeah? What have you found?"

"Sheriff, this is the car that black dude got away in after shooting up those PD units out near *The Mile*. Nothing in it though—clean as a whistle … except for that bullet hole in the windshield."

The Sheriff started to say something, but stopped as he noticed his newly arrived patrol Captain had a puzzled look spreading across his face.

"What's wrong, Matthews?"

"Boss—I just talked to some Feds about this guy, just before I headed out here. They wanted to pass some info on to the PD and, I suppose, get some back. You know that no one in the City will talk to them now … after the Grand Jury … so they came to me."

The Sheriff looked hard at the Captain for a moment before asking, "Think they know enough about this to be of help?"

Matthews shrugged, "I'll see if I can locate them. They've got some kind of operation going, so I'm sure their dispatcher can raise them." He started to move off toward his dark-green and unmarked prowler but was stopped momentarily by the Sheriff's angry growl, "Arrest the sorry bastards if you have to—I want their sorry asses standing tall in front of me with some real answers on their lying little federal lips."

Matthews muttered, "Oh, damn …" and moved on toward his car. As he passed the car used as a communications center, a deputy leaned out and said, "Hey, Cap', City Communications called to alert the Sheriff and the Chief Criminal Deputy, seems the city has a big-time homicide. One of those mobsters we *ain't supposed to have* got himself whacked. It's Carlo Malette. They said to tell the Sheriff since the big shit this hairball worked for lives out in the county."

....

THE SLIM, BALDING AND SUNBURNED patrol Lieutenant was just hanging up the telephone as Obregon and Simpson were ushered into his office. Before they could be speak or seated, the man rose and reached for his uniform hat. "We got something downtown you might be interested in. You can ride with me but, keep your mouths shut about who you are. The homicide dicks sure as hell won't appreciate having you on the scene … if they find out you're Feds. You're just visiting firemen from *where-the-hell-ever* … OK?"

They turned and followed as the Lieutenant brushed past and was out the door.

"Where we going?"

"Carlo Malette was found dead a little bit ago I hear. He left a note—Something about "Feds." Malette was something of a big shot mobster here a-bouts." He kept talking when he didn't get a response. "Yeah, I know. *There is no Mob*; and the Pope's a pulpit-pounding Southern Baptist. Maybe you guys can help … for a change … instead of just being a pain in the ass."

They took the elevator down three flights to the basement parking area and headed toward a dark, plain-on-plain, Dodge parked in a stall labeled "Patrol Watch Commander."

"We'll take mine—I'll drop you back later. You lock your car? I'd hate to think one of my guys put a rattler in it while we're gone …"

Neither Obregon nor Simpson laughed and the Lieutenant jerked the car door open and nodded for them to get in the other side. The Lieutenant pulled out of the parking garage, flipped on the grill-mounted emergency lights, and powered off toward midtown.

Less than ten minutes later, they pulled to a stop across the street from a combination warehouse and office complex stretching up to five floors. There were several patrol cars parked along the curb, their lights flipping multi-colored hues across the street and buildings. There were also three obviously "plain" cars detectives would drive. A close-sided station wagon was pulled across the sidewalk leading to the front door of the complex. The words "Medical Examiner" ran in red across its painted dark windows and its rear hatch was open. A young and bored patrol officer who looked all of sixteen blocked the front door.

The Lieutenant pushed through the front door, pulling Obregon and Simpson in his van, remarking only that, "They're with me ..."

The young patrolman, not knowing them, only gave them the look of a man that would rather be somewhere else and turned back to his guardianship of the space around the door, pulling up his gun belt and resuming his imitation old-timer's slouch.

Lieutenant Hansen crossed the lobby area and pushed the up button on a bank of three elevators. He turned to Obregon and Simpson as the elevator door opened and he stepped in, "Keep quiet around the Sergeant running the scene. You guys got his brother indicted during the Grand Jury sweep. He's honest—but he won't forget. His brother ate his pistol during the trial ... hell of a mess."

Obregon winced, nodded, and all three lapsed into silence as the elevator jerked upward and bounced to a stop at the 5th floor. They exited the elevator and found themselves in another open lobby area. There were four doors opening into the lobby area, all were closed except the one straight-ahead, gilt lettering on the door announcing, "C. Malette, Ltd." As they brushed by a second guard at the elevator, the activity inside the room became visible.

Several women, all looking frazzled and frightened, crowded along the reception area rear wall, all under the watchful eye of a squat, heavy-jowled detective in shirt sleeves. A large-framed automatic rested under his left armpit in a shoulder holster. The man's jacket lay across a chair. His sleeves were rolled up. He was hot, sweaty and tired. It was easy to see that his patience was out of town for the day.

Hansen, Obregon and Simpson entered the room just as the detective slammed his notebook down on a coffee table and in a hard and tired voice, snarled, "Goddamn it—you broads seen somethin'. The asshole just didn't fly in and outa here. You did see him … I know you did, you know you did. Now, let's start all over. What did the son of a bitch look like? Tall? Short? Ugly? Queer? Come on, dammit."

The exasperated detective only gave them a glance out of the corner of his eye as they quietly passed on into the inner office. All three men stopped just inside of the office door and stood there in a rather uncomfortable holding pattern. The Detective Sergeant running the crime scene seemed to not even see them and went on moving around the room, pointing to this and to that, giving instructions that were hurriedly scribbled into a notepad of another detective, who followed him around the room like a loyal puppy dog.

Obregon looked about the room. It was a large rectangle, perhaps thirty feet by twenty feet in length and width, darkly paneled and carpeted in thick, off-white, plush. The desk was large enough to fit the room, with its glass-topped, deep mahogany finish gleaming under layers of polish. The walls were covered in ornately framed paintings and prints. Though it was a business office, its walls strangely lacked the usual *scare wall* of diplomas and certificates. But, one doesn't rise to Malette's place in *business* through formal education. The only things out of place were the detectives, a pair of white-coated medical examiners, a folding metal-framed gurney with a green-black body bag lying on it, and a large and dark stain on the carpet. A slight grin came to his face as Obregon became conscious of Simpson staring at the floor, trying hard not to see the body bag and the bloodstain.

As if suddenly discovering them, the Detective Sergeant turned to them and, staring hard at the two strangers, said, "Hey, Bud … didn't see you. Got something the brass might want to know about." Then, grinning a bit, he added, "Ain't you just upset as hell about this fine member of Tucson society gettin' whacked?"

He turned and walked across the room and whisked a clear plastic evidence bag from the desk, then turned back to the Lieutenant. He never took his eyes off the two strangers as he spoke, "Good and fair lieutenant, my overworked detectives found this under the wop when they rolled him over." There was a pause, before he said, "Who're your friends, Bud?"

Hansen passed it by as if it were unimportant and took the envelope from the Sergeant, holding it up to the light for examination. "Friends ... from Denver. Introduce yourselves." No one did and the moment passed.

The Lieutenant paused a moment, then said, "Looks like it says *Fed* ... or *Feds* ... and I'm not sure ... this might be *Kirkpa*, whatever that is. Could be part of a name, if that's what it says."

"Yeah. Looks that way to me too. Mean anything to you? You know the creep in the bag. It's Carlo Malette. He's the prick that sued you a couple a' years ago ... right? I doubt he'll ever collect now. Sure as hell no real loss. The fuckin' bum shoulda been dead a long time ago, but this is number sixty-four for the year, not counting wets, and we got a long way to go. The chief will not a happy man be until he sees a cleared and closed stamp on this asshole's forehead. That buncha bimbos in the outer office claim they didn't see a damn thing."

"You sure Nick?"

"Yeah—talk to 'em yourself. Better get your buddies out of here pretty quick though ... unless you want them on the 5 O'clock news or in the morning rag. The press picked up our last broadcasts. Dave says the TV twits will be here in less than ten." There was a short pause before he said, "Say, your kids did a good job on the initial scene. Thank 'em for us."

"Thanks, Nick, I will ... see you later. Let me know if you dig up anything, OK?"

"OK"

Hansen handed the plastic evidence envelope back to the Sergeant and all three turned and filed back out of the office. They paused in the reception area while the Lieutenant looked hard at first one, then the other, as he asked, "That scribbling mean anything to you?"

Simpson nodded negatively and turned to Obregon, who seemed in deep and closed thought. He was silent for a moment, then asked very quietly, "Can I talk to whoever sits at that desk," as he pointed to the desk with the call director on its edge, "… the one closest to the elevators?"

The Lieutenant looked at him a long, puzzled moment, then said, "Sure, why not?" He turned to the detective who had been trying to get information out of the women, "Detective …"

The stocky, perspiring and exasperated detective turned toward them and said, "Yeah, Lou … what do you need?"

"Can I see whoever sits at that desk?" pointing at the receptionist's desk.

"Sure." He turned back to the harried looking women crowded into two couches backed along the far wall. He nodded toward a young, mousy-haired, but well-dressed woman, and then said, "OK, Babe? See that nice man in the policeman's suit? Get'cher ass over there and tell him how goddamn blind you are."

There was no movement for a bit. Finally, the smallish woman, with what Obregon called *the-thousand-yard-stare* got up from the couch and minced across the room. She stopped a few feet short of the uniformed officer and, in an almost strangled whisper, said, "I already told the detective I didn't see …"

Obregon cut her off in a tight and edged voice that Simpson had never heard from him before and even snapped the head of the Lieutenant around, a startled look on his face.

Obregon was leaning forward, his face scant inches from the woman's terrified eyes, "Look, you stupid bitch, this is not one of the little games you sorry punching bags want to play with me. I'm going to ask you just once and if I don't hear what I need, you'll never see the daylight again. This man, he about 6'2" … maybe 6'3", big shoulders, dark hair, combed straight back, real pale eyes? Hard looking guy? Dress real good? Yes or no?"

The woman just stood there, silent and shaking, "I … I just can't …"

"Lady, this is no hit by the pond scum you work for—I'll tell you again, if you want to be alive tomorrow …"

She stood a few more seconds, then tears and makeup began making dark rivulets down her face and she began to nod her head up and down. She still hadn't spoken.

"Dammit! Answer me,"

"Yes—yes … a tall guy. Looked all gray and hard. Dressed real well and he had the coldest smile I think I've ever seen. He was almost out the door before I saw him leaving … had a map in his hands."

Obregon's voice went soft again and there was quiet, "Thanks—now tell that detective over there the same thing—and I mean everything," before he turned to the Lieutenant and said, "We need to get to a secure phone—*now.*" He started toward the door, Hansen and Simpson following in confusion.

"What you got that we need, fella?" The Lieutenant's voice was tired and had an irritated edge to it.

Obregon was repeatedly pushing the call button for the elevators when they really caught up to him and began to ask questions again. He looked hard into Simpson's eyes, "The hardhitter, Dave, the *hardhitter.* I know who he is. If I'm right, it's a mechanic named Kirkpatrick. Everything I got from back east makes sense now."

Simpson answered, "What the hell are you talking about? This mess here can't be connected to that … can it?"

The Lieutenant was swiveling his eyes from one to the other in a puzzled and dismayed state, "What's going on here? Come on, you two spooks talk to me!"

"Lieutenant, Matthews said we could trust you … anyway, right now we don't have much choice and neither do you. Can you get us to the Federal Building? We can pick our car up later. You have to trust us enough to hold this close to your vest … at least for now.

We'll tell you a hell of a tale on the way there and while I make a couple of calls. Stick with us and we'll give you this case on a platter. Oh, and when they get finished talking to that woman, put her in protective custody—right then, *if* you want a live witness anytime down the road."

"Uhh, sure ... but," there was anger creeping into his voice as he concluded, "What have you two assholes got going? You trying to get some of my men killed?"

"No—but we have been a part of the problem—and not much of the solution."

The elevator bounced twice at the main floor and the door glided open. The three men hurried past the youthful guard and trotted toward the Lieutenant's car. They hurriedly piled in and the Lieutenant popped the car in gear and squealed away from the curb. Siren silent, lights flashing, he pushed the patrol car into the mid-sixties and blew across town in a scant few minutes.

The blue Dodge was pulled into the vacated *Official Vehicles Only* spaces in front of the Federal Building and all three exited the car, hurrying to the building's locked front door. They paused long enough for Simpson to use a key-card on the front door and quickly hustled on to his office. There, things seemed to temporarily go into a nervous and anxious pause. Obregon paced back and forth for what seemed minutes, then turned to Simpson and said, "I need a secure line."

"I doubt there is such a thing in this outfit—but, here ... this is the best I can do."

Obregon nodded, paused, and seemed to be thinking before saying "Well, hell—let me sit down." He pulled the small leather notebook from his jacket's inner pocket again, leafed beyond the back pages of telephone numbers and pulled a small card from a half-pocket on the notebook's backing. He studied a list in tiny print for a bit and then dialed a number with thirteen digits. The phone rang for several turns before Obregon said, "Ken, I need to know where Kirkpatrick is ... *now* ... can you help?"

Both men stared hard at him while he listened and nodded for a scant thirty seconds. Obregon sighed and simply said, "Thank you," in a low and flat voice and then he just hung up.

He turned to stare at both Hansen and Simpson before saying, "Kirkpatrick got a call to see Jorgensen. I owe Ken one. I'm not supposed to know it. We've got big problems …"

"What are you talking about? You're even beginning to make me nervous," Hansen said, "and just who is Kirkpatrick."

"To begin with, I think he's the man who put the guy we just saw down for the body bag … Malette, I think his name was. Lieutenant, we have some things to tell you. You won't like them, but you need to know. I need to make one more phone call, but start with the fact that, as old-fashioned as it seems today, Kirkpatrick is a *shooter*, and about as good as they come at that business. And I mean whether it is point blank or at 1500 yards, he's the man. You remember that little thug in Guatemala? They claim he removed the guards from over 700 yards, then walked up and shot the general from across his desk."

The men fell silent as Obregon pushed in another set of numbers and waited. There was only a short wait before he spoke into the telephone, "Jake … Mike Obregon. Yeah, it's me. Look, I don't want to get you in trouble … but, I'm in deep, very deep, trouble. The hitter … you talking about, he wouldn't be Kirkpatrick, would he?" There was a strained silence, "Jake, I need to know." After bit more silence, finally, "OK. Thanks. Jake, one last question, is Jorgensen out here too? Yeah? Thanks—which one? A Grumman … OK. Jake, just forget we talked—*please*. Thanks again buddy."

He sat there for what seemed several minutes, drumming his fingers on the desk. His companions said nothing, just stared at the visibly troubled man. After almost five minutes, he reached for the telephone again, punched in another set of numbers from the card and, after only a few seconds, said, "This is Obregon in Tucson. Give the Director this number," and spit out a scanline number. "I need to talk to him now—*right fucking now*. I don't care where he is … and, yes … as soon as possible. Yes, I'll wait right here. Sure … I'll tell you.

It's got to do with Deputy Director Jorgensen and Guthrie Mobutu. That's right. OK. Hurry up." He slowly and almost soundlessly laid the handset back into its cradle.

Obregon turned back to his two companions. Both looked puzzled, but too confused to ask questions other than with their eyes. He stared at them for a while, smiled wanly and said, "Let's go over it—from the start."

He focused on Hansen and cautioned, "I don't really want to get you in the middle of this, but there's not really much choice right now. I'd ask you to remember that a lot of what you'll hear is not a local affair and that I'll get my nuts fried if anyone finds out we've talked."

Hansen nodded slowly and said, "Maybe so, but you're leaving nasty little corpses here and there on my turf and I …"

Obregon interrupted him and went on, "Yeah, I know, I know, but … please … take only what you need and forget—forever—the rest. You have to know we don't usually work this way … and," turning to Simpson, "this is one hell of a mess."

Simpson only nodded and Obregon began to recount what he knew of the story. Hanson sat with a blank stare and said nothing. Just as Obregon began to fit Kirkpatrick into the scheme of things, the telephone interrupted with a dull buzz.

Obregon lifted the receiver, quietly saying, "Yes?"

The voice at the other end was tense and strained, "Obregon? What is going on out there?" and in weary redundancy, Obregon began to talk his way through the story again. There was an almost silent vacuum on the other end, though several times he thought he could hear another muffled voice in the background.

The tale took only about five minutes this time. There had been no need for the explanations Hansen required. When Obregon had finished, the Director came back on with, "Just a moment."

In less than sixty seconds, he returned, "Obregon, I know you're worried about being put in the middle, but you've done what you could. I need some very aggressive damage control. *Right now*. You seem to be doing OK with the local folks. So, keep it up and try to maintain their silence about anything beyond their immediate issues."

"I'm sure—absolutely sure—that Kirkpatrick is their man; and we'll handle that aspect of things. He worked through the Mob net for a long time and knew all of their hitters of any competence. And, yes, Duncan says Gunnar is out there."

There was a pause before he continued, "Obregon, just sit tight a bit. I'm sending a man down from Phoenix. His name is Barrington. He has my full confidence … remember that. He'll be in charge of all our assets *except* you and Simpson. Work with him. He'll be there in, oh—two hours, probably closer to an hour. Meet him at International. He'll be in a company jet." Then the Director simply hung up.

Hansen startled as his pager buzzed, looked at the number and grabbed up a telephone from the desk he sat near. His call was short. When he'd hung the telephone up, he turned back to Simpson and Obregon, "Matthews is looking for you. He says to arrest you if I have to—but he wants to see you. Yesterday would be just fine." He grinned as he said it.

. . . .

T HE DRONE OF THE DC-3'S ENGINES filled every nook and cranny of the cockpit and the craft had begun to buffet with increasing violence and irregularity.

Bailey pressed the intercom button and asked, "Any *honest* idea of where we are?"

The question was beginning to feel rhetorical, even to Bailey. The terrain below was as black and indistinct as velvet. The sky above, though sprinkled here and there with stars, was growing darker also. Ahead, the storm could be seen filling more of the horizon, frequent lightning bracketing cloud formations.

Stoudamyre, constantly fiddling with the stack of avionics, muttered something indistinguishable and fell silent, as he moved a straightedge across a chart and nervously checked and rechecked an old aluminum E6B flight computer.

He leaned a little closer to Bailey and pointed to a spot on the chart. "I finally got Nogales, intermittent as hell, out there at about 350 degrees. I pulled in Libby at 020. That's a thin slice I know, but I also got Bisbee at 040—here. There's not squat down here, but run those out and that puts us here—just north of Magdalena. I think that's it just off my wing tip. We oughta swing over to 100 degrees indicated. We'll be on that course, or thereabouts, for a while."

He leaned into the side-window, looking down, then said, "Oh, off my wing again, headlights down below—that has to be the highway south out of Nogales. That makes me a little more comfortable."

Bailey only nodded and asked, "How about altitude? We're cutting a skinny 7,000 ASL now—if you believe the altimeter and the iffy setting we started with." Bailey glanced at Stoudamyre as he was asking and swinging left to the new course.

Stoudamyre responded, "I'd bump it up to 7,500 for now. We'll be passing just to the left of a peak topping 6,700 in just a few—damn! Did you know there's a plane out there half a mile or so? Just there … dammit … don't see it now."

Bailey hit the button again and said, "Yeah. I saw it a couple of lightning flashes ago. Looks like a bizjet of some kind. Seems to be paralleling us … kind of wallowing along slow … no nav lights."

"Mex Airforce?" Stoudamyre asked.

Bailey thought about it a moment and said, "Doubt it, if it was Air Force, they'd have probably stuck one up our stacks a long time ago." He paused for a moment, searching the ever-darkening sky off his wing, and went on, "I'd say we're still flying because someone wants us, or *some* of us, to be flying. If I had to guess, my money would be on our black friend. The rest of us are hardly worth the trouble."

"Whatta we do?"

Bailey grinned and said, "Straight ahead, old buddy, straight ahead—and try our best to avoid those clouds I told you about.

Remember, some might have rocks in them. Do what we do best … OK?"

Stoudamyre leaned toward the small radar screen for a moment, finally straightened up and unbuckled his lap belt. His eyes were still on the small radar screen. "Hmm … we're not high enough to be sure, but it looks like most of the weather is left of our course—out to the edge of radar range anyway." He started to pull himself out of the seat, stopped, and leaned across Bailey's shoulder to stare out the window into the darkness. "Our friend still there?"

"Yeah, caught a glimpse of him a bit ago."

....

Jorgensen sat, collar open, with his chair reclined. Beads of sweat crowned his brow and his face was drained of color. Still, he stared constantly into the dark, trying to make his quarry appear.

Finally, mopping his face with an already soggy handkerchief, he reached for a button on the small console at his right and pushed it. The returning "Yes sir?" was almost immediate.

"You sure they're still there?"

"Why, yes sir. They're about … oh, three-quarters of a mile off our right wing. They are a bit lower that we are, so you probably won't see them unless they get back- lit somehow. They went to a course of about 100 degrees a while ago."

"Uhh, Bud, why are we … ahh, slewing around like this?"

Chapter 15

An angry swarm of senior sheriff's officers crowded closely around Obregon and Simpson, seemingly forestalled from violence only by the large, almost unmarked, business jet trundling across empty end of the tarmac directly toward their waiting place at the transient gate. The Sheriff himself headed the unhappy lot. He'd made up his mind that there was probably nothing the incoming federal agent could do to ease his discontent, no matter which agency he fronted. He had also made up his mind that if any of the agencies represented here were going in pursuit of the people responsible for the death of his officers, someone from his office would be going along, irrespective of *what the incompetent bastards from the Potomac thought.* But even that salving of the vanities would help little; he was sick to his very core. The bloody carnage at the overturned sheriff's cruiser would haunt him all of his days. Jill Ryan was the niece of his oldest friend and, small department that it was, he had shared a long-ago working relationship with Cass. Only his anger kept him from tears.

The jet bounced across a dry and shallow rainwater runoff swale in the tarmac and came to a whining stop at the fence separating the parking ramp and the officers crowded along its opposite side. As the engines began to wind down, a side door swung out and down, stopping just above the cracked and pitted parking surface. A tall and lanky man clad in black and wearing a sidearm high on his left hip stepped down to the ground in two hurried movements and headed toward them.

He paused just across the fence from the group and seemed to look at each one in turn for a moment, then turned back to Obregon and said, "You're Obregon, I think, right?" At Obregon's affirmative nod, he continued, "I'm Barrington. We need to be out of here as soon as they top off the tanks," nodding toward the approaching fuel tanker, "I need a rep from the sheriff's office to go with us—can you arrange that? Oh, and he needs to be someone who can forget he even went."

That surprise seemed to take the wind out of the Sheriff's sails before he'd even had a chance to offer a feeble bluster. He looked both shocked and puzzled. He opened his mouth to say something, but Barrington went on, looking directly at Obregon and ignoring the Sheriff, went on playing to his audience, "We heard about the deputies on the flight down—they'll need someone in on the finish, one way or the other. It's only right. I have room for only one of their men though … he needs to come out of uniform and armed and he needs to be able to make decisions blessed by the department."

The Sheriff finally found words and blurted, "Whoa, back up! Go where? And who the hell are you?" He started to go on, but Barrington raised a hand that, for some reason, stopped him mid-breath. "Look, we haven't got time to discuss this. I'll say this, who I am is not important—but know, without a doubt, I will see that those responsible for the murder of your deputies will not go unpunished. They are in Mexican airspace now—headed to … God only knows, so that makes it tough. There are some issues involved that I cannot discuss and what you *do* find out, you will have to keep quiet. I want one of your men to go with us to see the end of this debacle for himself. That go down OK with you?"

The Sheriff only stared back for a while and then, without any argument turned to Captain Matthews and asked, "How fast can you be in civies?" To Matthews questioning look, he pointed off toward the main terminal and went on, "Get over to the terminal to one of those shops and get something—right now!" Matthews turned and headed across the parking lot at an awkward trot.

He turned back to Barrington and, in a flat, hard tone said, "I'm sending one of my Patrol Captains with you. The deputies were two of his people; don't get him hurt too. We've already lost more than you can imagine today."

There was a short pause as the sheriff thought back over the pain of the losses, then he said, "And know this, if this is just another big brother screw-around, I will make your life a living hell … forever; no matter who you are. I don't care what or who it costs. It is likely none of this would have happened if your little group of know-it-alls had played it straight with us to begin with."

Barrington stood quietly for a moment before going on, "Sheriff, that may well be so, we do have a lot to apologize for in this circle jerk. Within the next few days, likely as soon as tomorrow afternoon, a man named Duncan will probably be here to see you. You will recognize him—I suspect he'll have been all over the papers and television by then. I think he'll explain what's going on here better than I ever could. In the meantime, we need to get out of here."

Barrington turned back to Obregon, "Who's Simpson? I need the both of you on the plane. We'll talk operations on the way south … and, before you ask, *no*, I am not taking over your case. You have your job … and I have mine—they will parallel most of the way from here on out. Come on out to the plane. I've got some written and faxed instructions from our respective hierarchies to give you."

He turned back to the others at the fence, "Excuse us, please, and send your Captain … Matthews … out when he gets back. Hurry him along." He stopped for a moment, looking at the ground and then back up and directly into the eyes of the Sheriff, "Look, I know this is hard to swallow—but, we'll salvage as much of this as possible. You want *vengeance*? We'll give you vengeance in spades." He glanced back at the aircraft and saw one of his men waving the handset from a telephone at him, motioning for him hurry. "Look, I have to go— your Captain will keep in touch as much as possible." He hurried off toward the open door of the aircraft as he eyed the coming darkness and the beginnings of lightning flashes and thunderstorms coming down off the hills on the southern horizon.

The man at the door handed Barrington the handset and retreated out of immediate earshot. Barrington settled himself into a seat opposite the door where he could look out at the activities on the tarmac and, taking a deep breath, pushed the transmit button and started, "Ed, I'll cut to the chase—I assume Will Duncan has at least partially filled you in?"

There was a brief pause, a bit of open-air rush, then a reply in slightly Spanish accented, but perfect English, "Yes, but do you mind if I ask just what the hell is going on?" There was a bit more of the open-mike rush, and he continued, "I have allowed Mr. Jorgensen to, in effect, freely violate our airspace—and ignore the criminal activity of the aircraft he was playing with when he called. This could develop into a major international incident if the wrong people get in the middle of it. Our President will not be happy. If he hears of this, I will spend a long, very long, time in one of our prisons. Do you have any idea of how unpleasant that eventuality would be for me?"

Barrington took advantage of the pause and broke in, and reverting to the formal, "Sir, General Mendez, ah … I know all that—I can only apologize and tell you we will keep you out of this one way or another. You know we have our ways—this could just as easily work out with you becoming something of a real folk hero. Keep an aircraft ready, just in case we need you to pose for the photographers and make a well-timed statement. If things begin to crumble," he paused a second and then lied through his teeth, "we are arranging a soft spot for you to land. I know that is not what you want sir; neither do we. We still need your help and … ah … a blind eye for a bit."

The silence was long and seemed even longer. Finally, "Alright, I will make the right things happen as long as you are in our airspace." There was a slight chuckle, before he went on, "You must understand that you may well have ended the career of General Eduardo Mendez-Sanchez—and that his poor wife and children will be most unhappy with you. Certain *jackals* will love you … but that is not the point at this moment. Now … what do you need?"

"General Mendez, I need to know where you think they are right now … and their general direction of flight. Can you keep your boundary flights off of them for the time being?"

"I can't say where they are going, but they have been generally following a track of about 100, 105—varying to as far southerly as 120 degrees—and," the puzzled tone to his voice increased, "you should know I got that from your own controllers in … right there in Phoenix. You know more about their accuracy than I."

"They should be approaching the edge of that tropical storm that has come in from the Gulf, but, nonetheless, their course has remained relatively consistent. I think their little variance to starboard has been to avoid pieces of the storm. I couldn't even begin to guess where they are going." He paused before asking, "Isn't the range of that DC-3 somewhat limited … particularly with their alleged heavy load and the headwinds they must be hitting?"

There was another short silence before Barrington replied, "I can't be sure, but I believe they left with topped tanks. I know Jorgensen's Grumman did, he fueled up here in Tucson. I've seen fax copies of receipts for that. I'm also just guessing, but I believe the DC-3 is right at gross when it took off. His range will be … well, not so great. We can *guesstimate* that in a minute. I just don't know where they are going— but I'd suspect it is somewhere up on the Gulf side of South America … Colombia or Venezuela maybe. There are some spots there they could off-load without too much interference, given the doper traffic and their relations with local governments of late and all."

"Mr. Barrington, I don't believe the DC-3 could survive the crossing of the Gulf without a fuel stop. I am, shall we say, marginally *acquainted* with Mr. Cooper, one of the passengers *assumed* to be on board. I do know that he has an arrangement of some standing with the, shall we say, *management* at a strip just outside Vera Cruz, Aqua Blanca it is called. The strip would handle the DC-3 … load and all— but that can't be the final destination. It is too far from the sea and in the wrong place for a transatlantic jump-off site. I would suspect they are heading somewhere their load can be transferred to a ship."

Barrington and the copilot, who had now joined him, were looking at the sectional chart that covered that part of Mexico and running out the rough 100–105 degree radial to the coast with a finger. Barrington keyed the handset and replied, "Is there fuel and everything there … at Aqua Blanca?"

"Well, yes … that's what I understand; but if Cooper's boss back in Tucson thinks of it too he can change the welcome there into one that is very uncomfortable for everyone involved. The relationship at the strip has belonged to Mr. Colisimo for much longer than Cooper knows. You will need to deter that eventuality if you can."

"I think I can handle that. Can you keep me up what your people hear and see? I particularly need to know when and where they land to fuel and any changes in course."

"Of course … let me give you a better number for us to talk." And after hurriedly running through the number twice, he broke the connection.

Barrington turned to his pilots and ordered, "Let's get moving … they are way out in front of us. Ah, here comes Matthews now … let me talk to the Sheriff for a minute. What's his name? Mason … that's it, Art Mason. … be right back." He stepped down from the aircraft and headed back to the knot of deputies standing at the fence.

He nodded to Matthews and said, "Better hop on, we're about to pull out … soon as the fuel truck unhooks." He turned to the Sheriff and began his lie with, "Sheriff Mason, I gotta guy down at the Federal building already putting together warrants to search Malette's office and home, Cooper's apartment, as well as Colisimo's home and office. Think you can meld in with his troops and help make that happen— taking as long as possible?"

"You take tactical command. We don't want the asshole interfering with us anywhere down the line. Keep him away from any and all telephones … and who knows? You might find something. I suspect that when we get back he will be getting salted away anyway. My man downtown will probably say it again, but confiscate any and all cash and immediate credit. We don't want him running. If we have to give it back, we'll give it back, *maybe*, sometime next year."

The Sheriff looked back at Barrington with a confused question forming on his lips that never quite made it to words. He'd tried for years to get behind Colisimo's lawyer covered façade. Now, it was to be this easy? Well, he thought, never look a gift horse in the mouth.

The business jet didn't seem so large when they had all crowded on and found seats. There were nine of them: Barrington and two thus far anonymous agents, Obregon, Simpson, Matthews, a wiry, dark-haired woman wearing a black jumpsuit and a headset. The woman was seated at a computer and radio consol just behind the flight deck wall and the two pilots seemed to fill the flight deck to overflowing. Everyone wore sidearms on their belts and several short automatic weapons lay across the only unoccupied seat. Two pump action shotguns and a scoped rifle filled in a rack against the side of the fuselage across from the open side hatch and a number of magazines and ammunition boxes filled a box on the decking next to them.

Barrington motioned for silence, and when he got it, said, "We'll talk this through in a minute, but I have a couple of calls to make first," and he motioned for the radiotelephone. His first call was to a number at the Tucson Federal Building and his conversation was short and almost one-way. "Gil, this is Barrington. I want search warrants put together for Malette's home and office and the same for Colisimo ... and don't forget Cooper. Get it done right now. Hit Colisimo first, hardest and longest. The Sheriff will be there in a few minutes, so hustle. I've told him you were already doing this. Don't let me down."

There was a series of questions from the other end that couldn't be heard by the other passengers, then Barrington spoke again, "Gil ... Gil ... shut the fuck up and listen. No, I don't have what you want. Do it anyhow. I don't care what the reasons are; we have to keep them occupied and off our back. Call Judge Raeburn if you have to. That nit will sign anything and, if he won't, have him talk to Duncan ... and then I can assure you that he will."

"Just get out there and stir the shit. If you can put anyone in jail … even for a few hours … do it. OK? … While you're at it, freeze all his bank accounts, screw with his credit cards, seize his aircraft, tow his cars—anything you think of that will send him running in circles. And, Gil, Sheriff Mason is in tactical command, for a lot of reasons I'm too busy to talk about. Thanks." He abruptly cut off the conversation and shook his head as if he didn't believe what he was doing himself, all the while smiling at what he knew would be Colisimo's anger and bewilderment.

He handed the handset back over his shoulder to the woman at the consol and turned to the men, "Let's get acquainted. My name is Zach Barrington. I generally work for the Director. I kind of … well … bat cleanup. These two guys are Donlevy and Moyer, the lady at the computer is Rivera, and the two pilots are Hawkins and Wallace. All of them are field agents in one capacity or another and, since we're headed south, they speak fluent Spanish—and that's good, because I don't."

"Let's see, you're Dave Simpson, Bureau, and you're Captain … Ross, is it? … Matthews from Pima County, and I've known about you, Mike … a long time."

The cabin door had swung up and closed and almost immediately the whine of engines winding up could be heard and, shortly thereafter, the aircraft began to waddle across the rough tarmac toward the active runway.

Everyone that wasn't occupied with other tasks nodded and reached across between the seats to shake hands and offer a greeting. "I want you guys to know, again, that this is Obregon's file and that we have very different jobs here. His is handling an extremely serious issue, of nothing less than international scope, and mine is … well, damage control. We have a couple of assholes that have stepped across the line—and they are my job. You may not like how that sounds, but the plane is moving now and it is a little too late to get off and walk. More than that, when we get back most of it *will have never happened* … and that's the end of *that*." Matthews and Simpson were the only ones who even changed their expressions.

As if on cue, the nose of the aircraft suddenly rotated upward to a steep angle and bounced into the air, accelerating rapidly. The noise of the runway disappeared behind them quickly and Barrington, pulling a sheaf of papers from a briefcase retrieved from beneath the seat, began to appear almost disinterested and, for the moment, ignored the men around him. He seemed to shuffle the papers into some sort of order before thumbing through them and pausing to read, or re-read, several of them. No one spoke for the few minutes he consumed with that task, each man staring at him and waiting for instructions, a comment, any sort of indication of what would happen next.

He finally looked up from the papers, which could then be seen to have small 4X6 inch photographs clipped to each page's upper left corner. "Let's talk about who we are after here, OK? Everybody knows who Jorgensen is—anybody need a refresher? No? Well, just to clear the air—and for your information particularly Captain, he is a Deputy Director at the Agency ... runs operations. It looks like he's gone sideways on us."

He paused for a moment, pulling two other sheets of paper out onto his lap, "These are the guys flying the aircraft. Y'know, I think they are victims of circumstance more than anything else. We have no real interest in them and certainly have no desire to hurt them— unless necessary."

Barrington looked at the forms for a long moment then passed them across the aisle to Obregon. "Look them over and pass them on. These guys are not part of either faction involved in this. Bailey, the older of the two, has been flying, oh, since Christ was a corporal is my guess. Of late, as his fortunes kind of went south, he has flown some flights that could get him jail time, but most of the time he has just stuck to the only business he knows: flying."

We interviewed some folks at the V.A. this afternoon late. If they are right, Bailey is about to hit the wall—he has inoperable stomach cancer." He shook his head, with a bit of sadness showing and went on, "The guy has an ex-wife and daughter—back in Virginia. Roanoke ... I think—where he grew up. Our guys there said she just broke down and cried when she found out he was really sick." She hasn't seen him in over ten years. You know, he has been flying since before World War II. God! He has flown everywhere from hell to breakfast in anything with wings. He is facing a crappy way to go out."

Obregon passed the form and photo on to Simpson, as he asked Barrington, "What about this other guy … Stoudamyre?"

"Bailey picked him up some years back during a stint in that airline we never owned, *Air America*. Until a week ago, Stoudamyre was teaching wannabes how to fly right back there in Tucson. Don't sell him short though—FAA says he has about 3,500 hours in DC-3s just like the one they are in now, a lot more in other stuff. Air Force gave him a Silver Star back in '70, one before that in '66 and three Bronze Stars … and a buncha Air Medals. They also say the son-of-a-bitch is a little nuts—and can be goddamn dangerous if the reason is right."

He looked down at the floor for a bit, and then looked Obregon straight in the eyes, "Hell, guys, these guys are only a complication—they are *not* the bad guys. Remember, I don't want to hurt them if we can avoid it."

He paused, then flipped the form containing Mobutu's photo out and handed it to Obregon, "And neither is this guy—he is just trying to help haul his dirty little country out of the dark ages." He looked hard at each man seated around the aircraft's cabin, then said, "You guys may not understand or like this, but, I intend to keep this man alive and get his ass out of the country, along with the pitiful little load of shit he has collected and I don't care where it came from. You can all read the story on this man—he is actually an honest-to-God hero. Not just to his people in Liberia, the Brits say he is one hell of a fine soldier and wish he was still with them. I don't know how this got fucked up, but I have directions to give him all the as close to *invisible* help I can muster. I, *we*, will do just that"

Barrington let that sink in before moving on to the last sheets and photographs. "This is a guy who has been in the Mob since he was in his early twenties. Obregon knows him and can fill you in more.

All I know is that he came down from Chicago several years ago and the other guy is his buddy, He is kinda stupid, but tough. They are … well … *expendable*."

He looked directly into Matthew's eyes and said, "It would be nice to have Cooper brought back to roll over on Colisimo if possible though. That would cure some of the irritation between the local law, the Bureau, and us. I have an idea that there is a connection between them and the deputies. It's rumored that wetback they found dead out there belongs to Cooper … and that isn't really his name."

"The last guy is Kirkpatrick … he does what we say we don't do. Do not, under any circumstances, sell this man short—he is one tough cookie … and is an old fashioned hitter that can use any piece ever made. Whatever you do though, remember that the man to watch is Mobutu. Head on, he is a killer. That makes the first few seconds of contact critical. We have to get across to him that he's not our target."

Barrington sat there quietly for a while, letting the others digest the information contained in the documents being passed around. Finally he collected all the material and pushed it back into the briefcase. "There is a lot we don't know: Who killed the Mexican the sheriff found with the deputies and, really, who killed the deputies are at the top of the list of unknowns. We think the wetback did it … but, who knows? Somebody sure as hell did that son of a bitch in hard. He had three holes in him—big holes." He sat there for a short moment, then mused on, "Cooper, or whatever you want to call him, works for Colisimo … 'bout two tiers down. He reported to Malette until a few hours ago … with a few side ventures of his own. He is tough, resourceful, but not in Kirkpatrick's or Mobutu's league; even though he probably thinks he is. We are pretty sure why Mobutu is here and where the stuff came from he is hauling—is there any more? Maybe."

"I hear that someone has been down in Argentina, Paraguay and parts south buying up some excess Czech crap and additional stuff they have made down there on license. It is hard to tell how much they might have on hand to sell. I hear … but don't know for sure … there is at least enough to fill the DC-6 that the guy down south already has … all small stuff … rifles, pistols, light machineguns, and things like that. The guy gathering up the stuff is another man cut from Mobutu style of cloth—works for him in fact. They could be a problem when … and if … we ever get face-to-face with them and if it turns hostile—so you'd better hope it doesn't."

No one had responded to Barrington yet and they were a good half-hour into the flight. Simpson finally broke the silence, "So … where are we going? And, like it or not, this is kind of out of my league … probably Matthews' too."

"Well … one thing at a time. I am not sure … yet … just where the hell we are going. That depends on them. Of course, after talking to Mendez, I have a suspicion they may be using Aqua Blanca as a refueling stop—if they use what Cooper's familiar with. We do have a course and a projected range of the most critical aircraft—that of the DC-3." He turned to the woman at the computer and radio console and asked for a packet of charts, which she shuffled out of a stack of papers and other charts on the deck beside her and handed to him.

He looked back at the men before focusing on the charts. "You're wondering how I know all of this so soon after every thing went down—right? Well, the simple answer is that not two electronic transmissions in all of Arizona have gone unmonitored today. As to the backgrounds on these people … hell, that took about thirty seconds." He smiled and then said, "Ah, yes, Big Brother is ever amongst us …"

He seemed to lapse into thought for a moment before spreading one of the charts out across his knees and beginning intensely study it and mark out distances with a rule. After a few minutes, he opened another and spread it across the first chart. Finally, he said, "Well, give or take a few, it is about twelve-hundred miles from where they took off to Aqua Blanca. They are loaded to the gills and taking on a headwind that isn't helping much. I'd suspect they would splash down short of landfall if they ignored a fuel stop"

"So-o, at about, let's say, a ground speed of maybe 140–145, yes, let's go high and cut directly for Aqua Blanca." He shook his head bemusedly and said, "You know, that old beast could actually go about twenty-five-hundred miles with a load if the conditions were right? Damn!" He turned and nodded to the man beside him, who moved to the open doorway between cabin and flight. He pushed the chart into the copilot's hands and they could be seen talking for a minute, then the aircraft began a slight bank to the right and abruptly started to climb steeply.

Barrington seemed to relax and slide down into the seat and drop into instant sleep. He suddenly blinked open and smiled, "Just sit back guys, we have a couple of hours to rest. You'll need it. Wonder what is happening to old man Colisimo 'bout now?" He chuckled, and then dropped back into the eyes-closed pretend-sleep. By the time the aircraft leveled off at 23,000 feet, he really was asleep, leaving his companions to stare at him in disbelief.

. . . .

T HE DARKNESS HAD GROWN ALMOST blue-black, making the long line of headlights winding their way up from the valley floor even more visible. Colisimo watched them approach for a few disquieting minutes before turning to his ever-present valet. "Cops. It has to be. Lots of them. Damn!" He shrugged on a dark-blue blazer on, moved to the large desk fronting the window and removed a small Walther .380 automatic from the top middle drawer and pushed it into his belt.

He quickly pulled open the large file drawer on the lower right of desk, tweaked a combination built into the metal drawer-top and pulled out a large packet of cash still carrying bank wrapers. As he moved about the room, gathering a cane, his hat and a flashlight, he hurriedly gave instructions to the valet.

"Marion, call Doctor Wallis, tell him to arrange a stay at any local and credible hospital. Let's say the issue is … oh, heart problems. Have him meet me where the trail over the ridge comes out on the gravel road that goes up to the water tank. He's been there … he'll know."

The valet was quiet, only nodding. Colisimo went on, "Tell the cops I was sick … went to town to see the Doc real early … you just don't know which one. Just let them hunt, OK? Take care of things. Don't get yourself in trouble resisting them—there's nothing here for them to find that they will recognize."

At the valet's continued nod, Colisimo walked off down the hall toward the back door opening onto the yard and pool. As he opened the door, a blinding light struck his eyes, illuminating the startled and dismayed look spreading across his face.

Two pleasant-faced, almost laughing, young men in police jump suits stood just at the edge of the light staring across the top of shotguns pointed directly at his chest. They looked as if they could hardly contain their mirth. Three Dobermans lay behind them, the tranquilizer darts that had silenced them lost from sight in the gloom. One of the young men wore a dark blue jump suit with the letters DEA stamped across the left chest pocket in yellow; the other was in dark green and had an embroidered sheriff's badge on the chest of his suit.

The deputy spoke first, almost in a chuckle, "Why, Mr. Colisimo, fancy meeting you here. It has been a while, hasn't it? Mind if we come in?" and he didn't wait for the invitation as Colisimo backed away from the advancing shotgun.

As they entered the door, the valet suddenly entered the hallway from a door to a small office. He couldn't see everything immediately and began to speak, "Mr. Colisimo, the tele …" and he froze at seeing the shotguns—one of which was now pointed at him.

"Telephone problems, *Marion*?" The deputy laughed then said, "Gee … maybe the line is down." the word *Marion* had come out in a mocking tone. The side-cutters in a flashlight pocket along his right leg gave mute testimony that the lines were indeed down.

The men were pushed back into the large front room of the home and motioned toward a low couch. "Sit … not you *Marion* … you get a search first. And, Mr. Colisimo, don't think I missed that dinky little pistol you have in your belt—relieve him of that, will you Jake?" When the frisk of Marion turned up another small automatic holstered in the small of his back, the deputy continued the taunt, and "You need this to serve tea, do you *Marion*? Must be rough tea parties."

He looked almost disappointed when the front door swung open and Sheriff Mason crossed into the light. Even he had a certain amused look on his face.

He ushered in some ten other officers in the various field uniforms of the agencies involved in the operation and then slowly walked across the room to face Colisimo. "Mr. Colisimo, this is a search warrant. Relax—we are going to be here a while. We can talk about old times later." At that he turned to the group of officers, "Alright, don't miss a thing—get to it … and grab every computer, file, safe, piece of paper, and address book you can find. Don't forget the trash cans."

The deputies and federal agents spread out throughout the large mansion and began to literally take the place apart.

Colisimo glared at the Sheriff for at least five minutes before speaking, "Sheriff, this is bullshit and you know it. I want my lawyer— and I am a sick man. Call my doctor."

"I'll just bet you are … and you'll get your lawyer … when I get around it. And fuck your doctor—I don't care if you croak right here on the fancy carpet."

....

ALL ACROSS THE CITY AND COUNTY, other raids had begun at exactly the same time the officers entered Colisimo's home. One raiding party entered the offices of the deceased Carlo Malette, another brought everything at J.D.S. to a halt and still another kicked down the door of the now absent Roy Cooper.

Sheriff Mason could only smile. One of the fools at J.D.S. had actually pulled out a handgun and tried to stop the raiding party. He was hauled away in a Medical Examiner's meat wagon and his demise only added to the indigestion that Colisimo suffered as he awaited a bevy of lawyers—some who would not be available as they would be sitting in adjoining cells and clamoring for their own lawyers. Within minutes, the trail of file cabinets, computers and employees were winding their way to the curbed vans and, later, on to the evidence and interrogation rooms of the Sheriff's main station.

. . . .

THE AIRCRAFT HAD BEEN ABOVE THE STORM and at cruise for less than half an hour when the husky young man who had been in quiet conversation with the copilot returned to nudge Barrington awake. He sat down at Barrington's left and laid out a chart across both their knees and began pointing at several sites toward the southeast of their position. Their conversation was quiet and in guarded monotones for a while, then the young man got up and moved back toward the flight deck entrance.

Barrington stared at the chart for a few more moments, then looked up at the rest of the men in the cabin. "Well, it looks like we were right about where they might stop for fuel."

"Here, take a look," and he swung the chart around for them to read.

"That old DC-3, according to the folks that ought to know, could go a lot further under better conditions. It still couldn't safely jump the Gulf though. They are fighting some significant turbulence and a hell of a headwind at their altitude. Combine the both of them and you have a need to stop at the corner gas station. Our folks monitoring their radio transmissions say they have made radio contact with some private radio in Aqua Blanca and asked for permission to land and refuel. Of course, the people on the ground there didn't know any better and OK'd it."

Obregon thought a second, grimaced and asked, "But doesn't that ace us out? I mean, Jorgensen is right on top of them. We sure as hell can't get there soon enough to make any difference."

"The General seems to have taken care of that for us. He got on the hook with Jorgensen and made sure he understood that absolutely nothing was going to happen on his turf. Jorgensen apparently bit on that." He grinned and shook his head, "Nobody is easier to con than a con."

He turned back to the chart and traced a line southwest from Aqua Blanca to a place titled *Pachuca*. "The General helped a bit more. He saw to it that Jorgensen and company were offered a refueling stop at a military strip about forty or fifty miles to the southwest of Aqua Blanca, provided he got in and out in half an hour. The thirty-minute timeline makes it look like he is trying to hurry them out of his airspace. It'll actually take longer than that by probably another thirty minutes. That oughta tie Jorgensen's shorts in a knot. All things going smoothly, that should get the '3 in and out of Aqua Blanca and put us a lot closer. It will still be tight."

Obregon stared hard at the chart for a while before saying, "looks rough around there. No room for mistakes." As an afterthought, he asked, "You don't suppose Colisimo has put the word out on Cooper, before we got a raid in on him and that the crew here at the airport has gotten wind of it, do you?"

Barrington pursed his lips in thought for a bit, shook his head and said, "No, probably not. Nodding toward the young man at the entryway to the flight deck, "He says our folks in Tucson have Colisimo and everyone even close to him tied up in search warrants. There might even be something there to find. They actually caught old man Colisimo trying to sneak out—on foot, of all things."

"I'd expect the sheriff is enjoying himself. He's had a hard-on for Colisimo for years," Simpson added grinning. "That about right Cap?" as he elbowed the Sheriff's Captain in the ribs.

Matthews only grinned and commented, "I wish I'd been there—should have been interesting."

Barrington nodded and turned toward the man leaning into the door of the flight deck, "Donlevy, he kicking this thing in the ass? How far out are we?"

The young man turned back to the men on the flight deck for a few words before moving back toward the seat alongside Barrington, "We're maybe an hour back and he's standing on it hard."

He paused and his expression changed to that of someone bringing up bad news. "In case you haven't noticed it, things are getting a bit bumpy. We're flying right into the corner of that storm. We need to slow down some to take the turbulence better. What do you have in mind for when we do get there?"

"Well ... our Mexican associate does not want an incident on his turf. Can't say I blame him, they've got something of a border war going on with the dopers on one side and DEA on the other and him right there in the middle. Hmmm ... looking at the timing, I'd say we should back off and let them get airborne again. Tell the pilot to 360 off to the left and stay out of range of Jorgensen's radar."

"OK—but, at the risk of being repetitive, do you have any ideas on how we'll handle this?"

Barrington offered a slight smile before saying, "Not yet—really, except that it won't be pretty. It depends on where they're going. We won't know anything about that until they break the coastline. Even then, it will be a guess. I'd suspect their course after leaving Aqua Blanca, particularly after crossing the coastline, should point roughly, I hope, at their next landing site."

Simpson arched an eyebrow and glanced sideways at Obregon, then said to Barrington, "We'd better have *some* kind of an idea where this will end up pretty soon and what we'll do about it."

"OK—but how? Anything right now is just a guess. We can assume, and safely, I think, that they're not heading anywhere else in Mexico for their off-load site. Honduras? Maybe. Guatemala? Maybe. Belize? Probably not. My guess is that we won't really know until they break out into the Gulf. I can only guess they're heading somewhere along the coast of Venezuela or Colombia. And that's just a dumb-ass guess,but, Cooper has been piddling around in the narco-trafficking world and has ... friends ... in Colombia. But, we don't know if he's actually running things anymore. I'm surprised he is even on board.

I'd bet Mobutu is the big guy now and we have no idea what his plans are. He does have someone down there buying more guns though."

When no one immediately responded, he pointed toward the firearms on the back row of seats and terminated the conversation with, "There—you'd better check out those toys before we have to use them—and, please, no holes in the aircraft. I borrowed it from a rich uncle."

....

Bailey could feel his arms tiring and sweat soaking his clothes, both a result of the struggle to maintain heading and altitude in the strong turbulence and a quartering wind. The burning pain in his belly made all that secondary. Finally, unable to stay focused on the aircraft, he reached for Stoudamyre's arm and, with his attention, signaled for him to fly *The Rose*. He sank back into the seat and closed his eyes for a few painful seconds before reaching for the small amber bottle of pills in the leg pocket of his coveralls. This was the first time he had not hidden the pills from everyone—including Stoudamyre. He popped two into his mouth—not one this time –and washed them down with a splash of water from a bottle he'd kept lodged between the seat and pedestal base.

The pills would take a few minutes before they washed him in a slight nausea and lifted him above the pain. He knew he was trading physical control of his body for less pain but it was a necessary compromise. He had a bad feeling about the stop at Aqua Blanca and he had to be ready for it.

Bailey knew Stoudamyre was watching and he turned to face his quizzical expression. "I'm sorry I got you into this mess without telling you everything first. I know I said there was more time—I lied." He stopped for a few seconds before going on, "Hurts like hell, but we have to finish this flight. It is all I have left."

Stoudamyre didn't respond for a bit, seeming to be involved in the bouncing of the instruments on the panel. Finally, he moved the switch on the mike control to intercom and asked, "We need to get you to a hospital once we hit the ground?"

"No—there is nothing a hospital could do. We have to play this through the way it is. Bill, I hate to admit this, even to myself, but I think you already know … time is a commodity I am really short on right now. I need just one more money trip. There won't be any more. I probably won't be able to go back with you … one way or the other."

Stoudamyre opened his mouth to speak, seemed to think better of it, and turned back to stare out into the darkness. Bailey could see his eyes tearing and heard him sniff a few times. After a bit Stoudamyre keyed the mike again and said, "We're twenty minutes out—what's the strip look like? Dammit, it's beginning to rain …"

Bailey replied, "Just a minute …" and began to dig through his flight bag.

In what seemed only a few minutes, they could see a twin row of lights marking the short runway at Aqua Blanca. The wind was gusting in from the right front quarter and the rain was becoming heavier. Bailey knew he didn't have to say it, but he did anyhow, "You want to be careful with the approach, Bill, you've got a piss-poor balanced and heavy load on old *Rose*. Keep her a little above the numbers if you can. We may have to go around."

Stoudamyre only nodded and kept boring ahead to split the lights. About two minutes out he keyed the mike again, "Our escort crossed over us a few minutes ago, headed southwest. I hope these fucks here are friendly."

Chapter 16

STOUDAMYRE PULLED THE NOSE OF 392 DELTA to a point just above the horizon as he flew her harder than he wanted onto the rough-surfaced runway and into spattering showers driven by the winds. Even then, the hard landing had a feeling of comfort and safety. He smiled and had just let the tail wheel come down to touch the asphalt when he was suddenly panicked as the runway lights flicked off. He started to slam the throttles against the stops and pull up and off of the runway but, before he could act, lights on the back of a pickup truck about half way down the runway bloomed with a large, yellow-lighted, *Follow me*. The truck sped up for a short distance and then bounced to the right onto a narrow taxiway and almost immediately began to slow.

Stoudamyre could just see dim, ground level, lights outlining the taxiway-runway intersection and stood on hard the right brake, swinging the already slowing *The Rose* onto the taxiway and following the lighted truck. The headlights of the pickup truck illuminated a low building with several other aircraft of various vintages parked in front of it. As he drew nearer, he could see a number of men, perhaps a dozen, scattered in front of the building. Most of the men had rifles slung across their shoulders. There was nothing about them that looked even remotely friendly.

A man in coveralls waving orange-coned flashlights waited near the end of the taxiway and motioned *The Rose* into a wide slot between a faded Convair and an early model Beech twin with both a missing prop on its starboard side and at least one flat tire. As *The Rose* pulled was into the space, he signaled for the engines to be cut. Stoudamyre began shutting the aircraft down and was conscious that Bailey had not said a word during the last of the landing process and the taxi to what passed for a terminal. He could see that the men in front of the terminal were moving their rifles from shouldered to cradled positions and that they were slowly moving toward the aircraft.

The two pilots sat still for a moment, watching the props tick to a stop, then one at a time they pulled their way off *The Rose's* flight deck and moved down the aisle between the packing crates to the side hatch. The space was almost without sound. Stoudamyre rotated the handle and pushed the hatch open, then dropped down to the rough and cracked tarmac as he warily eyeing the armed men edging in out of the building's dim light.

He watched as a slight man, silhouetted against the dim light, began a slow shuffling walk from the ramshackle building. He paused and stepped stiffly down from the low porch and pushed his way through the small throng of rifle carrying men. The man straightened a little and headed slowly toward him in a limping swagger, returning his silent stare. Stoudamyre remembered that the small revolver was still in the map case on the flight deck and that he'd left the machine pistol beside Mobutu. He muttered a profanity to no one in particular, knowing the little 5-shot pistol would be of no use against the rifles anyway.

The storm was moving in rapidly and a blast of rain and wind caused Stoudamyre to lean toward the man, squinting to keep him in focus. The thin, disheveled, man, dark and greasy, did not look friendly. Without taking his eyes from him, Stoudamyre reached back and slapped the metal decking near the open hatch hoping he had someone's attention, he growled, "Cooper—Cooper, get down here. You're supposed to know these assholes."

He heard Cooper mutter a quiet "OK" behind him and the sound of his dropping onto the ground. Stoudamyre jibed quietly, "Maybe you can get rid of Jess here too—huh?"

"Fuck you … flyboy … not here. We need to just get in and out of here. Fast."

"I say again, big shot, you know these … uh … assholes?"

"Each and every one of them—and you best stick to business or it'll be you that gets buried here … maybe all of us."

The dark and slight man had now entered the circle of dim light now spilling out of the open hatch. He was more than slight—he was a thin rail of a man, dark and dirty, dressed in a damp, limp, and once off-white linen suit. He did have a badge of office though: a large-framed and shiny automatic that he made sure was visible, stuffed very handily into the front of his belt.

He stopped and stood there for a bit, looking Stoudamyre and Cooper over in mock amusement. Finally, brushing the limp jacket farther back from the automatic, he focused on Cooper and asked, "Ah … Mister Cooper … what can we … uhh … do for you? 'S funny, I was talking to Mister C about you—and he got cut off. Real sudden. Wonder what was on his mind? Anythin' you can tell me 'bout that … huh? What say, Mr. Cooper.?" The "Mister" was emphasized in a way to make the word an insult.

Cooper did not bite on the push by the man, he launched into what might have passed for everyday business talk but for the stress edging his voice. "Couldn't tell you Tony, but it's good to see you. We need to gas this old hog up and get the hell out of here. We are late with a … delivery. Can you give us a hand?" The last unintentionally sounded almost as a plea.

The rail-thin Mexican moved closer to the open hatch, but it had suddenly gone black inside and he could see little, if anything. There was movement though and it was obvious that he sensed it. "What you hauling, Mr. Cooper? … an' why the hurry-up stop here. Mus' be important to fly the stuff yourself … in this weather." He nodded to the black of the rainy sky and gave a little shrug. He stared at Cooper and, alternately, the open hatch of the aircraft, then turned back toward the men behind him and yelled in Spanish for a flashlight.

Cooper wished for one of the guns on the aircraft and stepped between the open hatch and the skinny Mexican. "Tony, this is my haul—nothing you'd be interested in. Just get me some gas, huh?"

He turned back to Cooper and offered a one-sided and mirthless grin and said, "I'm interested in everythin', Mr. Cooper, everythin'. That's what your boss pays me for," and he reached for the flashlight that a tall, swarthy man with a Yankees baseball cap on held out to him. The skinny Mexican never managed to get turned all the way back around. His head jerked at more movement in the aircraft's open hatch and his hand dropped to the automatic in his belt and he began to fall into a crouch. That was the beginning of the end.

A sudden flash and rattle of gunfire erupted from the open hatch with nerve wrenching suddenness. It came in swift and short two and three shot bursts and was joined by the rhythmic booming crack of a large caliber pistol. The men closest to the open hatch were sent reeling and groveling onto the tarmac. Some of the men nearest the terminal building brought their rifles up, thought better of it, tossed them to the ground and scurried off into the darkness or hurriedly raised their hands in surrender.

Stoudamyre scrambled on his knees to the blank-faced Mexican's body, reached down and pulled the shiny automatic from his dead hand and brought it up toward the fleeing men as he eared the hammer back to fire. It was all over with before he could even fire a shot.

The silence was almost as startling as the sudden hammering of the shots had been. Cooper pushed himself upright, but just stood there, still breathless in sudden and consuming fear. In mere seconds, half a dozen men lay on the worn tarmac. Some did not move. The remaining men had either fled into the night or were in front of the ramshackle terminal building, hands still above their heads and their rifles on the ground at their feet. They no longer looked menacing, just scared and filthy. The silence was unnatural and even the rain stopped as if on unspoken command.

The lights inside the belly of *The Rose* blinked on again and Mobutu moved into view at the mouth of the open hatch. He was silent as he pushed another magazine into his machine pistol and looked over the scene in front of him. Finally, he gave Stoudamyre a nod toward the still fear-frozen men near the front of the building. "Get the rest of them over by the porch and police up those rifles. Give them a quick search for pistols. Hurry up … move! … you too, Mr. Cooper."

He pulled the bolt on his machine pistol, tossed the empty magazine back into the dimness behind him and jumped down from the aircraft. He immediately strode to the door of the small, dimly lighted building and booted it open, then followed the barrel of his machine pistol through the opening.

A pale and sweating fat man, obviously not Mexican, stared at him with wide and frightened eyes. He had a telephone pressed to his ear. Motutu motioned with the barrel of his machine pistol for him to put it down and the man slowly returned the telephone to its cradle. With Mobutu's nod toward the door, the fat man scurried past Mobutu, crabbing sideways to avoid contact as he went by. The stench of sweat and fear followed in his wake. He hurried on out the door and crowded in with the prisoners now under Porteros' gun as Stoudamyre and Cooper began trying to get the refueling process started.

For once, everyone did as ordered—in a military-like precision. In only minutes, the fuel truck was under the starboard wing and gas was being pumped into that side's fuel tank.

Bailey hadn't moved when Mobutu came back to the hatch. He sat hunched up against the open side of the hatch, silent and seemingly pre-occupied and lost in another place. He looked frail and old beyond his years. In truth, he was struggling to stay conscious. The pain in his gut had long ago exceeded the pills' ability to push it away into the darkness at the corners of his soul. He kept his mind busy with the routine of reloading the magazine from the .45 with fresh rounds gathered from a side pocket on his flight suit.

Mobutu stood there a while, taking in someone who had become much more than he first imagined. He reached out and grasped Bailey's shoulder and quietly said, "Thank you, Mr. Bailey. I appreciate your help. You do surprise me. You are a handy man with that old pistol."

He stopped for a moment and in what seemed real concern, asked, "You do look ill. Is there anything I can do?" He stared at Bailey for a while longer then went on, "I believe it is more than this little unpleasantness—yes?" There was care and sympathy in his face.

Bailey took a while answering, finally he quietly spoke, "Yeah … not your problem though. I'll get you to …"

Mobutu quietly interrupted, "Mr. Bailey—I am sorry. I have wondered about this all along. At first, I thought it was the heat and perhaps the alcohol—then I saw what you thought you were hiding … the pills. This is serious." The last was a statement, not a question.

"About as serious as it gets," Bailey replied so quietly he was scarcely heard.

"Hmmm … I was afraid of that. We need to discuss this—without other ears at hand … and after we get out of here. Please, rest until we are ready to go." He turned away as he saw the fuel truck moving up under the port wing. Things were moving well and he knew they would be airborne in a few scant minutes. He began to feel a small bit of hope begin to grow.

He turned back to Bailey, "We can talk once we are back in the air … perhaps? Possibly there is something I can arrange that might help for a while."

Bailey merely nodded an affirmative reply and continued to stuff rounds into the magazine in clumsy and distracted determination.

The rain and wind returned with an unwelcome vigor just as Stoudamyre capped the tank on the port wing. "We're not totally topped off—but I'd hate to use what is in the bottom of the tank and, besides, it'll get us where we need to go. … Hope we kept the rain out."

He jumped down to the ground from the trailing edge of the wing and motioned for Cooper to drive the rusted and weathered tanker away. He moved on around to where Bailey still sat in the open hatch of the aircraft, leaning against the cold metal edge of the door. He noticed that Bailey's eyes had brightened and he seemed more attentive to the activity around him.

"You gonna be able to help me get *The Rose* back in the air"

Bailey replied with the best humor he could muster "Yeah, sure, sonny boy, I wouldn't be this tired if I didn't spend so much time looking after your sorry ass … help me up."

Stoudamyre didn't laugh. His face was set and grim. He shook his head slowly, before turning back to look at the small group of men being guarded by the mechanic and saw Mobutu waving him toward the aircraft. He watched as the mechanic ran toward the aircraft through a passing squall and then pulled himself up into onto the metal decking and helped Bailey to his feet. He could see the men from in front of the terminal building running off into the dark, probably very glad to just be alive.

He could also see the fat man back inside the building, barely visible in the dim light. He had the telephone against his head and he was motioning wildly toward the aircraft. He nodded toward the building and the man as Mobutu climbed back into the aircraft. Mobutu looked back at the man and shook his head.

"He's probably already told whoever he needs to … so let it go."

"I don't give a damn about that—pop a few in his direction so he won't turn off the few runway lights we have. I had to look all over the place to find the switch and get them on in the first place."

Mobutu nodded and loosed a long burst from the machine pistol into the front of the terminal. The fat man disappeared from view and runway lights stayed on.

There was no preflight. They just cranked up *The Rose*, trundled her back onto the runway and climbed into the worsening storm.

....

Jorgensen's Grumman, still coupled to a faded red GMC fuel tanker, sat on the hanger side of a wide concrete parking ramp that also supported a long row of Mexican Air Force fighter jets, prop-driven transports and training aircraft. The ground crew refueling the jet seemed to be incessantly busy with little tasks here and there and the process of getting the tanks topped off was taking an inordinate amount of time. That had finally soaked in on Jorgensen and his temper went red hot. His patience was already strained with the loss of contact with the DC-3 and her crew, not to mention having to cope with the tail end of an airsickness bout, and he began the uncontrollable flare into a rage.

He brushed by the coverall clad Sergeant running the ramp and refueling process and went straight to the scrambled radiotelephone on the desk in front of his seat. He could see the refueling still going on ever so slowly outside the window as he punched in the series of number that would ordinarily ring on General Mendez's desk. There was no answer—ten rings and there was no answer.

Jorgensen felt the first pangs of being trapped. He was being played for the fool and felt it. He slammed the handset back into its cradle and lunged for the open hatch, yelling at his crew as soon as he poked his shoulders through the opening.

"You—get us loose from that tanker—get the fuck back in here and let's get out of here—now!" His voice was up a tight and unnatural step and harsher in tone than normal and it sounded odd, even to him, but his anger was too visible for those around him to resist. The pilot shoved one of Jorgensen's khaki-clad little lapdogs toward the Mexican military refueling the Grumman and turned back toward the remaining crew and passengers lounging on the fence between ramp and parking lot, waving them back toward the aircraft. They immediately began to scramble toward the aircraft, brushing aside a young soldier at the gate. He verbally protested but did not bring his rifle into play to stop them.

The Mexican at the fuel truck shrugged his lack of English to Jorgensen's excited aide but immediately began to unhook the hose and grounding cable from the Grumman. A closer look would have revealed a slight smile. The rest of the ramp crew just stood and watched, the same humor playing across their faces. The crew did a hurried walk-around in preparation for engine start-up.

No one offered to stop them as they began the swaying and hurried taxi to the active runway. As they neared the end of the long asphalt strip, a youngish-looking Air Force Colonel stepped out of a door in the building below the tower and stood watching, still keeping to the shadows. He quietly watched as they turned onto the active and began their takeoff roll and then turned and went back to the telephone on a desk just inside the door. He punched the single lighted button on the telephone base and, nodding to no one that could see him, spoke into the mouthpiece, "They are outbound, General. No—no incident. We stalled them almost an additional half an hour. Yes. Thanks."

His General was happy and that brought a smile to the Colonel's face as he hung up the telephone and stepped back to the door to watch the Grumman climbing to the northeast and a bank of darkening clouds. He wasn't sure what these Americans were doing—and he was absolutely positive that he didn't want to know.

At the other end of that short conversation, General Eduardo Mendez-Sanchez stared off into space for a while before hanging up the telephone and nodding to the middle-aged Captain waiting across the desk. "Make sure any record of that telephone call goes away—and get me Mr. Barrington on the line." A thoughtful look crossed his face and he raised a hand to stop the Captain, "No, wait a minute—get Mr. Duncan first."

He shook his head in mock amusement, "Pepe, do you know anyone more ill-equipped to play these silly games than the Americans? They are—a pain in the ass." He sat in silence for a moment and then saw the light on his telephone blink on. He looked up at the Captain, now across the large office at a bank of telephones and radio transceiver stations and saw him nod. He reached for the telephone.

"Director Duncan," deliberately using the title Duncan only wished he held, "… ah, it is so good to talk to you again."

"General … and what is happening with our little … problem?"

"Mr. Jorgensen is back airborne again. I can only assume he is trying to get back onto our grubby little DC-3's tail again. I am about to notify your man Barrington of this. I thought I would inform you first—just in case you have any additional information or requests. So, … what would Washington like from me now?"

"General, I am not in Washington—and have not been for some time. I am just coming out over the Gulf as we speak. I must be there when this ends—wherever and whenever that happens. I have … additional resources for Mr. Barrington and crew."

"Sir … this is not to happen on Mexican soil, under any circumstances. Do you understand that? I already have word that there was some sort of shooting where the DC-3 refueled. I cannot have any more."

"Patience, General, you cannot believe they are headed anywhere in Mexico. I think you should let Barrington know what has transpired. I doubt it would serve any purpose to tell him that I am also headed his way. He probably already knows though; he is most resourceful."

"As you wish, Director Duncan. Just remember what I said. I cannot tolerate any, shall we say, *unacceptable* actions on my turf. You know the outcome of anything like that." He hung up the handset and nodded to his aide, "Now get Barrington's aircraft on the line for me, will you please?"

The call from Mendez came just as Barrington's pilot had completed another left hand 360-degree turn and was finding smoother air away from the towering cumulus and flashing lightning of the storm forging its way in from the Gulf. The call was brief, only indicating that the old DC-3 was again airborne and headed toward the coast. Mendez gave a last position report for the aged aircraft and warned him that the weather would worsen—and soon.

Just before breaking the connection he dropped a more troubling warning. Mendez almost too casually offered that Barrington needed to know that not only was Jorgensen out bound from his refueling and headed for the DC-3's track, but that Duncan was headed his way and with *help*, as he so neutrally had put it, and they were, he added, at that moment out over the Gulf, some distance south of Houston.

They were, he believed, running above the eastern part of the storm and on a south by southwest course that should put him somewhere east of where the DC-3 should clear the coast. He closed with, "There are enough of you people out there milling around the in dark to need angels directing traffic." He had also included that Duncan had asked him not to tell Barrington that he was inbound. He smiled at his mischief and cut the connection.

Barrington thought about that information for a very long and quiet minute, then shrugged and turned toward the other men seated in the cabin. He seemed startled to suddenly notice the copilot still crouched silently in the aisle beside him, awaiting directions. Barrington stared off into space, mulling over the information just received from Mendez, before turning to the man. "'scuse me, get Rivera back here and crowd 'round." The gathering took only a few seconds and he began again, "Mobutu and company are back in the air."

The aircraft bounced a few times in the turbulence and, with the weight of its occupants changing positions, a couple of the passengers took on the slightly green hue of airsickness. Barrington enjoyed, but ignored, their discomfort.

"As I said, the DC-3 is back in the air. Rivera, see if you can have the pilot pick them up on the scope. Be aware that Jorgensen is also airborne again. See if you can come up with some sort of plan to keep beyond his radar for a while." He turned his attention back to the others seated around him.

"It looks like they are swinging more easterly … say 100 degrees … or so. On this course, they should break the coast in 110 or 120 nautical miles—somewhere around here," pointing at the chart he held across his knees, "about 20 miles up the coast from Vera Cruz. That will put them out over the Bay of Campeche. If they keep that heading, they make landfall here again—still in Mexico."

He stared off into space a few seconds and continued, "That course will, eventually, bring them over Guatemala." Almost as an afterthought he added, "I wonder if that's where they are going? Of course, that isn't the only problem this surfaces … if they cross into

Mexico again, we just might get a fighter up our collective asses. The good ol' boy network will only go so far."

He shrugged again and looked back up at the men staring at him, "Well, at any rate, we have a little time to think on that."

Barrington turned to the man next to him and went on with what was almost a monologue, "Donlevy, You have any idea why Duncan would be headed this way too? Mendez says he asked him not to tell us he was already out over the Gulf … with help. You ever know him to get off of his desk-bound butt, except to party with the beltway bums?"

Donlevy started to answer, but Barrington went on, "I don't like the feel of this. There is too much self-serving political heat floating around—and we usually get covered in shit when that happens." There was silence in the aircraft's cabin for several moments, before the copilot appeared back at Barrington's side. He had a chart folded onto a clipboard and balanced in on the armrest of between them as he knelt in the aisle.

"Boss," be began, as he pointed at a spot on the chart, "The '3 is about here—moving along this track … should come out where you thought … a bit above Vera Cruz."

Barrington nodded, "Yeah, thought so …"

The copilot went on, "Unless I'm mistaken, Jorgensen is here," jabbing at another spot on the chart. "It looks like he is running parallel and about ten miles off to their starboard." Barrington only nodded and the copilot went on, "I'd guess they have all systems pointed ahead and to their left, focused on the '3. If we stand on it for a while, circle around here," again pointing at the chart, "we will be behind and to the 5 O'clock position on both of them. We can keep them both on scope and be on the landward side when they break the coast. If either of them notice us at all, they'll probably figure we are Mexican fighters just following them out of the country. The ground scatter may help confuse them."

"OK—do it."

The copilot stood to return to the flight deck and grinned, "… and the air will be a hell of a lot less bumpy."

He had hardly seated himself in the right-hand seat when the aircraft swung hard left and began to climb. It continued to turn toward an imaginary spot in the air somewhere behind the other two aircraft.

....

Bailey began trimming for level flight as *The Rose* grudgingly clawed up through 7,000 feet. Though she rattled with the vibration and rain leaked in around the window seals, *The Rose's* engines managed a smooth and even roar of power. The old ship felt good to him and he smiled in satisfaction as he scanned over the instrument panel. After twice scanning every instrument, he eased back on the throttles and toyed with mixture and props as they settled into level flight. *The Rose* ceased the groan of climb and mushed into a relatively steady and smooth cruise.

Bailey turned to Stoudamyre and nodded, raising his hands from the yoke and turning control of the aircraft over to him. "The good Colonel wants to talk to me—keep the current heading for now. We should cross the coastline in about forty-five minutes or less. If the weather worsens I'll get back here to help."

"You feelin' better?" asked Stoudamyre, a look of concern in his eyes.

"Yeah—as a matter of fact, I am. We're doing what I do best now. Everything will be OK."

"Sure—you are looking better. You looked pretty doggy back there on the strip."

"Well, it was a bit tense ... you don't do that sort of stuff every day." He shook his head in what had the look of sadness, "Anyway, I'll be back shortly." He was conscious of a slight out-of-sync sound from the starboard engine as he started to unhook himself from his lap belt. He listened a moment, shook his head in relief as the sound went away, then pulled himself up and made his way off of the flight deck. He steadied himself on the stacks of crates as he swayed down the narrow alleyway toward Mobutu.

The man, his thoughts hidden behind an impassive expression, watched Bailey approach and motioned him to an unoccupied canvas seat riveted against the side of the fuselage. The blanket wrapped body of the dead mobster lay a bit farther back, just beyond the side hatch, and it made Bailey momentarily shudder.

"You are ill, Mr. Bailey." It was not a question and there was concern, but no pity, neither in his eyes nor his voice.

Bailey merely nodded, not yet sure he wanted to open himself to the man.

"I thought so. May I ask the problem?"

"Colonel, I can fly your plane, it that's the concern ..."

Mobutu dismissed the response with a wave of his hand, "No—Mr. Bailey, that is not the concern. You are indeed a fine airman and, but, for that matter, our copilot is perfectly capable of flying this old relic very satisfactorily. I am concerned about you. Accept that someone can be. You are obviously quite ill, yet so many times in the past few days you have risen to all challenges and proven to be much more than you appear." He stared intently into Bailey's eyes and seemed to study him for what seemed a long time. Bailey only stared back, uncomfortable, but expressionless.

"I have led men a long time, Mr. Bailey—good ones and bad ones—yet they never cease to amaze me. You have been one of the more puzzling ones. I am sorry to say that I thought you, pardon my bluntness, a tired old drunk, probably more trouble than you could ever be worth."

Bailey was still a moment before he shifted in his seat and relaxed in the warmth of the medication. He leaned toward Mobutu and in a barely audible voice said, "Perhaps that is all I am ... a worthless old drunk."

A slow smile crossed Mobutu's face and he too leaned forward and replied, "You have managed to get this corroded old hulk to fly—I never thought it possible. You've built a truce, however tenuous, with our gangster friend. I think we all underestimated you … I know the little Mexican back at the airstrip did. I am sure you were quite a surprise for him and I was certainly grateful for your help at the refueling stop. Now, what is it that you fight and keep to yourself?"

"Colonel, what I fight is really only my concern. You can't really help very much. I needed this last job and this thing … this thing … in my gut couldn't stand in the way."

He fished in a pocket and came out with a small notebook, propped it on his leg and scribbled across the face of a page. "What I do need is for you to see that whatever I end up making from this little trip—if anything—goes to this to this person."

Mobutu squinted at the scrawled name and address, carefully folded it and pushed it into his shirt pocket. "She is …?"

"She is—used to be—my wife. My daughter lives with her. I won't get a chance to help again. This is my last trip. I have a cancer—and it's a lot tougher than me. I will get you to where you need to go—probably no farther. I'd appreciate it if you took care of Bill for me too. He is—my friend; maybe the only one."

Mobutu nodded and leaned back against the seat. He was silent a while, then just above the din of the aircraft, said, "Yes, Mr. Bailey, there is quite a bit more to you than I thought. All right, know that I will do all that I possibly can. Before you go back up front, I have something for you to consider." He waited until he knew he had Bailey's attention, and said, "You know that I have a ship awaiting us at the end of our flight and, hopefully, another aircraft better loaded than this one. Perhaps you would consider going on with me? I doubt you can go back. There is nothing there."

Bailey stared at Mobutu for a bit, then hoisted himself to his feet, nodded a wordless thank you, and moved back toward the flight deck. He could see the first tinges of daylight through the windscreen as he slumped back into his seat.

"We have some problems, Boss, and we don't need any more just now." Stoudamyre's greeting was expected but not welcome.

"Oh?" Bailey said, as he seated the headset tightly over his ears.

"Yeah—look out there at that stuff. The tops look like they go to maybe 40K. I thought … hoped anyhow … we'd miss most of it this far south. It looks *rough*. We can dodge the big ones though," Bailey hadn't had time to really look over the squall lines they were approaching before Stoudamyre went on, "And that starboard engine is beginning to run some rough … a bit hotter too."

Bailey shook his head and said, "OK … let's work on it …" and Stoudamyre cut him off, "And we got company."

Chapter 17

JORGENSEN ABANDONED HIS BELTED SECURITY behind the mahogany desktop and surrendered to the questions filling a mind beginning to suffocate in real and growing fear. Swaying forward down the narrow aisle, he leaned through the open hatch and stared in confusion at the panel and its instruments.

He finally focused on the little green blip periodically appearing on the screen between the pilots that, according to the copilot, represented the DC-3 they followed. They were, also according to the graying and leather-faced copilot, just over six miles from the aircraft and a few degrees off to its right. Not that its position on the screen made any sense to Jorgensen, but the copilot claimed it was on the same general heading that they sickeningly wallowed along.

He swallowed rising nausea and croaked, "They haven't varied much from that heading, have they?"

"No sir, not much. They moved back to 120 degrees magnetic about an hour ago and that's where it's stuck. They'll be back over Mexican soil in a few minutes—45 at the most. I don't like that much—and it looks like there are two fighters off our six just a few miles back. I'd bet your buddy Mendez just might be getting serious. I wonder where in hell they're taking that old beast." The copilot started to go on, but turbulence caused the aircraft to begin to slop into the stall shudder and he quickly returned his attention to helping keep the Grumman on the high side of the stall. He did offer a plaintive, "Sir ... we have to get up out of this crap if we're going to stay this low and slow. I don't need to auger in to some damn hill to celebrate this fucking little exercise."

Jorgensen felt the nausea rise in his throat again, as a cold sweat break out across his face. "Damn! This is awful! Can you do anything to stop this wallowing around?"

"Well—we can climb above the weather—or most of it … go back to cruise and do some three-sixties … keep 'em on the scope. If we can figure out where they are likely headed, we got lots speed on them … we can get there first. Your little helpers can be waiting on them."

"Damn … anything … just do it. I'll be back in my seat. Uhh … you've been looking at that chart a long time—any idea where they're going?"

"Not yet. They keep this course long enough, they'll cross some more of Mexico, split Guatemala … now, that ought to be fun … cross Belize, more water and make landfall again in Colombia or Venezuela. You run a line out and it looks like it goes to Maracaibo. But it doesn't make sense that they'd be going there, be a certain hot welcome. Hell, to tell you the truth, Boss, I can't be sure they'll even make it through that squall line out there."

Jorgensen stood there a moment, considering what he'd been told, before saying, "Just keep an eye on them and let me know if anything changes. Jesus! I gotta sit down." He had barely made to his seat when he felt the sensation of the aircraft gaining speed and a downward pressure on his body that spoke of the aircraft rapidly climbing. The wallowing and sickening crawl through the sky became something more tolerable and he tried to force the airsickness from his mind.

He looked across the cabin and saw that Kirkpatrick was intently watching him, a stare of absolute contempt chiseled into his face. He dismissed thoughts of Kirkpatrick for the moment, motioned to one of his khaki-clad lap-dummies and watched the man struggle across the few feet to his side. "Get me some of that airsickness shit from the first aid kit … and pour me another drink." Then he almost retched, but never let his expression change—even as he saw his career, maybe even his life, begin to circle the drain.

....

Assistant to the Deputy Director and Director-hopeful Will Duncan looked up from the chart he was pretending to study so intently and nodded for the young aide hunched against the textured carpet wall of the flight deck. The young man stood and took the three steps to the seat across from his Rabbi in the Agency's difficult corridors. "Yes sir?"

The young man was recently out of the Navy—a SEAL—and he looked hard as nails. The man was handsome, except for the very livid scar across his forehead that disappeared into the hairline and caused his left eyelid and socket to appear slightly misshapen. He could just as well have been an All-American up for a conference with his coach. The thick belt with four magazines and a black automatic cinched around his middle spoiled that image though. "What can I do for you?" he asked, a Virginia version of a southern accent mellowing his words.

"Look, I don't know where these … people … are going yet, but we will be far past friendly turf. Get your crew ready for something that may not be pleasant. I don't want to screw around with the Mexicans again, but you never know. Can you get me someone off of the flight deck? I need to talk with them."

He watched the man move back to the four similarly armed men and begin to talk. The noise of the jet made hearing what they had to say impossible but he did notice that they didn't return his comments. Their acknowledgement was a slightly more awakened look and brief smiles. A few seconds later the man leaned into the flight deck and exchanged quiet words with the flight deck crew. That finished, he returned to his seat and seemed to relax into a restful nonchalance. Three minutes later the pilot plopped into the seat across from Duncan. He had a clipboard with a folded chart on it in his hand. "Yes sir?

"What's going on? Can you give me an update on things?"

"Sure … we've at 30K … doing about 380 knots, along this course line … here," he jabbed at a spot near the end of a red-penciled line on the blue-green of the chart. "The DC-3 is about here. We are coming up fast on their left."

Pointing his pencil at another spot to the southwest of their position, he went on, "A tin can down in the gulf tells me they are now on a relatively constant heading of 120 degrees. They'll be going to be back over Mexican turf in a few minutes, all things being equal. I don't know yet where they are going. There is nothing close for them to use—not in Mexico or Guatemala, too much DEA and military there for them to be comfortable with that."

"Where's Gunnar?"

"He's about here—the tin can also says they have given up on simply following the Gooney and have moved to altitude and just cutting 360s above and behind them. I suppose they know it, but they have Mexican Air Defense shadowing them as well as Barrington. There's every possibility the jets will whack them if they re-enter Mexican air space. You heard what the General said about his airspace. I doubt he's kidding … can't blame him. You might want to get on the horn to Mendez before this is all just so much bad history and front page hype."

"Yeah … much as I hate to, I'll do that. You got a fix on Barrington and company too?"

"Sure. Like I said, they are about here—staying away from Jorgensen but following the '3. They probably look like Mexican Air Force to Jorgensen's crew. Why don't you just let him handle this? It's his bag, y'know … and he's damn good at it."

Duncan didn't directly answer the man. He just sat there a bit before answering, "Yeah … I'll think about it. Keep tabs on all of them—and stay close enough to get to them—really fast … if we have to." He ran all that through his mind, knowing he'd like to let Barrington handle the whole thing—and yet understanding, with all there was to lose or gain—that he would have to be there looking over the man's shoulder when it all ended. He could feel both the pangs of fear and, at the same time, the first bit of gloating. Jorgensen, foul, uncouth and always-looking-down-his-nose Jorgensen—the end would be sweet. He had to see it. His soul demanded it.

....

BARRINGTON SMOOTHED OUT THE CHART he had unfolded across the pullout table between Obregon, Simpson, and himself. He studied it a bit, steadied a ruler across the chart's face, and began an absent-minded frown. "There is no place close that makes any sense—Guatemala, maybe; Belize, … hmm … no. You see anyplace in this bit of Mexico that they might be headed for?"

Obregon and Simpson stared hard at the chart, more confused than informed. Obregon finally said, "Well, there's lots of little dirt strips, but none of them are anywhere near a port that can get a ship of size in and out. And, hell, I don't know squat about Belize. I thought we had a bunch of drug guys and those State Department advisors down here—particularly in Guatemala. It doesn't seem likely that they'd chance running into one of those outfits. I guess anything is possible though."

The thin, dark-haired agent, Rivera, had moved from her place at the small bank of radio equipment and was staring over Barrington's shoulder at the chart. She started to turn away, stopped and leaned closer and a look of recognition crossed her face. "Zach, let me borrow the chart a minute—get right back to you."

She gathered the chart quickly and turned back to the console behind her. She spent a bare five minutes in hurried conversation with someone at the other end of her connection, then pulled off the headset and tossed it back on the table. The chart was hurriedly spread back on the table in front of Barrington.

"They're not going to Guatemala or Belize … certainly not Mexico—they're headed here," and she pointed to a spot on the coast of Venezuela.

Barrington looked up at her, "How ... what makes you think that?"

"Well, run the course out ... straight." She pointed a spot barely in Venezuela and a stone's throw from Colombia. "see? It comes in here on the Gulf. The only strip around that will take a DC-3 heavy is here ... *you* pronounce it. Something I heard yesterday caught my attention. The guys working with the Colombians have played fast and loose with the border the last couple of days and said they saw a freighter laying right off the coast near this old patrol bomber strip. They also said there's a couple of powered barges tied up to an old pier that's part of what used to be the base. They have to get the stuff out someway—and you know they are not going into Mariciabo. There's too much official heat for that."

Barrington studied the chart before looking up to Obregon, "What do you think? I mean, it does make sense."

"You're asking me? Hell, I don't know. Should we maybe take a chance and get there first?" Obregon asked, exchanging glances with Matthews and Simpson.

Rivera spoke before anyone else could speak, "How about, instead, I get hold of someone on the ground nearby ... if I can ... and have *them* do a quick flyby. Maybe they can see what's going on first. In the meantime, we can still shadow them and not have lost anything. Anyhow, I'd hate to be wrong and be sitting on the ground and have them go somewhere else. It would probably be better to follow them in."

Barrington nodded affirmatively, "Do it," and leaned back in his seat, a look of concern on his face. Rivera moved back to her console and began to transmit in the clear.

....

Bailey reached across and touched Stoudamyre's arm and nodded toward the yolk, signaling that he was about to take control of the aircraft. He wrapped his hands around its leather-wrapped surface and pulled himself up a bit taller in the seat, staring out at the squall line spread across the horizon. He could see that the thunderheads were more intense to his left, but noted that the lightning and rain lines were still strong all along their path of flight. He keyed his mike and said, "Doesn't look as rough as what we've already bumped though, but … you never know. I'm betting this is the last of the storm. I think most of it is behind us and to the left."

"Hope so. Seen our company lately?"

"No—but they're still there; I can feel them. I think I'm a hell of a lot more worried about the goddamn Mexican Air Force. If we don't lose a wing, we'll be back over their turf in a few minutes." He paused a bit, looked at his watch, grimaced and went on, "Why don't you try to fix our exact position while it is relatively smooth. We'll hit that squall line in about five minutes and it'll get rough again."

Stoudamyre leaned back into the seat before beginning to gather his maps and charts. "It's been pretty rough but except for that engine overheating, she's handled it all pretty well. Damn fine craft, these old birds.

Bailey nodded, "Yeah, these down-south storm cells can be tough." He stared off into space a few moments, then went on, "You ought to see how it could get in … Syracuse in, oh, January … all of this and ice too."

Stoudamyre stared at him a bit, saw that he was far away, and went back to working on a position. *The Rose* began to buffet in the unstable air ahead of the squall line as Stoudamyre pulled the clipboard, with the chart attached to it, onto his lap and began toying with the knobs on the radio-navigation stack. Bailey simply sighed and kept the nose of *The Rose* tight onto the course he'd followed since entering the Gulf.

It hit with a vengeance. The squall line came at them like a giant fist and smashed into *The Rose* and threw her at the ocean below. Just when it seemed the screaming downward fall would not end, *The Rose* slammed into what felt like a rocky floor, banked roughly left, leveled momentarily before the altimeter began to rewind as they were sucked rapidly upward. The squall line turned black around them and they were blinded by both driving rain and a seemingly never-ending array of lightening that turned the cloud-filled canyons into multi-colored, yet impenetrable walls of fire and water.

Bailey could feel the aircraft flex, actually see the wings bow first up, then down, and hear the starboard engine sputter and surge. A strong greenish glow began to play along the leading edge of the wings and on the arc of the turning propellers. Stoudamyre had grabbed the yolk and was struggling to follow him through each control movement, trying to keep the aircraft in the air.

Suddenly, they had leveled again at somewhere around 7,000 feet, but it only lasted seconds. The aircraft was grabbed again by the storm gods and flung downward. This time there was the sound of something breaking and the noise of men yelling, with more sounds of metal and wood smashing and grating on the metal decking. Bailey glanced back over his shoulder and could see Mobutu and Cooper struggling to stay upright and push a large wooden crate back into position.

Bailey quickly turned back to handling the aircraft. The men in back would have to be on their own. His job was to keep them in the air. The aircraft buffeted again but, this time, the aircraft's sickening plunge downward toward the sea stopped sooner and Bailey could see he still held over 5,000 feet of altitude. The starboard engine still sputtered, but continued to provide power, even though its temperature had begun to climb more rapidly. The aircraft began to steady up some and the turbulence decreased to a still rough, but manageable, buffeting.

They could see a thinner and lighter wall of clouds and the lightening began to fall astern of the aircraft. Bailey looked across at Stoudamyre and watched as he released his hands from the controls and turned to stare back at him, fear and shock still on his face. The whole episode had consumed less than three minutes and, yet, they were both exhausted.

Bailey breathed a sigh and looked back at the cabin again. He could see they were in the final stages of tying down the break-away crate. They would live—for now. He turned slowly back to stare out the windscreen and reached out and stroked the crucifix swinging from a knob on the panel.

Just under half an hour more of bounce and buffet had gone by the time *The Rose* broke through into clear air behind the squall lines and the turbulence immediately began to fade away. He could feel the tightness ease in his jaws and shoulder muscles as he raised himself up to look out across the nose of *The Rose*. The ribbon of sand along the coast was clear and bright and just beginning to slide under the wings. Dense tropical forest stretched ahead as far as he could see.

He leaned toward the instrument panel and tapped the glass cover on the starboard engine's cylinder head temperature gauge, hoping that would lower it back into the normal range. It didn't, but it was running more smoothly and he tried to push his mind off to other thoughts. *The Rose* was still in the air and there was not a lot more he could ask for at the moment.

....

THE SQUALL LINE LAY MILES ASTERN as Barrington, Rivera, and their crew crowded around the open chart. Rivera pointed at a spot along the line she had penciled in earlier and said, "They're still on the same course—and we're some thirty clicks into Belize airspace now. I'm still betting on that little strip near Mariciabo."

Barrington studied the map a while longer then looked up; glancing back and forth between the three men across the table "Looks right. I think you've probably got it nailed cold. What a crappy place to have a face-off. We've got no clue how many people with guns are there." Before they could answer, he turned back to Rivera, "Anything from your DEA friends?"

"No—uhh, wait a minute on that." She pressed the earpiece of the headset a little tighter to her ear and moved back to the console, reaching for the microphone. She was back in less than a minute.

"They say there's an old DC-6 on the strip now—and a bunch of folks manhandling crates out to one of the barges at the pier. They say it looks like the DC-6 is damaged, maybe one side of the landing gear has collapsed."

"Anything else?"

"No. They just skipped by … quiet and out a ways. Didn't want to spook 'em."

"Ask up front if they can still see anyone following the '3."

She moved off toward the flight deck and Barrington turned back to the other men, "I'd like to say this is just a good plan coming together but we're running on dumb-ass luck and I think it is about to get messy."

He started to say something else, but Rivera returned from the door of the flight deck, a concerned look on her face. "The DC-3 is still on the original course but Jorgensen has fallen off the face of the earth."

"What?"

"Yeah, they were trying to see if he'd just dropped back more, but about the time the Mex fighters veered off, Jorgensen's plane moved to the right and went beyond our radar."

"Shit! You suppose he's got a fix on where they're going?"

"Could be. I don't think we can count on the storm getting them. Someone back in Signals might have monitored my traffic and relayed it to him. You know that he's an old hand down here and, on top of that, has stooges all over the agency. Why not in communications? Give him that and he probably figured it out on his own. I'm still betting on that little airstrip in Venezuela, boss."

"I think you're right, but I don't think we can put all our eggs in that basket just yet. We still have to lay back and follow them in to wherever they go. Better let Duncan know—and does your DEA source have any clout there that can keep this just our thing? I'd hate to be bargaining with some jerk-off from the Venezuelan Army when we get there and the lead is about to start flying."

Rivera started to answer, when Obregon raised his hand for silence and spoke, "I know someone. You have some secure communications?"

Rivera nodded, shrugged questioningly. "Close as we've got—go ahead," and pointed to one of the black handsets at her workstation.

Obregon moved around her and took the seat at the console. He picked up the handset and punched in a series of numbers from memory. He waited a long minute and began to talk in low and earnest tones. The call took less time than it had to make the connection. He pushed the phone back into its cradle, sat there a bit, shook his head and moved back to his seat. "We have until 0800 local tomorrow. Damn, that's a marker I wasn't ready to cash in just yet. We'd better hope this … this … *Plain of the Dogs* is where they're headed. My man says Jorgensen has already been on the hook to someone farther up his food chain—and asking for the same thing. So much for the storm having eaten his lunch."

…..

BAILEY LOOKED BACK TO HIS WATCH for the third time in as many minutes and again found his eyes focused back on the cylinder head temperature gauge. He was right. It was slowly moving away from the normal zone, creeping toward his nightmare. Tinkering with the mixture and cowl flaps had not made any difference—it still crept slowly upward. He tried to tell himself it was all imagination as he saw the coast of Belize slide behind and the turquoise of the Gulf stretched out ahead.

He became conscious of someone at his shoulder, looked back, and saw Mobutu leaning through the flight deck hatch. He was staring intently through the windscreen. Before Mobutu could speak, Bailey pulled up one of his earpieces and nodded to him. "Thanks for handling things back there. We didn't need that stuff flying around much longer."

"You're welcome. How far out are we?"

"We'll give you an answer to that in a few minutes." He nodded to Stoudamyre, "He's working on that now. We'll be headed down in a bit though. We'll want to come up on the coast pretty low. Try not to attract any local heat. We couldn't outrun shit in this old bucket." He paused for a moment and nodded out to his right, "I also think I'm about to lose that starboard engine. That sure as hell won't help."

"How about the folks who were following us? We can't outrun them either."

"Oh, I'm sure they're still there—just off our radar. Colonel, you must be a very important man. I'm sure they didn't come all this way on my account. What do you think will happen when we hit the ground?"

"A lot of variables, Mr. Bailey, a lot of variables. I think our fate depends on a number of things: Who gets to us first, if my associates already there, and just who all of our *company* happens to be, just to name a few of the variables. I suspect it may be more of a party than we have paid admission for."

"I was afraid of that."

Stoudamyre looked up, wincing at the last exchange between Mobutu and Bailey, "Damn! You guys sure know how to make a fella feel good." He shook his head and pulled up the clipboarded chart, holding it for the other men to see. He pointed at a spot along a thinly penciled line, "We need to be at a couple hundred feet by here ... so you can start your decent in, oh, about twenty minutes."

Stoudamyre dropped the clipboard back into his lap, seemed to think better of it, holding it up again for Bailey's attention. He ignored Mobutu. "We probably ought to run in here—along this ridge, "as he pointed to a splash of color on the chart, "and be inland from the airstrip. The clutter from the hills will mask us longer.

He waited until Bailey looked up from the chart, "... that seem best to you?"

Bailey only nodded and finally pushed a finger out toward the cylinder head temperature gauge, "You noticed that?"

"Yeah. I hoped that if I ignored it the damn thing would go away. How far can we fly this thing on one engine … with all that iron back there?"

"All the way to the scene of the crash, I imagine—unless we dump some of … that iron … in a hurry when the time comes. I doubt if anyone back there will want to dump the stuff though."

"Any chance it'll hold up long enough?"

"Well—I don't know. The temp is going up gradually, so nothing is really busted. We'll just keep an eye on it and—hope. It does feel like she's dying though; maybe just to spite us. I can't say I blame her. If we do lose the engine I think I can still keep her in the air to our strip … maybe. These old birds are tough."

Bailey pulled his attention back to flying *The Rose* but the long, thin, light-grey line of smoke trailing the starboard engine stayed centermost in his mind. He only nodded when Stoudamyre tapped him on the shoulder and motioned for him to begin the decent.

....

THE GRUMMAN SCREAMED IN ALONG THE COAST, low and fast, ignoring the challenge from Maracaibo radio. They dropped even lower and skimmed by too fast to read the flag of a dark gray and rusting freighter anchored a hundred yards off of a rickety pier jutting out from the jungle rimmed coastline. The pilot pulled the nose up and swept to seven hundred feet, and, as they began swinging left, moved on through the turn to point the nose at the length of a long and patched asphalt runway. Jorgensen could see the two barges spaced out between the ship and the shore and wondered how many shooters were among the labor force on the ground.

The pilot brought the Grumman down steeply toward the end of the runway, watching the men around the strangely angled DC-6 scatter and run toward the brush along the edge of the asphalt. He'd wanted to do a slow flyby, but Jorgensen had ordered him to come in hot and steep, getting them on the ground as fast as possible, providing what he hoped would be something of a surprise.

The Grumman rolled on by the DC-6 and the reason for the aircraft's odd angle became apparent. The left landing gear was folded up under the wing and both propellers on the wing were bent back at the ends. The side hatch was wide open and the interior looked dark and empty.

When Jorgensen stepped onto the ground, the only sound was the spooling down of the jet engines. The runway, busy with ant-like laborers only a few minutes before, almost appeared to be abandoned. He knew those seen earlier around the damaged aircraft were watching him from the darkness and cover of the jungle and his throat tightened and went dry. He motioned for the others to follow him and began walking slowly toward the DC-6 that sat half way up and on the water side of the airstrip.

There were only five of them; the pilot had been left aboard to keep the Grumman ready for a quick departure. They were too few to unwisely seek battle. He had to stall until his ace-in-the-hole arrived in the form of his friends in Venezuelan's military intelligence forces. He felt secure in his own opinion that most of those who had fled on their arrival were little more than laborers, certainly not fighters. He intended to move aggressively, as if he held all the cards. He cranked the bolt back on the Uzi he cradled and walked on, wishing he picked up a second magazine for the weapon.

They spread out in a thin line, the two tan-suited camp followers off to his right, the copilot and Kirkpatrick to his left. And he had to keep Kirkpatrick in view—all the time. They neared the crippled DC-6 and moved in on the airstrip side of it, staring into the open hatch.

That's when Jorgensen saw the tall black man step out of shadows at the edge of the jungle. He wore a faded green, many-pocketed flight suit, bloused above shiny jump boots, and there was a web belt at his waist and a holstered pistol on his hip. The immediate problem though was the AK47 in his right hand, its barrel pointed skyward and stock resting against his hip. He appeared to be alone, but Jorgensen knew he wasn't.

They had moved a few feet past the DC-6, Jorgensen never moving his eyes from the face of the man standing just at the edge of the asphalt. They were finally close enough to talk and the black man spoke first, lowering the barrel of the AK47 to somewhere about waist high on the men in front of him.

"What do you want ... and who ...?" Jorgensen had started to swing the Uzi toward the man and stopped—hearing the same sound the tall black man did: The distinctive sound of a large helicopter. The sound was growing louder, coming in from out over the jungle. Both men looked upward, scanning the sky toward the sound. It seemed to be out there in sound only, its echo bouncing among the small green hills at the end of the runway, out beyond the idling Grumman. Then it rose, appearing to spring from the jungle floor, a matte black UH-1B, with its intentionally faded insignia barely visible and unreadable. The Huey poised there a moment, then dipped back toward the earth and swept down the runway toward where Jorgensen and the black man faced each other.

The helicopter flared and settled quickly to the hard surfaced strip, some 50 yards from the wing tip of the DC-6 and ten camouflage-clad and armed men spilled from the side hatches. They began spreading out in a long line and moving toward the jungle behind Jorgensen. He breathed a sigh of relief at the arrival of his back-up and turned toward the black man, a smile on his face. He was too late. The man was just disappearing into the foliage along the edge of the strip. He cursed, lowered the Uzi to waist level and fired a burst after the man. He began to look about for cover and motioning the uniformed men forward. An almost instant roar of automatic weapons fire began and rose in intensity.

Jorgensen settled for a spot behind the wheel and under the starboard wing of the DC-6. He could see his two young aides scurrying for the scant cover afforded by several overturned barrels. One of them seemed to trip and fall, his handgun bouncing across the asphalt ahead of him. He raised his head and stretched out an arm, straining to reach his partner, and collapsed. One down, Jorgensen thought and he could feel chest muscles constricting around his heart and his breathing become more labored. It was not supposed to be this way.

Jorgensen loosed a few rounds toward the jungle, with no particular target; as there was nothing to see. He could hear the sound of automatic rifle fire—somewhere out in the undergrowth— but there was only an occasional flash to see and target on. He turned back toward the runway and slid down to sit behind the cover of the large aircraft tire. He could see that the uniformed men were still advancing toward the tree line, firing as they moved. There was a price though; three of them already lay crumpled on the runway surface, unmoving and in widening pools of blood.

He looked around for Kirkpatrick, but the man was nowhere to be seen. Only the copilot was off to his left, laying flat on the asphalt, looking frantically about for cover. Jorgensen cursed, knowing he could not just let Kirkpatrick walk away and, at the same time, feeling the knot of fear grow in his belly. Either side of the Kirkpatrick coin could be very dangerous.

Jorgensen brought his attention back to his own situation. He had to gain control of the airstrip before the DC-3—and Mobutu— arrived. He mused that the tall black man had to be one of Mobutu's deputies, someone close to him, and probably just as much of a physical threat. But Mobutu was the one with covert ties to him that could be officially—politically—damning. Mobutu had to be eliminated.

He pulled the magazine from the Uzi, saw that there were only a few rounds left in it, and knew that it would soon be useless. He'd not brought additional magazines from the aircraft, foolishly expecting no firefight with the extra show of force the helicopter afforded. That had not happened though and, even as the men now neared the edge of the jungle, there was still fire from out in the dark undergrowth. He saw that two more men had fallen, one of them his copilot, but that they still kept up a steady stream of fire and slowly advanced. He could … might … win, with time. He needed time.

Chapter 18

BAILEY BROUGHT THE DC3 IN LOW OVER THE COAST, skimming just above the masts of fishing boats scattered across the shallow waters. Barely above the gentle swells, he could see the fishermen staring up at *The Rose*, shielding their eyes from the sun and waving. Sweat beaded his brow as he struggled to keep the aircraft level and in the air, the increasing loss of power from the starboard engine making the work more exacting and difficult, a straining physical labor. He'd been forced to push the port engine closer to its maximum and it was consuming fuel at an alarming rate and hastening its mechanical failure at the same time.

A long stream of thickening gray smoke now trailed from the starboard wing, almost as though the engine housed an as yet unseen fire. At landfall, he nodded to Stoudamyre for help and they managed to force the aircraft up another three hundred feet, gradually pulling the yoke back toward their gut as they slowly eased in more trim and stood hard on a rudder. The strain on the engine caused it to begin a periodic pattern of the backfiring and belching of darker puffs of smoke to mix with the gray. They were sweating and straining, but the effort kept them limping along the course they hoped would lead to the airstrip.

Bailey felt weak, beaten, even nauseous, but knew—for the moment—that he was in control of the aircraft. Somewhere out there, just a few miles, stretched a small airstrip; cut a long time ago from the jungle and small squares of farmland. There he could stop and nothing would matter anymore. That was as far as the contract with his soul went. He would get there. It was, to him at that moment, thirty-odd years ago, and, despite his illness, he felt young again. There, at The Plain of the Dogs, the whole game could end. Behind him there was nothing.

Stoudamyre reached over and slapped at his hand to gain attention, "We're going to lose what's left of that engine at any second. We need a place to set down." There was a look of intense worry on his face and he'd pulled his hands back to hover near the yoke, ready to reach in and help again.

"Not yet. Not here. There is no place to even try to set down here. The place we need is out there waiting for us, just another ten, maybe fifteen, minutes max. I can handle it for now. Go back and let them know we are getting close and might come down hard … and get back up here in a hurry. I'll need you to help get her down."

Stoudamyre nodded and quickly scrambled back into the cabin and saw that Mobutu and Cooper were prying the lids from some of the poorly marked crates, pulling out ammunition from one and magazines from another and loading some of them. Several M-16s lay in a clutter on the metal decking. He shrugged, and started to turn around, heading back to the flight deck. He noticed that Mobutu was looking at him, so he raised his hand, with fingers outspread, and closed and opened his hand two times, while mouthing "ten minutes." Mobutu nodded in acknowledgement and Stoudamyre turned and squeezed himself back into the right seat of the flight deck.

As he was sliding past Bailey, he glanced past him and out into the sky to their left and noticed the light reflect off of something, stared again and recognized another aircraft, less than a mile away. He slapped Bailey on the shoulder and pointed off toward the aircraft, "Did you know about that other jet? It's not the one from earlier. It's paralleling us—flaps and wheels down." Bailey only stared straight ahead and shook his head in the negative, replying, "I can't screw with it now—give me some help here."

Exactly eight minutes later, a long cut in the green surface of the earth appeared off to their left and ahead. They might just make it, Bailey thought ... *maybe.* The long black and grey splotched asphalt strip lay between small farm fields and clumps of undergrowth and jungle, and ran roughly north and south. The thought ran through his mind, "welcome back to the Plain of the Dogs," but he pushed that from his mind. There was more to be done. He set up a slow descent and tried to ignore the coughing and backfiring of the ailing engine. His muscles ached, but the heady joy of having won even this little victory kept strength flowing and his senses alert.

There was no formality or sharpness to his approach though, just a long, shallow, and bumpy turn to the left and then left again onto a short final. At about two hundred feet and a quarter mile out, the starboard engine belched fire and smoke again and just stopped. A flickering flame could be seen at the edge of the cowl flaps and it appeared as if it were spreading back toward the nacelle's juncture with the wing. Stoudamyre hurriedly punched the feathering button and fire extinguisher and was relieved to see them both work this time as the prop began slowing and turned edge-on to the wind. He dropped his hands back to the yoke to help Bailey keep *The Rose* level as they plowed on toward the end of the asphalt. The runway seemed so far away and their progress so agonizingly slow, yet in seconds it passed under the nose of the aircraft.

They hit the runway hard, just past the brush at its end and bounced twice. The smoke from the dead engine blossomed once more and began to leave a widening trail as they rolled out. The flames flickered only momentarily though and died again, even as the smoke increased. Bailey headed toward the far end of the runway, near where a mid-sized business jet could be seen.

....

Jorgensen started to pull himself up and move closer to the fight when he saw, rather than heard, the DC-3. He watched it come in low and followed its line of flight as it moved in from out over the jungle with a steady stream of smoke marking its path. He strained, but still didn't immediately hear the aircraft over the noise of the gunfire. He cursed his luck as he saw the DC-3 dip its port wing and begin a slow, sinking, turn to the left, toward the far end of the airstrip.

Then, suddenly, it became very quiet. The gunfire from the jungle stopped and the men just approaching the line between airstrip and jungle looked around in confusion before going to ground, crouching behind the few scattered fuel barrels and an old and abandoned and rusting truck, left there by long-ago users of the airstrip.

Jorgensen watched as the DC-3 crossed the end of the runway and raised its nose just before both main gear crunched down with a squawk and bounced, bounced again, and settled. The aircraft barreled straight down the runway toward where the Grumman still sat and Jorgensen's panic grew anew and with increased intensity.

He stood quickly and waved the confused men on toward the jungle, screaming for them to keep firing—*to get the bastards*. He fired the few remaining rounds in the Uzi, tossed it aside, and continued to follow the men toward the jungle, pulling a worn Browning from his belt as he did. His last look back at the airstrip saw the DC-3 stopped at the far end and, glancing around, he still couldn't see Kirkpatrick. That worry stuck in the back of his throat and ran though his mind along with icy spasms of fear. The sound of gunfire became louder and more frequent. He felt and heard the snap of bullets as they passed near his head, yet he was still not hit. Desperation and adrenaline drove him on. Fear fed that flame.

....

BAILEY STOOD ON THE BRAKE AND PIVOTED *The Rose* in a slow half-circle to the left. He could see back up the runway to the awkwardly canted DC-6 and the little mounds of camouflage lying near it. The noise of the still-turning port engine smothered all sounds of gunfire, but he could see the men crouched at the edge of the strip, pointing rifles at the dark of the undergrowth and he could tell that they were firing. There was a large and bulky man in a light colored suit waving the men on toward the jungle with a hand that clutched a pistol.

He quickly began to shut down the remaining engine and pulled loose his seatbelt. Stoudamyre pushed himself off the flight deck ahead of him, pausing only to look out at the badly smoking starboard engine, its prop still moving around ever-so- slowly. There was a look of relief on his face.

The side hatch was already open and Bailey could see that Mobutu was on the ground, strapping on a pistol belt that held several long magazine pouches for the machine pistol he carried on a canvas strap across his shoulder. Cooper was rummaging through an open crate, pulling out several boxes of ammunition and passing them to the open hatch. The mechanic just stood there, a look of uncertainty and fear on his face.

Cooper looked up at him, shook his head in contempt, but managed a calm voice as he said, "Look, Mac, you didn't sign up for a war—don't get your shorts in a knot. Stay here."

"Uhhh ... think I'll go with you. Don't think I want to be here by myself. Gotta gun?"

"Know how to use it if I do?"

"Probably not in this league—but I'll figure it out."

Cooper straightened up, stared at the man for a moment, and said, "Aww, hell ... just stay here with Bailey."

As he jumped down from the door, Bailey muttered, "I'm not staying here." The mechanic looked hopelessly after him for a moment, then reached out and took the rifle Cooper had just loaded and followed Bailey out the hatch.

Less than five minutes later they were all standing at the edge of the undergrowth, gathered around Mobutu, the only one they were sure knew what he was doing. Each was, in one form or another, armed. The crates and boxes of small arms in the aircraft had made that easy. Mobutu had quickly searched the Grumman and found the pilot, who offered no resistance, cowering inside. He started to just shoot the man, thought better of it and, instead, left him tied securely and safely prone on the metal decking of the DC-3.

Mobutu looked from one man to another and shook his head in silent wonder. His little force wasn't much and it raised his doubts for an outcome anywhere close to the success he needed. As he considered each in turn, the thought remained that it might all end here—so far from his intended destination.

He knew Cooper was little more than a mid-level street thug, dressed and polished in mobster finery. True, the man was fighting for survival and knew how to use the weapons he carried, but he could never be trusted. The man was running on nerves and bluster, his courage and resolution slowly fading.

The mechanic was just that: a mechanic, and little more. He was a casualty waiting to happen if things turned bad; more of a liability than a team member. His eyes constantly flicked from one side to the other and any little unexpected noise caused him to flinch. The rifle he now carried was more for his comfort than a useful tool.

Stoudamyre was different though. True, he was not a ground soldier, but it was obvious he knew his way around the weapon he carried. His hands were casually familiar and comfortable with the 9-mm machine pistol hanging in the crook of his right arm as well as the nickle-plated pistol he'd taken from the dead Mexican at their last stop. But Stoudamyre worried too much about Bailey and watched him with an obvious concern. Loyalty was a good thing, but his focus on the task at hand was less than continuous and a concern.

Bailey worried him the most and, at the same time, he knew the man was the most dependable of the lot. He'd found the man seemed to have no real fear and he was steady and very dangerous with the old and worn .45 he carried in his belt. But he was sick, very sick it appeared, and short on time. His pale face was almost slack, and yet there was alertness in his eyes. He was almost placid and calm to a fault. For reasons he didn't understand at the moment, Mobutu had grown to like, even respect, him. It seemed there had to be a better place than this for the man to end his days.

Bailey could read the look on the black man's face and smiled. He felt calm and, for some reason, even the pain in his stomach was subdued for the moment. He was tired and light-headed though and queasy from the last pills in his bottle. But the sound of the gunfire drew him to it and he wanted to be moving. He listened to the rattle of gunfire, off in the distance toward the crippled DC-6, and watched the jungle edge for movement. He could feel the yesterdays begin to run through his mind again and, this day, none of them were sad. Turning back to look at *The Rose*, the darkness began to creep back into his mind a little and the better memories faded.

Mobutu's voice brought him back, "We'll move around the edge on the left—in the bush—back toward the firing. Keep some distance apart and don't bunch up. Whatever you do though, don't lose sight of the airstrip or the man in front of you or you'll get lost. I'll take the lead. My men won't know you so they'll need to see me first. There's no sense in us shooting each other."

They fell in behind Mobutu and strung out along a narrow and spongy trail that bordered the airstrip, headed toward the sounds of what had become intermittent gunfire. They were spread out no more than fifty yards from Mobutu, in the lead, to Stoudamyre at the drag, yet no one could see more than two others in the little group. The brush and towering growth was thick and crowded in on them as they trudged on along the edge of the strip following a very faint trail. They moved slowly and as quietly as possible, all but Mobutu totally out of their element. The sounds of the shooting had slackened even more as they moved, but an occasional burst of automatic weapons fire told them that they were within a few yards of the outer edge of the firefight.

Suddenly, Mobutu froze in place, crouched, and raised his left hand to stop the small column. He stayed in the crouch a bit, searching the undergrowth with knowing eyes and complete awareness. As if on cue, two men rose from the jungle floor. They stood there quietly for a brief moment before the taller of the two smiled and stepped forward. He cradled an AK47 across muscled forearms and was clad in a faded green flight suit. He didn't speak until he was within a few feet of Mobutu.

"It is good to see you are well, my Colonel. You may have arrived just in time."

Mobutu raised himself to his full height again and very quietly replied, "Ah, Captain, it is good to see you too. You have been successful?"

"Until now. Do you know these people?" canting his head off toward the runway and the sporadic firing.

"Probably. We shall have to make their presence insignificant though and then get out of here—fast."

"We have already reduced their numbers."

"I saw that. Excellent, Captain, you have done well. If we remove the big white man, the others will go away," Mobutu offered.

"He is near that old rusted out truck. He *does* seem to be in charge."

"He is—get me to where I can see him. Oh, Mr. Bailey here is my friend. He is ill, very ill. Watch over him, very carefully, Sergeant, very carefully."

The second man, who still had not spoken, nodded, but showed no change of expression. He fell in behind Bailey and they again edged on up the narrow trail. Some 150 feet further, Mobutu raised his hand again and stopped the short column. He edged back toward the runway, the tall black man at his elbow, and stopped, still in the dark of the undergrowth at the edge of the crumbling asphalt. He could see the old truck, about 75 feet ahead, squatting low to the ground on rotted tires. A large and bulky man couched by the front bumper of the truck, talking with another smaller and darker man in the camouflage uniform of the military. The large man was pointing toward the undergrowth and the smaller of the two was shaking his head in an emphatic disagreement, his face a mask of fear.

Mobutu counted five men in camouflage lying sprawled on the hard surface of the runway. Off to the right and rear of the truck, near some old metal barrels, a man in a tan suit lay twisted, partially on his side, his face turned upward. A large and dark stain could be seen on the front of his white shirt. He was still and stared unseeing at the bright sky. Mobutu could see occasional movement behind the barrels, another man in a tan suit who appeared none too anxious to leave his cover, though he occasionally snapped a shot at the wall of undergrowth bordering the airstrip.

Mobutu turned back to the trail and gathered his little group into a quiet huddle. "It appears my Captain has cut the odds down a quite a bit." He turned to the man who had been with Bailey, "Stay close to these people—bring them on slowly. Kill anyone coming in from the airstrip. They are not our friends and we have no room for prisoners. I think this shall soon be over. The military out there seems to be losing heart." Motioning to the man he had addressed as Captain, he simply said, "Let's go." They padded off up the trail and were out of sight in less than a minute.

They followed, bunched up now, but still wary and slow. After about five minutes, they stopped short, hearing Mobutu yelling, "Is that you, Gunnar? It's me—Guthrie Mobutu ... can we talk?"

They could hear someone answer, but couldn't make out the words. They spread out and, weapons in hand, crawled on toward the airstrip.

As Bailey approached the edge of the undergrowth, he could see a graying, tall and bulky man leaning across the fender of the old truck. He had a pistol in his hand and stared intently out at the jungle.

"That's really you—huh, Guthrie? You're right, we *do* need to talk—right now. No guns, OK?

The bulky man pushed the uniformed man near him to the far end of the truck and put a forefinger to his lips to indicate silence.

"Guthrie ...?"

Bailey heard a muffled, "Alright, I'm coming out." He craned his neck to see on down along the edge of the undergrowth and saw nothing but the dark and dense green brush and vegetation. Suddenly, he was there, in the open.

Mobutu was standing at the edge of the runway, empty handed and still. The man at the front fender of the truck motioned for the other man at the rear of the truck to move on around toward Mobutu and laid his pistol on the fender in front of him. He stood up to his full height, still crowding close to the abandoned truck for cover, only his head, shoulders, and part of his upper torso showing to Mobutu.

They stood there staring at each other, this bulky and graying man in a rumpled and sweat-stained suit, and Mobutu, quiet and appearing indistinct against the wall of jungle. Bailey snaked a little closer to the edge of the grass and weeds, pushing the .45 in front of him. The big man's head lay just atop Bailey's front sight. The temptation was great.

"It's been a long time, Guthrie."

"Yes."

"You've caused me some real heartburn lately."

"I can imagine. It didn't have to happen. You weren't paying attention to everyday business—to your old friends."

Mobutu still didn't move, the conversation seeming pointless and without meaning. The man's hand edged toward the pistol on the fender.

"Guthrie, you know I can't let this go on. There's too much at stake—why don't you just forget about getting home. It's a lost cause there anyway. It always was. Come on back to work with me—we're a good team. You know the pay will be good. You've sampled it before."

"You know I can't do that. Your people fouled this up—shouldn't have happened. You need to fix it. You can, can't you?" The question and tone was mocking as he went on, "I've always heard you could fix *anything.*"

"Not this one. I've already told you there's too much at stake here." His hand now lay atop the pistol. "My name is about to go to the senate—nominated as the Director—unless you fuck it up. I can't let that happen."

The shooting had stopped completely and the uniformed men along the edge of the jungle were turned back toward the truck, watching Jorgensen and their commander, who was crouched near the rear of the truck. They awaited some order, direction, some sense of what was going on.

Jorgensen shifted his gaze to the now confused soldiers and swiveled to look at the man with the pleading eyes at the rear of the truck. He looked back to Mobutu and knew that if the black man were gone he might still be able to talk his way out of this morass. Maybe he wouldn't be Director—but an honorable and quietly elegant retirement, considering the funds he'd hidden offshore, would be better than prison—or a nameless grave. It was hot and humid, but he could not remember ever feeling this cold and clammy before.

The roar behind him spun him around to face the runway. His eyes opened wide and he loosed a string of profanities as another Grumman business jet floated in and hit the end of the runway with a screech of tires and rolled on by where he stood. Jorgensen stared unbelievingly at it for a moment, then spun back to face Mobutu, raising the Browning to fire.

Bailey could see the pistol coming up and knew that it was hidden behind the hood of the truck, Mobutu couldn't see it and was too close to be missed by any half-competent shooter. He heard himself yelling as he pushed himself to his feet and crashed through the last bit of underbrush, stumbling over some rusted wire strung between rotting posts. He pushed the .45 pushed out in front of him and ran clumsily and crouched over across the rough and broken asphalt. He fired his first shot when the bulky man shifted the pistol and his attention toward him. He knew he hadn't hit the man for he brought his other hand up and looked back across the top of the pistol at him, holding it in both hands now.

Bailey kept pulling the trigger, not feeling the recoil, and saw a man in camouflage rise up behind the man with the gun, then spill backwards throwing his hands to his chest. He pulled the trigger one more time and the big man spun back and sideways, smacking into the side of the truck and falling to one knee.

Suddenly, Bailey's legs gave away and he fell forward to his knees and began retching, a froth of blood spattering his clothing. He collapsed onto the pavement as he saw the big man struggling back to his feet.

Bailey blinked away the haze filling his vision and pushed himself back upright. There was no pain, but he felt outside his own body, loose, disconnected from the world, and seeing it all from afar. He pushed the .45 out at the man one more time and pulled the trigger. The gun boomed one more time and the slide locked back. He looked at it in a fog of confusion while he tried to drop the magazine and fumbled for another in a side pocket. He couldn't see that the last round had struck the truck door, just beside the man's head, spraying rust and metal fragments into his face. Bailey slowly folded in and down, pushed himself back to a sitting position, then collapsed again onto his side. He could hear the shooting fade and saw the sky grow brighter then fade out completely. There was still no pain, only a spreading and paralyzing weakness.

Jorgensen scooped up his pistol from the ground and looked out at the airstrip to see the Grumman off-loading men—men he couldn't recognize, but knew they could only mean him harm. The pain in his hip was intense and he could see a part of his trouser leg turning a bright red, but he could still stand and even move, though clumsily. He heaved himself around and looked at the jungle wall, trying to find a place to run, to hide. The men from the aircraft drew nearer and he recognized a man he knew only as Barrington, someone he'd often seen slip in and out of Duncan's office. His panic became almost uncontrollable.

Jorgensen started to move around the back of the truck and off at an angle toward the jungle, away from the shadows where he'd seen Mobutu. The little Venezuelan Major lay on his back, looking up at him with wide and pain-filled eyes, a growing patch of dark blood bubbling out onto his chest and soaking his uniform. Jorgensen's movement was slow, the numbness beginning to leave his hip and sharp pain invading to replace it.

He didn't bother to shoot back at the man who now lay on the asphalt, out in the open, but hobbled on around the back of the truck, stepping over the little Venezuelan Major, and slowly began to stagger for the jungle's cover. Other sounds of gunfire were heard and he turned to see that the man he knew as Barrington was shooting at him, though he was too far away for accuracy, and that three other men were breaking into a run toward him, bringing up machine pistols to shoot. Was one of them a woman? They were coming on so fast and he turned and lunged and staggered to the edge of the undergrowth, then threw himself across what was left of the rusted wire fence. No one had shot at him from the jungle and he knew they didn't have to anymore. He had lost. He smacked down hard on his knees and the pain in his hip grew as he crawled deeper into the darkness. As he moved away from the airstrip he could hear yet another jet approaching and the sound of tire on asphalt. He groaned at the pain in his hip, struggled to his feet, and staggered on almost blindly.

....

BAILEY FELT CONSCIOUSNESS COME BACK SLOWLY, but the nausea was still there and when he looked down at the dampness across his shirt, he saw that it was mottled with dingy flecks of drying blood. Though everything around him was still swirling and a pale gray, he struggled to get back to his feet. He managed to get to a low crouch and then his balance went and he sank back to his knees, swayed and fell forward as all turned dark again. There were noises in the distance, then nothing.

He had no idea how long he'd been there. There was a feeling of someone, something, touching his face. It was cool and damp. He tried to open his eyes but the light was painful and he closed them again, before slowly opening them slowly to bare slits. There was someone crouched over him, wiping at his face gently with a cloth. It was no one he knew—a woman—dark and with her hair pulled back tightly away from her face. He could see that she was in a black uniform of some kind, but that there was no insignia visible. The world started to spin again and the woman seemed so very far away. He could see Mobutu and Bill Stoudamyre standing behind her—or they could have all been part of a dream—then they too were gone.

What seemed hours, even days, his thoughts were beginning to make sense and his vision was clear again. The world around him slowly came back into complete focus. The heat was still oppressive, bearing down on his face relentlessly. He could see small and distinctly separate groups milling around on the hot surface of the runway. The uniformed Venezuelans had apparently gathered up their dead and wounded and stood in sullen silence at the open hatch to the helicopter on which they'd arrived. Bailey could see covered and prone bodies lying on the decking of the helicopter. A second official-looking UH-1B sat beside it now and other uniformed men were loading rifles, boxy television cameras and cases marked with the red crosses of medical gear into its open doors.

A slight man in a dark suit and a starkly white shirt and a tall, paunchy and dark man, resplendent in a be-ribboned olive-green uniform stood near the helicopter's nose in earnest and animated conversation. The uniformed man, from the gold on his collar and the riding crop he continually slapped across his hand, was obviously a high-ranking officer and he was angry-faced and agitated, his hands jerking about to emphasize whatever points he made. Two heavily armed men stood on either side of the officer, silent but threatening. The man in the dark suit seemed to be nodding in agreement most of the time, his few comments short, his demeanor calm. Finally, he shrugged, reached out and placed a hand on the officer's shoulder and began to talk in quiet tones far too low for Bailey to hear.

After a bit, the uniformed man nodded and they shook hands. He stiffly saluted, waved to the others at the strip, and turned back to the helicopters and motioned for the men to mount for departure. In less than five minutes they were well south of the airstrip, growing smaller as their sound grew faint.

Bailey could see the man watch the helicopters fade into the distance. He seemed to breathe a sigh of relief, turned and walked slowly back to where Mobutu stood talking with a man in a black jumpsuit who carried a machine pistol pointed down toward the ground. Bailey could see he had a self-satisfied but small smile on his face.

The man with Mobutu stopped mid-sentence and waited until he was close enough, "How'd it go?"

Bailey could hear the man respond as he shook his head, "You can buy just about anything down here. It didn't even cost much."

"How's he explain ..."

"You mean the ... casualties? Easy. He just lost some troops chasing rebels up in the hills last night. These will just be added to the list." The man paused a moment, then went to what seemed his real concern, "Where's Jorgensen?"

So, that was the big man's name, *Jorgensen.*

Mobutu answered first, "Out there—somewhere." He nodded toward Bailey, now on a stretcher under some meager shade at the edge of the asphalt, "Bailey shot him, how bad I don't know, but Jorgensen managed to make it to the brush." He nodded toward Bailey again, "You need to meet this man, Mr. Duncan."

The man looked down at the ground a moment, then back to Mobutu, ignoring his comment and continuing his verbal search for Jorgensen, "How long ago?"

"Oh, about an hour now. You want him—*really* want him—right now?"

Mobutu nodded back toward Bailey again and the man looked down at him, saw that he was conscious and took the two steps to his side, kneeling there. "Ah, you're back in the world again." The man's expression softened and he looked straight into Bailey's eyes. "I'm Will Duncan." He thumbed a motion at the others standing behind him and said, "They say you've had a rough time. How do you feel now?"

Bailey started to push himself up, but Duncan gently laid a hand on his shoulder, "Come on now, lay still. You'll be getting to a doctor soon. You and I need to talk—but rest first." He nodded as Bailey faded back into a drugged stupor. Then Duncan stood up, and picked up his conversation with Mobutu where he'd stopped earlier.

"It would be better if he's found—don't want him turning up later at the wrong time and place. If he's dead, we'll make him a hero. If he isn't, we just might make it so—and we'll still make him a hero. Use what time we have as best you can." Turning to Mobutu, "It'll be dark in less than three hours. You have that long to get your stuff and your crew out of here—can you do it?"

Mobutu only nodded and moved the few steps to Captain Davis and quietly gave directions. The man moved off barking orders to the men scattered along the edge of the strip. He then stopped a moment near Stoudamyre and they both quickly trotted off toward the end of the runway and the parked DC-3. A few minutes later, they had started the one remaining engine and were slowly taxiing the aircraft back to the head of the trail leading down to the pier for off-loading. The other men were already gathered around with wheeled dollies and handcarts and were ready to begin the work.

Mobutu started to join the workers when Duncan stopped him with a hand on his arm and a nod toward Bailey. He could hear the man say "What about him?"

"As you can see, Mr. Bailey is very ill. I am surprised he's made it this far. He has amazed me—the man is about done with life and yet he still held up better than most of these others. And he really handled that worn out aircraft. I want him taken care of well—as long as he needs it."

Duncan pursed his lips and seemed lost in thought for a while. When he replied, the words sounded as if they were distasteful to him, "It would be better if he didn't come back to the States, particularly if he's sick enough that he might not know what he's saying."

Mobutu only nodded and looked out at the bay and the freighter. Duncan followed his gaze and slowly continued, "You suppose there's a medic of some kind ... maybe even a doctor ... on board?"

"There is supposed to be, I ordered one when the ship was leased. I'll have the man with the radio check."

"Do that. Then I need to talk to you a minute."

Bailey's mind had crawled out of the darkness somewhere in the middle of their conversation and he'd just lain there, listening. He'd been moved to what passed for shade and, without the sun beating down into his face, he felt almost cool. The pain was still there, but somewhere off in the background, replaced with a growing lightheadedness and a craving for water.

He pushed himself up into a sitting position and had watched Mobutu walk off toward a man kneeling at a field radio and was silent until he returned after a few minutes. The first loaded carts had begun the short trip down to the pier. He was still silent as they moved away from the noise of men's labor and Duncan began his pitch. Bailey listened, hearing but not understanding most of the conversation.

"Colonel, there's not much I can say to make any of this better—and we don't have the time anyway."

Mobutu was silent and just stared into the man's eyes, seeing the discomfort that brought and enjoying it.

"I can't promise you squat—except that if you get out of here by dark, it will never have happened. Understand? I will take care of mollifying the law back in Arizona, handle Mr. Cooper's future ... all that ... OK?"

"Yes—I understand. But, there needs to be more, Mr. Duncan, much more. Do *you* understand?"

"Of course I understand. If I am in a position to do more, I will. Know that I am only making an assumption that I will be getting the nomination to fill the position Jorgensen was vying for with such ... intensity. I will be a good friend to have in the Agency. But I will have to be *your* friend, not President St. Claude's. Presidents come and go—you will be there a long time. He must not know of our relationship for the time being."

"That is acceptable—for now. What else do you want?"

"Nothing—well, you could help my men police up Mr. Jorgensen. You know where he entered this ... this smelly weed patch. This is, after all, your type of game. I would be very grateful for your help."

"It is not a game, Mr. Duncan. How grateful?"

"If you find him, you will always be most *comfortable*, regardless of your president's political future. I should tell you that if you find him here, he may be in the company of a very dangerous man ... Kirkpatrick is his name. He too has become ... redundant. But, be careful—very careful."

Mobutu turned and walked back to where Captain Davis stood, retrieved his machine pistol and joined Barrington and his men at the edge of the dark and dank undergrowth. They talked for a few minutes, Obregon, Simpson, and the sheriff's captain broke away from the group and returned toward where Bailey lay. He began losing his focus as Mobutu and the remaining three men spread out some ten yards apart and, heading generally downhill, stepped off in to the brush.

Bailey could hear Stoudamyre's voice through the fog and he pulled consciousness back and looked around to locate him. He motioned toward them and asked Stoudamyre, kneeling there by his side, where they were going. He looked around at the other men moving in and out of *The Rose*'s hatch, like so many ants on a carcass and shook his head in disbelief.

Stoudamyre spread a smile across his face and gave Bailey a gentle pat on the shoulder. "Ah, you're awake. Well, they're going in after that big dude you shot. Jorgensen is his name, I believe. Seems that boss man over there," indicating Duncan with a nod, "wants him pretty bad. How're you doing now, huh?"

Bailey didn't answer, but there was question in his face and it could be easily read.

Stoudamyre squatted by him and went on, "Hmm, where to start ... well, they'll have *The Rose* empty in a bit and we'll—those spooks and us—well, we'll be outa here. Old *Rose* will have to stay though –she's had it. Duncan wants us to torch the both of them. Too bad. She's been a good old bird. It'll be a little like murder." He paused and looked away, as if considering a difficult thing to say, then cleared his throat and quietly said, "We're not leaving together old friend. Mobutu—good ol'

Colonel Guthrie Mobutu—wants to take you with him. He says there is some kind of doctor on that tub in the bay. He –all of us now—know you're pretty sick. Figure the sea voyage, in the lap of luxury, y'know, won't hurt you any. He says his family will take care of you; and I don't think he lives in a stick and mud shack in the outback. And, besides, that guy," again nodding toward Duncan, "wants you gone."

"What about you?"

"Me? I'm going to fly back with that nervous looking fella over there. He flew that guy Jorgensen in here. He's just dying to get back on his boss' good side, so we'll fly Cooper and those other Feds back to Tucson. Duncan says they have a job for me—flying—somewhere. Maybe they do, maybe they don't. I'll be OK ... you just take it easy."

He still squatted there though, his face tense with the look of an unasked question, finally he blurted, "Ah, hell, you feel good enough to talk to these guys a minute?" He motioned to the three men standing behind him. "They want to talk about the airstrip back in the desert—and Cooper ... and that isn't even his damn name. You don't have to, y'know."

Bailey thought about it a moment, shook his head affirmatively, and stuck his hand out to Stoudamyre. "Help me up—so I can sit." He could see the relief on Stoudamyre's face.

One of the men pulled up an empty packing crate and guided Bailey to it. He sat slowly down as the earth canted and spun a bit, then settled. He could see Cooper, leaning against a fender of the old truck, watching them and carrying a look of dismal dejection. His clothes were dirty and torn and there were several smudges on his face. He appeared to have lost a very physical argument. He shrugged and nodded at Bailey, as if giving him permission to go on.

One of the men approached Bailey, pulling off silvered dark glasses as he did. "Mr. Bailey, my name is Obregon. As your buddy told you, I'm a Federal Agent—one you wouldn't normally meet." He motioned at the man on his right and went on, "This is Special Agent Simpson, he's from the FBI—and this man," nodding at the stocky and gray man on his left, "is Captain Matthews, Pima County Sheriff."

Bailey didn't respond. He just sat on the edge of the crate and stared at them. The man went on, "Look, I know you don't have to talk to us—we'd appreciate it though. We just want to make this all go away. You're already out of the sticky stuff on this fiasco. Mr. Duncan tells us they're gonna let you go with Colonel Mobutu. Your buddy is clear too, but he is flying back to Tucson … sort of insurance for when we get where Cooper has to produce."

"Produce?" Bailey raised an eyebrow and stared back at the man.

"Yeah—produce. Between you, your mechanic and your buddy Stoudamyre, there's enough to get him extradited from just about any country in the world, and, truth is, we wouldn't even bother. He can become part of the flora and fauna hereabouts if he doesn't play the game. We're trading him for a bigger fish—he can give us Colisimo. We wouldn't do it this way, but you already took care of the guy who killed the deputies. It just might be worth the trade."

Bailey sat there a moment, the fog still drifting through his mind. He began to see and feel the gritty little Arizona airstrip again. He could hear its sounds, feel its heat, and part of its despair seeped into his soul again. The images slowly rolled through his mind in a disjointed and random manner. He could feel the suffocating heat of the flight deck as he struggled to remove an instrument and smell the moldering cabin. The ghastly pale and dead face of the woman deputy seemed to just hang there in front of his thoughts. He seemed to watch from afar as the foul little Mexican spun to face him and then convulsed again and again with the impact of each bullet.

His mind seemed to clear a bit and he realized he must have been talking, for the men around him were nodding, wide-eyed but understanding. And he was crying, unashamedly crying. The man identified to him as Matthews knelt, to stare into Bailey's face, "So— *you* shot the little wetback." It was not a question. "You know who hired him?"

Bailey stuck out a hand, "Help me up," and was pulled to his feet. He stood there, feeling the earth spin crazily again, and a few moments, stop. He looked around the airstrip again, at *The Rose* and the DC-6 behind her, and thought that where he now stood was no place to die. He looked back at Cooper again and then back to Matthews, "What did you say Cooper's real name was?"

"I didn't—but it is Leonetti."

"Well, he hired us to fly—I just thought it was some work, meant to be below the radar. I needed the job—bad. As you can tell, there won't be another. The filthy little wetback was at the airstrip when we got there. Cooper … uhh, Leonetti, hired him to keep watch on us. He killed the deputies, the sorry bastard. I … I've not shot anyone since—well, never mind—but I'd shoot him again … a thousand times if he could feel it. What'll happen to him?" pointing off toward Cooper.

Simpson cut in, "Nothing good. He won't get the money from Mobutu. Duncan is sending it back to Liberia with him—except for 250 grand he is sending to your ex-wife and daughter. He's got about $500 on him and I doubt he'd get far with it down here. We could just bury him over there by that big fella we found dead on your airplane, or we could throw his ass back on a plane for Tucson and let him loose on the streets about the time Colisimo gets bailed out. That ought to be fun to watch."

"But, what will you really do? You're talking bullshit now."

"Yeah, I know. Well, believe it or not, Cooper actually has value now, temporary as it is. He'll trade his sorry-assed boss for a stint in the Witness Protection Program. You know, all that crap about honor among thieves has a really thin veneer. And, from what I hear, if he runs his mouth well, he can really stir up Tucson society." Simpson started to go on, but Obregon interrupted.

"Mr. Bailey, you have any idea who did the armory holdups? … Hear any talk about that?"

Bailey shook his head in the negative and pointed off at Cooper again, "No, bet'cha five bucks he knows though—ask him."

"Oh, we will." He paused a moment, then asked, "If we get this on paper and get it to you, where ever that happens to be, will you sign it?"

Bailey only nodded and sat wearily back down on the crate. Everything around him had a blurred and distant look to it. The woman in the black jumpsuit moved in close again and smiled, "You need to lay back down. Here, I'll give you a hand. I'm going to give you a little something that will ease the pain a bit. Just lay back and relax."

....

Bᴀɪʟᴇʏ ᴀᴡᴏᴋᴇ ᴛᴏ ᴛʜᴇ ʀᴏʟʟɪɴɢ sᴡᴀʏ of the sea and a slight rumble and vibration that he could feel through the bed on which he huddled. It was some minutes before he recognized it as the noise and feel of a ship, apparently underway and in light seas. It was dark but he could see a round spot across the room that was of a lighter blue-black and he thought he could see stars. He groaned a bit as he moved and a small dim and yellowish light flicked on across the room and he could see the dim outline of Guthrie Mobutu.

"Ah, Wes, you are back with us."

He lay there a bit and slowly sat up, swung his legs out and felt his feet touching a soft and thick carpet. He could still feel the vibration of a ships movement through the floor.

Finally, he asked, "Where are we?"

He could see a calm smile on Guthrie Mobutu's face, "We are on our way home, my friend, on our way home."

Epilogue

J UNE IN THE NORTHWEST CAN BE a tantalizingly beautiful month—when it is not raining. This day it rained. It came down in hammering torrents punctuated by periodic flashes of heavy and close lightning that framed the tall firs, cedars, and hemlocks lining the far side of the runway. It all gave multiple colors to the sheets of water being driven by the strong and gusting northwesterly winds.

Bill Stoudamyre, Chief Pilot William J. Stoudamyre, Kinney-Leigh Development Corporation, stood at the window and watched the rain. He had the window open a few inches, just enough to smell the freshness of the storm and still keep the rain out, but his thoughts were elsewhere and his mind was filled with a gloomy despair.

His thoughts wandered back almost a whole year. He saw and felt the old and worn DC3, relived the nightmare in the desert, remembered the noise and chaos of the crumbling airstrip on The Plain of the Dogs and, most of all, he remembered Wes Bailey. There'd been no word in over two months and he knew the end had to be near, if it had not already passed. He felt the loss bearing down on him as if it weighed tons and there was nothing he could do, except feel the loss and pain—and slowly drown in it.

He still didn't understand everything there was to know about the *official* side of their nightmare—but he knew enough about the journey of *The Rose* to have it ever etched in his mind and on his soul. He'd made several small attempts to dig out the facts and found he was out of his league. The unknown would remain unknown.

Guthrie Mobutu had finally, in January, told him as much as he could, he guessed, given the circumstances. He said that Jorgensen had been found that day at the airstrip in Venezuela. He had been propped against a tree at the edge of a little dirt road winding from the pier to a small nearby Indian village. Dead, he was stone cold dead. Bailey's shot had not killed him though, nor had those that found him. There was a single bullet hole in his forehead.

At first they'd thought he simply given up and committed suicide. He did have an old Browning clutched in his hand. Then they'd found several discarded passports tossed in a nearby ditch. They had another man's face on them and Barrington had recognized the man known by a few within the Agency as a shadowy and rarely seen agent called only *Kirkpatrick*. Just Kirkpatrick. He had long-held ties to the IRA and, though he generally lived in London, and was considered by some to be more myth than man, perhaps to not to even really exist.

A short, no more than a 15 minute hike to a little nearby village confirmed that a tall and hard-looking man had walked in and rented a man and his rickety truck to take him into Maracaibo. He'd paid a lot they said. It was a long drive—and he wouldn't take no for an answer. They had been gone for over an hour, maybe more. No, they were not really sure it was Maracaibo, but that's what they thought the man said. Duncan had been unhappy with that, Mobutu recalled, and made a flurry of calls from a radiotelephone on one of the corporate jets.

Stoudamyre let the thoughts slip away and reminded himself that he really had no complaints—no, none at all. Duncan had certainly not forgotten him. Barrington had come by his sadly empty and tacky little Tucson apartment less than a week after he'd gotten back, dropped off $25,000 in hundred dollar bills and told him to just relax for a while. And so he did, new women friends and all. But it wasn't the same. He didn't drink so much and found himself home early and the evenings were spent staring into yesterday's space. Alone.

Barrington had also left him with a two-day old newspaper from

San Diego. He told him to read it and that he would find it interesting. The headlines touted some new police department hero, the winner of a face-to-face shoot out with an IRA assassin.

An IRA shooter in San Diego? Strange. The picture, Barrington said, was Kirkpatrick. He had apparently come back to the States to gather in hidden money and passports and ran afoul of some young hotshot in blue.

Stoudamyre wondered how the cop had known who to look for and how he happened to be better at the end game than a true professional. He shook his head and mused on that and then decided it made no difference and tossed the newspaper into the trash.

Two weeks later a letter came—registered mail—from someone named Barbara Keefer, with a title of Human Resources Director, Kinney-Leigh Development Corporation, in Olympia, Washington. Develop *what*, he thought, but the letter went on to say that someone had recommended him for the position of Chief Pilot. They'd accepted that recommendation. He was, she said, about to be in their employ and if he would just call, she would arrange an advance in the form of a direct deposit to an account of mutual agreement.

Welcome aboard, she said. She went on to say that they had arranged for him to *freshen up* his ticket—to include Lear and Grumman Gulfstream and, she said, he was to report to work October 15th—if that was consistent with his schedule. His salary was, well, out of sight. It was signed with a neat and proper flourish, right out of the Parker Penmanship book.

He remembered thinking that good old Duncan had certainly come through—more than he had ever imagined. He also knew that he had just been bought body and soul and it had a foul taste. He packed his bags and went by the Sheriff's office on the way out of town—just to check one last time with Captain Matthews. He found the Captain was now Under-Sheriff and quite happy not to talk about Venezuela any more.

Yes, he had said, the rumor was true. He was about to be appointed Acting-Sheriff. Sheriff Mason was now back east, at some Federal charm school, and about to be frocked the United States Marshall for the district headquartered in Phoenix. Matthews would run for the office of Sheriff, in his own right, with the coming fall elections.

He wished Stoudamyre well and nervously hurried him out the door. He did say that the articles in all the local paper were true: Colisimo had been indicted on enough counts to cause cardiac arrest in the healthiest of men. Cooper? No, he had no idea what had happened to Cooper. The deputies? Well, things like that happened, sad as it was. Yes, he was sorry, but *we* are expendable he'd said with false humility. Funny how a guy that's alive always can think to say that, thought Stoudamyre as he had walked out the door and into the sun again.

That was the last time he saw Matthews. He promptly left for Georgia and the flight service where he was to get his up-graded tickets and begin his new life. He tried not to think of how odd it was that he was the only student on site and that they all looked at him as if he was a refugee from another planet. But, on October 15th, he was in Olympia, Washington, resplendent in new gabardines and a power red tie, nervously staring across the reception counter and offering up his name.

Stoudamyre turned around and looked over the office that was now his daytime home and marveled at his fortune. The office was right out of a designer's magazine—filled almost to excess with rich wood and leather, paintings beyond his comprehension, and superb little display models of aircraft ancient and contemporary poised here and there in mock flight. Everything he should want. Yes, he was lucky. More or less.

He walked back to the desk and pulled out the chair, sat down again, and stared at the letter that lay centermost on the large and thick leather writing pad. It was the fourth time he had come back to it and still had not been able to open it. The envelope was off-white and of good, thick stock. The stamps of Liberia were distinctive and colorful. The return was simply: Mobutu, 38 Government Plaza, Monrovia, Liberia.

This time though, he picked it up and softly bounced it in his hand, as if weighing it. Finally, breathing a small and sad sigh, he snatched up a letter opener and quickly sliced the length of the envelope's top and pulled it open. It contained three things: a single folded page of the same stock as the envelope, a photograph, and a many leafed airline ticket to Monrovia on Air Canada and BOAC out of Vancouver, British Columbia.

Stoudamyre dropped the airline ticket back on the desk without considering it and unfolded the letter. It was brief and he quickly skimmed through its carefully hand-written paragraphs. He had known this day would come, but his vision blurred with tears as he read, "Mr. Bailey has passed from us..." He read the letter again and smiled at how Mobutu said that his Julianna had cared for him until the end and that she had insisted on a very formal funeral mass. It was over at last, he thought.

He read the last paragraph over several more times. Mr. Bailey had, Mobutu said, thought very highly of him. Mobutu also said he had need of a person like him. He had a job for him, no, a position of some rank and importance, if he so desired. The ticket, through several roundabout stops, was his for the using—or disposal. The choice was his. The letter was signed above a title block that said: General Guthrie Mobutu, Commanding.

The writing on the back of the photograph said simply: *Remember him this way*. Stoudamyre stared at the photograph a long time. Bailey sat at a wooden table on what appeared to be the porch of a large whitewashed house. Behind him, her hand resting on his shoulder stood a small, darkly brown, and totally elegant, woman. She leaned back against the whitewashed wall and smiled into the camera. Beside her stood a teenaged version of Guthrie Mobutu. He was sober and serious looking, with intelligence keen in his eyes. Across the table from Bailey sat Guthrie Mobutu himself. He was dressed in khaki and multiple rows of awards and decorations shown above his left shirt pocket. The gold bullion devices of a general crowned his epaulets. But it was Bailey that drew his eye. True, he did appear pale, even drawn, but the smile that creased his face was real and it went all the way to his eyes. He would remember him this way.

Stoudamyre flicked off the light on his desk and walked back to the window. He stood for a long time, staring into the rain, not seeing it for the tears clouding his vision. Finally, he turned back to the desk and picked up an old and scuffed flight case from the floor near the desk. He opened it and dropped the letter, photograph, and airline ticket inside and started to walk out the door. He paused for a second, turned back and picked up the *William J. Stoudamyre* nameplate from the desk, dropped it into the trash bin alongside his desk, smiled, and walked out the door, down the long, empty hall and out into the rain.